THE
JERUSALEM
INCEPTION

A NOVEL

By Avraham Azrieli

Printed by CreateSpace, Charleston, SC

ISBN: 1451549512
ISBN-13: 9781451549515
Library of Congress Control Number: 2010903795

Also by Avraham Azrieli

Fiction:

The Masada Complex

Non-Fiction:

Your Lawyer on a Short Leash

One Step Ahead – A Mother of Seven Escaping Hitler

The Alps, December 31, 1944

Chapter 1

His wool uniform was rough against her cheek, but Tanya continued to cling to his arm. It was silent inside the Mercedes, only a restrained murmur from its powerful engine. The supple backseat absorbed all but the deepest ruts in the Alpine road. The hands on the dashboard clock glowed in the dark, approaching midnight. In a moment, 1944 would end, and with it, their way of life.

They watched the driver struggle to keep the large staff car on the icy road, which slithered up into the formidable mountains toward the Swiss border. The headlights were painted over, only thin blades of light left to illuminate snapshots of steel barriers, pine trees, and mounds of fresh snow.

Klaus cracked the window, and cold air invaded the car, together with the engine roar of the loaded truck that followed them close behind. Tanya's hand crawled into his, her fingers curled against his warm palm. The car entered a tunnel, and the phosphorous hands of the dashboard clock merged into one.

Midnight.

As the Mercedes emerged from the tunnel, the western horizon exploded—red, blue, and white lights, bursting into the black sky—a New Year's salute from thousands of artillery guns, orchestrated by General Patton, the irascible commander of the American Third Army. In the front seat, the driver cursed under his breath.

"Happy birthday." With a finger under her chin, Klaus brought up Tanya's face and kissed her lips. "Seventeen," he said, "and many more."

"Together." She pressed his hand to her lower abdomen, where a new life was growing.

Meanwhile, the driver began searching the radio frequencies through static and bursts of music until Adolf Hitler's voice emerged. "Like a phoenix," the Führer yelled, "*Deutschland* will rise again!"

Tanya felt Klaus tense up beside her, his arm rising for the customary *Heil Hitler!*

But the flame of excitement died instantly, his hand turned into a fist, and he grunted. She remembered the Wehrmacht's intelligence reports he had shown her, patiently explaining the military jargon and the implications of color-coded arrows. The Ardennes Offensive continued in full force, with all surviving Panzer divisions thrown against U.S. forces. Hitler had refused a negotiated surrender and boasted of turning the tide with a wonder weapon of destruction. But the Führer was delusional. The most Germany could expect was a brief reprieve from Allied pressure on the Bulge. "And then," Klaus had said, "the total destruction of the Third Reich."

The Mercedes took another hairpin turn. In the windshield, Tanya could see the emblem glisten at the far end of the hood like a gun sight seeking a target.

The road leveled off, and the thin headlights hit a steel gate that blocked the way. A sign warned: *Halt! Schweizerische Grenze!*

The driver stopped the car, came out, and opened the door. "*Herr Obergruppenführer!*"

Klaus put on his gloves. He helped Tanya out of the Mercedes and raised the hood of her fur coat to shelter her from the biting frost.

A moment later the truck stopped behind the Mercedes. It was enormous, with a solid, steel-braced box resembling a train car.

Klaus took out a silver cigarette lighter and used it to signal up and down.

A reply came from the other side of the border, a point of light moving from right to left.

The Swiss guards opened the gate, and a dark Rolls Royce limousine glided through. A young man in a dark suit stepped out from behind the wheel. He knocked his heels together, bowed curtly, and opened the rear door. "*Guten Abend, Herr General!*"

"And to you, Günter," Klaus said. He helped Tanya into the Rolls Royce, and the door closed.

The rear section of the vehicle was arranged like a cozy sitting room, with two leather sofas facing each other. A Wagner opera, *Götterdämmerung – Twilight of the Gods*, played softly. Dim lights illuminated the mahogany woodwork. Curtains covered the windows.

Armande Hoffgeitz shook Klaus's hand and pecked Tanya's cheek. "You're three minutes late," he said. "Do you need a new watch?"

The two men laughed, and Klaus pointed at the truck. "More than sixteen thousand gold watches in there. Maybe I'll keep one." He pulled off his gloves.

Armande Hoffgeitz looked at his hand. "You're not wearing the ring." He held his own hand to the ambient lamp. A serpent intertwined with the letters *LASN*, which stood for Lyceum Alpin St. Nicholas, the Swiss boarding school they had attended together.

"Regulations allow only one." Klaus tapped his SS ring. "*Treu. Tapfer. Gehorsam.*"

"And are you still *loyal, valiant, obedient?*"

"I'm down to valiant only." Klaus reached into his coat and took out a pocket-size ledger, bound in black leather and marked with a red swastika. "How's business in Zurich?"

"The war has been very good for us. Too bad it's about to end." His grin faded when he met Tanya's eyes. "I'm only joking, Fräulein, yes?"

Tanya smiled. After three years in their world, she had learned to smile well, even to the most piggish remarks.

Klaus handed him the ledger. "The total numbers include all the previous deliveries. This truckload is my last."

"Everything is still in the original boxes, stored in our cellar vaults, per your instructions." The banker opened the ledger.

"We took back what they stole from Europe over the centuries. One day, I will use it to build the Fourth Reich."

"A noble aspiration." Armande glanced at Tanya before holding the ledger up against the lamp. "But it will take time for the world to forget this war."

"I have time." At thirty-four, Klaus von Koenig was the youngest Nazi general, thanks to a talent for finance and Himmler's patronage.

The banker was no longer listening. He browsed the black ledger, his stubby finger running down to the totals at the bottom of each page. "This is fantastic. *Fantastic!*" His gold-rimmed glasses slipped down to the tip of his nose, and he pushed them back. "Diamonds, total weight, nine and one-quarter tons? God in heavens! Thirteen point four tons of pearls? Sixteen tons, eight hundred and ninety-two kilos of emeralds? Three tons, nine hundred and thirty-four kilos of red rubies?" He pulled the curtain aside and looked at the truck across the road. "The Jews had so much?"

Klaus patted his chest. "They swallowed more stones than breadcrumbs."

Armande Hoffgeitz looked at him, puzzled. "So how?"

"Crematoria. The fire consumes everything but precious stones. The gold teeth had to be removed beforehand, of course." Klaus didn't miss the shiver that passed through Tanya, who would have been gassed and cremated had he not pulled her out of line at Dachau. "It's almost over now," he said. "We're shutting down the camps, thank God."

Tanya knew his itinerary, the names on his routine travel route—Maidanek, Belzec, Auschwitz, Dachau, Mauthausen, Gross-Rosen, Chelmno, and back to Herr Himmler's compound near Treblinka, where she had overheard Commandant Franz Stangl brag of killing seventeen thousand Jews in a single day—stripped, shaved, herded into the showers, gassed, searched for gold teeth, and burned to thin powder, which was then combed for precious stones.

The banker's thick forefinger pushed his spectacles up his stubby nose. "What did you do with the gold?"

"Shipped to Argentina by U-boats. The last one is waiting for us in Kiel."

Armande Hoffgeitz held up the ledger, shaking it. "How could they have so much?"

"Why not? They were educated people. Scientists, engineers, doctors, businessmen. Even bankers, like you. But the Führer's doctrine required cleansing Europe of the Jews to free up opportunities and wealth for the Aryan race. Turned out to be a tragic waste, in my opinion."

"The costs of elimination?"

"The whole thing. Anti-Jew policies were useful initially to galvanize our political power, fire up the street. But actually rounding them up, transporting them, exterminating them? Huge waste of resources. And those who survived are helping our enemies defeat us." Klaus motioned vaguely. "Anyway, the largest stones are in a steel case in the cabin, strapped to the passenger seat. Ten to thirty-five karats each. Museum quality. You'll need to be very discreet when you sell those."

The banker pulled down a mahogany tray, which formed a small working space. He produced a sheet of paper and copied the total quantities of each category of stones and jewelry, checking the numbers twice against the ledger. "You must choose an account number and a password that you'll remember easily."

Klaus took the pen and glanced at Tanya. In the space for the account number he wrote *829111*. For the password he entered *AYNAT*. He sighed below: *Klaus von Koenig, 00:16 a.m., January 1, 1945*

Armande took the form and held it high, blowing on the wet ink. When he was satisfied, he folded it and tucked it away. "Regarding the conversion of all your deposits into liquid assets, I recommend a basket of currencies."

"With all due respect, I prefer American stocks. Sell everything and buy shares of American corporations."

"But America is broke. After the war, their economy will crash. How about—"

"The Americans are winning. Not the British, Canadians, Australians, or the Russian swine. The Americans have spirit. Forget *Deutschland Über Alles*. From now on, it will be *America Über Alles*. That's the future!" He sat back with sudden weariness. "Buy me American stocks—manufacturing, food, oil, chemicals."

"As you wish." The banker opened the ledger on the last page and scribbled at the bottom: *Deposit of above-listed goods is acknowledged this day, 1.1.1945 by the Hoffgeitz Bank of Zurich. Signed: Armande Hoffgeitz, President.* "We can't just dump huge quantities of stones on the market—prices will collapse."

"Take your time." Klaus took the ledger and handed it to Tanya, who slipped it under her shirt, where it rested against her chest.

Armande asked, "When will I hear from you?"

"I will contact you from Argentina when it's safe." Klaus rolled down the window. "Felix!"

His driver hurried across the road.

"Tell your cousin to show Günter how to drive that monster." He pointed at the truck. "I don't want him to lose control on the way downhill."

"*Jawohl, Herr Obergruppenführer!*" Felix ran to the truck.

"What about him?" Armande put the papers back in a briefcase. "Will you take Felix to Argentina?"

"I offered. He's loyal and obedient, but no longer valiant. He wants to go with his cousin back to Bavaria, till the fields, milk the cows. Fools' dreams."

Armande Hoffgeitz's assistant climbed into the cabin of the truck. The engine roared, and the truck proceeded through the gate into Switzerland.

They got out of the Rolls Royce. It felt even colder than before. The banker rubbed his hands. "A U-Boat ride across the Atlantic is risky. Why don't you come with me to Zurich?"

"It's too close to Germany," Klaus said. "I must be far away when the Reich surrenders. The Allies will hunt us down, put up show trials, and march us one by one to the gallows."

Tanya clutched his arm.

"Good luck, my friend." Armande Hoffgeitz got behind the wheel.

"*Auf Wiedersehen.*"

The Rolls Royce slid backward across the border, and Klaus led Tanya to the Mercedes.

Felix held the door open. His cousin stood at attention.

"Excellent driving," Klaus said. "You'll be rewarded."

They saluted. "*Danke, Herr Obergruppenführer!*"

He helped Tanya into the car and was about to follow, but paused. "What was that?"

The two soldiers looked around, uncertain.

"I heard something!" He drew his service Mauser.

Felix and Karl cocked their submachine guns and followed him around the hood of the car. The night was quiet, the moon exposed by the thin clouds. He stayed back as the two soldiers advanced toward the trees, their boots sinking into the snow, their weapons ready.

He raised his arm, aimed, and pressed the trigger once. The shot caused a flock of birds to scramble off a nearby tree. Felix turned to his cousin, who collapsed, blood trickling from a hole in the back of his head. The Mauser shifted, aligning with Felix's head, silhouetted against the snow-weighted branches. The next bullet entered Felix's temple and exited on the other side. The driver's knees folded under him and he knelt down, blood oozing down both sides of his face. His mouth gaped as if attempting to speak, and he fell forward in the snow.

Klaus got behind the wheel and shut the door. "I'm sorry you had to see this," he said. "But they knew too much."

Tanya didn't answer. She forced her mind to recall the photos he had shown her of the ranch in Argentina, the rolling hills and lush pasture, the sturdy cattle and proud horses. She imagined the sound of chirpy children.

Elie Weiss crouched in the snow by the roadside. The wool coat, stripped from a corpse a month earlier, was too big. The gloves were tattered, the knuckles bare. Another hour of exposure could cost him a finger, or worse.

"We're too late," Abraham Gerster said, clapping his hands to keep the circulation going. "We missed them. Let's go back to the village, steal some food."

"Not yet. They might come back this way."

Abraham obeyed without argument. Elie was barely two years older, but they had known each other since childhood, when such age differences fix seniority in concrete. But Elie envied Abraham's vitality, his youthful energy, the strength he hadn't lost despite the harsh weather, constant hunger, and bursts of violence. At eighteen, Abraham was still running at full speed, four years after they had escaped the German slaughter of their shtetl. They had learned to survive in the thick forests, stealing food when possible and killing Germans at every opportunity. But as the war dragged on, hiding became harder, and the dwindling German units had little food left to steal.

"Maybe they took another route," Abraham said.

"I heard them clearly." Elie had eavesdropped on two German soldiers smoking outside the inn at the village. They were cousins, serving as drivers for SS General Klaus von Koenig, who was transferring loot from the camps to the Swiss border. Elie and Abraham had climbed the steep mountainside, plowing through deep snow and treacherous boulders, to set a trap. But they must have been late.

"Listen!" Abraham tensed, inching closer to the road.

An engine sounded from uphill. Elie watched the next turn up the steep road. His eyes never disappointed him. Back in Kolno, his father had been the village *shoykhet* – the kosher butcher. People had said that Elie had the devil's eyes, small and black and all-seeing, even in darkness. People had strange ideas where death was involved.

The engine noise came closer. A single car.

Abraham got up on one knee, ready for action. His hands were strong, his shoulders wide. He was no longer the rabbi's dutiful son. Gone were his side locks, the black coat, and the hat. He grabbed the trunk of a fallen tree and dragged it into the road.

The car made the last turn. Its headlights painted over, it headed downhill, gaining speed, oblivious to the impending disaster. The front tires hit the tree trunk. The car lost its ability to steer, missed the next turn, and crashed into the ditch, landing on its roof.

Elie crossed the road and approached through the snow. It was a Mercedes sedan. Steam hissed from its engine, fading into the cold air.

The driver's door opened, and a man crawled out, coughing hard. The SS insignia glistened on the collar of the gray uniform. A general.

Elie drew his long blade and stabbed the Nazi through the back, just above the right kidney, puncturing the lung. He pulled the blade straight out, careful not to damage a major artery. Searching the man's pockets, Elie found a cigarette lighter and a wallet filled with cash. He held the lighter flame to the face— sculpted, Aryan features, square jaw, thin lips pressed in pain. Elie recognized him from newspaper photos: General Klaus von Koenig, Heinrich Himmler's deputy.

A wave of hatred flooded Elie, but the caution that had kept him alive through the war made him pause. Why was the general driving himself? Elie looked up the road and listened carefully. No escort vehicle, no guards, no entourage. What happened to the drivers? Had they continued to Switzerland with the truck? Elie remembered one of them speak of the general's exactness in recording the details of the loot in a small ledger. He felt the pockets again. Nothing. Was it in the car? He turned and saw Abraham drag something out of the overturned Mercedes—a black bag, or an animal?

Up close, Elie realized it was a fur coat. The hood fell back, releasing a cascade of black hair. A white hand emerged and punched Abraham in the crotch. He cursed, clenched her hair, and slapped her across the face. With the speed of a snake she grabbed his hand and sank her teeth into it. He yelled and stumbled back, holding his hand. Then he leaped forward, his right boot rising behind for a kick that would surely kill her.

Elie stepped between them. "Not yet!"

Abraham bent over in pain. "Nazi bitch!"

"Watch them." Elie got down on his knees and hands to search the car, using the cigarette lighter to illuminate every corner of the plush sedan. Nothing resembling a ledger, but he found a handgun, its handle plated with ivory.

He tossed the gun to Abraham, who prodded the general with his boot. "Stand up! *Schnell!*"

Elie watched with satisfaction—the rabbi's son was doing the butcher's work.

General Klaus von Koenig pulled himself up on one elbow. His breathing was labored, a gurgling Elie recognized as the sound of foamy blood filling the chest. His eyes squinted with pain as he looked at the woman. "*Auf Wiedersehen, meine geliebte.*"

"She'll see you in hell!" Abraham's ragged boot banged against the German's back. "On your feet!"

With great effort, the Nazi rose.

"We are Jews," Abraham said, aiming the gun at his head. "*Juden!*"

General von Koenig straightened up, pulled back his shoulders, and raised his right hand at the dark sky. "*Heil Hitler!*"

Abraham shot him in the face.

The woman gasped.

"*Nekamah!*" Elie's frozen lips hurt, reciting the Hebrew word for revenge. "*Nekamah!*"

She stared at the dead German a few feet away. Tears lined her cheeks.

"Whore!" Elie addressed her in German. "Where is the truck?"

She tilted her head up the hill, where they had come from.

He kicked snow in her face. "Who took it? Which bank? Tell me!"

Clawing at the snow, she edged away, leaving a dark trail of blood. The car wreck must have injured her.

"Shoot her in the leg," Elie ordered. "Pain will make her talk."

"She's bleeding already," Abraham said. "A lot."

"Do it!"

She raised her hand to stop him, shut her eyes, and recited, "*Shmah Israel, Hear, O Israel, Adonai is our God, Adonai is one.*"

Elie was shocked by the words of the ancient covenant. A Jewish woman travelling with a Nazi general? Shedding tears for the dead monster? He ignited the cigarette lighter. In the small flame, her face was shockingly beautiful, the angelic features of a woman-child, her green eyes wide and moist.

Abraham stashed the gun in his belt, dropped to his knees, and took her hand. His face was fresh, cheeks red from cold, chin marked by the shadow of a beard. His blue eyes sat large in his face, filled with compassion under the shock of blond hair. "*Hear, O Israel, Adonai is our God.*" He pulled out a dirty handkerchief and wiped her forehead. "But there's no God. No *Adonai*. If only He existed!"

She touched Abraham's lips, silencing him, and Elie killed the lighter.

"What's your name?" Abraham slipped his hands under her and lifted her up effortlessly.

"Tanya." Her eyes turned to the dead Nazi lying in the snow. "Tanya Galinski."

Grabbing her arm, Elie said, "You grieve for him? Why?"

"Leave her alone," Abraham said.

"Where is his ledger?" Elie pointed to the corpse. "He kept a record!"

"Enough with the questions." Abraham turned, carrying her, and stumbled. But he regained his footing and kept going. "She needs a doctor."

"Did he give it to you?" Elie felt up the fur coat. "Tell me!"

Tanya rested her head in the small of Abraham's neck, and he carried her through the snow back to the road and down toward the village. It started snowing again, and the ground quivered under the distant bombardment. The Battle of the Bulge lit up the western horizon with a glowing, man-made dawn, as if the first day of 1945 was eager to begin.

Four months later ...

Chapter 2

Tanya woke up warm. She felt Abraham's breath on the back of her neck, found his hand, and guided it to her breast. The morning sun filtered through the pitched tarp they used as a makeshift tent, the light accentuating the printed swastikas that lined the edges. The forest around them was quiet after an early spring storm had left a thick, white layer that buried all sounds.

The night at the border seemed to belong in another lifetime. The tumbling Mercedes had left her with a badly slashed thigh. The bleeding would have killed her, but Abraham had brought her downhill to the village and found a doctor, who cleaned the wound and stitched it up. For several weeks, the three of them had hidden in the forest while a feverish Tanya teetered between reality and delusion. Abraham nursed her while Elie kept his distance. One day, when she was well enough to wash in a stream, two armed German deserters happened upon her, grinning at the sight of a young woman to be had. Elie cut one's throat while Abraham broke the other's neck. Their ruthlessness left Tanya both shaken and reassured.

Once she had recovered, Abraham and Elie resumed their daily hunting for vulnerable Germans and scraps of food. She stayed in the forest, scouring for edible plants. Her past life of Nazi upper-crust luxury had become a distant memory, replaced by a struggle for survival. The occasional longing she felt for Klaus and his calm affection grew rare while an overwhelming passion ignited between her and Abraham, who treated her growing belly as lovingly as he treated the rest of her body.

Tanya reached back, found his head, and caressed the blond hair, which had grown long enough to curl at the ends. He purred, his mouth against her nape, making her shiver. The air was cold, and she blew through rounded lips, her breath making saucers of steam.

Abraham pulled the blankets back over their heads, pressed his naked body against her back, and kissed her ear. He capped her breast with one hand while the other went down and began to pleasure her. She surrendered to the rhythm of his touch, focusing on this utter joy that filled her world, and groaned with delight as he entered her.

Elie Weiss bit his fingernail, tearing it off with a length of skin. He listened to their lovemaking with a mix of fascination and fury. After so many mornings like this, he knew their whispers, giggles, squeaky kisses, and muffled groans. It left him aroused and incensed.

But this morning, as he lay in the snow wrapped in sheets of tarp and stolen Wehrmacht blankets, within reach of their tent, he heard something different after they climaxed. It took him a moment to realize the sounds were whimpers. It was Tanya, sobbing mutedly. Was her face buried in Abraham's bare chest, or turned away? Why was she crying after such ecstasy? Was it sadness, or overwhelming happiness?

Then Abraham began to sing, the words too soft to decipher outside the tent.

Elie crawled out of his shelter and put his ear to the tarp.

It was Hebrew, from King Solomon's *Song of Songs*. Abraham chanted for Tanya the tune that had celebrated the beginning of Sabbath in the synagogue, back in the shtetl:

"Your neck is ivory, your nose the ridge of Lebanon, gazing over Damascus; I long for my beloved, passion upon me."

Tanya's sobs subsided. Only Abraham's voice filtered through the frosted tarp:

"Let's run in the fields, in the farms, explore the vineyards; have the vines flowered, have the poppies reddened, have the pomegranates sprouted? There I shall give myself to you, my beloved."

Elie and Abraham settled in a clump of boulders overlooking the narrow road. It was an unpaved stretch of muddy, brown dirt that parted the snow-covered, untended fields all the way to the eastern horizon, where the frontline was delineated with flares of explosions. The American forces would be here in a day or two, but meanwhile, this country road showed signs of recent use, most likely by cowardly German officers escaping to Potsdam and Berlin.

Elie focused the binoculars on the spot where the road meandered between low-lying hills. He smoked a Lande Mokri cigarette—the last one from a pack he had found on a warm corpse the previous week. Abraham sat against a rock, reading a Karl May western, which he had found in the wreckage of a German command truck. He was whistling the tune of the *Song of Songs*, which irritated Elie. General von Koenig's handgun rested on a rock by his arm, its ivory plated handle bright in the sun, which peeked through the clouds.

A vehicle appeared. Elie adjusted the binoculars, following it. "An open staff car. A driver and three officers. Field uniform."

Abraham cocked the handgun and stuck it in his belt. He reached for one of the Sturmgewehr 44 machine guns that leaned against the rock. "Here comes breakfast."

Elie stubbed the cigarette carefully and placed it on the ground for later. "They're moving fast." He cradled his machine gun and leaned against the side of a boulder. He would be invisible to the Germans until they reached the nearest section of the road, where they would have to look up to notice him—too late for evasive maneuvers or a counter attack. "They got no escort. Idiots."

Abraham took the binoculars and gazed. "Is that a white flag on the antenna?"

Elie took back the binoculars and examined the approaching vehicle. The fluttering cloth on the antenna wasn't a unit banner.

It was a white rag. What did it mean? Had the war ended? Then why were the front lines still alive with artillery shells? "Must be a trick," he said.

"I'll question them." Abraham was already halfway down the hillside, running toward the road. "Cover me from above." He reached the road when the German staff car was close enough to hear its engine. He stepped into the middle of the road, aimed his submachine gun at the approaching vehicle, and raised his hand to stop them.

Elie made sure his own Sturmgewehr 44 was set to *Automatic*, leaned against the boulder, and watched.

The staff car slowed down. The driver downshifted. The three officers sat straight, as immobile as mannequins. None of them reached for a weapon.

The driver came to a full stop a stone-throw away from Abraham. From above, Elie could see them clearly. The field uniform wasn't Wehrmacht. It was SS.

The driver raised his hands.

Abraham stepped closer and yelled at them in German to get out of the vehicle.

The officers in the rear exchanged a quick word. The one in the front raised a stick with another white rag. It was then that Elie saw the driver reach down for something and instinctively pulled the trigger. The brief spray of bullets hit the driver. But Elie's gun suddenly jammed. He tried to pull the trigger again.

Nothing.

Meanwhile, the officer in the front drew his handgun and aimed upward to the general area where Elie was hiding. His first bullet hit the boulder, and Elie ducked, struggling to pull out the magazine and reload.

There was more shooting below. Automatic weapons.

The jam released, Elie aimed downward and pulled the trigger. But the staff car was vacant, and the trail of his bullets followed the three Germans as they sprinted to the opposite side of the road. He got one of them in the back. The remaining two dropped into a ditch.

Abraham was lying in the middle of the road, his chest bloodied.

Elie made his way down the hillside, taking shelter behind boulders, waiting for the first bullet to chase him. But the SS officers were not shooting. Perhaps they didn't have time to grab their guns, or they were out of bullets. He dropped low near the road and peeked over it, the barrel of his gun aimed forward.

Two sets of hands stuck up from the ditch. "Don't shoot," one of them yelled. "We surrender!"

"Come out!" He glanced at Abraham, who wasn't moving.

The two Germans climbed out from the ditch, their hands up in the air. "It's over," one of them said. "The Führer killed himself!"

That explained it. The war would go on for a little while, until someone else assumed power and officially surrendered. But the SS was already running for cover.

"The Führer is dead," the other German said, as if the news bore repeating.

"*Mazal Tov.*" Elie pressed the trigger, perforating them. But as his gun quieted, he heard the distant staccato of shooting, and bullets shrieked over his head. Down the road, another German vehicle was approaching fast.

He ran, passing by Abraham, whose eyes were open, his lips moving, a puddle of blood spreading around him. General von Koenig's handgun rested on the road by Abraham's limp hand.

Tanya spent most of that gray day clearing snow between trees in search of edible remnants of last summer's vegetation. The cannon fire was getting closer. The Allies were winning. Soon, the war would end, Abraham would take her to Palestine, and the warm sun would shine over their future.

In the early afternoon, she found the shriveled stalks of chicory and worked two more hours to dig up the roots from the frozen earth. She started a fire, melted snow in a pot, and by twilight it smelled almost like soup.

Elie showed up next to her like an apparition, no sound preceding him. He had lost his wool cap and one of his gloves. He crouched by the fire, shivering, panting, not looking up at her.

She turned, searching for Abraham. He wasn't there. Fear smacked her chest.

When his breathing returned to normal and the bluish hue of his face receded, Elie ladled a bowlful and sipped the hot liquid, spitting out bits of roots. He handed her the bowl and sat on his heels, taking apart his weapon. He held up the dismantled barrel and looked through it at the fire. "Damn thing jammed at the worst moment."

Unable to hold back any longer, Tanya said, "Where is he?"

"They turned Abraham into a bloody sieve."

"*No!*" Her scream echoed through the forest. "*Abraham!*"

Elie reached for her hand. "I'll take care of you."

She ran into the dark woods, bumping blindly into trees, and fell in the snow, shaking, crying, refusing to believe. How could he be dead? He had been so alive only hours ago, hugging her, kissing her, loving her.

A bloody sieve.

Elie came for her. He was a diminutive man, but his grip was tight. He supported her back to the fire, forced her to drink what was left of the soup, and helped her into the tent. She could tell he had searched through her few belongings. She pressed her hand to her chest, feeling the contours of the small ledger through her clothes. His dark eyes followed her hand, but he said nothing.

She thought he would lie beside her, but he backed out of the tent. And why should he push it? She was now at his mercy, pregnant, without a soul in the world.

He waited for her to remove her coat, gloves, and hat, and placed them all under his head as he lay down to sleep at the foot of the tent, gripping his gun.

Curled up under the coarse blankets, Tanya shook with tremors that travelled like waves through her body. She could smell Abraham all around her, feel his presence, his love. But the words rang in her ears. *A bloody sieve.*

An hour passed, maybe more. Her hand reached to his side of the tent and found a shirt he had tossed aside the previous night. She pressed it to her face, inhaling his sweet smell, and sobs swelled in her chest. But she steeled herself. There would be plenty of time to cry, but only a brief window to escape.

Elie seemed asleep, but she didn't trust him. He was clever, devious. She listened to the pace of his breathing, the slight snoring, and waited.

It started snowing again, and soon he shifted, drawing deeper into his cocoon of tarp and blankets. Yet she waited another hour before starting the tedious work of undoing the threads that bound the head of the tent. When the opening was wide enough, she inched forward until her trembling body was out.

A wolf howled far inside the forest.

Elie grunted. His gun rattled as he turned under the covers.

She waited, holding her breath.

His snoring resumed.

Reaching into the tent, Tanya slowly pulled out a blanket, which she wrapped around herself. She listened for the sounds of the front, where fighting had not paused for the night, and headed toward it through the thick woods. Under the canopies, the snow was still deep, reaching up to her thighs. She pulled one leg after the other.

The wolf howled again, closer this time. Another one joined him. And a third.

She tried to go faster. The heat from her body melted the snow, soaking her long underpants and the blanket on her back. The boots filled with snow, which turned into freezing, muddy slush. She progressed, maddeningly slow. Her teeth clattered, her muscles twitched, and a rustle of branches nearby made her shout, "Who's there?"

More howling. From all directions. Or was it a single wolf, circling, closing in?

She wanted to lie down, to cover herself with snow, to sleep. "*No!*"

She pulled off her boots and swung them around as weapons. She took another step, her legs as heavy as logs. Another step.

Voices nearby. Was it Elie Weiss?

No! The words were foreign! *English!*

"Help me," She yelled. "Please! Help!"

An animal ran at her, eyes like darts of light. Tanya held up her arms, and the animal rammed her. Hot, foul breath, followed by a sharp pain.

She fell backwards, crying his name, *"Abraham!"*

Twenty-one years later ...

Chapter 3

Rabbi Abraham Gerster led his men up the dirt path. Behind them, West Jerusalem glowed in the reddish evening sun. At the top of the hill, he mounted a squat, massive boulder, which overlooked the Armistice border that cut Jerusalem in half. The wind suddenly lashed at him, trying to snatch away his black hat, but he held it and recited in a booming voice, "*Hear us, God! Gentiles defiled your Temple, turned Jerusalem to ruins!*"

Psalms seventy-nine, Lemmy thought as he climbed after his father onto the boulder.

"*They fed your chosen to the vultures, your faithful to the wild beasts.*" Rabbi Gerster paused as the men repeated the words.

Lemmy pressed down his hat, shading his eyes, and stepped to the edge of the boulder while chanting the next line, "*Spilled our blood like water around Jerusalem.*" He gazed at the rolls of barbed wire below, running north-south like rough stitches left by a careless surgeon. Beyond the serpentine wires, he saw the Jordanian bunkers, gun barrels sticking out of shooting slats. They occasionally fired across the border, killing or maiming a passerby on the Jewish side. But they never did it on a Friday, Islam's holy day.

"*Pour your wrath, God,*" Rabbi Abraham Gerster continued, "*upon the Gentiles.*"

As the men repeated the words, Lemmy looked further up, beyond the border and bunkers, at the Old City. It had been in Arab hands since 1948, and he could smell the familiar mix of smoke and dust and reeking human waste. The Dome of the Rock dominated the skyline, a golden mosque built atop the ruins of the holy Temple. The Old City seemed to float in the air, *on wings of holiness,* as his father had once said. It was built on Mount Moriah, where God had once told the patriarch Abraham to sacrifice his only son. Lemmy imagined little Isaac following Abraham up that hill—

"Pssst!" His father motioned him to get off the boulder.

Lemmy jumped down and rejoined the group. He bumped into Benjamin, his best friend and study companion, who was rocking devoutly, his eyes shut in devotion. Benjamin stumbled back, and they pushed each other, laughing. A young scholar nicknamed Redhead Dan turned and glared at them. Benjamin resumed murmuring Psalms, and Lemmy pretended to do the same.

Up on the boulder, Rabbi Gerster opened his arms and sang, *"Bring us back to you, God, and we shall come."*

The men of Neturay Karta—"City Sentinels" in Aramaic— sang with him as they had done every Friday afternoon for eighteen years, *"Return us to the old days of glory!"*

The wind picked up again. It had risen from the Dead Sea, through the barren canyons of the Judean Desert, collecting dust, which lodged in their beards and spiral side locks. They swayed in prayer, fists pressed to their chests, clustered behind the boulder and their rabbi's open arms. Behind them, the red ball of the sun descended toward the distant Mediterranean Sea.

In the back of the group, Lemmy picked up a pebble and tossed it up in the air, catching it with a fast hand. He watched his father's arms reach wide in a symbolic embrace of the Old City, the same arms that had used to carry him onto the boulder. He had grown since, almost eighteen, almost ready for marriage and children of his own. But still, even now, his father seemed like a giant to him.

The pebble by his ear, he imagined hearing swords clinking as men in armor marched by. Were they Absalom's rabble rousers, seizing Jerusalem from his aging father, King David? Or the crusaders, rushing to the Church of the Holy Sepulcher? In his mind he walked the narrow alleys of the Old City, smelled the bittersweet aroma of burning hashish and camel feces, heard the chimes of bells and the prayers of muezzins.

"*If I forget thee, Jerusalem,*" Rabbi Gerster led his men in a mournful chant, "*my right hand shall wither.*" They repeated the chant, and the rabbi glanced over his shoulder at his son. Lemmy joined the chant, swaying back and forth, "*My right hand shall wither.*"

Rabbi Gerster turned back to face the Old City, his voice louder than the wind. "*My tongue shall stick to my palate, if I don't remember Jerusalem!*" He raised his right hand, his fist clenched.

A shot sounded in the distance, and the black hat flew from the rabbi's head.

Lemmy stared at his father up on the boulder, expecting him to collapse.

A second shot. Dirt blew up near the rabbi's feet.

The men yelled and fell to the ground, cowering behind the boulder.

But Rabbi Abraham Gerster kept his fist up in defiance of the anonymous Jordanian sniper and continued the chant, "*If I don't remember thee—*"

Another shot, the bullet shrieking above.

Peeking over the rock, Lemmy tried to locate the source of the fire, but the echoes bounced from all directions.

"*If I don't put Jerusalem above my own happiness!*"

With the chant concluded, Rabbi Gerster bowed in the direction of Temple Mount and stepped toward the edge of the rock. A final shot popped, and the bullet hit the ground where his shoe had rested a second before.

This last one sounded like it came from the north, an area under Israeli control, but Lemmy knew that was impossible. He heard a distant siren from the UN observers' station to the south.

Bent over in fear, the men ran downhill, except for their rabbi, who paced calmly, indifferent to the shrieking bullets. Lemmy chased his father's hat, catching it halfway down the hill, and brought it back. Rabbi Gerster examined the hat and poked a finger through the bullet hole. The bearded men congregated around their leader, watching in awe. Redhead Dan yelled, "A miracle! A miracle!"

The sun's last rays touched the roofs. Sabbath was about to begin, time to return to Meah Shearim, the enclosed neighborhood where the insular sect of Neturay Karta lived in strict observance of the Torah, insulated from the sinful ways of the surrounding Zionist society.

"It was a close call." Rabbi Gerster put an arm on his son's shoulders. "Blessed be He, Master of the Universe."

"Amen," Lemmy said.

They walked down the steep path, worn from eighteen years of weekly visits. The men glanced at the rabbi, their anxiety mixed with elation at having witnessed a miracle. They were devoted to him, a holy man who had emerged from the ashes of the Holocaust alone, not yet twenty years old. Lemmy had heard the stories from others, how his father had come to Neturay Karta to seek refuge among the faithful. His payos had barely started to regrow, the scars on his chest still fresh. But he was the scion of the famous Gerster rabbinical line, and the sect's elders took him in. They matched him with a wife, Temimah, another survivor of the war. In 1948, when the Jordanians had exiled the Jews from the Old City, Abraham Gerster took a vow not to travel away from Jerusalem until Temple Mount was restored to Jewish sovereignty. And when a son was born to him, he named him Jerusalem, though everyone called the boy Lemmy, as if his given name was too holy to be used lightly. With the passing years, Abraham Gerster had gained a vast knowledge of Talmud and a reputation for calm wisdom, becoming the leader of Neturay Karta.

As they reached Shivtay Israel Street, Lemmy saw a woman standing by the roadside. She was petite and slender, her dark hair collected in a bun. A sleeveless dress exposed her shoulders, and her plain sandals revealed tanned ankles.

Lemmy was shocked. Zionist women never ventured near Neturay Karta with their hair and limbs so immodestly exposed.

The men murmured contemptuously and pulled down the brims of their hats to hide the sinful sight.

The woman stepped forward and blocked Rabbi Gerster's way. She stared up at him with piercing green eyes. And before anyone managed to interfere, she reached up and touched his beard.

This unimaginable violation—a woman's impure hand touching the rabbi!—unleashed Redhead Dan, who charged forward like a bull, ramming her. Her heel caught the curb, and she fell backward and banged her head on the sidewalk.

The men closed in, cursing in Yiddish, fists clenched. Redhead Dan shouted, "*Shanda! Shanda!*" He plucked off his shoe and lifted it over the woman's head.

Without thinking Lemmy hurled himself at Redhead Dan and knocked him to the ground.

"Stop!" Rabbi Gerster raised his hand. "*Enough!*"

The men stepped back.

She sat up. A thin stream of blood dripped from her forehead, down her cheek, and onto her plain dress.

The rabbi kneeled by her side. He said nothing, but his face was pale. The woman pushed a lock of hair away from her face. He offered her a white handkerchief. She took it, pressed it to her bruised forehead, and began to laugh.

She laughed!

Lemmy realized she must be mad. Why else would she laugh?

She continued to laugh, yet tears flowed from her eyes.

The men watched their rabbi to see how he would react to her madness.

"Please visit us tomorrow." He gestured at the gate. "Over there."

She nodded.

He stood and walked away. His men hurried after him. Lemmy offered a hand to Redhead Dan, who refused it with an angry grunt and sprang to his feet unaided.

Just before entering the neighborhood gate, Lemmy glanced back. The woman was still sitting on the ground. She waved at him with his father's handkerchief, stained with her blood.

Elie Weiss crouched on the rooftop of a deserted house near the border. The gray beggar's cloak kept him warm, but the hood made his bald scalp itch. He unscrewed the sniper scope from the rifle and gazed through it as a monocular, watching Abraham and his bearded men disappear through the gate into Meah Shearim. Elie shifted his focus to Tanya. She pulled herself up and walked away. Unlike Abraham, the years had left no mark on her. She had remained delicate and childlike, a porcelain doll. But her appearance no longer matched her inner substance. The pregnant, teenage orphan had turned into a confident Mossad agent. It had been a stroke of luck when he had noticed her name, after all these years, on a secret list of decorated agents. He knew not to approach her directly, but had found a way to pass the information to her about the rabbi of Neturay Karta, whose name matched her dead lover. Yet throwing the two lovers back together was a gamble. It could set off a conflagration of passions that would derail his plans. But Elie had weighed the chances and bet on the idealistic innocence Abraham and Tanya shared, which would keep them from rushing into each other's arms at the expense of their respective missions. And having watched Abraham's son leap to Tanya's defense so impulsively, Elie suspected the youth might prove to be the key to effectively manipulating both his father and Tanya.

The UN siren, which his shots had awakened, died down. The armistice observers would assume it had been another bored Jordanian soldier and do nothing about it, as was their custom. He used the rifle scope to watch the UN Mideast Command at the old Government House across the border. Other than the guards kicking a ball in the courtyard, there was no activity. On the hill behind the UN compound, a rotary radar antenna turned lazily, curved as a giant sail, full with wind. It monitored the airspace constantly, enforcing the ban on aircraft operations in the region.

Elie put down the scope and sat on the tar roof to wait. He leaned back against the low wall surrounding the rooftop and pulled a cigarette from a pack of Lucky Strike. He smoked slowly, drawing deep, savoring the flavor of toasted burley. He didn't mind waiting. Darkness wasn't far off.

Chapter 4

On Sabbath morning, Lemmy accompanied his father to the synagogue, a large hall where prayers and studying took place daily from early morning to late night. It was filled to capacity. Cantor Toiterlich recited the morning prayers, and the men repeated after him. Children ran around, and the women in the upstairs mezzanine whispered gossip behind the lace partition. Abundant light came from the tall windows. The crossbeam ceiling, high above, carried an enormous crystal chandelier that glowed from Friday afternoon until Saturday night.

Midway through the service, the Torah scroll was carried to the dais for reading. The cantor called Rabbi Abraham Gerster up to the dais. The rabbi covered his head with the prayer shawl and recited the *Hagomel*—the prayer of gratitude for having survived mortal danger. When he finished, the men yelled, "Amen!" They had witnessed God reach down yesterday to spoil the sniper's aim and deflect the deadly projectiles from the rabbi.

When the reading ended, Cantor Toiterlich chanted a prayer for the rabbi's health and longevity. He followed with a special prayer for the rabbi's wife, Temimah, that God may cure her infertility and grace her with more sons, who would grow up to study Torah. With the rabbi and his wife approaching forty, the congregants murmured, "May His will be so!"

As soon as morning prayers ended, the women hurried to their small apartments to set up for the Sabbath lunch. The children ran between the wooden benches, their colorful clothes lively against the black attire of their fathers. The men stepped outside, squinting at the bright sun, and strolled down the alleys in groups, discussing Talmudic conundrums.

Waiting in the synagogue courtyard, Lemmy unbuttoned his black coat and raised his face to the sun, enjoying its warmth. Benjamin nudged him, and he saw his father and Cantor Toiterlich emerge through the double-doors.

"Good Sabbath," he said and shook their hands. Cantor Toiterlich lived with his wife and nine children in a two-room apartment three doors down from the rabbi. The eldest, a daughter named Sorkeh, stood behind her father.

Rabbi Gerster said, "Why don't you and Sorkeh talk a bit while we walk home?"

"Yes, Father." Lemmy's face flushed. The separation between the genders in Neturay Karta allowed for no youthful socializing. But Talmud prescribed: *At eighteen to the chuppah.* So when a boy of eighteen was told to chat with a girl after prayers, it meant that the matchmaker had already proposed to both sets of parents, the fathers had negotiated terms for providing the basic needs for the couple, and the mothers had found each other agreeable to share in helping the young mother with soon-to-arrive babies, while the groom continued to study Talmud. Marriage in Neturay Karta was a serious business, handled by the parents, who knew their sons and daughters better than the youths knew themselves.

Rabbi Gerster walked with Cantor Toiterlich and Benjamin down the alley. "We're facing a crisis," he said, "with the abortion law proposal in the Zionist Knesset."

"A desecration of God," the Cantor agreed, and they launched into a discussion.

Lemmy and Sorkeh followed a short distance behind.

"Nice weather today," he said.

"Warm! I like it!" She was a head shorter than he. Her flowery dress reached down to her shoes, fitting loosely on her plump, feminine figure. She must have just turned sixteen, the age at which Neturay Karta girls were added to the matchmaker's list. Unlike married women, the girls didn't cover their heads. Sorkeh's hair was her prettiest asset—a dark, reddish mass of curls that framed her round face.

"How are your studies going?" She smiled and touched her hair.

"Very well. Thank you." Lemmy thought how, moments after she would become a married woman, her head would be shaved smooth and covered with a kerchief—one of several fine, cotton headdresses she would receive as wedding gifts. The image of Sorkeh with a bald head made him grin.

She looked at him with an uncertain smile.

"I'm sorry," Lemmy said, "I just remembered something funny."

She nodded eagerly. "It happens to me too."

He felt the need to explain, but thought better of it.

"Sometimes," Sorkeh said, "I think of a funny occurrence, like when my mother was making the *keegel* for Sabbath, and the noodles overcooked and stuck together and she couldn't mix in the sugar!"

Lemmy chuckled politely.

Encouraged, she continued, "So we tried to mix the noodles with oil to separate them, and I was holding the pot—"

Tuning her out, Lemmy thought of yesterday's dramatic events. He recalled the Jordanian shooting, his father's arm on his shoulders, and the petite woman who touched his father's beard, her arm exposed, her skin smooth. He shuddered as the sun disappeared behind a gray cloud. The narrow alley had been neatly swept before the Sabbath, and the air was sweetened by the aroma of cooking pots that had been simmering since Friday. His mouth watered. Talmud forbade eating until after morning prayers, and he was famished.

"—and it took us an hour to clean up the mess!" Sorkeh burst out laughing.

Realizing she had reached the punch line, Lemmy smiled. "That's funny. Do you like to cook?"

"Oh, yes!" She launched into a long monologue about food preparations for Sabbath and various holidays.

With occasional head nodding, Lemmy paced along the connected row of apartment buildings, which had originally been designed as a wall of defense against Arab nomads, but now kept out the immoral, secular Israeli society.

He was relieved when they reached home. After further greetings, Cantor Toiterlich and his daughter left.

Rabbi Gerster entered the apartment first, touching the mezuzah on the doorframe and then his lips. They hung their coats in the foyer and entered the dining room, where the table had been set with silver utensils and white cloth.

Temimah and Benjamin's mother, Rachel, shuttled dishes from the kitchen. The mother and son had come to lunch every Sabbath since Benjamin's father had left the sect many years ago, never to be heard from again.

Benjamin's dark eyes glistened, and he whispered, "How was it?"

Lemmy crinkled his face.

Rabbi Gerster began to sing: "*Tranquility and joy, beacon for Israel, day of Sabbath, of rest, day of delight.*"

Benjamin and Lemmy joined him, singing the familiar tunes until the women were ready to serve the meal.

The rabbi recited the blessing on the wine goblet and the braided challah bread, which he sliced with a long, toothed knife. They ate *gefilteh* fish in jellied broth and wiped the plates with chunks of challah. The three of them sang again while Temimah and Rachel cleared the table.

Next came a large pot of *tcholent*—a concoction of meat, beans, vegetables, and spices that had been cooking overnight. Temimah's ladle broke through the crust, and she served her husband. He pointed at the steaming, generous portion. "My dear wife wants me to get fat!"

Temimah emptied a full ladle in Benjamin's plate, then in Lemmy's. Her face, framed by a headdress tied behind, was bright with sweat. "So?" she asked. "How is Sorkeh?"

Everyone looked at Lemmy.

"Sorkeh?" He creased his forehead. "Who's Sorkeh?"

They laughed, and the rabbi started chanting, "*Sabbath today, Sabbath the sacred day,*" saving Lemmy from further inquiries.

After the meal, while the women were busy in the kitchen, Rabbi Gerster leaned back in his armchair, sipped tea, and quoted from memory: "*The heaven and the earth were completed in all their glory, and on the seventh day God finished the work and blessed the Sabbath.*"

Lemmy listened carefully. Every Sabbath lunch, his father followed the same routine: A quote from the Torah and a trick question.

"Torah and Talmud," the rabbi intoned, "what's the difference?"

"Torah is God's word," Lemmy answered. "Cast in stone. Talmud, on the other hand, is a compilation of transcribed arguments between Talmudic scholars."

"I disagree," Benjamin said. "The sages' arguments originated from God's words, which had been passed down the generations by memorizing until the Babylonian exile, when every word was transcribed." As always, he ran out of breath before he ran out of words.

Rabbi Gerster turned to Lemmy. "*Nooo?*"

"How can Talmud be cast in stone? It's a collection of oral debates about law, rituals, business, science, ethics, animal sacrifices, and everything else."

"Since when," Benjamin asked, "does the style determine the substance?"

"Ah!" Rabbi Gerster lifted a finger. "A disagreement between two promising scholars!"

Lemmy noticed his father glance at his watch. Was he also thinking of the woman from yesterday? Would she come to visit?

"Talmud," the rabbi said, "just like Torah, is divine, and therefore solid and unchangeable. The sages were inspired when they expressed their arguments, channeling, so to speak, God's own words."

"But how can we apply fixed rules to a changing world?" Lemmy swayed in the manner of Talmudic scholars. "Torah says not to start a fire during the Sabbath. It made sense when starting a fire was hard work. But today we can flip a light switch with a finger."

"Good question!" Rabbi Abraham Gerster clapped his hands. "Why keep the rules? And why continue to wear long black coats and black hats even when the summer comes?"

"Tradition," Benjamin said.

"Correct." Rabbi Gerster lifted his tea cup but didn't slurp from it. "For thousands of years, Jews have kept a fire burning from before sunset on Friday and devoted the whole Sabbath to rest and study. Should we throw away those traditions just because men invented electricity?"

"Men didn't invent electricity," Lemmy said. "God did."

"True." Rabbi Gerster chuckled. "Good point."

"So maybe," Lemmy pressed on, "God expects us to understand that He created electricity for our use, Sabbath included, even though men had not discovered electricity until centuries after Talmud was written."

"God had reasons to delay such discovery," Benjamin said. "But the rule remains, because we turn the light on by closing an electrical circuit and creating something new, which is forbidden during Sabbath."

"Beautifully spoken!" Rabbi Gerster knuckled the table.

As if in response, someone knocked on the front door.

Lemmy went to the foyer and opened the door.

It was the woman from the alley. "Shalom," she said.

He nodded, unable to speak. Her black hair was again tied up in a knot, revealing a small bandage on her forehead, which otherwise was as white as marble. She wore a long dress with sleeves down to her wrists. Her eyes were accentuated by slanted cheekbones and pencil-thin eyebrows. Her beauty made Lemmy think of a sentence from morning prayers: *How wondrous your creation is, God. How wondrous!*

"I'm Tanya Galinski." She offered her hand.

He made a slight bow, but didn't take the hand.

"I forgot." She smiled and dropped her hand. "It's a sin to touch a female."

Lemmy beckoned her into the foyer.

"You must be Abraham's son."

He nodded.

"You inherited his good looks and his gallantry. Thanks for defending me yesterday."

Lemmy turned before she could see his blushing face and went to the dining room.

Benjamin was saying, "That's why Rabbi Eliezer said that—"

"Excuse me," Lemmy said. "It's the woman from yesterday."

Rabbi Gerster put down his teacup, which clanked against the saucer. He got up and went to the foyer, where he ushered her into his study and shut the door.

Lemmy stared at the door, astonished. Talmud forbade a man to be alone in a room with a woman other than his wife. How could his father shutter himself in his study like this? And with a secular woman, no less!

Chapter 5

When the door closed, Tanya handed him the white handkerchief, washed and neatly folded. He pocketed it and took her in his arms. Pressed to his chest, she could hear his heart beating through the black coat, which smelled of cooked food and mothballs. She held him tightly, expecting the surge of love and longing that had swept over her every time she had thought of Abraham over the years. But this man did not feel like *her* Abraham, and the tickle of his beard on her forehead suddenly overwhelmed her with something close to revulsion. She tore away from him, turning to face the wall of books.

He blew his nose. "Oh, Tanya! To see you alive!"

She looked up at him, this bearded, imposing rabbi, who had somehow evolved from the electrifying youth she had loved. The last months of World War II had been a burst of joy within a world of blood and suffering. But his death had hacked her spirit in half, turned her into an emotional amputee. During the intervening two decades, she had missed him constantly—the warmth of his skin, the firmness of his muscles, the taste of his lips. In her dreams, he appeared unchanged, stimulating her like nerve-ends on a missing limb. In her mind, he had remained young and fierce, full of venom for the Nazis and passion for her in an emotional dichotomy of equal intensity—an eighteen-year-old who killed and loved quickly, wholeheartedly, before his world came to an untimely end.

But this man radiated neither rage nor passion, and his blue eyes were filled not with fire, but with tears.

Tanya gestured at the small study, the walls of books, a plain desk, and a narrow cot with white linen. "For this you survived?"

"No! For *you* I survived. For you!" He unbuttoned his coat. "They picked me up from the road and threw me in the back of a truck. A field hospital, full of wounded, dying soldiers." He fumbled with the buttons of his white shirt. "It stunk of rotting flesh and gangrene, the ground muddy with blood." His shirt parted, exposing the scars—crests and cavities, red and blotchy. "But I wouldn't die!"

Tanya placed the palm of her hand on his rutted skin.

"I wouldn't give up," he said. "I was certain you were coming for me."

"My God," she whispered, moving her hand on his disfigured chest, "how terrible!"

"Through high fever and torturous chills, lungs filled with my own blood, I saw your face, felt your hand on my forehead. *She's coming! She's coming!*"

"But I—"

"Every time they cleaned my wounds, every time they squeezed the pus from my chest, I screamed. *She's coming! My Tanya is coming!*" His rabbinical facade was gone, his face twisted with agony. "But you didn't! Why?"

"You're blaming *me*?"

"Blame?" He groaned. "It's not about blame."

"Yes, it is! Why did you go with him that morning? To kill a few more Germans? They were losing the war anyway. You left me in the forest, and he came back. I was at his mercy!"

"You should have given Elie that bloody ledger."

"It wouldn't have satisfied him. I had to escape."

Abraham stepped closer, his head leaning forward to look down at her face. "Oh, God Almighty, you've remained the same. So beautiful."

Tanya stepped backward. "Elie told me. *They turned Abraham into a bloody sieve.* Those were his words: *Bloody sieve.* And the image has stayed with me since."

"So you ran away."

"What was I supposed to do?"

He seemed hurt by her very question. "Search for me!"

"For another rotting body among thousands?" She breathed deeply. "Why didn't you search for me?"

He used the handkerchief to wipe his eyes. "How I missed you. All these years!"

"Your loyalty wasn't to me."

"True." He buttoned up his white shirt and black coat. "I was filled with hate."

A lifetime had passed since she had last seen him, a youth with blond hair, walking off into the forest with Elie Weiss, fearless, eager to hunt down the retreating Nazi troops. *Bloody sieve.* But he had somehow survived and now, not yet forty, he looked like a biblical prophet, his beard long and gray, the odd, spiraling side locks dangling by his face. His blue eyes, still young, were set in wrinkles that didn't originate in smiling.

She fought back her tears, then gave in, letting them flow down her cheeks.

He took her hands and began to sing. "*Let's run in the fields, in the farms, explore the vineyards.*"

She couldn't breathe. His voice was the same—deep and solid, like the roots of a strong tree.

"*Have the vines flowered? Have the poppies reddened? Have the pomegranates sprouted?*"

She cried, and he cradled her face in his big hands. "*There,*" he sang, "*there I shall give myself to you, my beloved.*"

Tanya's hand reached up, the tips of her fingers on his moist forehead.

"I did search for you," he finally said, his voice cracked. "But I found Elie instead, and he showed me your boots and blanket, all chewed up, encrusted with your blood. He said there were bones too, even some hair, which he buried in the forest."

Tanya sighed. "I ran from him. The front was getting close, but the wolves, they smelled my fear, my desperation, and attacked me. American soldiers heard my screams. They shot some wolves, and the pack attacked the wounded." She shuddered. "I don't remember the rest."

His shoulders sank, deflated. "It's my fault. I left you defenseless. And for what? To hunt down Germans—an infantile revenge when the ultimate payback would have been *us!*"

"Us?"

"A family. Children. A new life. Isn't that what the Nazis had set out to destroy?"

She looked at him, finding traces of *her* Abraham under the untrimmed beard and premature wrinkles.

"When I saw those boots, the blood," he cleared his throat, as if the memory was choking him, "I lost hope, felt like I was dead, but still alive."

"So you rediscovered God?"

He sneered. "There's no God."

"But—"

"You of all people should know. You saw their assembly-lines of death, the factories of extermination, whole families, whole villages."

She nodded.

"You saw the innocent children. Pregnant women. Rabbis whose lives had been dedicated to worship, to the glory of God. How could He exist? It makes no sense, unless He is ruthless and evil and a menace, a graceless Almighty, who deserves neither undue recognition, nor unanswered prayers!"

Tanya glanced at the volumes of Talmud and other holy books lining the bookshelves.

He waved his hand in dismissal at the wall of books. "The Holocaust proved God doesn't exist. No God worth His divinity would allow it to happen."

"So why are you here?" She touched his beard. "I don't understand."

"After the war, Elie and I went to the camps. We saw the gas chambers, the crematoria, the skeletal survivors. I realized there was a purpose to my survival. I must prevent another Holocaust." He raised his hands in surrender. "My life belonged to the dead, to their legacy."

"And to Elie Weiss?"

"To the Jewish people." He showed her the palms of his hands. "I lost my faith, it's true, but I had been raised to be a rabbi, and those were useful skills."

She nodded, smiling sadly. "You're a mole among the fanatics."

"An agent of peace among Jews."

"How would this prevent another Holocaust?"

"A strong Jewish state is a national shelter and deterrence against our enemies. As rabbi of Neturay Karta, the most extreme fundamentalist sect in Israel, I fight internal strife among Jews, which has caused the destruction of every Jewish state in history. It's the biggest risk to our sovereign continuity. No one could do it better—I possess the rabbinical skills, but I am a realist, a secret atheist, a devout nationalist who's willing to do what it takes to control Jewish fanatics from destroying Israel. It's my destiny! Don't you see it?"

Again she saw a biblical prophet, not her Abraham. "And what's *our* destiny? You and I. To be apart?"

"That's our private tragedy. Yes." He sighed. "Where did you hide all these years?"

"I went where Elie wouldn't find me. Berlin."

Redness spread from his eyebrows upward through his forehead, the sign of anger she remembered from the snowy forests in 1945. "How could you go back? To *them?*"

"It's easier to hide in ruins."

"Did you find another Nazi lover?"

It felt like a slap in the face. "I gave birth at an American field hospital and helped them interrogate SS captives. Later, I joined *Aliyah Bet*, then the Mossad."

He sat on the cot, shaking his head. "I'm sorry. I don't have the right to judge you."

She noticed he didn't ask about the child. "I've been happy, considering. I work with terrific, idealistic colleagues. Israel is stronger because of our clandestine work."

"How smart, to hide within the secret service. But Elie found you eventually."

"Took him twenty-one years."

"How?"

"I earned a citation for a successful operation. He saw my name at the prime minister's office. A stroke of bad luck, I guess. But we can turn it into *good* luck." She watched his expression. "We can defy his manipulations, start all over, together!"

Abraham smiled. "Oh, how I wish we could."

"We're still young enough to start a new family, raise kids together." She held her breath, hoping he would ask about the child she had raised alone.

"How can I leave my people? Without me there will be religious riots, violence—"

"Elie can find another mole."

For a moment, Abraham's eyes brightened up, the sadness chased away by the prospect of handing over this mission to someone else, of starting over as a free man, reunited with the only woman he had ever loved. Tanya saw it in his face, and hope flooded her.

But the moment passed, and his sadness returned. "Maybe, one day. But not now. I can't."

"Why?"

"Because my mission needs me here."

"I need you." Her voice choked. "I've needed you for so long."

"I wish we could."

"Better to live a lie?" Her hopes dashed, Tanya was filled with rage. "To deceive your people?" She pointed at the narrow cot. "To deceive your wife? And your son?"

"He doesn't know any different. One day he'll assume the leadership—"

"And that makes it kosher?"

"Please, keep it down."

"How can you raise him to lead a bunch of misguided, religious fanatics?" Tanya hit the line of books with an open hand. "You teach him to obey a God whom you don't believe exists—"

"*Shhhh!*"

Tanya stormed out of the study. In the foyer she saw his teenage son, who quickly opened the door for her.

"Wait!" Abraham chased after her. "Be reasonable! It's a matter of life and death!"

"It's a sham!" She slapped his black coat.

"You don't understand!"

She tugged at his beard. "A fraud!"

"*Tanya!*"

"The hell with you, Abraham Gerster! I wish you had really died—at least it would have been an honorable death!"

He grabbed her arm. "This is bigger than you and me! Just listen—"

"Listen to a dead man?" Tanya jerked her arm free and hurried down the stairs.

Lemmy stepped back, flat against the wall. The fear in his father's face was inconceivable. No one had ever intimidated Rabbi Gerster, certainly not a woman.

He prodded Lemmy out the door. "Go, accompany her!"

Lemmy hesitated.

"Go on, son!"

Glancing back into the apartment, Lemmy noticed his mother watching from the kitchen door. Temimah Gerster's face was inscrutable, her mouth slightly open. Her hand held the doorpost, the knuckles bleached.

He caught up with Tanya, and they left Meah Shearim through the gate on Shivtay Israel Street. She turned north, walking fast, saying nothing. On the right, high rolls of rusted barbed wire marked the strip of no-man's land along the border with Jordan. They passed by Mandelbaum Gate—the only crossing between the two parts of Jerusalem. In addition to Israeli and Jordanian posts, it was guarded by the UN Truce Supervision Force, composed of Norwegian and Indian soldiers in blue caps. Tanya stayed close to the buildings, whose walls were pockmarked with shrapnel and bullet holes, left untended since 1948. Lemmy wondered if she knew about the Jordanian sniper's attempt on his father's life the day before.

He stole a quick glance at Tanya, who seemed oblivious to his presence. It was hard to guess her age. *Thirty? Forty?*

They reached a scarred, one-story house made of uncut stone. The east section was reduced to rubble, and two formerly internal doorways were sealed with bare bricks. Rusty metal shutters covered all the windows, shedding off dry flakes of turquoise paint. A wall of sandbags shielded the front door. The border was a stone-throw away, and he wondered why Tanya lived in such a perilous location.

She unlocked the door. "What's your name?"

"Lemmy," he said. "It's short for Jerusalem."

"How inspiring." Her sudden smile revealed a perfect set of white teeth. "Do you have any siblings?"

"None."

She went inside, leaving the door open, and reappeared with a book. "Here. A reward for your gallantry."

He looked at the cover. *The Fountainhead* by Ayn Rand. "Thanks, but I don't read such books."

"Why?"

"A good Jew devotes all his time to studying Talmud."

"Does Talmud forbid reading Ayn Rand?"

"Not specifically, but—"

"Aren't we supposed to be a guiding light for the Gentiles?" He nodded.

"How could Jerusalem Gerster be a guiding light to the *Goyim* if he's not allowed to become acquainted with their way of life?"

Embarrassed to keep staring at her, Lemmy examined the photo on the back of the book. "Is she a Gentile?"

"Ayn Rand?" Tanya laughed. "Actually, I think she's Jewish."

"Oh. Then I can read it."

"Bring the book back when you're done. I'd like to hear your impressions."

Lemmy stuffed *The Fountainhead* in the pocket of his black coat and headed back to Meah Shearim.

Elie Weiss sat in his gray Citroën Deux Chevaux, parked up the street from Tanya's house. He drew on his cigarette, watching Abraham's son. The black-garbed youth walked fast, his payos angled back in the wind like a girl's braids. Elie held up a black-and-white photograph that showed Jerusalem Gerster, his hand raised in emphasis of a Talmudic argument, while his study companion buried his face in his hands in mock desperation.

The second photo in Elie's hand was smaller, its edges fraying, yellow with age. He had taken this photo during the war with a camera that had previously hung from the neck of a Nazi officer. Abraham had twisted the leather strap tighter and tighter until the German's tongue grew out of his mouth like a baby eggplant and his black boots stopped twitching. In the photo, Abraham was already wearing the boots, which had fit him perfectly.

Elie held the two photos together, the face of young Abraham in 1945 next to the face of his son in last week's photo, which Elie had taken from a rooftop near Meah Shearim. The resemblance was astonishing, which meant Tanya was now very confused.

He dropped the photos on the passenger seat, drew once more from his Lucky Strike, and tossed it out the window. A gust of wind blew smoke back in his face, and his eyes moistened. He closed the window and latched it in place. Pressing the lever into first gear, he made a U-turn and drove away, leaving behind a wake of blue engine fumes.

Chapter 6

Lemmy had memorized the landmarks along the way, which he now followed in reverse order. He thought of Tanya's sculpted face, one moment serious, the next smiling. *The Fountainhead*, in his coat pocket, banged against his thigh with every step. Should he read it? Should he know more about the *Goyim*, as Tanya had argued? Father had once said that Talmud contained all the knowledge a man needed. But that obviously wasn't accurate. Electric lights, for example, weren't mentioned anywhere in the thousands of pages of Talmud. Perhaps *The Fountainhead* would also illuminate things that were not mentioned in the Talmud? He reached into his pocket and touched the book, feeling a quiver of excitement. He remembered a Yiddish idiom: *Stolen water is so much sweeter.*

Along the way he passed through a secular neighborhood. A group of teenage boys and girls played soccer in an empty lot. They wore short-sleeved shirts, three-quarter pants, and leather sandals. The girls wore ponytails, but the boys' hair was short, even where their payos should have been left untouched according to Jewish law. He stood at a distance, intrigued by the ease with which they played together, the girls as aggressive as the boys. The ball found its way into the goal, marked by two rocks, and the scoring team cheered and hugged. A girl locked her arms around a boy's torso and hoisted him up in the air.

They noticed Lemmy and stopped playing. He tipped his black hat and resumed walking. One of them started imitating the calls of a crow. Several others joined in, and a choir of crows sounded behind him.

Lemmy paused and turned. He stretched his arms sideways like wings and mimicked a flying bird. They laughed, and the crowing ceased. A girl put her hands around her mouth and yelled, "Good Sabbath!"

He waved. "Good Sabbath to you."

Twenty minutes later, Lemmy turned the corner on Shivtay Israel Street. He stopped and stared. What he saw seemed unreal. The gate leading into Meah Shearim was closed. Chairs and tables were piled against it from within. The metal shades had been shut over all the windows in the outer walls. A crowd of Neturay Karta men in black coats and red faces filled the alley behind the gate. Someone shouted, "The rabbi's son!" Others yelled at him to run away.

A bunch of policemen in riot gear hid behind their vehicles from a steady shower of eggs and vegetables. One of them ran toward Lemmy. Brass fig leaves adorned his shoulders, and egg yolk smeared his chest. He raised his club, his eyes wide under the gray helmet, and shouted in Hebrew, "Where are you going?"

Lemmy pointed to the gate.

The officer grabbed his arm and pulled him toward a police van. "You're under arrest!"

Angry protests sounded from the gate.

A policeman aimed a shotgun, and his colleague slipped a cylindrical grenade into the open end of the barrel.

"Don't!" Lemmy struggled to get free.

The policeman pressed the butt of the shotgun to his shoulder.

Lemmy wriggled free, sprinted at the policeman, and knocked him down. An explosion slapped a wave of heat at his face, and the world turned dark.

Elie Weiss entered the police compound at the Russian Yard and headed downstairs. The operations center, a beehive of activity during the week, was manned by a single policewoman. Her feet were on the table, and she was humming *Jerusalem of Gold* along with Shuli Natan on the radio.

She gave him a casual salute. "What's happening?"

"You tell me."

"Major Buskilah is in Meah Shearim, making an arrest."

"*Trying* to make an arrest."

"Whatever."

"Has he called for reinforcement yet?"

"On a Sabbath? I don't have anyone to send there." She took her feet off the table. "You want Buskilah on the wireless?"

"I have a feeling he'll call us soon." Elie sat down and lit a cigarette.

When Lemmy's vision recovered, he saw the grenade spewing teargas under a truck. The policeman, shotgun still in hand, struggled to get up. *Where's the officer?* Lemmy turned his head in time to see the club coming down on his buttocks. He screamed in agony and rolled away. Faint shouts came from the gate, and a bunch of shoes flew over, landing on the cowering policemen. The officer chased Lemmy, the club raised for another blow, his face a mask of hate. He missed and raised the club again, yelling in Hebrew.

Lemmy ran faster. *I'm going to die!*

Picking up speed, he glanced back, stumbled, and fell. The officer had no time to avoid him and tripped, and rolled over. Lemmy saw an opening, landed a punch into the officer's crotch, and sprinted toward the gate. A hoard of policemen were chasing him, but he didn't look back. He reached the gate and turned right, running around the outside wall of Meah Shearim. Farther down, a metal shade swung open, and Benjamin's head emerged. Lemmy raced to the window, the policemen's steps thudding behind him. The window was high. As he came closer, he did not slow but instead sent one foot forward and kicked the wall, which catapulted him high enough to grab the window sill. Benjamin caught his arms, someone else got his coat, and they hauled him inside.

He found himself on the floor, the room full of men, Benjamin talking excitedly, calling him "*meshuggah!*"

There was havoc around the window. Club strokes rang on the wall and the metal shutters. A helmeted head appeared, and then another one. Lemmy realized the Zionist police would soon get through, beating in heads and slapping on handcuffs. He got up and stood aside as someone carried a pot of steaming *tcholent* to the window. A second later the policemen screamed outside.

They hurried through the small apartment, which was missing furniture and its front door. The crowd by the gate jeered as the policemen ran back and hunkered down behind their vehicles. The road was dotted with black shoes, vegetables, and patches of yolk and eggshells.

Lemmy realized that his hat was gone, his black coat was torn in two places, and blood stained his white shirt. His buttocks ached badly.

"Coming through!" Redhead Dan pushed through the crowd with a wheelbarrow loaded with bricks. He reached the gate and handed out bricks.

The officer shouted at his subordinates, and they advanced at the gate.

Redhead Dan yelled, "Heretics!" He hurled a brick, hitting the windshield on one of the vans. A cheer came from the crowd, and he shouted: "Death to the Zionists! Death to the enemies of God!"

The officer pulled out his handgun. He aimed upward and released one shot.

All the black-garbed men turned as one and fled up the narrow alley toward the synagogue, except for Redhead Dan, who stayed by the gate and shouted, "Don't run! God is great! Don't run!"

Lemmy took refuge in a doorway. He heard someone yell, "The rabbi! The rabbi!"

Rabbi Abraham Gerster appeared at the synagogue doors up the alley. He walked in measured steps toward the gate. The men parted to give him a wide berth, bowing their heads in respect, or embarrassment. He was dressed in Sabbath clothes—black coat, white shirt, and a wide-brimmed, black velvet hat, which cast a shadow over his bearded face.

The officer watched from across the gate, gun in hand, deputies wielding their clubs.

The rabbi waved a hand, and a handful of men removed the chairs, tables, and doors. The hinges screeched as the gate opened.

He walked into the street, approaching the officer, who holstered his gun and took off his helmet, revealing gray hair. They spoke for a few moments. The officer kept shaking his head, and Rabbi Gerster pointed at the van. The officer pulled out a mouthpiece attached to a spiral cord. He stood in a pool of shattered glass, engaged in an angry exchange with a person on the other end of the radio. He threw the mouthpiece onto the driver's seat and beckoned his men.

Rabbi Gerster spoke to him, and the officer gestured at his crotch, his eyes searching the silent crowd. He pointed. "There! The punk with blond hair!"

Rabbi Gerster curled his finger at Lemmy.

Benjamin muttered, "*Oy vey!*"

"Say Kaddish for me." Lemmy limped out the gate.

His father looked at him—the dirty pants, the bloodied shirt, and torn coat. "Major Buskilah says you punched him."

"He clubbed me. Here!" Lemmy motioned at his behind.

The major took a step forward. "You little—"

"*Jerusalem!*" Rabbi Gerster pointed. "Apologize to this man."

"I'm very sorry." Lemmy smiled at Major Buskilah. "May God ease your pain in a week or two."

"That's enough!" Rabbi Gerster waved his hand. "Go home and clean up!"

Benjamin waited at the gate. "What did he say?"

"We discussed the weather. Why are they here, anyway?"

"You don't know?"

"What?"

"There was a demonstration downtown!"

Cheering sounded as Major Buskilah and his men drove off. Rabbi Gerster crossed the soiled street. The cheering quieted down. He entered the gate and walked up the alley. The men watched in silence until he entered the synagogue.

"Did you see that? Your father scared away the police!"

"What demonstration?"

"Redhead Dan organized a group. They went to King George Street to protest the abortion law. The drivers were honking, so Dan threw a rock at a car. They say the driver was injured." Benjamin nodded knowingly. "God punished him for driving a car on Sabbath."

"Throwing rocks is also forbidden on Sabbath." Lemmy had heard his father say it. "Let's find my hat."

Chapter 7

After instructing Major Buskilah over the radio to leave Meah Shearim, Elie Weiss waited at the Russian Yard police headquarters until the force returned. The major was fuming. "We should have arrested them! Stone throwing is a crime!"

"Count your blessings," Elie said. "The event ended without serious injury and, even more importantly, without any media presence."

"Appeasement will only empower these fanatics!"

"Leave the strategy to me."

"You're a civilian. This is a police matter."

"It's a political matter, and I speak for the prime minister. From now on, you'll consult with me before taking any action against the ultra-Orthodox. Understood?"

Major Buskilah grunted, but he didn't argue anymore.

From the Russian Yard, Elie drove to Premier Eshkol's official residence in the Rehavia neighborhood. The house rested in the shade of a giant elm tree. The previous meeting had just ended, and Elie saw Chief of Staff General Yitzhak Rabin cross the small courtyard and get into his staff car, which drove off.

An assistant showed Elie in.

Like David Ben Gurion before him, in addition to being prime minister, Levi Eshkol also held the defense portfolio. The meeting with General Rabin had left him with a red face. "They're sucking my blood, Weiss, and spitting it in my face!" Eshkol dropped into a chair. "I'll be remembered as the klutz who got lost in Ben Gurion's big shoes."

"You're doing a fine job," Elie said.

"And what about your job? You told me they'll only chant Psalms and go home to eat tcholent. Now they've put a driver in the hospital, and the opposition is drafting a no-confidence resolution for tomorrow's Knesset session over my government's failure to rein in the *meshuggeneh* black hats. I don't need this! I have President Nasser and King Hussein and the crazy Syrians to deal with!"

Elie lit a cigarette. "It was an accident."

"Accident is the incompetent's fig leaf." Levi Eshkol had been pressed into leadership by Golda Meir and the other old-guard Labor leaders, who used him to block the younger politicians from ascending to the top. But now the Arabs were gearing up for another wholesale attack on Israel, and the media was pressuring Eshkol to yield the defense portfolio to the famed General Moshe Dayan. "Are you losing your touch, Weiss? My people were able to cut deals with the religious parties on the abortion vote in the Knesset—"

"Neturay Karta is not a party." Elie stubbed his cigarette in an ashtray that was already full. "It's a fundamentalist sect that cuts no deals, a fuse that can ignite a nationwide religious revolt."

"My point exactly. They are your responsibility." He shook his finger at Elie. "I inherited you, Weiss. I was told that your Special Operations Department can handle them, but I'm starting to have doubts."

"Why?"

"With food comes appetite. Now rocks, tomorrow guns."

"Shooting is not a Talmudic skill," Elie said. "My reports outline our strategy. Neturay Karta is the epicenter of Jewish fundamentalism, of fervent anti-Zionists. We've been monitoring them for two decades. Ben Gurion had expected bloody religious riots within five years of declaring independence. It's been almost two decades, and I've been able to contain them."

The mention of Ben Gurion's name had the desired effect. Prime Minister Eshkol seemed deflated. "I don't read the Bible every day like he does. Maybe I should."

"A small disturbance here and there is a small price to pay for civic order."

"Not so small if you're the poor driver who paid with a cracked skull." The prime minister took off his thick glasses and started polishing them. "If they go *meshuggah* again, you must crush them like flies."

"Neturay Karta might be a small sect, but thousands of ultra-Orthodox citizens would come to its defense from all over Israel—Haifa, Tel Aviv, Beersheba. I have informers everywhere. The black hats despise the Jewish state as a sin against God. They view the secular majority of Israelis as heretics."

"You exaggerate." The prime minister pulled off his shoes and rested his feet on a chair. "How many do we have nationwide?"

"Altogether about seven percent of the population. And they believe only God and his Messiah may rebuild the Jewish homeland." Elie snapped his fingers. "Miracle making is reserved for God. They deny the authority of the government, and if they choose to go from Talmudic pontifications to action, they could destroy the Zionist dream."

"They can sit back and let the Arabs do the job." Prime Minister Eshkol sighed. "The Soviets have been arming the Arabs to the teeth—planes, ships, tanks, rockets, guns. The wars of 'forty-eight and 'fifty-six were child's play compared to what's awaiting us. They won't repeat their mistakes. And if the Jordanians join Egypt and Syria? A unified Arab force, trained and armed by the Soviets, attacking us simultaneously on all three fronts! *Armageddon!*"

"What about the UN?" Elie was referring to the Truce Supervision Force, which had monitored the borders since 1948.

"General Bull is useless." Eshkol was referring to the former chief of the Norwegian air force, with the unlikely name Odd Bull, who commanded UN forces in the Middle East. "He's a like a castrated sperm bull who knows what he's supposed to do but can't perform."

Elie chuckled. The prime minister's metaphor was poignant. The UN observers, sent to keep the peace, had no power to counter belligerence.

"The Arabs," Eshkol said, "learned the lessons of past defeats—"

"We also learned some lessons."

"We have one tank to their hundred! One rifle to their thousand! One soldier to their ten thousand!"

"One smart Jew is better than ten thousand Arab soldiers. And don't worry about Neturay Karta. My guy can handle them."

"With one man inside you hope to contain such a fire?"

"It would help if you could delay the abortion vote."

Eshkol shook his head. "We're socialists. Our labor unions and the kibbutzim want to see progressive legislation, gender equality, women's rights. Otherwise, what differentiates us from the Arabs?"

"I understand." Elie stood to leave. "Oh, almost forgot. I have a favor to ask."

The prime minister peered at him through his thick eyeglasses. "Money?"

"My department is self-funded, as you know."

"Then maybe you can spare some cash for a few tanks?"

"Of course, as soon as you appoint me chief of the Mossad."

Prime Minister Eshkol laughed.

Elie didn't mind. He would eventually get his wish. He had bankrolled the Special Operations Department with money and valuables he and Abraham had taken from the Nazis they had killed. In the past twenty years, he had traveled to Paris regularly to withdraw cash from several accounts he maintained there under a false identity. It allowed him to finance SOD activities outside the Israeli government's budgetary controls. But SOD was nothing compared with Mossad. His secret plan was to gain possession of General von Koenig's fortune and win control over Mossad. With both money and the infrastructure of overseas espionage, he would become the master of a formidable clandestine apparatus with limitless powers.

"So, what's the favor?"

"There's someone," Elie said, "a Mossad operative whom I need. A temporary assignment."

"Yes?"

"It will only be part-time, nothing too involved."

Prime Minister Eshkol grabbed a pencil and opened his notebook. "What's his name?"

"Tanya Galinski. She's currently—"

"*Ohhhh!*" Eshkol grinned, taking off his glasses. "Tanya Galinski! *Ah scheinah meidaleh.*"

Elie didn't respond.

"And what do you want with Mossad's loveliest secret?"

"She's been brought back for an eavesdropping assignment. What I need from her won't interfere with her current duties."

"I'll approve it. Maybe you'll get lucky with Miss Galinski."

Chapter 8

Lemmy could not sit for the rest of the day. After sunset, when Sabbath was over, Temimah crushed a block of ice and wrapped it in a kitchen towel. "Lie on your belly and put it on."

"Thanks." He turned to go to his room.

"It's time you grow up," she said. "Your father expects you to take over some of his responsibilities."

"Like what?"

She scrubbed a pot, which had waited in the sink for Sabbath to end. "Sorkeh Toiterlich is a wonderful girl, and you're almost eighteen."

Most of his contemporaries were already engaged, except Benjamin who, without a father, was a more challenging match. "I don't feel ready," Lemmy said.

"It's not a question of being ready." His mother filled the pot with soapy water. "It's your duty to God. To the Jewish people. And to me."

This surprised Lemmy. He had never thought of starting a family as a duty to his mother, whose daily life consisted of fulfilling her duties to others—to his father, to him, to the sect and its needy members. It had never occurred to him that she was also entitled, that she could be the beneficiary of someone else's duty.

Temimah resumed scrubbing the deep pot with an iron brush. "It's not enough for me, taking joy in other people's children." The brush scrubbed faster. "I'm not asking very much."

"Asking me to marry isn't much?" Lemmy shifted the pack of ice between his hands.

"She'll be a good wife. I'll help her with everything. And you can keep studying in the synagogue with Benjamin every day as if nothing happened."

"But I don't feel anything for her."

Temimah's hand stopped scrubbing. She looked at him, her eyes moist under the tight headdress. "Do you feel something for me?"

He didn't know what to say.

"I've prayed for more children of my own." She glanced at the ceiling. "But your father is a special man. He knows what's best and I, well, I'm his wife. That's my duty. But I crave to hold a baby. If not mine, at least yours." She turned back to the sink.

Lemmy watched her shoulders tremble. What could he say? He wanted to relieve her sorrow, but the thought of standing with Sorkeh under the *chuppah* made him cringe. "Good night, Mother," he said.

She didn't answer.

He locked himself in his room, stretched on the bed with the pack of ice on his buttocks, and began reading *The Fountainhead*.

Hours later, his full bladder tore him away from the story. He hurried down the dark hallway to the bathroom and back to his room to continue reading. When he finished the book, the morning sun shone through the window above his bed. He closed his eyes and imagined the tall, square-jawed Howard Roark, the architect who defied the masters of his profession, mocking their grotesque imitations of ancient Rome in American cities, their pasting of motifs from a French chateau or a Spanish villa onto modern towers of wealth. Instead, Roark designed functional buildings in furious, brutal objectivism. Lemmy admired Roark's unyielding integrity, his willingness to sacrifice everything for his beliefs, and his love for Dominique Francon, who loved him back but joined the enemies, who swore to silence his genius.

The Fountainhead excited Lemmy in an unfamiliar way. He could recite from memory full chapters of Torah and Talmud, which he had studied since the age of three. He loved the scriptures' poetic beauty and logical wisdom, and until now believed nothing else was worth reading. But here was a book that had absolutely no Torah or Talmud in it, and yet from its pages emerged a universe rich with men and women who fought for their beliefs, suffered for their idealistic goals, and served as the fountainhead of human progress while experiencing pain, love, and physical lust in ways he had always thought sinful.

Chapter 9

During the following days, Lemmy's bruises prevented him from sitting down. He spent the day on his feet, studying Talmud with Benjamin in the synagogue. When his legs ached, he went outside to stretch out on a bench. At night, he stayed up for hours, lying on his belly with ice on his buttocks, reading *The Fountainhead* again.

The next Sabbath, after the meal, he ran all the way to Tanya's house. He circled the wall of sandbags and knocked on the door. She appeared barefoot, in a sleeveless shirt and khaki shorts that revealed sculpted legs.

"I brought back your book." He averted his eyes.

"You don't like the way I look?"

He swallowed. "You look the way God made you, but I'm not supposed to see so much of it."

Tanya laughed and took his hand, pulling him inside. Her hand was dry and cool and pleasant to touch. She placed *The Fountainhead* on a shelf among other books.

He asked, "Has Ayn Rand written other novels?"

"So you liked it?"

"It's a good story." He felt foolish for keeping the real depth of his excitement from her. "America is a great country. I hope to visit it one day."

"What did your father think of the book?"

Lemmy hesitated. "He didn't see it."

"Why?"

"He would tell me not to read it."

"You always do what your father tells you?"

"Pretty much."

"And your own desire, it has no meaning?"

"My desire is to obey my father."

"And what about your mother?"

"She obeys him too."

Tanya smiled. "You know what I mean."

"My mother doesn't expect my obedience."

"That's your father's prerogative?"

He nodded.

She collected a pile of papers from her desk and put them in a drawer. "Would you like some coffee?"

"No, thank you."

"Tea? Water? You must be thirsty after such a long walk."

"I'm fine. Really."

"Are you afraid my dishes aren't kosher?" She sat on the sofa. "You needn't worry. I'm a vegetarian."

Lemmy wasn't sure what it meant. He had never heard the term. Did she eat only vegetables? That would make for a very limited diet, especially in the winter, when fresh produce was meager. He wandered around the room, touching the old furniture and the books. A framed photo on the wall showed a teenage girl with light hair and Tanya's smile. "Who's that?"

"My daughter, Bira."

In Hebrew, *Bira* meant a capital city, but he had never heard it used as a name. "You named her for Jerusalem?"

"That would have been a nice coincidence, wouldn't it?"

"Where is she now?"

"In the army, defending Israel. Not hiding in the synagogue like the men of Neturay Karta."

"We're not hiding."

"I didn't mean you personally. You're too young, anyway."

"I'll be eighteen soon."

"Will you enlist?"

"In the Zionist army?" He rolled one of his payos around his forefinger and played with it. "We defend the Jewish people by praying and studying Talmud."

"You really believe that prayer and study would protect Israel from three hundred million Arabs armed with the best Soviet weaponry?"

"Torah says: *God shall fight for you, and you shall be silent.* For the righteous Jew, faith is the mightiest shield from enemies."

"Do you know the story about the Jew who complained to God that he was so poor that he couldn't feed his cow?"

"There are many of them."

"That's true. Well, this Jew got an answer. God told him that he would win the lottery."

Lemmy leaned against the wall, watching her.

"A week later, when he complained to God that he didn't win the lottery, God asked: Did you buy a ticket?"

Lemmy laughed. He paced along the wall, returning to Bira's photo. She stood against a background of large buildings and signs in foreign letters. "How old is she?"

"Twenty-one. She even has a boyfriend."

"*Mazal Tov.* When is the wedding?"

"It's too early to think of a wedding. They're dating, that's all. Movies, dancing, kissing, you know, being young."

He examined the photo. The signs in the background were in German. "Is she really your daughter?"

"Excuse me?"

"I mean, you look too young."

Tanya touched her face. "I was seventeen when Bira was born."

"And your husband?"

"He was already dead."

For a few moments, neither of them spoke. He saw a newspaper on the coffee table, *Ha'aretz*, a Hebrew daily that was banned in Meah Shearim. The date was October 7, 1966, yesterday's paper. He read through the headlines. China's Independence Day marked by a conciliatory letter from Moscow. U.S. government proclaiming optimism that Hanoi would accept the peace initiative to end the Vietnam War. Syrian diplomats, in a meeting with UN General Odd Bull, threatened an attack on Israeli air bases. Terrorists infiltrate through the border with Egypt and sabotage fuel lines. Shots from the Jordanian side of Jerusalem injure an eleven-year-old boy playing soccer with friends, while UN observers stood by. Ben Gurion celebrated his eightieth birthday at his Negev Desert kibbutz with President Shazar and the author S.Y. Agnon, but without Prime Minister Eshkol.

Lemmy turned the page and read the first paragraph of an article about the release from jail in Germany of Nazi leaders Albert Speer and Baldur von Schirach. The writer expressed regret that the two men had not been executed twenty years earlier with the rest of Hitler's henchmen.

A photograph on the opposite page shocked Lemmy. It was his father! Under it, the paper reported:

NETURAY KARTA RABBI: ABORTION IS MURDER!
The Knesset Committee on Health heard testimony from Rabbi Abraham Gerster, leader of ultra-Orthodox sect Neturay Karta, regarding proposed legislation to permit abortions for out-of-wedlock, incestuous pregnancies, or when the mother's physical or mental well-being is at risk. Rabbi Gerster declared: "Laws are made by God, not by democracy. God said, Thou shall not kill! Did God set a minimum age for murder victims? No! A viable fetus is a live person, created in God's image! How could you allow doctors to kill babies inside their mothers' wombs?" Security officials fear anti-abortion riots by ultra-Orthodox extremists, especially after last Saturday's rock-throwing incident.

Tanya asked, "What do you think? Will history repeat itself? Like the Jews who killed each other inside the Temple during the Roman siege?"

"I don't know. God will decide our fate."

"What's the word inside Neturay Karta?"

"Abortions are a symptom of Zionist decay, like driving during Sabbath, eating pork, violating sacred gravesites for antiques. That's why we shun the secular Zionist society that surrounds us. Most Talmudic scholars believe God will soon punish Israel. Some want to throw rocks, attack government buildings, maybe burn police cars."

"And you?"

"Me? I'm too young to decide those things."

Her hand rested on his shoulder, her face very close. "So who's going to decide if Jewish blood will run again in the streets of Jerusalem? Rabbi Abraham Gerster?"

Mint, Lemmy decided, that's what her breath smelled like. He knew he should get up and leave, but he couldn't. The fire from her hand had spread to his loins. "My father is a great scholar of Talmud. Our people listen to him."

"Because they think he's a *tzadik*?"

"Yes. He is a righteous man."

"Oh, Jerusalem." Tanya's hand slipped off his shoulder. "It must be nice to be so innocent."

He stood up and glanced at the bookshelf.

"Would you like another novel?" Tanya picked one. "That's a good one."

Lemmy couldn't contain his smile. It was Ayn Rand's *Atlas Shrugged*.

Elie Weiss watched from his Deux Chevaux as Abraham's son left Tanya's house and walked down the street, his black coat unbuttoned, his black hat tilted jauntily. When the boy was out of sight, Elie got out of his car and knocked on Tanya's door.

She stood in the doorway. "What do you want?"

"A bit of your time. May I come in?"

She moved aside.

He entered a large, tidy room. The closed door to his left probably led to the equipment room where she listened in on UN radio traffic. He sat on the sofa.

Tanya remained standing. "I need to go back to my work."

He pulled out a pack of Lucky Strike.

"Don't smoke here."

"No problem." Elie slid the pack back into his pocket. "How was your reunion with Abraham? Lots of hugs and kisses?"

"You told him I was dead!"

"I told him the facts. He drew the conclusion."

"You tricked him, just like you had tricked me about his death. *Bloody sieve!*"

"It's a miracle he recovered, and it was a miracle the wolves didn't eat you."

Tanya's pretty face was red with anger, making her even more attractive. "We needed one more miracle, but you're still around!"

"I saw your new friend leave. Good-looking boy, Abraham's son. Snip off those payos and strip the black clothes, and he's a carbon copy of the Gerster you once loved."

Tanya's face grew even redder. "You're a sick man!"

He was pleased with her reaction, which confirmed his strategy. "I need to know what he told you. Anything about Neturay Karta?"

"You haven't changed."

"He must have told you something." Elie wanted her to think this was just about snooping for information on the fundamentalist sect, let her believe he had given up on the fortune her Nazi lover had stashed in Switzerland.

Tanya walked to the opposite end of the room. "You already have Abraham in position. He's your agent. Leave his son alone."

"Why?"

"Because he's an innocent victim."

"You read too many novels."

"He's just a boy."

"He's the same age Abraham was in forty-five. You remember the boy he was, yes? The heads he blew? The necks he squeezed? The hearts he stabbed, or broke?"

Tanya turned away. She released her hair and held it to her cheek like a child seeking comfort in a familiar rag. "You couldn't make me betray Klaus twenty years ago. You think I'll betray Abraham now?"

"Your loyalty to ex-lovers is commendable."

"A snake," she said, "is what you are."

"A very powerful snake." Elie looked around. He knew she would not leave the Nazi's ledger in plain sight, but he hoped to see something useful, a hint of where she had hidden the key to the dormant fortune. "You're taking it too personally. This is not about me or you or Abraham. This is about the future of Israel.

We won't survive the Arabs' attacks while a Talmudic Trojan horse spews religious violence in our midst."

"A few hundred fragile scholars are a threat to the state?"

"Neturay Karta's fundamentalist ideology is like a spark that could start a brushfire, which will spread to every religious community in Israel."

"You're being paranoid."

Elie put a cigarette between his lips. "Orthodox Jews believe that one day the Messiah will ride into Jerusalem on his white donkey and twiddle a magic wand to recreate King David's empire and bring us back to the Promised Land. Therefore, they perceive modern Zionism as a blasphemous usurpation of God. Remember the zealots who killed the great priest and caused Roman victory over Jerusalem two thousand years ago? Neturay Karta is the reincarnation of those ancient fanatics, the modern-day progenitors of a violent rebellion against the secular Israeli democratic government—"

"You're wasting time. I work for Mossad, not for you."

"Actually, soon you'll also be working for my Special Operations Department." He could see her face tense up. "I won't interfere with your regular duties, but you'll have to follow my orders and provide me with all information and *items* that you possess."

Tanya shook her head sharply, her hair flying about her, making her look like a young girl. "General Amit won't force me."

Elie thought for a moment. "Are you sleeping with the chief of Mossad?"

"You're repulsive!" She picked up a book and threw it on the desk in frustration. "Yes, Elie Weiss. I sleep with General Amit, I sleep with Abraham *and* his son, I sleep with dogs and pigs, and I sleep with everybody except you. Now leave my house!"

He got up and paced to the framed photo on the wall. "Your daughter's lovely."

"Leave!"

"Bira Galinski. Private First Class, mandatory service, IDF Media Department, Central Command." He looked at the photo closely. "Not as pretty as her mother. Light hair, blue eyes, big bones. Must be her father's looks. I hear she wants to be a historian, a scholar, not a spy. Odd, if you consider her parents' career choices."

He turned to Tanya, whose face went pale. She said nothing.

"Now, let's see. She was born in Berlin on July eleventh, nineteen forty five. A healthy baby—three kilos two hundred grams. Her birth certificate refers to the father as deceased. But he must have been alive and well back in," Elie counted on his fingers, "say, late winter, nineteen forty four, which was when you and Herr Obergruppenführer Klaus von Koenig—"

"Go to hell." She threw open the door.

"To hell?" Elie crossed the room slowly and stood close enough to smell her. "I've been there, Tanya, long nights, listening to Abraham Gerster making love to you, not even bothering to be quiet, as if I were blind and deaf and without my own desires." He paused, regretting his momentary sincerity. "Treat me with respect, or I'll expose your daughter's Nazi paternal lineage. Can you imagine the consequences?"

Chapter 10

The following Sabbath, Lemmy found a week's worth of newspapers on Tanya's coffee table. A headline read: *General Bull's Demand for Reinforcements Rejected by UN Secretary General U-Thant*. Another headline: *Eshkol Blames Egypt and Syria for the Growing Tension at the Borders*. The paper quoted opposition Knesset member Shimon Peres: *Levi Eshkol and Abba Eban Sacrifice Israel's Security for the Interests of America and the Soviet Union!*

Reading through the headlines, Lemmy realized how distorted his perception of Israeli society had been. Within the insular Neturay Karta, everyone believed the godless Israelis to be uniformly immoral, rejoicing in promiscuity and porcine gluttony. But Tanya's newspapers reflected the dedication of the Zionist leaders to the survival of the young state. Their ideological bickering appeared sincere and passionate, not the cynical materialism that he had expected.

Before he left, Tanya gave him a thin book by Emile Zola: *I Accuse*.

Back home, his parents were taking a Sabbath-afternoon nap. He shut himself up in his room and began reading. Written in 1898, it was the story of a Jew named Dreyfus, whose career as a French army officer had ended in a disgraceful conviction for treason. The book argued that Dreyfus had in fact been framed as a scapegoat by the French establishment to cover for one of their own.

I Accuse enraged Lemmy. Here was a Jew who lived with the *Goyim*, attended their schools, served in their army, and risked his life in their wars, expecting in return only the honor of equality and fraternity, as promised by the new French Republic. But his reward was injustice, humiliation, and suffering. Wasn't Dreyfus a perfect example of the Gentiles' pathological hatred of Jews?

A week later, on Sabbath afternoon, Lemmy entered Tanya's house and declared, "This book is the ultimate proof that Neturay Karta is correct, that a Jew can only live safely among other Jews who observe the strict teachings of Talmud!"

"Only Neturay Karta?" Wearing shorts and a tank top, Tanya sat cross-legged on the floor. "This whole country is Jewish. Israel offers true equality for the Jewish people as a nation, not as a religion."

"Zionism is a rebellion against God, who told us to wait for His Messiah to bring us back and restore our independence."

"But didn't God give us the Promised Land and told us to go there? The Zionist pioneers have fulfilled that promise, didn't they?"

"The Zionists violate the Sabbath, shave off their payos and beards, and don't pray. Instead of studying Talmud, they study fragments of clay they dig up from the ground, as if those remnants of ancient dwellings could give them heritage and identity. They don't care about God!"

"Have you ever met a Zionist?"

"Aren't you a Zionist?"

She laughed and gave him another book. "It's the story of the first Zionist. Let's see what you think after reading it."

Lemmy looked at the cover. *Theodor Herzl, a Biography.*

His face burned as he entered the apartment with the book under his coat. This was not a novel that could be excused as youthful indiscretion. This volume carried on its cover the face of Theodor Herzl—the visionary of modern Zionism. It was worse than hiding a pig under his coat.

That night, Lemmy tiptoed through the apartment to make sure the lights were off in his father's study and his mother's bedroom. Back in his room, he pulled the book from behind the shelved Talmud volumes and lay in bed to read Herzl's life story.

An assimilated Austrian Jew, Herzl was a reporter for the *Vienna Neue Freie Presse* who believed in modernity and freedom as a basis for a peaceful humanity. He did not observe Jewish laws and saw himself as a free citizen of Europe. But while covering the 1894 trial of Alfred Dreyfus in Paris, Herzl had witnessed fervent anti-Semitism, both within the quiet halls of justice and on the streets, where the mob chanted, "Kill all the Jews!" He became convinced that the Jews in Europe faced a grave danger, and the only way to save them was the creation of a Jewish state. In a pamphlet titled, *Der Judenstaat, The Jewish State,* he outlined a new home for the Jews in the Holy Land, based on political freedom, religious tolerance, and racial equality. Herzl called for a secular democracy that would include the indigenous Arabs and bring progress to the desolate Ottoman colony of Palestine. He summoned the first Zionist Congress in Basel and called on Jews everywhere to end their twenty centuries of exile and return to their ancestral homeland. He travelled to Palestine, met Keiser Wilhelm II, and negotiated with the Ottoman Grand Vizier, as well as Sultan Abdulhamid II himself. From Constantinople, Herzl travelled to London, obtaining tacit support from Great Britain. Meanwhile, Zionist activists took his message to countless Jewish *shtetls* across Russia, Poland, Germany, Hungary, and Romania, where millions of religious Jews recited daily: *Next year in Jerusalem.* But the rabbis rejected Zionism and ordered their followers to continue the long wait for the Messiah. Herzl died eight years after publishing *Der Judenstaat,* lonely and disappointed, never to find out that his premonition of disaster would be validated in the Nazi Holocaust that killed six million Jews.

Herzl had written: *If you wish, this is not a fable; in fifty years, we can have a Jewish state.* Lemmy calculated quickly in his head and was awed by Herzl's prescience: The 1948 founding of Israel came fifty-two years after Herzl had made that prediction.

It was tragic, Lemmy thought, that the rabbis had rejected Herzl's vision. Their reasoning was familiar—it was still the foundation of Neturay Karta's anti-Zionist stand. But the irony didn't escape him. The small minority of European Jews, who had defied their rabbis and left Europe to build a Jewish homeland in Palestine, lived to mourn their families and friends who had obeyed the rabbis, rejected Zionism, and died in Hitler's gas chambers, crying, *"Hear, O Israel, Adonai is our God, Adonai is one."*

Chapter 11

As the weeks passed, Lemmy's buttocks healed, and another winter descended on Jerusalem. He visited Tanya every Saturday afternoon, exchanging books and browsing the newspapers. She served him tea in a glass cup, and they discussed the news or the book he had just read. He was often tempted to ask how she knew his father but sensed that the subject was taboo. She gave him the works of major writers, such as Tolstoy, Edgar Allen Poe, and Jack London, which were available in the Hebrew translation. Some novels, such as *Gone with the Wind, Madame Bovary, Tom Sawyer, A Tale of Two Cities, and Martin Eden,* led to discussions in which Tanya described European history and the American civil war with knowledge that hinted of extensive study and travel. And certain books aroused feelings inside Lemmy that he had never experienced before, especially when it came to the relationship between men and women, so different from the rigid division that was strictly applied in Neturay Karta. He began to read books in German, using a dictionary to bridge the gap between the spoken Yiddish he was fluent in, and the more proper German grammar and vocabulary of literature. He read some of the books more than once, gaining better understanding of the characters, subjects, and meaning. The stories of S.Y. Agnon, for example, were populated with religious Jews like himself, yet described their innermost feelings and passions in a way that Lemmy found irresistible.

With time, his life divided into two separate tracks. His days as a Talmudic scholar started shortly after dawn, with a quick rinsing of his face and off to the synagogue for morning service. Breakfast was bread, jam, and milk in the foyer of the synagogue, followed by studying Talmud with Benjamin. Lunch was followed by Rabbi Gerster's daily lecture and independent study until sunset and the evening prayers. Lemmy and Benjamin usually stayed in the synagogue for another hour to settle their arguments.

Dinner at home was the conclusion of a day of studying. While Temimah served them soup and a dish of meat and potatoes or fish with vegetables, his father always asked the same question: "What do you know tonight that you didn't know this morning?"

This question led to a discussion of the pages of Talmud that Lemmy had studied with Benjamin. Invariably, Rabbi Gerster shed new light on the subject, revealing hidden threads and subtle concepts that had escaped Lemmy.

Each scholarly day ended when his father recited the final prayer after the meal and retired to his study. Lemmy always helped his mother clear the dinner table before wishing her good night.

He read Tanya's books every night, including books she borrowed for him at the public library. His nights filled with excitement as his eyes raced across printed pages filled with strange characters, foreign societies, and human conflicts. When his eyes burned, he'd go to the bathroom, splash cold water on his face, and return to reading. The forbidden books transported him to locations far beyond the walls of Meah Shearim, and the excitement lingered even when his eyelids refused to stay open and he fell asleep for a couple of hours before another day started.

Lemmy learned to juggle his daily studies and nightly escapades. The days were filled with the intellectual intensity of cracking Talmudic riddles with Benjamin among the companionship of a synagogue filled with cigarette smoke and familiar faces. The nights were spent in literary forays outside Neturay Karta. He erected a virtual wall between the life he shared with Talmud, family and friends, and the solitary adventures of his nights. He knew that a crack in the wall could precipitate a deluge of acrimony—his father's wrath, his mother's tears, Benjamin's hurtful betrayal. But the books' allure was too great.

Chapter 12

On a frosty morning in late December, Tanya switched the eavesdropping equipment to automatic recording and left her home for the long walk to the bus station in West Jerusalem. Across the border, in the Armenian Quarter of the Old City, church bells tolled to summon the faithful to Christmas mass.

The bus took almost three hours to reach Tel Aviv, often stopping to wait for the army to scout the road ahead for Arab terrorists. Getting off the bus at the central station, Tanya walked west toward the Mediterranean coast.

The first Jewish city in modern times, Tel Aviv, which meant *Spring Hill*, was nothing like Jerusalem. Its inhabitants were secular Israelis. Women wore outfits that revealed the contours of their bodies, and men were muscular and sun-beaten in a healthy, exuberant way that contrasted with the pale Jews of Jerusalem. The sea air was fresh, and the sun shone as if summer hadn't yet departed.

She changed into a bathing suit in the public showers at the beach and walked across the strip of soft sand to the water. The sea was almost flat, only shallow waves lapping at her feet. She took a deep breath and ran into the chilly water of the Mediterranean.

By early afternoon, the unseasonably mild weather had drawn hundreds of bathers, who rose and fell with the waves, squealing in a blend of Hebrew, English, German, and Arabic. A lifeguard with bronze skin and a hairy chest rowed his white fiberglass board toward Tanya and offered to take her for a ride. She declined, and he continued on his patrol.

After drying herself, she spread a towel on the sand and lay down in the sun.

Bira and Eytan met her for dinner at an outdoor café near the beach. He was a dark Israeli with a sunny smile, and seemed unconcerned when the two women lapsed into German, reminiscing how Tanya had taught Bira to ride a bicycle in a Munich park until they both fell into a shallow reflecting pool.

Tanya spent the night in the tiny apartment Bira shared with five other soldiers. They chatted late into the night, and Tanya went to bed content that her daughter had acclimated to life in Israel. Bira had grown up in a succession of European cities, their frequent relocations dictated by Mossad needs. But the disadvantage of a rootless childhood was balanced out by a multilingual fluency that served Bira well in her IDF research duties, while she easily made new friends among her fellow troops.

W ell before sunrise, Tanya walked the short distance to the Kirya, the fenced-off IDF headquarters in the center of Tel Aviv. She passed through several checkpoints, and took a long elevator ride down to the Pit—the underground command center.

The meeting convened in a large room with solid concrete walls and mechanical ventilation. Prime Minster Levi Eshkol sat at one end of a long table, his thick eyeglasses on his forehead, his eyes buried in a document. The IDF chief of staff, General Yitzhak Rabin, sat at the other end, puffing on a cigarette. The rest of the seats around the table were taken by IDF generals and the civilian chiefs of Shin Bet and Mossad, all much younger than Eshkol. Plastic chairs lined the walls, occupied by aides and advisors.

On the opposite side of the room Tanya noticed Elie Weiss, diminutive and brooding. His wool cap covered his ears. He beckoned Tanya to an adjoining seat, but she sat near the door.

General Rabin approached a large wall map, the cigarette dangling from his lips. "*Boker Tov,*" he said.

A few voices replied, "Good morning."

"What morning?" the prime minister asked, looking up from his papers. "It's still the middle of the night!"

Rabin smiled. At forty-five, he was a handsome man with reddish-brown hair and a healthy tan. "As I see it, our goal is to avoid war. But our duty is to prepare for one."

Several generals nodded. They seemed accustomed to Rabin's slow, deliberate manner of speech.

"The tension on the borders," Rabin continued, "is growing. In the north, Syrian bombardments rain down from the Golan Heights. In the east, PLO terrorists infiltrate from Jordan and kill civilians. In the south, Egypt is building up its forces in Sinai. In the west, terrorists attack us from Gaza. The daily casualties on every front erode our citizens' morale."

"It's a chronic disease," the prime minister said, "like bronchitis, or cataract."

Everyone laughed, knowing that he was suffering from both.

"It's becoming a fatal disease," Rabin said. "The Arabs smell blood. They're finally strong enough to overrun Israel."

"The world won't allow it," the prime minister argued. "The UN will confront the Arab leaders. I sent Abba Eban to urge General Bull."

"Our intelligence reports," Rabin continued, "indicate that Egypt might block the Straits of Tiran."

"Impossible!" Prime Minister Eshkol shook a finger at Rabin. "We have guarantees from the Americans. That's why we agreed to withdraw from Sinai after the 'fifty-six campaign! Egypt will never have the chutzpah!"

"The Soviet Union is arming the Egyptians and Syrians in hopes of creating another Vietnam here. But our eastern border is the longest. To succeed against us, Egypt and Syria need Jordan." With the point of a long stick, Rabin traced the meandering border down the middle of the Sea of Galilee to the mouth of the Jordan River and inland toward the Mediterranean Sea, where it ran parallel to the coast, creating a narrow strip where Israel was less than ten miles wide. Near the northern suburbs of Tel Aviv, the border veered east to the Judean Mountains. It sliced Jerusalem in half, with the Old City on the Jordanian side and the Jewish neighborhoods in a small peninsula. The border immediately dropped back west, circling the southern bulge of the West Bank, under Jordanian control, then east again to the desert valleys below the Dead Sea. The southern part of Israel, almost two-thirds of its odd-shaped territory, was the Negev Desert. It was dotted with isolated kibbutzim, collective farms that defied the harsh desert with green islands of alfalfa, carrots, and tomatoes.

General Rabin's pointer returned to the narrow coastal strip north of Tel Aviv. "Here is our soft belly. Unlike the south and the north, where we have a bit of territorial depth to fight, a massive Jordan bombardment of West Jerusalem and the coastal strip will destroy us."

"They won't dare!" Prime Minister Eshkol leaned forward, his elbows on the table. "It would be a violation of every UN resolution!"

Drawing long from his cigarette, Rabin took his time. "If diplomacy fails, we'll have to fend off King Hussein, or war will be lost on the first day."

"I can't spare any troops," said General Dado Elazar, CO northern command. "The Syrians sit in their bunkers on the Golan Heights and shoot down at our kibbutzniks in the valleys. We have casualties every day. How long are we going to tolerate it?"

"My lines are stretched to the max," said General Gavish, CO Southern Command. "Three hundred kilometers of desert. I have gaps wide enough for an entire Egyptian battalion to march through. We operate a phantom division in the middle section— three old tanks driving back and forth, raising dust to fool the Egyptians about our size. But if they actually attack, we'd better prepare white flags and learn Arabic."

"Imagine that," said a voice from the corner, "the Israelites going into Egyptian captivity all over again."

Tanya had not noticed him before. General Moshe Dayan, veteran IDF chief of staff, wore plain khakis and his black eye patch. He joined his fingers, forming a peak. "We'd better pull out the old blueprints for the pyramids."

"Happy Passover," someone said, and the room erupted in laughter.

"War is coming," Dayan said, suddenly serious. "The IDF must attack first, or we'll all die."

"Madness!" Prime Minister Eshkol was red in the face. "We are a tiny country, an island of Yids in an ocean of Goyim! The United Nations guaranteed our sovereignty. It's General Bull's responsibility!"

"What's he going to do?" Dayan smirked. "Order his thousand UN observers to observe more closely?"

"We can't fight alone." Eshkol's voice trembled. "We need America. Or France. Alone, we'll be squashed!"

A wiry, tall man leaped from his seat and went to the map. "My team has prepared plans for a first strike." Ezer Weitzman, nephew of Israel's first president, had until recently commanded the air force. He was now CO operations, second only to Rabin.

Weitzman grabbed the pointer from Rabin. "A first-strike by the Arabs would disable our airfields, blast the Dimona nuclear reactor, and destroy our cities." The pointer moved rapidly between different spots on the map. "The north and south will be cut off from central command." He tapped the Golan Heights, the Galilee, and the Negev. "No supply lines. No reinforcements. No spare parts, ammunition, or oil refills. Our tanks and infantry will be disabled and wiped out. End of story." Weitzman threw the stick on the table, and it slid lengthwise until it stopped, the pointer touching Prime Minister Eshkol's white shirt. "Authorize a preemptive air strike on them, or prepare for a second Holocaust!"

Having kept the defense portfolio to himself, Eshkol was now stuck with the challenge of reining in the military brass. Tanya saw him scribble something in a little notebook. "Here we are," he said, "an ancient nation with a great military force. But still, the people of Israel are afraid. We're like *Samson the nebishdicker.*"

They laughed, and Tanya understood Eshkol's clever metaphor of the biblical superhero, *Samson the nerd*, Israel being simultaneously mighty and meek, ferocious and fearful. In contrast to the Israeli-born sabra generals, who were confident and eager to fight, Eshkol belonged to the older, Diaspora-born politicians, whose worldview had been formed in Eastern Europe, where Jewish men cowered under kitchen tables while the Goyim ransacked their homes and raped their wives and daughters.

"We should avoid both complacency and hysteria," General Rabin said. "If the Egyptians blockade the Straits of Tiran, our oil supplies from Iran will be cut. Our factories will stop. Buses and trains too. And our reservists won't be able to reach their units."

"We could," Eshkol said, "ask the Iranians to ship the oil around Africa to Haifa."

"The real wild card is Jordan," said Moshe Dayan. "King Hussein doesn't want to risk losing East Jerusalem and the West Bank, but he can't appear disloyal to his Arab brothers."

"Which is fine," General Weitzman said. "We'll capture Temple Mount and reunite Jerusalem!"

"We don't want the West Bank, though," Rabin said.

"Why not?" Weitzman asked. "The hills of Judea and Samaria are filled with the biblical sites where Abraham, Isaac, and Jacob lived. Imagine the Cave of the Patriarchs in Hebron, the first piece of land Abraham bought in the Promised Land. Jericho, which Joshua captured upon returning from Egyptian slavery—"

"And imagine," Rabin said, "ruling over a half-million Arabs."

"They'll run away," Weitzman said, waving his hand, "like they did in 'forty-eight."

"I don't think so," Rabin said. "The IDF is a defense force. The military occupation of a large Arab population will be morally problematic."

Prime Minister Eshkol pointed at Elie. "Weiss, tell us about the Jewish fundamentalists. Will they be grateful to the government if we capture the holy places?"

"They'll be grateful to God." Elie stood up. "I estimate that capturing the biblical sites will cause a rise in religious nationalism centered on old ruins and ancient tombs. Thousands of observant families will pick up and move to Hebron, Jericho, and Bethlehem. Depending on your political leaning, this could be viewed as a wonderful new wave of laudable Zionist pioneering or as a power grab of territories needed for a future bargain with the Arabs. I believe that if Israel conquers the West Bank and East Jerusalem, future governments will face a political *fait accompli*—no withdrawals and no peace with the Arabs."

There was a long silence, broken by Ezer Weitzman. "That's a bunch of nonsense. Who is this guy?"

The chief of Mossad, Meir Amit, cleared his throat. "Until recently, our assessment was that the Arabs would not be ready for war before 1970. However, six months ago the Soviet Union began shipping massive amounts of arms, accompanied by thousands of military personnel, including field commanders, tank officers, and fighter pilots. They're acting as advisors, but they'll fight, just like in Vietnam."

"Why?" The question came from Rabin.

"Dimona," the Mossad chief responded without hesitation. "The Kremlin considers our nuclear program to be a direct challenge to Soviet influence in the Middle East. By early summer, June or July, they'll have Egypt, Jordan, and the Syrians, as well as supporting brigades from Iraq, Saudi Arabia, and Lebanon, ready to attack Israel."

"They won't!" Prime Minister Eshkol sat back, removed his glasses. "The UN will stop them!"

The Mossad chief glanced at Tanya. "A very telling conversation took place when the General Bull called King Hussein to wish him a happy birthday."

"Some neutrality," Prime Minister Eshkol said. "He didn't call on my birthday!"

Amit smiled. "They're friends. The young king is a flying enthusiast, so Bull treats him as sort of a protégé. He invited Hussein to tour the new UN radar station at Government House. We're still gathering intel on it. But when Bull told King Hussein that his family will be visiting Jerusalem in the spring, the king offered his villa in the south of France instead."

Tanya had her notes ready. "The king responded that it's going to be a very hot spring in the Middle East, but by summer they'll be able to vacation together in Tel Aviv."

The prime minster swiveled his chair to face Tanya. "What was Bull's reply?"

She quoted from her notes. "*It's a date!*"

Lemmy woke up to an explosion of banging and knocking that made him sit up in his bed fighting for air. The room was completely dark, and it took him a moment to realize the noise was coming from his alarm clock. He hit it, and the noise died.

The apartment was not heated during the night, and the sweat on his forehead was icy. The wind rattled the window. He turned on his reading light and sat for a moment. His body ached. He wished he could stay in bed. He had slept for less than two hours, having finished a novel about young Italian lovers whose passion led to tragedy.

Lowering his feet to the cold floor, Lemmy resisted an overwhelming desire to slip back under the warm blanket. In a moment, he would be late for morning prayers. He dressed quickly, grabbed the black hat from the hook, and rushed out of his room.

The small sink by the bathroom had a single iron faucet. He used the copper cup to rinse his hands three times as prescribed by Talmud. He splashed cold water on his face and dried his hands and face on a towel while reciting the blessing: "*Grateful I am before you, Master of the Universe, for giving my soul back to me in your mercy. I believe in your grace.*"

His father had already gone to the synagogue for an hour of predawn studying. Lemmy passed by the kitchen without stopping, crossed the foyer, and reached for the door handle.

"Jerusalem?" His mother's quick footsteps sounded, and she appeared in the foyer. "Here. Drink it."

He took the mug and filled his mouth with sweet, hot chocolate. It was always at the right temperature, soothing away the bitter residue of a restless night without burning his palate. He gulped it, looking at his mother over the mug. The vapor between them softened her untimely wrinkles.

"Thanks." He handed her the empty mug.

"May God bless your day," she said while he headed down the stairs.

He knew she was watching from the window as he ran through the rain, holding his hat, his shoes splashing through puddles.

He entered the synagogue foyer and brushed the drops off his coat. Monotonous chanting came through the open doors of the main sanctuary. In the far corner of the foyer, Benjamin stood with Redhead Dan and his study companion, Yoram.

Lemmy approached them. "What nasty weather!"

"It's better than famine," Benjamin said. "You want us to starve?"

"Why starve?" Lemmy waved his hand. "Couldn't God create a better irrigation system? This rain gets everything wet—buildings, roads, dogs, roaches. Even the sea gets wet! It's stupid, isn't it?"

Redhead Dan said, "God isn't stupid!"

"He didn't say it about God." Benjamin said. "Just about getting wet in the rain. Surely our merciful God knows best how to run the world He created, right?"

"That's a given," Lemmy said. "But God should deliver water where it's needed—olive groves in the Galilee, orange trees near Jaffa, and so on. The current system—"

"Are you questioning God's wisdom?" Redhead Dan folded his arms on his chest.   He was in his early twenties, burly and freckle-faced. His red hair, spiraling payos, and bushy beard created a blaze that kept his head constantly boiling. His young wife had given birth a few days earlier to a baby boy—their first child. "God will punish the sinners! The filthy Zionists will pay for their abortion law." His voice grew louder. "We'll destroy their Knesset, flush their law books down the toilet, and drown their heresy in a bath of blood!"

"You mean a river," Lemmy said, "not a bath."

"What?"

"A river of blood. It's hard to drown in a bath."

"Whatever!" Redhead Dan made a cutting gesture with his hand.

"And whose blood will it be," Lemmy inquired, "in which they'll drown?"

"Zionist blood! What else?"

"You mean *Jewish* blood?"

"No!" Redhead Dan stepped back, his fists clenched as if he was about to attack. "*Zionist* blood! Zionists are Goyim!"

"But according to Talmud every child of a Jewish mother is a Jew. Even a Jew who converts to Christianity remains a Jew. So how could Zionists become Gentiles?"

Redhead Dan glared at Lemmy. "Don't you hate the Zionists?"

"Hate is a sin. Rabbi Akivah said, *Love your fellow Jew as you love yourself.*"

Benjamin said, "Come on, who has energy to hate the Zionists before breakfast?"

"Heretics aren't Jews!" Redhead Dan poked Lemmy's chest with his finger. "We must stone them to death at the city gates. It's written!"

"A lot of things are written." Lemmy left them and entered the main sanctuary. Benjamin followed him to their bench, and they joined the rest of the men in chanting *Adon Olam, Master of the Universe.*

When the chanting ended, Rabbi Gerster walked up to the elevated dais in the center and recited the first Blessing of Dawn: "*Greatness to You, Master of the Universe, for giving the rooster eyesight to know day from night.*"

The men repeated after Rabbi Gerster, and he continued to the next blessing, "*For not making me a Gentile.*"

They recited the line.

Benjamin whispered, "What's gotten into you?"

Lemmy shrugged, repeating the next blessing, "*Greatness to You, Master of the Universe, for not making me a woman.*"

"You should be more careful," Benjamin whispered, "Redhead Dan is crazy."

"What, he'll smash my face with a brick?"

Benjamin grinned. "Only if you perform an abortion."

Elie Weiss watched Tanya exit the main gate of the IDF headquarters. His Citroën's two-stroke engine idled noisily. He was parked under a large eucalyptus tree on Kiryat Shaul Street, waiting for her after the strategy conference. She headed north toward the bus station. It was a busy morning, with many soldiers and civilians on their way to work. She walked fast in sensible shoes, blue pants, and a beige shirt that resembled a uniform. Her hair was collected in a bun, and large sunglasses covered most of her face. He turned on the engine and proceeded slowly. A gap in traffic allowed him to jump the curb and come abreast with her, moving at the same pace.

"Hi there," he called through the open window. "Need a lift?"

Tanya glanced at him, not slowing down.

"That's no way to treat your commanding officer."

She stopped walking.

Elie hit the brakes, and the little car rocked back and forth on its soft springs. A bus screeched to a halt behind the Citroën and honked repeatedly. A few pedestrians stopped to look.

Tanya got into the car and slammed the door.

He started driving, keeping pace with traffic. "I like Tel Aviv. Not as cold as Jerusalem."

"I won't work for you."

Making a right-hand turn, Elie accelerated. The tiny boxer engine rattled like a lawnmower. "You're a soldier, an expert in gathering information about Israel's enemies. What's the difference between spying on Arabs or on nutty Jews who threaten Israel from within?"

"It's the difference between a soldier, which I'm proud to be, and a snitch, which I won't become. And anyway, I don't buy your theory. Religious Jews will never turn violent."

"It's not a theory. Last time we had an independent Jewish state, the zealots killed the high priest and butchered all fellow Jews who opposed them, which allowed the Romans to burn down Jerusalem. It can happen again. Don't you want to save Jerusalem?"

She pointed. "There, drop me off at the bus station."

"How close are you getting with Abraham's son? Is he in love with you yet?"

Tanya removed her sunglasses and looked at him.

"Be reasonable." Elie stopped at the curb. "Mossad agreed to share your services with my department. Work with me."

"You don't need my work. I know what you really want."

"Whatever it is, you have no choice."

"But I do." Tanya opened the door. "I have records of interesting conversations between the UN observers on a certain Friday afternoon. There was a shooting. The bullets barely missed Abraham."

"It happens. The Jordanian soldiers get bored."

"According to the UN observers, the shooter was sitting on a roof on the Israeli side of the border. They got a pretty good description of him. A smallish guy in a beggar's cloak. They didn't miss the prominent nose."

He chuckled, touching his nose.

"Keep yours out of my business, and I'll keep mine out of yours. If you try to force me to work for you, I'll share the information with my colleagues. They would like nothing better than to investigate you. *Verstehen Sie mich?*"

"I understand." Elie knew there was no point in lying to her. Perhaps a dose of openness would work better. "It's all part of the plan. Religious fanatics love miracles. These Neturay Karta men saw God interfere to save their rabbi from the sniper. They revere Abraham even more now, which helps him do his job, control them, prevent a repeat of our sad history."

"History doesn't repeat itself."

"But Ecclesiastes said: *What happened then shall happen again, and what was done then shall be done again, for there's nothing new under the sun.* And as you have correctly guessed, what I wanted back then, I still want."

"Elie Weiss speaks honestly?" Tanya closed the door. "I'm shocked."

"Do you still have the ledger?"

"Let's drive. I hate to travel by bus."

Leaving Tel Aviv behind, they crossed open fields and passed by the airport. The road dropped into a wide valley, approaching the Judean Mountains and a thick layer of clouds. He took his time gathering enough resolve to speak openly to her.

"The wealth," he said, "which General Klaus von Koenig deposited in Switzerland, was Jewish property. You spent four years with him, so you know how he collected all those precious stones and jewelry."

She nodded.

"The dead Jews are gone. They'll never reclaim it. But Israel is their moral heir. Imagine what we could accomplish with such a fortune."

"You're right. I'll hand over Klaus's ledger to the Ministry of the Treasury."

Finally! She admitted to possessing the ledger! Elie knew he had to speak the truth, or her sudden openness would vanish for another twenty years. "In the hands of the government the money will come to nothing. They'll waste it, pay more bureaucrats. We must use this fortune, which came from the Holocaust, to prevent another Holocaust."

"How?"

"A formidable, global network of trained agents to monitor Arab leaders and sympathizers, weapon scientists and arms dealers, and those who finance the war against the Jews. We will eliminate our enemies before they manage to hurt us!"

"You're right," Tanya said. "I'll hand it over to the prime minister on the condition that the money is earmarked for Mossad and Shin Bet."

Elie downshifted and veered to the shoulder, where a convoy of vehicles was assembling for the last leg of the trip to Jerusalem, the steep climb up the mountains, where the slow pace of travel provided easy targets for the Arabs. He glanced at Tanya. Was she teasing him? Rage blurred his eyesight. He should draw his father's *shoykhet* blade and put it to her throat. But the car came to a stop, the wind disappeared from the open window, and he smelled her delicate perfume. Truth was, he could never bring himself to hurt Tanya Galinski.

He lit a Lucky Strike and drew deeply, holding the smoke for a long moment. "Why are you toying with me?"

"A taste of your own medicine?"

The convoy began to move, and a truck ahead of them spewed a cloud of sooty fumes. Elie drove faster, changing gears to accelerate past the truck.

"You want that fortune," she said, "as leverage for more power."

"Power to defend our people. I will prevent another Holocaust."

"You alone?"

He ignored her sarcastic tone. "I can do a better job than those desk people, who lack the stomach for action. We're at war, and the world is our battlefield. I'll get results!"

Tanya looked at him, saying nothing.

"You can work with me as an equal partner, apply your field experience to commanding an international army of agents. You'll be the most powerful woman in Israel, maybe in the world."

"I'm happy at Mossad."

Elie didn't tell her of his plan to become chief of Mossad, as well. She would find out in due time, become his subordinate, and despite her hostility, she would end up admiring him. "I'll split the money with you."

"I don't need money." She loosened her hair and retied it in a bun. "But there's something else I need."

Was she offering a trade? A dip in the road caused the car to sway from side to side. Elie struggled to control it.

"Abraham's son deserves a chance for a normal life."

Even though her words were uttered without intonation or dramatic gesticulations, Elie knew Tanya had just allowed him a peek into her innermost passion. "Why would he want a normal life? He's a black hat, lives the good life in Neturay Karta, studies with his friends all day, not a worry in the world. He doesn't know any better."

"He does now."

"So?"

"Tell Abraham to let him go."

Elie considered this unexpected development. "It won't be easy. He's counting on the boy to get married, become a great Talmudic scholar, a leader in the sect."

"Abraham will obey you."

The incline slowed down the Deux Chevaux. Elie downshifted to maintain momentum. "What will you do with—what's his name?"

"Jerusalem. I want him free of their insular religious extremism."

"He was born into it."

"And you were born in a kosher butcher shop in a shtetl on the eastern border of Germany. I don't see you pursuing your birthright."

"Abraham won't like it."

"I want the boy to leave the sect, enlist in the army like any young Israeli, and go on to study in the university. He'll be a doctor, a scientist, a businessman. He has a good mind."

"The IDF might decline to draft a religious fanatic."

"You could pull some strings."

"I could." Elie threw the cigarette out the window.

"The day he starts boot camp, I'll give you Klaus's ledger."

Elie downshifted to second gear. The engine struggled uphill, the noise an effective masquerade for the joy in his voice. "How do I know you won't cross me?"

"I'm not like you."

"Would you prove your good intentions by telling me the name of the bank?"

"The Hoffgeitz Bank of Zurich. Armande Hoffgeitz signed the ledger as the bank's president. He and Klaus—"

"Attended boarding school together at Lyceum Alpin St. Nicholas."

"You've done your homework."

"Information is my business." Since that night near the Swiss border, Elie had investigated General Klaus von Koenig's personal history in detail. As a teenager, Klaus had been sent by his parents from Munich to the most prestigious Swiss boarding school in the Alps. Elie had traced each of his classmates, finding twenty-nine who in 1945 had served in senior banking positions. Armande Hoffgeitz was on Elie's list of possible bankers in possession of the Nazi general's loot.

"Do we have a deal?"

Elie offered his hand. "I'll do my part, but what if Abraham refuses?"

"First day of boot camp. Or nothing."

They shook hands, and when she let go of his hand, Elie gripped the steering wheel to conceal a tremor.

Chapter 13

After morning prayers, all the married men lined up in front of Rabbi Gerster to receive their *gelt*—a weekly allowance that sustained the scholars and their families. He handed each man a sealed white envelope containing a sum based on each family's needs. Only the rabbi knew the source of the *tsedaka*, the charity funds that sustained the sect.

Lemmy went outside to the courtyard, filled with chatty wives who waited for their husbands to come out. The rain had stopped, and a blue window opened in the clouds. His mother was surrounded by bags of children's clothes. A cluster of mothers picked little shirts and pants, which they measured against their toddlers. Temimah sorted through the bags to help them find the best sizes and colors. When the selection process ended, she collected the remaining clothes into a large sack and handed it to Lemmy. Meanwhile the men emerged from the synagogue and gave their wives the white envelopes.

As always, the women did not leave until the last man came out, followed by Rabbi Gerster. They lined up, and the rabbi blessed each family as they passed before him.

After all the women and children left, and the men returned inside to take their breakfast in the foyer, Rabbi Gerster beckoned Lemmy, who followed him with the sack of used clothes, wondering why his father was going into town.

They left Meah Shearim through the gate on Shivtay Israel Street and walked down to Jaffa Street. The rabbi held a hard-bound book, his long black coat buttoned up, his wide-brimmed hat pulled down over his eyes. Most pedestrians were secular Israelis, and occasionally someone pointed at him and whispered to another.

"Your mother told me you're nervous about the marriage."

The comment caught Lemmy off guard.

"What's the problem?"

"I'd like a little more time, Father."

"You want to delay fulfilling the most important *mitzvah?*" Rabbi Gerster was speaking of the first divine order in Genesis: *Procreate and multiply, and fill the land.*

"Just for another year. Maybe two."

"What's next?" Rabbi Gerster stopped and turned to his son. "Recite the midday prayers at night? Put off the fast of Yom Kippur until Passover?"

Lemmy looked down, thankful for a noisy bus that allowed him a moment to think. He couldn't tell his father the truth, that Tanya's books had confused him, that he dreamt of falling in love with a beautiful woman and sharing a passionate attraction of body and soul that would last forever.

"You must remember," Rabbi Gerster said, "what King Solomon wrote: *Each want has its time, and there is a time for each desire.* The time for marriage is at eighteen."

There was a lull in traffic, creating quietness that made Lemmy's silence even louder. He forced the words out of his mouth. "I'm not sure about Sorkeh."

"The cantor's daughter isn't good enough?"

"She's very good, but—"

"What's wrong with her?"

"Nothing."

"Cantor Toiterlich is a righteous man who raises his children with Torah and faith in the Master of the Universe. Do you agree?"

Lemmy didn't answer.

Rabbi Gerster put his finger under Lemmy's chin and made him look up. "Our creator said in the Torah: *And a man shall adhere to his wife, and they shall become one flesh.* You are not the first young man to find this mitzvah a tad daunting. That's why parents choose a good match for their son or daughter. Do you understand?"

What could he say? That he feared watching Sorkeh become as wrinkled and lusterless as his mother? Lemmy picked up the sack of clothes. "Yes, Father."

The rest of the way they did not speak.

Shmattas ran her clothing exchange from an enclosed passage between two buildings, fitted with a tin roof. Rabbi Gerster waited outside while Lemmy entered.

The space was cluttered with open boxes of used pants and shirts. Wood hangers carried coats, jackets, suits, and dresses. There were black clothes for the ultra-Orthodox residents of the neighborhoods to the north and east, and colorful clothes for modern Zionists in the secular neighborhoods to the south and west. Lemmy found himself gazing into a box of colored ladies' underwear.

Shmattas emerged from the dark end of the store. She was an old hunchback, shorter than a ten-year-old child, who smelled of dust and mold and sweat. She plucked the sack from his hand and gave him another sack. "God bless *Rabbitzen* Gerster."

"Amen," he said.

Outside, his father closed the book and headed down King George Street. Lemmy followed him into a small market of wooden stalls piled with shining oranges, grapefruit and lemons, dried Lebanese figs, apricots, carob, prunes, and dates. Glass-fronted counters held blocks of sesame halvah, chocolate dotted with nuts, and peanuts in dried honey. Flies swarmed the stalls while vendors lauded their goods. He followed his father along the open sacks of herbs and spices and ground exotic roots. The sights and sweet aroma made him salivate.

Beyond the market, they passed through a narrow walkway into an enclosed courtyard that stunk of urine. A beggar in a hooded cloak sat by a swinging door, his legs interwoven, his eyes behind sunshades. He swayed slowly, murmuring Psalms from memory. Lemmy wondered if the beggar was blind.

Rabbi Gerster put the brown book in the beggar's lap and entered into the public restroom, beckoning Lemmy to follow.

The narrow, rectangular room was poorly lit and damp. A dozen or so urinals lined the wall.

When Lemmy stepped outside, the beggar was in the same position. Rabbi Gerster dropped a coin in his cup, picked up the book, and kissed it as one did with sacred books.

Elie Weiss continued reciting Psalms long enough for Abraham and his son to be halfway back to Meah Shearim. The swinging door let out bursts of stench, and he tried to breathe through his mouth. He stood up, the cloak loose on his gaunt body. It was heavy and itchy, and he longed to lower the hood. The cup was filled with coins. He emptied it into the pocket of his cloak and walked through the passageway to King George Street.

The gray Citroën Deux Chevaux was parked in a side street of four-story apartment buildings. A group of kids stopped playing ball when they saw him. He slumped behind the steering wheel, pulled back the hood, and scratched his bald head until the itching eased. He took off the sunglasses and lit a Lucky Strike, holding the smoke inside for as long as he could, and read the note that Abraham had hidden inside the book:

1. A demonstration will take place Saturday PM. I can't hold them back without raising suspicion. Tell Major Buskilah to look for a redhead named Dan. No broken bones, but make him bloody and keep him locked up for a few days.
2. Abortion is a black-and-white issue under Jewish law. I have to voice the loudest protest or they'll notice a discrepancy and question my judgment. If the law passes Second Call in the Knesset, expect intense protests.
3. Money is running short. Increase is essential to maintain dependency.
4. About Tanya: Her appearance was a shock. I'm happy she's alive, but ache to be with her. I made up my mind that, once my son marries, I'll start transitioning to him. He'll be able to assume the leadership within 2-3 years. Then I want out. Tell Tanya to wait for me!

Elie placed the note on the passenger seat. The situation presented a delicate challenge. If Tanya knew that Abraham decided to join her, yet his freedom depended on his son's staying in—and leading!—Neturay Karta, she would call off the deal. But Abraham was fooling himself. That boy was already lost to fundamentalism. In a contest between 3,000 years of glorious Jewish heritage and the beauty of Tanya Galinski, there was no question who would win Jerusalem Gerster's soul.

He turned on the ignition, and the car shuddered before it coughed out a blue cloud and rumbled up the narrow street. The kids in the rearview mirror watched as he made a left turn onto King George Street and headed to Rehavia.

Chapter 14

It took them an hour to walk back to Meah Shearim. Lemmy carried the sack of clothes on his shoulder, keeping pace with his father. They spoke of the Talmud page Lemmy was studying with Benjamin, involving a dispute between two men who found a prayer shawl in the street. "What's the logic," Rabbi Gerster asked, "of giving them both equal ownership shares? They can't split the *tallis* in half, right?"

"Maybe it's a metaphor."

"For what?"

"A person?"

"What kind of a person?"

"A child?"

Rabbi Gerster nodded. "Explain."

"A baby is like a sacred thing, a gift from God to two people. But as with a prayer shawl, a child cannot be divided in two. The parents must enjoy the child in partnership."

"Or have more children?"

"Right." He glanced at his father.

"Are you worried about your mother?"

Lemmy nodded.

"You shouldn't worry. These things are in God's hand."

"She's very sad."

Rabbi Gerster was quiet for a moment. "My Temimah is a righteous woman. The Master of the Universe is not giving her more children, and we accept His judgment. We shall continue to pray that He grants her renewed fertility and more children."

"Amen."

"Or grandchildren."

Lemmy didn't say Amen to that. Fortunately, they had arrived back at the synagogue, which welcomed them with the noise of Talmudic arguments and the sting of cigarette smoke. Rabbi Gerster walked down the aisle to his elevated seat up front, and Lemmy headed to the rear. He threw the sack on the floor by the bench.

Benjamin asked, "Anything for sale?"

"Your mother's underwear."

"*Shush!*" Benjamin laughed. "You're disgusting!"

"Let's study."

They began reading the Talmud page. All around, men argued with each other. Some sat, some stood, swaying back and forth in a meditative motion. A few still wore their *tefillin,* and those who were married also had their prayer shawls draped around their shoulders, fringes darting about.

The crystal chandelier hung above the *bimah,* the center dais, like a giant cluster of glassy stars. It was the only item of splendor in Meah Shearim, a community sewn together with threads of frugality and modesty. Lemmy had heard the story many times, how his father had appeared one day with a horse-drawn cart. It took seven men to unload, and when Rabbi Gerster pried open the crate, each of the tiny crystal leaves was individually wrapped in vinegar-soaked cotton. Nothing like that had ever been seen in Neturay Karta, and a debate erupted on whether such extravagance should be allowed. But Rabbi Gerster explained that the chandelier had once hung in his father's synagogue in the eastern reaches of Germany. The elders of Neturay Karta decided that the chandelier was a Holocaust survivor from an extinct Jewish congregation, just like Abraham Gerster himself, and therefore should be accepted. And so, as it had once lit the faithful faces of Jews in Germany, it was shining again in Jerusalem—but only on Sabbath and holidays. On regular days, its tiny leaves merely glittered in the natural rays of the sun or the long fluorescent lamps that lined the ceiling.

The men prepared for Rabbi Gerster's lecture by analyzing the designated page of Talmud, debating each point with their study companion. Lemmy's Talmud volume was open before him on the slanted shelf attached to the back of the next bench.

Benjamin stood, embracing a Talmud volume to his chest, his face creased in concentration. "Two men hold a prayer shawl," he recited. "David says, I found it, it's mine. Jonathan says, I found it, it's mine. Each will swear that he owns at least half, and they will share it."

Lemmy threw his hands up. "One of them must be lying, which makes the solution unjust! The truthful owner is losing half of his property."

"But they're both honest!" Benjamin raised his voice over the noise of the surrounding scholars. "They're two pedestrians who simultaneously noticed a *tallis* lost in the street. They grabbed it at the same time, and each of them honestly believes he was the first to reach it. Partition is fair!"

"Fair, but impractical. How do you share a prayer shawl? Alternate days?"

"Maybe."

"It's too simplistic," Lemmy said. "Talmud must have another layer of meaning here." He leaned over the page. His fingers followed the lines of text. The aging, wrinkled page felt coarse. This was only one out of thousands of pages in many volumes of Talmud, written down by the sages in the Babylonian exile more than a thousand years ago. The main text appeared in the center of each page, discussing sins and good deeds, prayers, holidays, repentance, business rules and ethical theories, and even astronomy and geography, governance of the kingdom, and trade with the Gentiles. Printed in the margins were notations of later scholars.

Lemmy sat back and gazed at the ceiling. He rubbed his eyes with the back of his hand until tears surfaced.

Benjamin rapped the bench with his hand. "Wake up!"

"It's the damn smoke." Lemmy waved at the full synagogue. "Bunch of hypocrites!"

"Are you crazy?"

He tugged on his earlobe. "Why is it forbidden to pierce your ear?"

"The sanctity of our body." Benjamin scratched his head through the large black yarmulke. "We're created in God's image, as written in the—"

"Aren't lungs part of the sacred body too?" Lemmy pointed in a circle. "Look at them, hundreds of supposedly God-fearing Talmudists, destroying the lungs God gave them."

"*Shush!*" Benjamin pulled him down.

"They should hear!" Looking around, he saw they were all too involved in Talmudic discussions to notice his outburst. He punched Benjamin's shoulder. "Even you don't hear me!"

"I do. The answer is simple. Smoking is allowed because it keeps the mind sharp and alert, so that you can study Talmud all day, which is the most important mitzvah of all."

"Another Talmudic hoop."

"Right." Benjamin's white teeth flashed. "Now, do you agree with my explanation, that because each of them honestly believes he was the first to reach it, they share it?"

"What would you do with half of a prayer shawl? Drape it around one shoulder?"

Benjamin threaded his finger through his cylindrical side lock, pulling and releasing it like a spring. "Maybe sell it and split the money?"

"That makes sense. But Talmud still avoids the real issue. What if each of them claims to be the original owner, who had lost it and came back to pick it up? What do we do when it's clear that one of them is a liar?"

"In such case," Benjamin chanted in the argumentative tune of Talmudic scholars, "Rabbi Sumchus says that the *tallis* should be kept in a safe place until the Messiah comes and the liar is exposed. But Rabbi Yossi says it should be sold and the proceeds split so that the true owner at least gets half of his property now."

"I think the owner should grab it," Lemmy argued, "go to the police station downtown, and get the bastard arrested. Who cares about Rabbi Sumchus and Rabbi Yossi? They've been dead and buried for a long time."

"*Oy vey!*" Benjamin looked around to see if anyone heard Lemmy. "What's wrong with you? One minute you're falling asleep, the next you're saying crazy things."

Lemmy leaned forward, his elbows on the book of Talmud. "I've been reading stuff."

"What kind of stuff?" Benjamin leaned closer, as if someone could hear him over the surrounding noise. "You're not reading Kabbalah, are you?"

His friend's conclusion was logical. Kabbalah, the secret world of Jewish mysticism, was forbidden to anyone but the most pious rabbis, whose strength of faith qualified them to study it. There was a rumor in Meah Shearim that Rabbi Gerster was one of the few scholars allowed to explore the secrets of Kabbalah.

Benjamin grabbed Lemmy's arm and shook it. "Tell me!"

He could not tell Benjamin the truth. If the burden was so heavy on him, how terrible would it be for Benjamin? "I read at night."

"What do you read?"

The Talmud page began to blur, the print no longer discernible. "The smoke is killing me," Lemmy said, though he wasn't sure it was the smoke that brought up his tears.

At noon, everybody went out to the foyer and formed a line before a table loaded with sliced bread, jars of jam, and a tall samovar of hot tea. Lemmy and Benjamin took their lunch outside to the sunny forecourt, where the air was crisp and fresh.

After lunch, the men returned to the synagogue for Rabbi Gerster's lecture. He mounted the front dais and stood before the wooden ark of the Torah, his back to the men. A blue velvet curtain, embroidered with Torah verses in gold threads, covered the ark. Rabbi Gerster kissed the curtain and turned to the podium. He was wearing his prayer shawl over the black coat, his wide-brimmed black hat contrasting with the blond-gray payos and beard.

Lemmy glanced at Benjamin, whose face was filled with anticipation. Everyone else was similarly entranced, holding their breath for the surprise opening Rabbi Gerster was certain to deliver.

The rabbi caressed his beard and rocked slowly over the lectern. "We're all smart," he roared, his voice filling the sanctuary.

"We're all wise. We all know Talmud. So why would two scholars yank on a tallis in opposite directions like silly boys fighting over a toy?"

The synagogue filled with laughter.

"Master of the Universe! Who would fight over such an object of small value and great spiritual significance? Imagine that I walk home with Cantor Toiterlich, and we find a prayer shawl—"

"You can have it," Cantor Toiterlich boomed.

"No way," Rabbi Gerster said. "You take it! In good health!"

Another burst of laughter came from the men, and Rabbi Gerster, whose own tallis was draped around his shoulders, held up one corner, looking at it with feigned astonishment. "Fighting over this? For what? To wear it later, when they repent for fighting a fellow Jew?"

Nachum Ha'Levi, an elderly man in the first row, raised his hand. "The commentators explain that property lost by its lawful owner becomes the property of the first person to notice and pick it up in a manner which manifests ownership."

The rabbi held his arms wide open. "Therefore?"

"Therefore," Ha'Levi continued, "if they just stood there and chatted politely, they would acquire nothing. That's why the example must include them grabbing it at the same time. Without the physical aspect, there's no claim for ownership."

"True," Rabbi Gerster said, "but the physical confrontation serves another purpose. It shows that an angry dispute must resolve in peace." He pointed up. "God's emissary was the learned rabbi, who brought about reconciliation. He's not explicitly mentioned, but a real scholar reads between the lines!"

Many in the crowd nodded and made notations with pencils on the margins of the Talmud page. Lemmy wrote on his: *Which rabbi? Why wasn't he mentioned?*

Benjamin read it over his shoulder and whispered, "What do you mean?"

Rabbi Gerster clapped his big hands. "Any questions?" His blue eyes surveyed the hall, searching for a raised hand or a doubtful expression. There was none. He closed the Talmud volume. "Let us take a break from studying to bring a Jewish baby boy into God's covenant."

In the rear, the doors opened. The foyer was full of women in headdresses. One of them handed a bundle to Redhead Dan, who carried it to the dais.

Shortly after 4:00 pm, Elie Weiss arrived at the central police compound at the Russian Yard. He found Major Buskilah at his office in the rear of the building.

"I've been expecting you." Buskilah was an Iraqi Jew, gray-haired with a weathered face and muscular arms. "My superiors ordered me to obey you, but I won't risk disaster with those black hats. Like all other hoodlums, they will interpret leniency as a weakness."

Elie sat down and lit a cigarette. He drew on it several times until the small room filled with smoke. "I sympathize with your frustration."

"We should have arrested them all. It was a stupid order!"

"My orders are always part of an established strategy."

"Next time my radio might be inoperative."

"You want to face a court-martial?"

"Better I face a court-martial than the wife and kids of a policeman lost under my command."

"There's going to be a demonstration on Saturday." Elie handed him a black-and-white photo, showing the face of a man with a beard and payos. "This is the ringleader. Red hair, burly fellow."

"I remember him. He threw the first rock."

"Beat him up and throw him in solitary confinement for a couple of days. I'll join him in the cell once he's softened up."

Major Buskilah pocketed the photo. "There's another one. The rabbi's son. I'm going to bust his balls."

"Little Jerusalem?" Elie was amused by the major's sudden anger. "What's he done to you?"

"That prick kicked me in the nuts!"

Lemmy joined his father on the dais. He set up the instruments on a small folding table, together with a bottle of sweet red wine and a silver goblet. Redhead Dan sat on a large, elevated chair, his sleeping baby on his lap. Lemmy tried to ignore the many eyes that watched his every move.

Rabbi Gerster released the safety pin on the cloth diaper. He pulled up the tiny feet, removed the diaper, and chanted, "*Every male among you shall be circumcised. Thus shall the covenant remain as an everlasting mark in your flesh.*"

The hall erupted in a loud, "Amen!"

Lemmy handed him the pressure gauze.

The baby suddenly opened his eyes and saw Rabbi Gerster's bearded face. The toothless gums opened wide, and he screamed.

The rabbi tied the strip of gauze around the base of the baby's tiny penis. The fiddling must have stimulated it, because a stream of urine emerged, passing over Rabbi Gerster's left shoulder. Redhead Dan chuckled nervously, and Lemmy held the blade forward. His father took it and brought it to the baby's loins.

Redhead Dan cleared his throat. "*Blessed you be, Master of the Universe, for the sacred mitzvah of bringing my son, Shimon ben Dan, into the covenant.*"

Lemmy held the baby's legs apart, Rabbi Gerster sliced off the foreskin with the blade, and blood gushed out of the cut.

Redhead Dan said, "*Oy!*"

The baby shrieked.

Lemmy let go of one of the baby's legs and received the blade from his father. The rabbi picked up the wine goblet and recited: "*Bless you be, Master of the Universe, creator of the fruit of wine.*" He sipped wine and bent down, bringing his lips to the fresh, bleeding wound. Lemmy reached for a fresh bandage.

The rabbi sucked on the open cut, turned his head, and spat a mouthful of wine and blood on the floor. Lemmy quickly pressed a bandage to the wound while his father swished a mouthful of red wine from the goblet and spat again. He wiped his lips and beard with his handkerchief. Meanwhile Lemmy fixed a clean diaper on the baby, dipped a piece of cotton in wine, and held it to the baby's lips. The screaming stopped.

The men chanted, "*Mazal Tov and Siman Tov*—Good Fortune and Good Omen."

Rabbi Gerster gulped from the wine, this time swallowing it, and joined the men's singing. Lemmy cleaned the knife and collected the bloody bandages and the foreskin. Later he would bury it behind the synagogue.

The men helped the shaken Redhead Dan down from the *bimah*, and a circle formed around him, dancing and singing, as he carried his son to the foyer, where a cluster of women was waiting with the tearful young mother.

Lemmy felt his father's arm on his shoulder. "I think you're ready," the rabbi said. "Next time, you'll conduct the ceremony."

Chapter 15

Hannah Arendt's book, *Eichmann in Jerusalem – a Report on the Banality of Evil*, left Lemmy confused and angry. Four years earlier, when the Nazi fugitive had been caught in Argentina and brought to stand trial in Jerusalem, Rabbi Gerster led the men in a special prayer of gratitude for the divine hand that had brought the mastermind of The Final Solution to judgment. But Arendt portrayed Eichmann as a man of average intelligence, mild temper, and clerical efficiency—a family man who happened to find himself at the top of a vast bureaucracy of mass extermination.

On the next Sabbath afternoon, he shared his frustration with Tanya.

"But it's true," she said. "What in retrospect seems like a monstrous enterprise was nothing but a day job for thousands of Germans. Their culture of obedience had conditioned these men to follow their leader's orders and do a good day's work—whether it was to manufacture trucks or to operate gas chambers."

"That's impossible! Any human being could tell the difference!" Lemmy clenched his fist. "Even a child knows that killing innocent people is evil!"

"But what if the people being killed aren't human? What if they have been stigmatized for generations as evil, as pests, as the cause for all social and economical problems? What if eliminating them is your national duty, dictated by the state's top authority?"

"A man has a mind to question authority."

"Do the men of Neturay Karta question Rabbi Abraham Gerster's authority?"

This argument shocked him, but before he could become angry, he noticed the hint of a smile on Tanya's lips and understood she was trying to provoke him. "My father speaks for God. Do you believe in God?"

"That's a trick question." She took his hand. "Come, let's have cake."

They shared a lemon tart she had bought at a kosher bakery near Meah Shearim. It was January 1, 1967—her thirty-ninth birthday.

When he left, she gave him two thin volumes: *Night* and *Dawn*, both by author Elie Wiesel. He read them both that night, and was left agonizing over a quandary that went to the core of his faith: Why had God allowed the Nazis to do this? What was God's purpose in causing so much suffering?

O ne afternoon, Rabbi Gerster posed a question from the podium: "Talmud says: *Create a rabbi for yourself, and acquire a friend.* I've always wondered: Why *create* a rabbi, but *acquire* a friend?"

Redhead Dan, sitting somewhere in the middle of the hall, raised his hand. "A friend could be acquired with gifts or favors. But a rabbi's blessing isn't for sale."

"I disagree," Cantor Toiterlich declared from the front row. "Talmud wouldn't direct us to *buy* friends!"

Benjamin stood up. "Maybe *acquire* means that it's mutual. But the relationship with one's rabbi is created by one's submission to a spiritual leader."

"Well put, young man!" Rabbi Gerster took a contemplative stroll across the dais, the men's eyes following him. "But as a rabbi, I'd rather have mutuality. So let me tell you a story." He leaned on the lectern, looking around the hall. "A few years ago, a man named Aaron traveled a whole day from Haifa to talk to me. Temimah brought us tea, and I inquired of the sights he'd seen along the way, how the country was changing."

Everyone knew of the vow he had taken not to leave Jerusalem until the Old City was freed from the Arabs.

Lemmy whispered in Benjamin's ear, "Obedience to the rabbi—that's the answer."

Benjamin nodded, but it was clear he wasn't listening. His eyes were locked on Rabbi Gerster, up on the dais. Everyone's face wore the same delighted expression. Lemmy imagined himself up at the podium. Could he be like his father, captivate hundreds of brilliant, inquisitive Talmudic scholars? And even if he could, did he want to?

"Finally," the rabbi continued, "Aaron told me his problem. He was a God-fearing Jew, who worked hard as a bookkeeper to raise five children with his righteous wife, Miriam. One Friday night, he got out of bed to use the bathroom, and noticed that his wife wasn't breathing!"

The men groaned, their bodies leaning forward in suspense.

"Complete silence on Miriam's side of the bed!" Rabbi Gerster turned to the ark and made like he was begging for relief of Aaron's agony. "So, even though it was Sabbath, he turned on the lights and discovered that his wife wasn't even in bed!"

An explosion of laughter rocked the hall.

"Aaron wasn't laughing! He ran through the house in panic, opening every door, turning on the lights in every room, until he found her asleep on the couch. He woke her up, and she started yelling at him for turning on the lights during Sabbath!"

He waited for the laughter to calm down.

"The rest of that night, Aaron couldn't sleep, because all the lights were on. The following night he still couldn't sleep, because Miriam refused to return to their bedroom. His snoring interfered with her sleep, she argued, and she could no longer bear children, so why share a bed? Aaron begged, yelled, threatened a divorce, but Miriam was deaf to his pleas. So he took her to their rabbi, who had married them many years before, circumcised their sons, blessed their daughters, and led them through life with his wise advice and knowledge of Talmud."

"Ah!" The men sighed in relief.

Rabbi Gerster clapped his hands. "Guess how the good rabbi from Haifa ruled. For Aaron?"

A forest of hands appeared.

"For Miriam?"

Lemmy looked around. No hand rose in support of the wife. The blood rushed to his face. Talmud didn't command marital slavery! He knew what Howard Roark would do now!

He raised his hand.

No one saw the lonely hand in the rear of the hall, except for his father, who ignored it and announced, "Mazal Tov! You voted wisely!"

The men applauded.

"Talmud commands a wife to serve her husband's bodily needs, notwithstanding her incapability to bear children anymore. It's part of the marriage. After all, Sarah, the mother of our nation, gave birth to Isaac when she was a hundred years old. It can happen." Rabbi Gerster looked down and sighed. "It's all in God's hands."

The silence was charged. Everyone knew of the rabbi's pain at his wife's inability to bear him more children.

"You voted wisely," he repeated, "but you guessed poorly!"

The crowd groaned.

"Their rabbi told Aaron to let her be. Now what do you say to that?"

The men shook their heads. They all had wives.

"It's true," the rabbi explained, "that a wife must serve her husband. Miriam sinned, but a sinner cannot be forced to repent. That's the essence of Judaism—a free choice to sin or to repent. It's between you and God. And that's what I told Aaron when he came to me for a second opinion." He caressed his beard. "But then I thought, does Talmud allow a second opinion when you don't like your rabbi's ruling?"

No one responded.

"*Create. Acquire.* Don't you see it?" Rabbi Gerster looked around the hall. "Friendships you acquire with kindness, generosity, or intellectual interaction. We are friends with our grocer, tailor, and barber, and we are friends with our study companion. Friendships vary by the nature of reciprocal exchanges. We go through life acquiring and losing friends. But a *rabbi*?"

Lemmy watched the nodding heads spread like a wave of comprehension.

"Every Jew must *create* his rabbi by embracing faith and knowledge. It is a permanent bond of trust, spirituality, confidence, and obedience to your rabbi's authority. *Create!* Your rabbi will conduct your marriage ceremony, pronounce your food kosher, settle your disputes, educate your children, and marry them to their chosen spouses. The relationship with your rabbi is like the relationship with your child. And let me ask you: When our child behaves disagreeably, do we go out to seek a new and better child? Of course not! Once we create the parental bond, it's inseparable, for better or for worse. Similarly, the bond of obedience to our rabbi is unbreakable." Rabbi Gerster paused, looking from one side of the crowded synagogue to the other. "And when I called to check on Aaron a few months later, he told me that Miriam had fallen sick, and he took care of her, which renewed their feelings for each other—better than ever!"

The men exhaled in relief. A story with a sweet and instructive ending was a perfect appetizer for the warm dinner that awaited each of the men at home, prepared by their loyal wives. The chandelier above the dais, while not lit up, glistened in red reflections of the setting sun, signaling the end of a day of studying.

But Lemmy could not think about dinner. How could hundreds of Talmudic scholars, critical and inquisitive minds, turn into the submissive crowd surrounding him? How could they not raise their voices in the same protest that boiled inside him?

As if in a dream, he raised his hand.

His father noticed. "Yes?"

The clatter subsided as all heads gradually turned to him.

"I think that, just like Talmud doesn't require a wife to obey her husband blindly, Talmud also doesn't require a husband to obey his rabbi blindly." Lemmy swallowed hard. "A rabbi is only flesh and blood. A rabbi could be wrong. Anyone could be wrong sometime, right?" He took a deep breath. The hall was silent. "Maybe the meaning of *create* is that we have a personal choice to seek a rabbi whose rulings we find to be wise?" He shifted his weight, his knees shaky.

His father's face remained expressionless. "Go on."

"A rabbi," Lemmy said, "might give his followers the wrong advice—not maliciously, but due to ignorance or poor judgment. Not always would it be a minor disagreement about sleeping arrangements. What if it's a matter of life and death?"

The silence grew deeper. All eyes focused on him.

"For example," Lemmy spoke louder to hide the tremor in his voice, "the rabbis in Europe told their congregations not to immigrate to Palestine, and the millions who obeyed their rabbis died in the Holocaust. And those who disobeyed the rabbis' rulings and joined the Zionists in Palestine? They survive! I think it proved that rabbis can be wrong. Deadly wrong, even." He wanted to continue, but the words never left his lips.

"Master of the Universe!" Rabbi Gerster grabbed the lectern. "Six million were chosen to join God, and you think it was their rabbis' fault?"

"It's not about fault, but about being wrong sometimes—"

"Silence!" Rabbi Gerster raised both hands. "Who are we to judge God's decision to gather His lambs under His merciful wings?" He swayed back and forth. "His decision to take my saintly mother, my eight young brothers, and two little sisters. Was my father, Rabbi Yakov Gerster, guilty of their death? And of the death of the rest of our shtetl?"

After a long moment, Cantor Toiterlich began chanting in a mournful voice: "*This world is only a very narrow bridge, leading to heaven.*"

More voices joined him. "*And the essence is not to be afraid, not to be afraid at all.*"

The second time, every man in the synagogue, except Lemmy, chanted the sad melody, eyes shut in devotion, voices growing stronger. "*Not to be afraid, not to be afraid at all.*"

Lemmy felt Benjamin tugging at his sleeve. He sat down. His throat was dry. No one looked at him.

Temimah served chicken soup with a slice of bread and a piece of meat with boiled potatoes. The silence was broken only by the clanking of forks and knives. Lemmy had expected his father to admonish him, but not a word was uttered since they had left the synagogue after evening prayers.

Temimah served tea and cookies.

Rabbi Gerster recited the blessing after the meal, ending with, "*God shall give courage to His people and bless us with peace.*"

"Amen," Temimah said.

"Father," Lemmy said, "I didn't mean to upset you."

"You didn't upset me." His father sighed. "The Nazis, their name be wiped from memory, *they* upset me."

Temimah stood up but did not start to collect the plates.

"I have doubts," Lemmy said. "I'm not sure I can accept what you said about obedience. My question about the Holocaust—"

The word *Holocaust* brought Rabbi Gerster's hand pounding the table with such force that the teacups jumped and landed noisily. "You think you're alone? *Everyone* has doubts about what happened. Everyone!" He pointed at Lemmy. "You are my son. When you speak, it's like I'm speaking. You can't say whatever comes to your mind. You have a responsibility, for God's sake!"

"Abraham, please," Temimah said softly, "he is only—"

"He's not a child anymore!" Rabbi Gerster stood. "He can defend himself!"

"It's good for him to express his doubts."

He glared at her. "To express blasphemy?"

Temimah lowered her eyes.

"And you," the rabbi turned back to Lemmy, "remember who you are! Our people need certainty, not misgivings. They look to us for answers, not for more questions. Do you understand?"

"I'm not a rabbi," Lemmy said.

"Not yet! And if you don't think before you speak, you'll never be one!" He left the kitchen, and a moment later, the front door slammed behind him.

Lemmy collected the plates from the table and placed them in the left sink, which was dedicated for meat dishes. His mother turned on the faucet and soaped the sponge. "For people like us," she said, "your father and me, the Holocaust is a demon. It's a terrible monster that's still haunting us."

He knew they had both lost their entire families in the Holocaust. That's why he didn't have grandparents, uncles, aunts, or cousins. Temimah had survived a mass execution by pretending to be dead, dug herself out, and was taken in by a Catholic nun who hid her in the basement for four years. After the war and two more years in a displaced persons' camp in Italy, she had arrived in Israel and found a distant relative in Neturay Karta, where a marriage was arranged with Abraham Gerster.

"And we're too small to question God." She caressed his cheek. "We have to accept His judgment, His decision to collect all those innocent souls to His paradise." She sighed. "It's a wonderful thing to know that I'll meet my parents and siblings again. It makes me so happy to imagine our reunion."

Watching his mother's face, suddenly aglow with inner joy, he held his tongue. How could he argue with her about the meaning of the Nazis' murder of those she had loved? How could he express doubts, when God's powers provided his mother with hope?

"Go now," Temimah said. "You should be with your father."

Lemmy took his coat and hat and went to the synagogue for evening study. Many of the men were back, swaying over open books. Cigarette smoke swirled up to the ceiling. But there was no sign of his father.

Elie Weiss leaned against the wall by the entrance to the public restroom. The beggar's cloak was not thick enough to deflect the bitterly cold wind, and he was shivering. Abraham had called for an emergency meeting—the first time ever.

He appeared out of the darkness in his long black coat and wide-brimmed hat. Elie led the way to his car. The alley was deserted, no children playing outside at this time of night. The dark interior of the car provided privacy against prying eyes. Elie considered turning on the engine for heat but gave up, not wanting to attract attention.

Abraham did not waste time. "Did you reach Tanya?"

"She's a Mossad agent. I can't just pick up the phone and call her."

"Is she in touch with my son?"

"What in the world are you talking about?"

"He accompanied her home that Saturday, a couple of months ago. And now he's talking about things he couldn't possibly know from studying Talmud all day inside Neturay Karta. It occurred to me that he might be communicating with her, maybe even seeing her in secret."

"Unlikely. Why would she waste time on an ultra-Orthodox kid?" Elie rubbed his hands. Abraham must not find out about his son's relationship with Tanya. "I'll sniff around my Mossad buddies. Maybe they'll tell me how to reach her."

"Do it!"

Elie had never seen him so anxious. "Still, a little exposure to the real world will give your son better tools as a leader."

"That's my decision! What if Jerusalem loses his faith in our teachings?"

"You could always expel him from Neturay Karta. He's practically an adult."

"He's my son!" Abraham's heavy hand grasped Elie's forearm. "And he has a mother too. He's everything to her. If he continues down this road, it'll kill Temimah. He's the focus of all her hopes."

"What if she has another child?"

"No! I can't even look at children, so similar to our siblings in the shtetl. Every time I see a child, I think of what happened to them."

The image appeared in Elie's mind, the sight from the crack in the attic's floor, where he and Abraham had hidden above the butcher shop. The Germans had separated the children from the older Jews and herded them into the corral outside. Elie's father had kept his knives in a wooden rack, sharpened daily to perfection, as Talmud required a *shoykhet* to slaughter an animal in a single pass of a smooth blade, causing no pain. But the SS men got bored with slicing the children's throats, so they started stabbing their bellies. Elie could still hear the screams, punctuated by the shooting in the street, where the rest of the Jews were being mowed down in groups of fifty. It had been the first time Abraham's unique talent emerged. The rabbi's son had an eerie ability to combine cold thinking with hot-tempered action. Abraham had waited until the four German soldiers were occupied with a girl, who wriggled and fought while they tried to undress her. Abraham slipped down from the attic through the flap door, collected two long knives from the rack, and stabbed the four soldiers in rapid succession. But there was a fifth soldier, who had been out of sight, smoking near the door. By the time Elie followed Abraham down, the German grabbed his machine gun, which was leaning against the wall. Elie managed to swing a knife at the man's wrist, a passing cut that separated the tendon connecting the muscle that operated his trigger finger. The German's momentary bewilderment about why his finger wasn't functioning gave Elie a chance to swing the blade a second time, separating his vocal cords and windpipe. Before the Germans upfront noticed that something was amiss, the two of them slipped through the rear of the shop into the forest. And for months after that, through hunger, danger and more killings, Abraham had continued to bemoan their failure to save even one of the children.

"And tell Tanya I want to see her again."

"You're the leader of Neturay Karta." Elie tapped the steering wheel. "Wasn't her first visit risky enough?"

"We'll meet in secret, just like you and I meet."

"You can't revive the past, you know?"

"That's not your business!"

"You are my agent, and therefore you are my business." Elie pulled a cigarette from a pack. "That son of yours won't be ready to lead Neturay Karta for another ten, fifteen years, if ever. There's no retirement from your job. You knew it from day one."

"I gave twenty years!" Abraham put a finger in Elie's face. "Find Tanya and tell her that I'll be free in one or two years. Do it!"

Elie lit the cigarette, keeping the match burning so that he could watch Abraham's reaction. "It's not so simple. She has feelings for others."

"What are you saying?"

Elie drew long on the cigarette. "Could I speak any clearer? Tanya has a reputation in the spy world. She's a very passionate woman. Highly sensual. Surely you remember?"

Abraham leaned closer, his wide shoulders filling the tight space in the car. The flame of the match danced in his eyes, and his bushy beard trembled as his lips pressed together. His left hand rose and rested on Elie's neck, almost encircling it. The hand tightened, four fingers at the nape, a large thumb pressing the windpipe.

Elie dropped the match, and the cigarette fell from his lips. He tried to undo Abraham's grip, realizing he had underestimated the intensity of Abraham's love for the woman he had thought dead for two decades. Reaching down, Elie's hand fumbled with the beggar's cloak, trying to reach the long shoykhet blade that was strapped to his lower leg.

The world fogged up.

His hand found the handle of the knife and tried to pull it from its sheath, but the folds of the cloak entangled it.

"One day," Abraham said, releasing his grip, "you'll push it too far."

His breath shrieking through his constricted airways, Elie watched through the windshield as Abraham walked away, his black coat and hat melting into the dark of the night.

Chapter 16

Later that night, when Lemmy returned from the synagogue, the door to his father's study was still open, the lights off. His mother was working in the kitchen. She asked, "Where's your father?"

"He wasn't in the synagogue."

She wiped her hands on her stained apron. "He likes to be alone when he's upset. Next time you should ask him whatever you want, but do it in private."

Lemmy thought of his father's expression. "He's angry because I questioned the authority of rabbis. It's like I told them not to obey him."

"Your father cares nothing for personal glory." Temimah smiled sadly. "Sometime I wish he did. But he carries too much guilt for having survived while everyone else died."

"How do you know?"

"Because I feel the same way. But your father can't afford to indulge in weakness. As a leader he must project strength. It has taken me years to understand, to accept some of his decisions. I must serve him without a question. It's my duty as a Jewish wife. And you must fulfill your duty, as well."

"To get married?"

Temimah sighed. "You think it's easy for me? But he is my husband. He is a *tzadik*, more righteous than all of Neturay Karta put together. We must trust his judgment." She fixed the collar of his shirt. Smell of dish soap came from her hands. "Good night, Jerusalem."

"Good night, Mother."

Locked in his room, Lemmy read Jerzy Kosinski's *The Painted Bird*, the story of a young boy with black hair and dark skin, who wandered around Europe during World War II, chased by primitive villagers and German soldiers. The boy told his own story, and Lemmy imagined he was hearing the boy's voice as he chronicled his torments.

Long past midnight, the pages became hazy. Lemmy closed his eyes. *Had the rabbis in Europe caused their faithful followers' deaths?* His father's blue eyes stared at him from the dais, dark with fury, or with terrible pain.

He turned off the reading light and gazed into the darkness. He wondered where his father had gone after they had argued. It wasn't safe in Jerusalem at night, especially near the border, where occasional Arab infiltrators from Jordan murdered Jews and slipped back across the border before getting caught. He had no desire to venture out from under the blanket, but he knew the pressure in his bladder would interfere with his sleep.

Walking down the dark hallway, his bare feet absorbed the coldness of the tiled floor, and he thought how long it would take to warm up again. He reached the foyer and found the door to his father's study open. Light from a street lamp outside came through the window onto his father's empty cot. Something must have happened to him!

Lemmy hurried to wake his mother up. Together they would go to a neighbor who owned the grocery store, which had the only telephone in Meah Shearim, and call the police. The thought of his father injured—or worse!—terrified Lemmy.

The sound of a sigh made him pause outside his mother's bedroom. Through the closed door, he heard it again. Was she crying? Had he upset her with his questions and doubts? He turned the knob and nudged the door.

A section of the wall came into view, then the headboard of his mother's bed, illuminated through the window by the same street lamp that shed light into his father's study.

Another sigh.

The door opened further. Lemmy saw his mother.

Temimah was on her back, her head slightly up, her shaved scalp shining with sweat. She sighed again, her face almost happy. Her hands reached back over her head, pressed to the headboard. Her left knee was bent to the side, the white kneecap pointing at Lemmy. Her nightgown was pulled up to her waist.

The bed shook.

The door opened all the way, revealing his father, who crouched over her, holding her thighs apart, thrusting into her again and again—a slow slide backward, another thrust, a slide backward, a thrust. His mother's sighs were hushed yet throaty. Her face twisted with each thrust in pained pleasure, her eyes locked on her husband's face. The thrusts came faster, his father staring at the wall over the headboard, his beard trembling. Suddenly, he paused and pulled backward, detaching from her, and sat on his ankles. His right hand reached into his groin and started shaking rapidly.

Startled, she looked up at her husband and groaned.

The light drew the lines of her full breasts, heaving under the nightgown, the valley between her thighs suddenly vacant. She sat up and grabbed onto his shoulders, trying to bring him down onto her, trying to embrace his hips with her thighs. She moved up and down, grinding against him. She attempted to force away his shaking hand, to pin herself onto him, to direct his seed into her body. He used his free hand to shove her away, down on the bed. His right hand shook faster and faster until he froze, and his whole body seemed to tense up in a hard, arched way, and he looked up at the ceiling and grunted.

His right hand still capped his groin as he stepped down from the bed. He stood with his back to the door, unaware of Lemmy's presence, and looked down at Temimah. "I'm sorry," he said quietly.

She was lying on her back, her lower body naked, her legs open. She turned to the window and whimpered.

His back slightly hunched, the rabbi turned, took a step toward the door, and froze.

Lemmy stood in the doorway.

His mother was sobbing now, facing the other way.

His father did not move. They looked at each other for a long moment.

Lemmy turned, entered the bathroom, and closed the door. He did not turn on the light, but lowered the hinged toilet seat and sat down. The wooden seat was cold, and he shuddered. He rested his elbows on his knees, his chin between his palms. He stared into the dark, absorbing what he had seen, comprehending his father's refusal to seed his mother. There was only one explanation. God had nothing to do with her infertility, and Lemmy realized that he had grown up without siblings because his father didn't want more children.

And then a terrible thought occurred to him: Had his father ever wanted *any* children?

Lemmy's lips trembled. Tears streamed down his cheeks.

Chapter 17

F riday was a day of study, but Lemmy could not concentrate on the page of Talmud before him. He tried not to gawk at his father, who sat at the front of the synagogue, where men came up to him with questions. Trying in vain to convince himself it had been a nightmare, Lemmy knew the truth: The great rabbi was a liar.

The evening meal was a big affair, as the whole Toiterlich family was invited for dinner to celebrate the impending engagement. Cantor Toiterlich sat at the opposite end from Rabbi Gerster. His children shared two to a chair, except for Sorkeh, who was placed across from Lemmy. While Mrs. Toiterlich helped Temimah with the food, the cantor filled the room with his rich tenor, chanting the traditional blessing for a new couple: *"Delight and enthuse, the beloved and betrothed, as you took joy in your creation, at Eden, in the beginning."*

Lemmy saw the joy on his mother's face as she filled the kids' plates and caressed their heads. He thought of her face the other night, the film of sweat, the pleasure, and the agony. He could not drive the image from his mind, could not forget that her utmost desire—to bear children—was denied by his father, who made everyone believe it was God who was keeping Temimah barren.

The meal lasted a long time, with singing and several toasts in honor of the young couple. Lemmy chatted with Sorkeh, doing his best to be cordial. But whenever his father spoke, he looked away, afraid that his eyes would betray his feelings.

That night he again read *The Painted Bird*, falling into a fitful sleep that left him tired and confused.

During Sabbath morning prayers, at the conclusion of his sermon, Rabbi Gerster said, "I understand that some of you wish to hold a protest later against the faithless Zionists. Remember, however, the words of the Torah: *You shall not raise your hand against your brother!* Your behavior must exemplify the righteousness of this community."

Sabbath lunch felt as if it would never end. Lemmy couldn't wait to go to Tanya's house. But after the blessing, Rabbi Gerster told Lemmy to join the other young members of Neturay Karta, who were leaving soon for the demonstration.

As soon as the group reached the intersection of Jaffa and King George streets, Lemmy noticed several police vans parked up the street.

Redhead Dan stepped into the road and waved his fists at passing cars. "Sabbath! Sabbath!"

The cars swerved into the opposite lane to avoid the black-garbed man. The drivers cursed through open windows. Some raised their middle finger.

Surrounded by other Neturay Karta men, his flaming beard and payos flapping in the wind, Redhead Dan shouted, "Sabbath! Sabbath!" He chased slow-moving cars and pounded on them with his fists. "*He who violated the Sabbath is destined to die! Stone him with rocks until his soul leaves his body!*"

The quote was correct, Lemmy knew, but Talmud disfavored capital punishment, saying that a Sanhedrin, a rabbinical court, which issued one death sentence in seventy years, was a deadly Sanhedrin.

The parked police vans turned on their flashing lights, their doors opened, and policemen jumped out. They put on their helmets and held up their shields and truncheons.

Redhead Dan grabbed Lemmy's arm, pulled him up front, and yelled, "Our rabbi sent his son! God will punish you if you touch the rabbi's son!"

Lemmy tried to free his arm. "Are you crazy? We can't fight them!"

"God will fight for us!"

"They knew we were coming!"

"Don't worry, the whole Zionist army couldn't silence God's voice!"

"It's a trap!"

Redhead Dan was too worked up to listen. "The Zionists are afraid of us! They're afraid of you, Gerster!"

Lemmy looked across the street at the policemen. The major stepped forward and smirked, swinging his baton.

Another attempt to release his arm from Redhead Dan's grip failed. The young man didn't even notice. He pulled Lemmy after him while the group clustered tightly, their faces touched by fear.

The policemen lined up along the opposite curb.

Redhead Dan dragged Lemmy with him to the side of the road and lifted a stone as big as a fist. "*He, who violated My Sabbath, stone him to death!*"

Lemmy shouted, "Don't!"

"It's God's war!"

Additional police cars blocked the surrounding streets. Traffic ceased, and the men of Neturay Karta faced the policemen in riot gear and truncheons.

Major Buskilah held a tin cone to his mouth. "Disperse immediately!"

In response, Redhead Dan raised his hand, reached back, and hurled the rock across the street. It flew in a wide arc and hit one of the policemen, who cried and fell down. Major Buskilah lowered the tin cone and shouted orders to his troops.

"God is with us! Repent, or go to hell!"

Across the street, the injured policeman was carried away, his cracked helmet remaining behind.

Redhead Dan took another step toward the middle of the road. "Sinners must be punished!"

Lemmy threw all his weight backward, certain that his arm was going to snap out of his shoulder. He saw Major Buskilah signal his men, and three things happened at once: The policemen rushed forward, Lemmy put his foot aside and tripped Redhead Dan, and the men of Neturay Karta fled.

The policemen circled the two of them. Redhead Dan got up, clenching his fists, and the major swung his truncheon and hit him on the side of the head. As he fell down, the truncheon landed on his back and thighs, again and again, making a sickening, hollow sound, while Redhead Dan screamed.

"Stop it!" Lemmy lunged toward the major, but two policemen restrained him.

The beating continued until Redhead Dan stopped screaming. Major Buskilah gave him a kick, which produced no response from the unconscious man. The major turned to Lemmy, panting, his face red, the truncheon clutched in his hand. "Who's laughing now, punk?"

"Satan, probably." Lemmy didn't lower his eyes.

The major holstered his truncheon, took Lemmy's arm, and pulled up the sleeve of his black coat, exposing the red skin left by Redhead Dan's grip. He showed the mark to his men. "Looks like evidence of resistance, boys?"

They laughed, and Major Buskilah shoved him. "Go home, boy. Tell your father that the Zionist police treated you fairly. Go on!"

Lemmy picked up his hat. "What about him?" He gestured at Redhead Dan.

"We'll take care of him," Major Buskilah said. "Go home!"

Chapter 18

Elie Weiss waited until Monday night, allowing Redhead Dan two days to stew in pain and fear in the windowless cell at the police lockup. Major Buskilah's deputies pushed Elie into the cell, where he collapsed on the floor, wrapped up in his beggar's cloak.

The young Neturay Karta man was sitting in the corner on the concrete floor, cuddled in his black coat, mumbling Psalms from memory. A light bulb hung from a wire, illuminating his bruised face.

Elie shuffled to the wall and propped himself up to a sitting position. "May God burn their souls in hell!"

"Amen." Redhead Dan coughed. "What happened to you?"

"The Zionists." The fake beard itched, and he scratched quickly. "They don't like what I have to say."

"They arrested you for talking?"

"Beat me up, too. With sticks, for speaking the words of the Prophet Ezekiel: *And He said to me, prophesy upon these bones, and tell them: Listen, dry bones, to the word of God!*"

Hearing the biblical words intoned in the manner of a learned scholar seemed to reassure Redhead Dan. "But why did the Vision of the Dry Bones upset them so much?"

"They said the prime minister couldn't sleep, that I was keeping him up."

"You recited Ezekiel by his house at night?"

"Is he home during the day?"

Redhead Dan described his own painful experience. Elie's sympathy was forthcoming as he listened to a lengthy rant against the state and its sinful ways. He steered the conversation to personal facts, asking the ultra-Orthodox man about his life in Meah Shearim, his family, and his studies. Elie reciprocated by sharing his own version of personal history, a mix of fact and fiction, of growing up in an Orthodox family in Germany, embracing modern socialist ideas, running away with a Zionist group to start a kibbutz near Lake Kinneret in Palestine, farming the land, fighting the British army for independence, and risking his life in the wars against the Arabs in 1948 and 1956. But Elie's invented biography veered off the common path of secular Zionism when he had supposedly regained his faith in God and started observing the Sabbath. The kibbutz expelled him with nothing but a few items of clothing and a sandwich, which he couldn't eat as it was not kosher. He settled in Jerusalem, working in construction and preaching Ezekiel, which had presently landed him in jail.

They spoke about the heretic Zionists, who were about to legalize abortions. As their discussion went from conceptual ideas to concrete facts, Elie led Redhead Dan to the eventual conclusion that, as the ultimate leader of the Zionist state, Prime Minister Levi Eshkol was responsible for a legislation process that would cause the murder of unborn, yet viable, Jewish children. "It's driven from the top," Elie said. "The prime minister must be made an example for all sinners!"

The Talmudic scholar in Redhead Dan emerged, and he quoted a whole section of Jewish law dealing with the concept of *Rodef,* where Talmud required the preemptive killing of a Jew who is actively attempting to hurt other Jews. The blood of such a *pursuer* must be spilled under the concept of collective self-defense before he succeeded in his attempt to hurt other Jews.

When first light showed in the barred window, Elie closed his eyes and said, "I think God wanted us to meet. It is written: *In a place where there are no men, be a man!* You and I must be men. We must bring down the Zionists and renew our people's faith in God!"

"We? How could we—"

"A man of faith can decide to smash the idols, just like Abraham the patriarch did." Elie leaned closer and whispered, "I have made that decision. And so can you."

"*Me?*"

"Why do you think God put us in the same cell? It's His design!"

Redhead Dan nodded slowly.

"God wants us to stop the Zionists, to prevent the killing of Jewish babies." Elie glanced at the door and spoke into the young man's ear. "I can't do it alone. I need two more men of strength and faith in the Master of the Universe."

"But how?"

"You feel powerless?"

"Yes!"

Elie showed him a fist. "God created explosives for a reason! To give us power!"

The guards' voices came through the steel door.

"Thursday at midnight, at the gate on Shivtay Israel Street. Be there, in God's name!"

Chapter 19

On Wednesday morning, as the men had their tea and bread in the forecourt of the synagogue, Lemmy saw Redhead Dan limping up the alley from the gate. Many of the younger men hurried to welcome him, singing, "*Connive and scheme—it shall not work! Conspire and curse—it shall not stand! For God is with us! God is with us!*"

They accompanied him into the synagogue and over to his seat next to Yoram. The forced smile on Redhead Dan's face contrasted with the bruises and the black eye. After a few moments, everyone returned to their open Talmud volumes, puffing on cigarettes.

At the conclusion of a morning of study, they recited the noon prayers and went outside to eat lunch and discuss the coming vote in the Knesset. Later that day, the proposed abortion law was scheduled to be presented to the assembly for a second call which, if passed, would allow the committee to submit it for a third and final call, when a majority vote would turn the proposal into law.

The religious parties in the Knesset had announced that they would abstain. Opposition leader Menachem Begin had yet to tell his caucus how to vote, but Prime Minister Levi Eshkol announced that the Labor party and its coalition partners would vote in favor of the proposed law. However, some in Neturay Karta speculated that many Knesset members would defy their party leaders and refuse to support the legalization of infanticide.

Lemmy stood with Benjamin, chewing on a piece of bread and listening to the discussions, which quieted down when Rabbi Gerster came out of the synagogue. He searched the crowd, saw Lemmy, and summoned him with a curled finger.

A half hour later, they arrived at the police compound at the Russian Yard on Jaffa Street. A policeman showed them into Major Buskilah's office.

"I want to know," Rabbi Gerster demanded, "why did you beat my disciple?"

"For the same reason I let your son go." The major pointed at his belt, which rested on the desk with the holstered gun and truncheon. "Violence will be met with violence, peaceful protest will be met with peaceful measures." He gestured at two metal chairs. "Please."

Rabbi Gerster sat down, but Lemmy remained standing.

"I hope the lesson was clear enough for the other Talmudic scholars."

"That violence must be met with violence?" The rabbi pointed at the truncheon. "This type of reasoning could go both ways, back and forth, worse and worse, until we lose control and spill blood."

"There won't be any violence on our side if your guys stop throwing rocks at people every time you disagree with something. We're not Neanderthals any longer, you know?"

Lemmy stepped forward, but his father raised a hand, stopping him, and said, "Hurtling insults is a common prelude to hurtling rocks. I'm here to make sure we don't have either."

Major Buskilah nodded. "I'm listening."

"If a Knesset majority supports the proposed abortion law, Neturay Karta will have to march in protest, bring out the word of God. But we will remain peaceful and hurt no one as long as we are not attacked by others."

"I will communicate the request to those who make such decisions."

"We seek Shalom," the rabbi said, using the Hebrew word for peace, "but Torah requires us to denounce sinners. We'll need safe passage and an opportunity to be heard without harassment." He stood and turned to leave, but when his eyes met Lemmy's, something in his expression communicated an implied license to act.

Without haste, Lemmy pulled the major's truncheon out of its holster, grasped it with both hands, lifted it high, and with all his strength landed it across the back of the metal chair. The wooden truncheon broke in half.

Lemmy put the handle on the desk, picked up the other part, and placed it next to the handle. "Good day," he said and followed his father.

They left the police compound and went through the market on Jaffa Street, with its clutter of shoppers and vendors under a whirl of dust. The noise jarred Lemmy's ears, and the dense air burned his tired eyes. He followed his father's wide back through the chaos.

The narrow passageway welcomed them with the familiar foul smell. The beggar in a hooded cloak was sitting by the door on crossed legs, his back to the wall, reciting from Psalms. Rabbi Gerster placed the sacred book in the beggar's lap and went inside. Lemmy followed.

They washed their hands, stepped outside, and recited the appropriate prayer. Rabbi Gerster took the book from the beggar's lap and dropped a coin in his cup. The beggar did not look up.

During the evening, news filtered into the synagogue that the abortion vote was delayed, as the Knesset was engaged in a heated debate over military issues. Earlier in the day, the Syrian defense minister, Hafez al-Assad, had accused Israel of planning an attack on Syria on behalf of the United States in order to topple the Syrian Ba'ath regime. He declared: "The Syrian army would destroy the Jews!" Egyptian president Nasser followed with a promise to "Recover the stolen Arab land and throw the Jews into the sea." Meanwhile, retired general Moshe Dayan opined from the Knesset podium that the government's sheepish response to Arab threats amounted to an invitation for attack: "The current leadership is putting our collective neck on the executioner's block," Dayan said.

The debate in the Knesset continued into the night, and many Neturay Karta men remained in the synagogue, praying and studying.

Shortly after four on Thursday morning, the Voice of Israel reported on the radio that, after a brief presentation and without much debate, a majority of the Knesset approved the proposed abortion law, which was sent back to the committee for fine-tuning before its submission for a final vote.

From the time the news came until sunrise, the synagogue bustled with anger over the new Zionist atrocity. A large group clustered around Redhead Dan, who explained that this law was not another instance of the Zionists committing personal sins, such as driving on Sabbath or digging up sacred graves. Rather, the Zionists had reached a new low, combining two of the greatest sins: Shedding the blood of another Jew and defiance of God's first *mitzvah* to procreate and fill the land with their seed.

After morning prayers, the men lined up before Rabbi Gerster to receive the white envelopes containing bundles of Israeli liras, which they took outside and handed to their wives to shop for the Sabbath. Rabbi Gerster did not come out to bless the families of Neturay Karta, but told the men to go home and change into their best clothes.

On hearing the news of the abortion vote, Elie Weiss drove to the Knesset building. The note inside Abraham's book yesterday had made it clear that a showdown was only a matter of time:

> *If the legislation passes second call in the Knesset, I'll have to lead the protests. Neturay Karta will be joined by many others. Buskilah must control his policemen. No shooting—we don't need martyrs. p.s. Did you reach Tanya?*

At the service entrance in the rear of the Knesset building, Elie was directed into the underground garage, through a second security checkpoint, to a long, gray Chevrolet, which was guarded by two men in short-sleeve shirts.

Prime Minister Levi Eshkol was in the back seat, reviewing a pile of documents. He glanced up when Elie got in and returned to his papers, penning brief notations on each document. When he finished, the prime minister lowered the window and handed the document to one of the guards. "So, Weiss," he said, "what bad news do you have for me today?"

"Religious riots against the abortion law."

"My enemies should have my luck." Eshkol sighed. "Abortions! My fellow *Yids* think we're in Holland. Next thing they'll be planting tulips. Can you believe it? Not a generation since the Nazis killed two million Jewish children, and we talk about abortions. We need babies, not abortions!"

"I think it's more about women, not babies."

"And why now? What's the urgency? The Arabs are gathering again to kill us, and I have to waste my time on abortions? I wish I had time to create such a problem for a pretty woman!"

Elie smiled. The clerical-looking prime minister's only known vice was his young and attractive wife—his third, who had formerly been the Knesset librarian.

"Speaking of pretty, how did you do with Tanya Galinski?"

"It came to nothing," Elie lied. "Now, about the abortion law, can you suspend the legislative process?"

"They won't listen." The prime minister sighed. "I'm under siege. Liberals on my left, Menachem Begin on my right, Dayan behind my back, the religious parties going through my pockets, and Ben Gurion's errand boy, Shimon Peres, crapping on my head without lowering his pants!"

Elie chuckled.

"It's not funny! The Soviets have delivered enough MiG jets to Nasser that he can line them up and skip from wing to wing all the way from Cairo to Tel Aviv without getting sand between his toes. And the newspapers say I'm unqualified to defend Israel! Why? Did I lose the Old City in 'forty-eight? Did I withdraw from Sinai in 'fifty-six in reliance on the incompetent UN? They think Dayan is better because he looks like a pirate!"

"I can make you popular again."

"Ha! I'm chewing pebbles and passing rocks. Popularity is far from my mind."

"I have a plan that will make everyone coalesce around your leadership."

"Man plans and God laughs," Eshkol said.

"It's a fail-safe plan."

"And what will it cost me?"

"Appoint me chief of Mossad."

"A summer-night's dream." Eshkol made a dismissive gesture. "You already have a job—keep those religious hotheads in the box. Or send in the police. They'll beat down those troublesome Talmudic scholars in ten minutes."

"The *Gestapo* was also capable."

The prime minister's face paled. Like most Israelis, he had lost most of his family in the Holocaust. Even two decades later, the trauma of the Final Solution remained the most dominant force in Israeli politics, a calamity that served as a yardstick against all other dangers. Many believed the Arabs were preparing to finish what the Germans had started and that the *Goyim*—the Western world—was content to *again* cluck its collective tongue and watch the Jews die. With the United States bogged down in Vietnam, and France smarting from an Algerian humiliation, Israel's only allies had declined to help. Prime Minister Eshkol's futile pleas to Washington and Paris were viewed by the Israeli public as groveling, further decimating his image.

Elie took out a cigarette, but didn't light it. "I've worked with my guy for nearly twenty years to draw to Neturay Karta the most extreme men from every Orthodox community, so that we can watch them in one place. It costs me a lot of money, but it works. Abortion, however, could potentially create an anti-Zionist consensus in the ultra-Orthodox community, not just in Jerusalem, but all over Israel. Neturay Karta will lead, but their protests will draw huge crowds."

"Then put a siege on them for a couple of weeks, until things calm down."

"That's the surest way to disaster."

"Why?"

"Imagine the media photos—policemen with guns and helmets, rolls of barbed wire, and bearded Jews in black hats. Shall we feed them rotten potato skins to complete the picture?"

"A Jewish ghetto."

"In Jerusalem, no less." Elie waited for the image to sink in. "The Jewish world would be outraged. However, if they are caught using weapons against the government, the balance of sympathy would reverse."

A guard put his head in. "They're calling for you upstairs."

"My plan," Elie said, "is to stage an event soon—a pretext—to justify harsh measures. The basic idea is to catch a couple of black hats in the act."

"What act?"

"An armed attack on you."

Eshkol removed his glasses. "Attack? On me?"

"Two birds with one shot. Not only would it give us a pretext to clamp down on the ultra-Orthodox, but you'll come out a hero. Assassination attempts are proven to give a shot of popularity even to the most downtrodden politician."

"Especially if they succeed!"

Elie smiled. "There won't be any real risk to your personal safety."

The prime minister gave Elie a long, searching look. "Talk about risk, does your guy on the inside realize what they'll do to him if he's exposed as a mole?"

"My guy," Elie said, "is not an easy man to kill."

Lemmy watched the men return to the synagogue in wide-brimmed hats, brushed-up black coats, and pressed white shirts. His father was sitting near the ark, his eyes buried in a book, rocking back and forth. The men sat on the wooden benches, watching him. When everyone was seated, the rabbi got up, kissed the blue curtain over the ark, and faced the silent throng.

"This is a test," he said. "Our God decided to test us!"

The men murmured their agreement.

"The Zionists want to kill innocent Jewish babies," he continued, his voice rising. "Zionist doctors will take pregnant daughters of Israel into clinics with white walls, lay them on white sheets, and slaughter their unborn babies!"

Men cried out and hit the tables with open hands. Lemmy looked around, astounded at how his father's few words impacted them.

Up on the dais, Rabbi Gerster stood hunched over the lectern, his beard coming down his chest, his white, striped prayer shawl draped around his shoulders. When the cries dwindled, his blue eyes turned upward, his hands clenched, pressed to his chest.

The men watched him.

"The Zionists think they know everything." He spoke very quietly. "They claim that unborn babies feel no pain, that they are nothing but senseless patchworks of flesh and bones. The Zionists claim that, until birth, a baby has no soul with which to rejoice or suffer, with which to serve God even in prematurity by being the very image of God, by demonstrating the miracle of God's creation and His wondrous powers."

A few men yelled, "Amen! Amen!"

"The Zionists think nothing of Torah, of God's words: *I shall make man in my image.* They think the unborn is disposable, like a skin-mole to be cut off and thrown away." Rabbi Gerster shook his head. "Not worthy of life." He took a deep breath and cried, "Pure, innocent Jewish souls, butchered inside their mothers' wombs!"

The men wailed.

"A carnage sanctioned by the Zionist state!"

Another wail, louder.

Rabbi Gerster paced across the dais, back and forth. "They say it's a matter of natural law, that the unborn fetus is completely dependent on his mother, a useless organ, which the pregnant mother may cut away." The rabbi stretched his right hand in front of him, raised the left hand, and dropped it on his right elbow like a guillotine, chopping off his own hand. "Slice it off!"

The men shivered with horror.

"The Zionists," he went on, "reject God for laws created by *Goyim* like Aristotle, Cicero, and hypocrites like Saint Thomas Aquinas. They ponder the works of so-called philosophers like Baruch Spinoza, who was rightly excommunicated by the rabbis of Amsterdam." Rabbi Gerster hit the lectern with an open hand. "The Zionists argue that dependency makes the fetus expendable. But a one-year-old child is also dependent upon his mother, right?"

His right hand gently caressed the head of an imaginary boy standing next to him.

"If the baby is still inside her, she may go to a doctor, who will insert a sharp steel rod between her thighs." He pierced the air in front of him with his hand. "And stab the baby, stab it and stab it and stab it until it becomes a perforated piece of dead, bloodied flesh!"

The crowd responded with a fearful groan.

"And what if the baby is born?" His right hand returned to caressing the imaginary boy's head. "A handsome boy, three or four years old, but still dependent on his mother for his survival. By the same logic, she may choose to care for her little boy, or bind him hand and foot and lay him on a table." The rabbi pretended to do so. "And shove her knitting needle through his brain!" He grabbed the imaginary boy and twisted, shouting, "Or break his little neck!"

A terrible howl tore through the air, and many of the men buried their faces in their hands, crying. Lemmy watched them cry to God through burning throats, beg for His mercy. Even Benjamin was crying, his fists pressed to his eyes.

A memory came to Lemmy's mind, his mother, lying on her bed. He drove the image from his mind, groaned to silence the persistent voice that told him he was the cause for his mother's childlessness. For a brief second he saw her again, trying desperately to pin herself onto his father, only to be shoved away with the same hand, with the same rage with which his father had just twisted the imaginary boy's neck. It was his fault, Lemmy knew. Somehow he had repulsed his father to the point of refusing to have more children, of preferring to live a lie, of depriving Temimah of what she so desperately longed for.

He looked at Benjamin, but his friend was too overwhelmed by the pantomimed killing of the little boy.

After a long time, the men of Neturay Karta fell back onto the wooden benches, exhausted. Only an occasional whimper sounded.

Rabbi Gerster wiped his face with a white handkerchief. "We'll now go to the streets of Jerusalem to proclaim the word of God: *You shall not kill!* We'll warn the Zionists not to pursue their abortion law, lest God's hand comes down to punish them. But we'll do it peacefully and pray for our misguided brothers, because a sinner who repents is more righteous than one who has never sinned."

He kissed the velvet curtain on the ark, his hands on the embroidered golden letters. He descended from the dais and walked through the synagogue, each row draining behind him into the center aisle. He led the column of men through the foyer to the forecourt and down to the gate. Cantor Toiterlich chanted verses from Psalms, which they repeated after him. As the long snake of black hats wriggled its tail against the rusted bars of the gate, Lemmy slipped away.

He entered the quiet apartment and shut the door, leaning against it, panting. On the opposite wall, above the door to his father's study, a square of exposed bricks contrasted with the white walls. Every house in Meah Shearim had a similar unfinished patch to symbolize the dwellers' constant mourning for the destruction of the Temple on Mount Moriah, which had stood in ruins for two thousand years. Roman hands had thrown the torches and catapulted the rocks that had demolished it, but Talmud said that the Temple was destroyed due to hatred among Jews. As he looked up at the naked bricks, Lemmy thought of his father, leading his disciples through the streets of Jerusalem to a certain confrontation with other Jews.

He entered his father's study. The desk was covered with books and papers. The chair had a tall back and padded armrests that ended with carved lion heads. Hundreds of books were lined on wooden shelves all the way to the ceiling.

Lemmy sat in the armchair and clenched the lion heads. He remembered sitting in his father's lap, embraced by the big hands, his own little hands tapping on the desk, the back of his neck tickled by his father's beard.

On the desk was the brown book his father always carried into town, a pencil resting in the crease. When Lemmy opened the book, the pencil fell out, together with a stack of Israeli liras. He turned the book to look at the cover. The title had faded with time. Lemmy traced the letters with his finger. *THE ZOHAR.*

His hands reflexively threw the book back on the desk. It was the book of Kabbalah!

He wanted to put the pencil and money back in the book, but could not bring himself to touch it again. He stumbled out of the study, ran to his room, and closed the door.

"Jerusalem? Is that you?"

He had assumed his mother was out. Had she seen him enter his father's study? He wished she would just go away.

Temimah entered his bedroom. "Why didn't you go to the demonstration?"

He avoided her eyes, afraid of remembering the way she had looked at the height of passion. "I'm not feeling well."

"What's wrong?" She reached the back of her head and tightened the knot on her plain headdress. Her fingers felt around it, ensuring it covered her head. The motion was mechanical, reassuring.

"I'm tired."

"You read too much." Her eyes lingered on the bookshelf, lined with volumes of Talmud.

Suddenly he realized it wasn't Talmud she was referring to. He jumped from the bed and stood between her and the bookshelf.

"I clean your room every day. You think I would miss those books?"

"Don't tell him!"

"Your father has enough to worry about. God knows what would happen here without him." Anxiety tightened her voice. "You must stop."

"No!"

"But these books are bad for you."

"That's a lie!"

Temimah seemed startled by his anger.

"I can't go back. I can't ignore what I know. I'm not a damn horse." He placed his hands by the sides of his face like horse blinders.

"Am I a damn horse?"

Her pain tied a knot in his throat. It was his father he was angry at, not her. "I didn't say that."

"You think I don't know what I'm missing? But I also know what I have—a husband, a son, a home, and a God, who has prescribed this life for me." She approached the bookshelf, inserted her hand behind the set of Talmud volumes, and pulled out *The Painted Bird*. The small book was wrapped in transparent plastic for protection. The cover illustration showed a bird with a human expression, its feathers red, yellow, and green, its beak crooked, its malicious eyes staring at the reader. A straw basket was strapped to its wings, and in it sat a boy with sad eyes.

"Please," Lemmy said, "put it back."

She opened the book. "Who is Tanya?"

He snatched *The Painted Bird* from her, shoved it behind the Talmud volumes, and headed to the door.

"Jerusalem!" His mother grabbed his forearm. "She gives you those books, doesn't she?"

He nodded.

"Who is she?"

"Ask your husband!" Lemmy shook off her hand and left the room.

She followed him to the hallway. "I've asked him."

Lemmy paused and turned.

"Your father used to have nightmares." Her face was ashen, the wrinkles of untimely aging growing deeper. "He cried her name in his sleep. *Tanya! Tanya!*"

"What did he say when you asked him?"

"Nothing." Temimah went to her room, pausing at the door. "He wouldn't answer."

"So you sent him to sleep in the study?"

His mother's voice cracked when she answered, "That was his decision."

"What a nice surprise!" Tanya embraced Lemmy. He had never visited her on a weekday, only on the Sabbath. And she had never embraced him, only touched him briefly, as if unintentionally. Now she was holding him to her, pressing her limbs against him. Without thinking, he kissed the top of her head. She must have just gotten out of the shower, her hair still wet, its scent fresh like flowers.

She took his hand and led him inside. A beige sweater hung loosely from her straight shoulders, her breasts erect under it. He forced his eyes away, dropped off his hat, and put on a black yarmulke.

Tanya walked to her desk and collected the documents that were scattered on it.

He came closer and looked over her shoulder. He saw documents in English, German, and French, hand-written notations in Hebrew. Everything was stamped in red: *Top Secret*

"Is this your work?"

"Watch it." She pinched his nose. "You only have one."

"I can keep a secret."

She steered him toward the old couch. "When you love Israel like I do, you do your best to defend it. I'm best in languages, so that's what I do." Her teeth sparkled, and he noticed that her face was flushed, as if she had spent time in the sun. "Talk about defending Israel, why aren't you studying Talmud today?"

"Nobody's studying today. My father is leading a demonstration against the abortion law."

Tanya turned on the radio—a wooden box with large, black plastic knobs for volume and tuning, and a round see-through frequency scale. Static sounds emanated from a square cloth over the speaker while the radio warmed up. Finally, the newscaster's voice came: "Thousands of ultra-Orthodox men gathered to protest the abortion legislation, which passed another legislative hurdle this morning in the Knesset. I'm looking at the intersection of Jaffa Street and King George Street, where all the stores have shut down, and the road is a river of black hats. Police officers have taken positions—"

The reporter paused as a roar came from the demonstrators.

"There he is! The leader of Neturay Karta, the famous Rabbi Abraham Gerster." The reporter was practically shouting now. "This rabbi vowed never to set foot outside Jerusalem as long as the Temple Mount is occupied by the Jordanians. He stands on a makeshift platform and recites from Psalms into a loudspeaker. We can only guess what King David would think if he heard his beautiful verses recited by a fanatic rabbi in a black coat as a battle cry against fellow Jews!"

Another roar came from the crowd.

"Something is happening near the platform! I can see men fighting—Orthodox and seculars beating each other! Policemen are rushing in, wielding clubs. My God! The platform is knocked over! Rabbi Gerster is down! It's a huge scuffle! I just saw some rocks flying overhead! More policemen are running over!"

Shouts of panic came from the radio. Lemmy leaned closer. Tanya put a hand on his knee, pressing it lightly.

The reporter's voice could hardly be heard over the background noise. "They are all rushing in that direction now. Teargas! At least ten canisters just flew over the crowd! Police snipers are shooting teargas from the roofs. It's real war!" He paused again and cried: "Rabbi Gerster is hurt!" After a moment of pure noise, he yelled, "They're picking him up! His face is bloody! They're running back to Meah Shearim!"

Tanya turned off the radio.

"I'd better get back home." Lemmy could barely breathe.

"Your father is fine, don't worry."

"He was bleeding!"

"How timely."

He looked at her, bewildered. "What do you mean?"

"His injury happened at the right time. It stopped the fighting just as it was getting out of hand, don't you think?"

"Thank God!"

She laughed, leaning toward him, her long hair against his cheek. Again, the smell of flowers sent a warm tide through his guts. He felt an urge to bury his face in the thick mass of her hair. He sat down on the edge of the sofa, weakened.

Tanya put her arm around him. His muscles tensed, and he felt hot. "Please don't." He could barely speak. "It's not allowed."

She touched his neck, her hand cool against his burning skin. "But I'm not a married woman."

"Still."

"Because I haven't dipped in the ritual mikvah?"

He was surprised how easily she read his mind. Every woman was sullied by her monthly menstrual discharge and therefore forbidden to touch a man until her impurity was cleansed by immersing in the mikvah, the community ritual bath of collected rainwater.

"But I'm pure," Tanya said. "I dipped in the sea last week. That's as good as a mikvah, right?"

Lemmy could tell by her tone that she was smiling. He wanted to say that, while the sea was indeed the best form of purifying a woman, the exacting rules prescribed by the rabbis required that she immerse while naked, to ensure that the cleansing water had unhindered access to her impure skin. But the thought of Tanya swimming in the nude paralyzed his tongue, and he bowed his head forward, submitting to her touch. His muscles softened under her firm fingers, which crept up from his nape, to the back of his head. His hair passed between her fingers. The world around him shrunk, nothing existed—no sound, no smell, no taste, no sight—nothing but the light touch of Tanya's hand.

His black yarmulke fell to the floor.

Her hand backtracked down to his lower nape, under his ears, brushed against his spiraling payos. He turned to face her.

Chapter 20

It was close to midnight when Lemmy left Tanya's house. He kept a fast pace along the border that crossed Jerusalem from north to south. A full moon illuminated the night. He was bursting with happiness and energy. Breaking into a run, the hard soles of his black shoes pounded the road.

Down Shivtay Israel Street, near the gate, he slowed down to catch his breath. His parents were likely awake, waiting for him. He had to calm down. There was much he had to tell them. He would make them understand his feelings and thoughts. How could he marry Sorkeh Toiterlich when his heart belonged to Tanya?

It was dark, except for a dim street lamp. The night breeze was cool on his face. He thought of what had happened with her, the all-consuming joy they had shared, joy like he'd never felt before. These feelings could not be sinful!

He entered the gate and hurried up the alley. A hand emerged out of the darkness and yanked him into a doorway. He was thrown against a wall. A whiff of body odor made him gag.

A hushed, urgent voice said, "It's the rabbi's son!"

Lemmy pulled his arm free.

A match was struck, and the bearded face of Redhead Dan appeared. "What are you doing here?"

"Taking a stroll. And you?"

"Don't mess with me, Gerster!"

A car engine sounded in the night. Two headlights appeared in the street, advancing toward the gate.

"Stay here!"

Lemmy watched Redhead Dan approach the car, accompanied by Yoram in his hesitant, stooped gait.

The car stopped. The two men bent over the driver's window. There was a lengthy discussion. Lemmy saw a box emerge from the window. There was more hushed talking, and the engine growled as the car began moving in reverse, retreating up Shivtay Israel Street.

Yoram carried the box through the gate. They stood under a lamp, and Redhead Dan opened the box. Inside were four fist-size metal balls, more elliptical than round, with black skin that resembled turtle shell. A ring was threaded through a lever at the top of each one.

Redhead Dan grabbed Lemmy's coat and shook him violently. "If you say anything to anybody about this, I'm going to turn you into chopped liver and feed you to the cats. Understood?"

Elie Weiss maneuvered the car in reverse all the way up the street and around the corner. He shifted into first gear and drove away. He had not expected to see Abraham's son with the two men. Had he stayed with Tanya so late? Things must be heating up between them faster than expected. Soon the boy would be ready for the picking, ready to assume his own clandestine destiny.

As Elie drove through the sleeping neighborhoods of West Jerusalem, he pulled off the fake beard and side locks. He had told Redhead Dan that the car was borrowed from a relative. A more thoughtful man would be suspicious, but the young hothead was eager to take revenge on his Zionist tormentors.

Abraham would be outraged if he ever found out. He had truly embraced his role-playing as the scion of rabbinical ancestry, fulfilling his preordainment as a Talmudic saint, a demigod for these fundamentalist Jews. Not bad for a man who had lost his faith in God. But the coming crisis would test Abraham's abilities. The attack on the prime minister would be visible, unquestionable, and dread-inciting beyond its actual nature. The secular Israeli majority would rally behind Eshkol while the state's security agencies clamped down on the ultra-Orthodox. Elie's reward would be the Mossad appointment he had coveted, finally providing him with trained personnel, overseas branches, vehicles and weaponry, which together with Klaus von Koenig's fortune, would enable Elie to pursue his grand vision of countering anti-Semitism worldwide.

There was light in the windows of the apartment. Lemmy ran up the steps. He had to warn his father immediately. The box contained some kind of explosives, he could tell, and Redhead Dan was up to no good.

He entered the foyer and closed the door. His parents were in the dining room.

"Master of the Universe!" His mother ran to him. "We were so worried about you!" Her eyes were red, and she hugged him.

"I'm fine." Lemmy detached from her and entered the dining room.

Rabbi Gerster had an open book of Talmud before him. A white bandage was tied around his head, an oval stain showing through in the middle of his forehead.

"Where did you go?" Temimah asked. "You could have been killed!"

"Father, I need to talk to you." Lemmy approached the table. "I saw—"

Rabbi Gerster got up and slapped him across the face. The blow knocked Lemmy off his feet. He heard his mother scream.

Getting up, he leaned on the table for support until the room stopped spinning. He slowly digested the fact that, for the first time ever, his father had struck him.

He heard the study door slam and went to the foyer. The left side of his face was burning. He banged on the door. "If you hit me again, I'll tell people what a cruel father you are. And a cruel husband."

His mother gasped.

The door opened, and Rabbi Gerster stepped out. He didn't say anything. The oval stain on his bandage had turned red and moist.

Lemmy did not retreat. "I'll tell your *flock* why my mother has no more children!"

Without a word, his father's hand rose again, flying at his face. But Lemmy was ready, blocking it with his forearm. "One son is too much for you?" He wiped his tears.

"Obviously," his father said.

"There's a solution. *He who repudiates his father or his mother shall be put to death.* Exodus, twenty-one, seventeen—"

"Wash your hands and your mouth before you quote from the Torah. Behave as a God-fearing Jew, or else—"

"Or else what? You'll call for a stoning?"

"Or else," Rabbi Gerster said, "I'll banish you from this community!"

Chapter 21

On Friday morning, Rabbi Abraham Gerster did not go to the synagogue. In the afternoon, he failed to lead his men to the boulder overlooking the Old City to pray for Jerusalem's reunification. On Sabbath morning, when the rabbi again didn't arrive, the men crowded around Lemmy, but he had no answers for them. After the service, the whole community congregated in the alley under the rabbi's apartment, and Cantor Toiterlich led them in recital of the prayer for the sick and infirm, followed by *God is my Shepherd.* Temimah sent Lemmy downstairs to thank the men and send them away, explaining that Rabbi Gerster needed rest to recover from his injury.

On Sunday, and on each of the following mornings, the rabbi did not come to the synagogue. On Thursday morning, Lemmy found a bundle of white envelopes on a chair by the door, each with a name written on it by his father. He took the envelopes to the synagogue and placed them in a pile on the lectern before his father's empty chair. After morning service, the men collected their weekly allowances from the pile.

Thursday passed without Rabbi Gerster's lecture. Lemmy and Benjamin labored together on the question of ownership of a cow that broke loose from its owner's field to graze on public land, where it was found by another man. When time came for evening service, Benjamin closed his Talmud volume and kissed it. "I wish your father would return already."

"I don't."

Benjamin knuckled Lemmy's head.

"Hey!" Lemmy grabbed his hand and twisted it.

"Ouch!" Benjamin tried to pull free, and they struggled for a moment, laughing until someone shushed them.

Lemmy had not told Benjamin what had happened between him and his father, or about Redhead Dan and his mysterious box, or about Tanya. He felt guilty keeping secrets from Benjamin. But would their friendship survive such revelations?

The cantor struck the large table on the center dais, and all the men stood to chant the prayers.

A few moments into the prayers, Lemmy felt Benjamin's hand on his shoulder. He glanced at his friend, who smiled while praying.

After the evening service, they walked together, resuming their argument about the cow's ownership. Benjamin's interpretation remained attached to the text, while Lemmy theorized that the cow, which wandered off its owner's field, got lost, and was found by another on a public land, was really a metaphor for the Jewish people. "The original owner of the cow was God. The field was the Promised Land. The cow was the Chosen People—the Jews, exiled from the Promised Land, lost in the countries of the Goyim, the Diaspora. Therefore, as a lost cow, the Jews were sold for slaughter by the Nazis. And God, like the original owner of the lost cow, took the survivors back to his field—the Promised Land."

"But a cow is not people," Benjamin argued, "the Promised Land is not a field, and the Diaspora is not green pasture. The sages talked about business policy. Good-faith buyers must obtain incontestable ownership no matter if the vendors actually owned the merchandise, including a cow. Otherwise, the markets would be paralyzed with distrust. And anyway, the sages wrote this hundreds of years before the Holocaust and Israel's establishment, right?"

When Lemmy argued that the Talmudic sages were unconsciously predicting the future, Benjamin laughed so hard that his laughter became contagious.

They were standing by the building where Benjamin lived with his mother in a one-room apartment. A group of men came from the direction of the synagogue, and Redhead Dan's voice traveled down the alley, "We're not alone! Others support us, and not only with words! We'll do to the Zionists what they plan to do to babies. *An eye for an eye!*"

On Friday, Rabbi Gerster remained in seclusion. An hour into the afternoon study session, Redhead Dan mounted the dais and announced that he would be leading a group to the great boulder to pray in view of the Old City. He invited everyone to join. Within minutes, the synagogue was empty. Benjamin tried to convince Lemmy to go, but gave up and left without him.

Lemmy sat alone in the large hall, his book of Talmud open before him. Unable to concentrate, he closed it and left.

On the way to Tanya's house he saw the group of secular teenagers playing in the parking lot. One of the boys noticed him and waved. Lemmy waved back. A girl in shorts and a ponytail beckoned him to join. He shook his head and kept walking.

A young woman in khaki uniform opened Tanya's door. She looked at the black coat and hat and said, "We don't give donations to yeshivas."

He felt his face flush. "I'm here to see Tanya."

Her blue eyes examined him as if she suspected he was lying. Unlike Tanya's delicate constitution, she was attractive in a strong, robust way. Her light hair was cropped at shoulder length, and her nose was small and straight.

"You must be Bira."

"Guilty as charged." She offered him a hand. "And you are?"

"Lemmy." He hesitated, and shook her hand.

Bira yelled, "Mom!"

Tanya hugged him and took his coat and hat. Bira disappeared into another room

They sat down, and Lemmy told her what had happened since he had left her house the previous week—the mysterious box, his father's slap, and the anxiety in the sect.

"But I don't understand. Why did he hit you? It makes no sense."

"My father demands complete obedience."

"He must be under enormous pressure," Tanya said. "To lead a fundamentalist sect in these tumultuous times. A great deal rests on his shoulders. I'm sure he regrets hitting you."

"I doubt it."

"So you never actually told him about the objects in the box?"

"No."

"Then I must pass the word to the appropriate people." Tanya kissed him. "You should go home now."

Bira appeared, carrying a duffel bag and an Uzi machine gun. "Time to head back to Tel Aviv," she said.

Tanya hugged her daughter. "You two can walk together."

Lemmy took her duffel bag. It was heavier than he had expected.

For a while they pretended to be occupied by the scenery. He pressed his hat down as the wind grew stronger. On the left, across the border, a Jordanian soldier shouted a slur in Arabic.

Bira said, "Soon we'll kick them out and reunite Jerusalem." She had an air of physical strength and confidence that befitted carrying an Uzi and kicking Jordanians.

"God will give it back to us," Lemmy said, "like He gave it to King David. Then we'll build a new temple."

"How about a new university? Or factories? That's what we need."

"Not in Jerusalem," Lemmy said. "Factories need water, materials, natural resources, but there's nothing here except proximity to God. That's the only reason every ruler in the history of the Middle East wanted to possess Jerusalem—Nebuchadnezzar the Babylonian, Cyrus of Persia, Alexander of Macedon, Antiochus the Syrian, and the Roman emperors Silvocuses, Pompey, Hadrian, and evil Titus."

"Because it was the capital city of the Jewish kingdom."

"And why was that? Because kings saw Jerusalem as proof that God was on their side. But God chose us, not them." He pointed at the golden Dome of the Rock, shining in the sun's midday rays.

"But they think God chose them." Bira grabbed the duffel gab, stopping Lemmy. She searched inside, found a crumpled magazine, and showed him a page with black-and-white photos of pieces of clay and primitive utensils. "This was found in Beit Zait, a two-hour mule ride from here." She pointed to one of the slivers of clay. "Star of David. And the piece was dated to King David's era as described in the Book of Samuel. That proves our ownership."

Lemmy examined the photo closely. "How can they date a piece of clay?"

"A chemical process. It's pretty accurate, and it proves Jews were here long before the Arabs, who are temporary squatters on our land, just like the Greeks, Romans, Crusaders, Caliphates, Ottomans, and the British." She folded the archeological magazine and stuffed it back in the duffel bag. "The Arabs can eat their headdresses until they choke. This piece of real estate is ours!"

A muezzin wailed from a tiny terrace atop a pointed minaret across the border. Bira pointed. "We lasted two thousand years in exile, including massacres, expulsions, forced conversions, and genocide. But now we're back!"

"You're nothing like Tanya."

Bira's intense expression broke into a grin. "I adore my mom, but the whole generation of Holocaust survivors is a little weird." Bira drew circles on her temple.

Lemmy had meant the two were different physically, but he didn't correct Bira, afraid she would notice the all-consuming lust that he felt for her mother.

They reached the corner of Shivtay Israel Street. Lemmy put down the duffel bag. He glanced at the gate to Meah Shearim. "You should keep going. Our people aren't very tolerant of women in Zionist uniforms."

Bira picked up the bag. "I read about your leader in the newspaper. He said that abortion is like murder." She twisted her face. "There was a picture of him. He looks like some crazy prophet."

"He's my father."

"*Oops.*"

He laughed.

"My big mouth. I always do that." Bira pecked him on the cheek. "See you soon."

He touched his face where she had kissed him and watched her walk away, her Uzi dangling from her shoulder. As she reached the next street corner, Bira looked back and waved. Lemmy waved back, and then she was gone.

Chapter 22

Tanya left a message for Elie Weiss with the SOD desk at the prime minister's office to meet her at a small café on Ben Yehuda Street. He pulled two of his agents from a surveillance assignment nearby and placed them at a table near the door, where they played backgammon. He sat at a corner table with his back to the wall.

When Tanya entered, he took off his wool cap and stood. It was Friday afternoon, and only a dozen other customers were in the café. He watched her cross the room and his breath quickened. What she radiated went beyond beauty. Perhaps it was the contrast between her black hair and the white skin, or between her physical smallness and the fierce posture. Or maybe the feline fluidity of her body's movements.

She sat down and removed the oversized sunglasses, revealing her turquoise-green eyes.

Elie swallowed with difficulty. "You make an unlikely spy," he said. "No one in this room will ever forget you."

"You'll be surprised."

"I'm serious. How do you survive in this line of work?"

"Ill-fitting clothes, out-of-fashion hats, and never meeting their eyes." Tanya shrugged. "I don't bother with it in Israel, but in Europe no one gives me a second look."

"I find it hard to believe." Elie flagged down the waitress. "Bring us tea with lemon."

"I have terrible news." She kept her voice low. "Abraham's son saw a box delivered to the most extreme guy in the sect, someone called Redhead Dan. The description fits hand grenades. Abraham hit the boy before he could tell him what he'd seen. *Hit him!* I don't understand it—why would Abraham hit his son?"

Elie was more concerned with why Redhead Dan had shown him the grenades. "Hand grenades in Neturay Karta?"

"Yes!"

"Impossible. The kid is confused."

"His description fits perfectly. And there's talk of violence. *An eye for an eye.* You must contact Abraham immediately. Only he can prevent disaster."

"Well, better safe than sorry." Elie rubbed his scalp with his hand. "I'll inform Abraham right away. Did his son tell you anything else?"

"No."

Elie was relieved, but he had to make sure. "Did he hear of any plans to actually use the grenades?"

"No."

"Does he know where they're hidden? Anything?"

"It was a coincidence. He ran into them—"

"Lucky for us, but what was he doing out there in the middle of the night?"

Tanya blushed and looked away.

"I see." Elie lit a cigarette. "He's a bit young for you, isn't he?"

"He's almost eighteen." She parted her hair with both hands, throwing it over her shoulders. "You have a problem with that?"

"On the contrary. How else would you suck information from him?"

"You disgust me." She glared at him, the blushing skin of her face as smooth as that of the seventeen-year-old girl he remembered.

"You are fortunate, Tanya. Few women get to go back in time, so to speak, do it over, save a lover from the wrong path."

She leaned on the table, her face close to his. "Abraham was on the wrong path because you manipulated him to keep hunting down Germans, and I was too naïve—"

"I manipulated Abraham?" Elie sneered. "He was obsessed with revenge after he saw the Nazis butcher our families. He wanted to keep killing Nazis, terminate them in the most painful way, every one of them, including Nazis like your sweetheart, Obergruppenführer Klaus von Koenig."

"Klaus was an accountant. He didn't butcher anyone."

"Himmler's deputy, the protégée who facilitated SS operations with his financial genius, was just an accountant?"

"He didn't kill Jews."

"Your dear Klaus was no less a mass murderer than the rest of the Nazi high command!"

"I thought we were talking about Abraham."

"Right. That's what drove him—avenge the Holocaust and prevent the next one. It still drives him today. Drives *us!*"

Tanya smiled bitterly. "How could I compete with that?"

Elie didn't answer. What could he say? The truth? That Abraham had changed his mind and wanted to quit his secret work to be with her? No. Telling her the truth would ruin everything.

"I don't have to atone for failing to save Abraham or for losing him," she said. "Abraham lost me then, and he lost me again a few months ago. He'd rather stay with those misguided Talmudic souls than live with me in happiness. But Lemmy is a different story. *Him* I can save!"

Elie clapped. "Bravo!"

For a moment he thought Tanya would hit him, but she turned and left. His agents put down the dice and started to rise, but Elie shook his head, and they sat back and watched her leave.

He took his seat and slurped cautiously from his tea. The waitress brought the check, and he dropped a few bills on the table. He had no intention of informing Abraham. The risk was small that Lemmy would approach his father again about the grenades before tomorrow morning. The boy was still smarting from a good fatherly beating.

Tanya left the café on the verge of tears, determined not to give Elie the satisfaction. She walked down the street, shielding her face from the wind. He was doing it again, the same as twenty years ago, during those few months in the forest with Abraham, when Elie's dark eyes had cast a constant shadow over their passion, his thin lips lopsided in a humorless grin. Now he was doing the same thing, mocking her relationship with Lemmy. But why was she so upset? Was there a grain of truth in it? Was she a pathetic middle-aged woman trying to relive the lost passion of her distant youth?

She reached a bus stop and huddled in the small canopy with a few other people. Lemmy would be preparing for the Sabbath now, changing into his best clothes. Earlier, when she had seen him stand next to Bira at the door, Tanya could hardly breathe. She had loved their fathers, one a Nazi general, the other a scion of a rabbinical line, two men who could not be more different. Yet Bira and Lemmy looked like siblings, with blue eyes, blond hair, and strong build. Even their different outfits—Lemmy's ultra-Orthodox black garb and Bira's IDF uniform—barely camouflaged their resemblance.

The bus approached, and the passengers lined up to board it. She glanced up the street at the café. Elie had not yet left, and his two goons were still bent over their game board. Why wasn't he rushing off to warn Abraham? Why was he unconcerned with the warning she had delivered with such urgency?

"Young lady?" The bus driver tapped the steering wheel. "I don't have all day!"

The realization hit her suddenly. She hurried back to the café. "How did you know?"

Elie put down the tea cup. "Back already?"

"How did you know it was the middle of the night?"

He lit a cigarette. "When else would anyone deliver contraband?"

"It was you!" She pointed a finger in his face. "You delivered the grenades!"

"Nonsense."

"You're an evil man!" Her voice rose.

He signaled his agents, who shooed out the few patrons.

She leaned on the table. "Abraham has kept them quiet for eighteen years, sacrificed everything to prevent violence, and now you'll destroy all his achievements!"

Elie clucked his tongue while stubbing the cigarette in the ashtray. "Even your darling Abraham can't control them forever. We always knew that one day it would turn bloody. Read the Bible, it's all there. Better it happens on my terms. My timing. My plan."

"Have you consulted Abraham about *your* plan?"

Elie brushed the question aside. "He's a soldier. Need-to-know basis. He managed to control them over Sabbath violations, their demonstrations at archeological sites, their window smashing at restaurants serving bread on Passover. Maybe he'll control them over the abortion issue. But it's getting harder. What I'm doing will eliminate his internal opposition in the sect. They'll tremble in fear."

"So why don't you tell him about it? These are his people. He knows them better than you!"

"I spent a night in a cell with that Redhead Dan character. We bonded, prayed together like kindred spirits, a pair of seditious fanatics determined to teach the Zionists a painful lesson." Elie chuckled hoarsely. "Physical pain and sleep deprivation are great fodder for brainstorming. He bought right into my act. We worked up a concept for a sensational attack."

Tanya felt weak. Was he just bragging? "When?"

"Tomorrow morning. I promised to create a diversion, so the two of them can escape back to Meah Shearim. But, as Eshkol likes to say, I didn't promise to keep my promise."

"Where?"

"The prime minister's residence, during a press conference about defending West Jerusalem in the event of a surprise Jordanian attack. Eshkol and Rabin will brief the journalists on the roof, and then—*boom!* They'll see it from above in live action, like a movie. As soon as the black-hat terrorists attack, they'll be cut down."

Tanya grabbed the table, making the empty tea cups rattle in their saucers. "What do you mean *cut down?*"

"They attack, the guards respond. Fair game. And the media will have photos of two ultra-Orthodox men, black coats and all."

"It's murder!"

"Don't be naïve. By tomorrow night, the public will rally behind Eshkol. I hired a professor at Tel Aviv University to do a whole analysis. He went back to Roman times, examined all cases since then, all the way through Queen Victoria—four attempts on her life, by the way. The American president, Andrew Jackson, who beat up his assassin with a cane. And Adolf Hitler, an excellent example too, attributing his survival to divine intervention. President De Gaulle, as well. Politicians who survive assassination attempts automatically gain hugely in popularity. Political scientists call it *Popularity by Misfire*. It's the twisted psychology of public sentiment."

"You're sick!"

"Desperate situations require desperate measures," Elie said. "The ultra-Orthodox fanatics will make Eshkol a hero to the secular majority."

Tanya dropped into the chair. "You must call it off! These Neturay Karta men are like children, living in the fairytale world of Talmud. And why give them live grenades? You could have given them smoke grenades!"

"It has to look real. Can you imagine the mocking headlines: *Assassins Believe Smoke Enough to Knock Down Eshkol*. It would defeat the whole purpose. We need a heroic survival, photos of an unscathed prime minister standing in the rubble, sipping coffee amidst the debris, laughing in the face of danger. Don't you see the brilliance of this plan?"

"Throwing grenades in a residential neighborhood, based on political science? Do you hear yourself?"

"You'll see. Eshkol will address the nation with confidence, reassuring the people of his control of the situation. With the war imminent, the army needs a popular prime minister. The silent majority will unite behind him, and the Orthodox will keep their black hats down to the floor for years."

"It will never work!" She could barely control her fury. "You'll produce a handful of martyrs, and the next day hundreds of other Orthodox youngsters will start collecting weapons in all the yeshivas. You'll start the very armed rebellion you're trying to prevent!"

"I disagree," Elie said. "The Orthodox will react with fear and self-flogging. And the few bad ones, we'll pick like blackberries and squash them."

The waitress showed up with a freshly brewed tea pot.

Elie filled his cup. "Remember what happened to weak Jews? Israel will be destroyed unless we eliminate our enemies." He slurped his tea, and the rising steam blurred his face for a moment.

"I won't let you go through with this madness!"

"It's way over your head." He warmed his hands over the tea pot. "Don't interfere."

"And if I do? You'll have me *cut down* as well?"

"Just a short vacation." Elie put on his wool cap and beckoned the two agents. "In seclusion."

When she saw the agents approach, Tanya grabbed the steaming tea pot and emptied it in Elie's face.

Lemmy was reading *The Painted Bird* when his mother knocked on the door and entered his room. "Benjamin is in the foyer to see you. Would you like some milk and cookies?"

"Thanks." He stuffed the book under his pillow and went to greet Benjamin. As he reached the foyer, the door to his father's study opened and Yoram, Redhead Dan's study companion, came out, quickly leaving the apartment.

Rabbi Gerster emerged from his study. He wore a white shirt and black pants held by suspenders. He looked tired. The bandage was gone from his forehead, the small wound covered by a scab.

"Good day, Rabbi," Benjamin said. "I hope you're feeling better."

"Seeing you here makes me feel better." Rabbi Gerster held a book in his hand, bound in rugged brown leather. *The Zohar.* "You know, boys, what's the difference between a sin against God and a sin against a fellow Jew?"

"Yes," Benjamin said. "God won't forgive the latter unless you sought forgiveness from the one you offended."

"Jerusalem?" His father waited until their eyes met. "Yoram told me about the box. I now understand what you wanted to tell me that night."

Lemmy shrugged.

"But I was too upset to listen. It was after midnight, and no one knew where you had gone. Your mother almost went out of her mind with worry. You understand?"

Another shrug.

"It was my duty to discipline you. Talmud says: *A father who deprives his son of the whip is like a father who hates his son.* Right?"

Lemmy glanced at Benjamin, whose mouth was slightly open, looking from father to son.

"You understand why I had to hit you, yes?"

"Are you asking for my forgiveness?"

The rabbi smiled sadly. "Yes, I am."

"Perhaps you should first ask Mother for her forgiveness? I mean, what's a slap on the face compared to what you're doing to her?"

Rabbi Gerster's shoulders sagged, and the strong hand that had slapped Lemmy a week ago came up and tugged at the graying beard. He turned and stepped back into his study.

Lemmy grabbed Benjamin's arm and led him to his room. A plate of warm cookies and two glasses of milk were waiting on his desk.

"Master of the Universe!" Benjamin took off his black hat. "What's going on?"

"It's complicated." Lemmy shut the door. "Here, have some milk."

"I can't." Benjamin looked at his watch. "I ate a late lunch, turkey sandwich, so I'm not allowed dairy for another two hours. Are the cookies dairy?"

"I'm sure they are. My mom uses milk chocolate chips." He felt angry at the sight of milk and cookies kept from Benjamin's enjoyment because of the six-hour wait required between eating meat and dairy. "This is all so idiotic!"

"What's so idiotic?"

"All God said in the Torah was: *Do not cook a calf in its mother's milk.* From this symbolic ethical rule we Jews have created a behemoth!"

"The dietary rules make sense," Benjamin said.

"To avoid the risk of cooking a calf in its mother's milk, the early sages banned cooking any calves in any cow's milk. The next generation of rabbis decided not to cook any cattle—young or old—in any milk, including goat, sheep, and camel's milk. The next generation decided to ban eating any meat simultaneously with any dairy product—just in case! Then Jews bought separate sets of pots and pans and plates and silverware for meat and dairy to make sure there's no risk of cooking a calf in its mother's milk!"

Benjamin laughed. "You know the answer. These are fences to guard us from an accidental sin."

"Accidental incestuous cooking? Is that the reason we treat chicken like beef, lest one day a clever *Yid* farmer would breed a chicken that gives milk, and his dumb wife might cook a little, soft-feathered *chick'aleh* in the milk of its mother hen!"

"Could happen!"

"And finally, the rabbis decided that we should wait six hours after eating meat or fowl because, if we ingested dairy, it might lead to cooking!" Lemmy leaned forward and pulled on Benjamin's side lock, extending the rolled hair until it straightened as long as his arm. "It's written: *Do not shave the side of your beard like the Gentiles.*" He let Benjamin's side lock spring back into place, dangling down to his shoulder. "God didn't want Israelites imitating the pagan hairstyle of biblical times. But over generations, *Don't shave* became *Don't trim, Don't cut, Don't touch your payos from birth to death,* as if this hair," he tugged again on Benjamin's side lock, "these dead cells are somehow sacred. It's ridiculous!"

"Is God ridiculous? Where do you get these ideas?"

Lemmy pulled out *The Painted Bird* and handed it to him.

Benjamin examined the front cover, the colorful drawings of a painted bird.

"This story is written so well that you feel like you're watching a movie."

It was an odd statement. Neither of them had ever seen a movie. Movies were for the sinful, empty-minded Zionists. Benjamin read a few lines, threw the book on the bed, and rubbed his hands against his pants. "It's a sin to read books like that!"

"It's about the life of a kid like us in a different time." He picked the book up from the bed. "It makes you think about the horrible things people do to each other, and—"

"Shush!" Benjamin's hand covered Lemmy's mouth. "A good Jew must devote all his time to studying Talmud!"

"Aren't we supposed to be a guiding light for the goyim?"

"So?"

"How could we be a guiding light for those about whom we know nothing?" It felt odd to repeat Tanya's argument to his friend.

"You don't need to commit sins to understand the sinners." Benjamin went to the door. "Sabbath starts soon. We should go to the synagogue."

"Wait!" Lemmy's impulsive sharing of his secret had placed them on a risky path, and he was determined to make his friend understand. "At least read a page, see how wonderful it is!"

"No! Don't you realize that Satan is trying to seduce you?"

He opened the book and started turning the pages of fine print. He was running out of time. "This boy's parents left him with an old woman at the beginning of the war. They were Jews, or Gypsies. A few months later the old woman dies, and the boy hits the road. He encounters all kinds of strange people who abuse him. And after every cruel experience he finds hope in a new method of worship. First he is superstitious, completely obsessed by witchcraft and evil spirits. Next he becomes a devout Catholic, counting each prayer against each indulgence. Finally he decides that, because all his devotion didn't save him from suffering, God doesn't exist. So he becomes a communist, constantly reciting party slogans about equality and freedom. At one point, a peasant paints a bird in different colors, and when it's released to rejoin its flock, they don't recognize it and attack. The boy sees a rain of feathers—red, blue, yellow, green, and orange—fall to the ground."

"And the same will happen to you!" Removing a volume of Talmud from a shelf, Benjamin opened it. "Generations of sages created this eternal wisdom for you. Why go to foreign pasture when your own field is already so lush?"

A loud knock sounded, and Rabbi Gerster entered the room. "Shall we go to the synagogue?"

Benjamin's face lit up. "Bless be He who cures the ill!"

"Amen," the rabbi said.

Despite his anger at his father, Lemmy was relieved. Eight days had passed since the abortion protest on King George Street. His father's self-imposed confinement had deepened the division in the sect. Redhead Dan had boasted that Rabbi Gerster would soon order a violent struggle against the Zionist government, whereas Cantor Toiterlich timidly gave voice to Neturay Karta's long-held principles of seclusion, prayer, and the study of Talmud. The debate in the sect had been brewing all week while the men had waited for their rabbi's return.

Rabbi Gerster noticed *The Painted Bird* and picked it up.

Benjamin shifted in place as if his feet stood on red embers.

"Cheap entertainment for the feebleminded." The rabbi tossed it on the bed. "Has my son become feebleminded?"

"It's neither cheap nor entertaining," Lemmy said. "It's a story about a boy who spends the long years of the war hiding from the Nazis, freezing in the winters, hungry, terrified. Weren't you once such a boy?"

Rabbi Gerster's lips pressed into a thin line. "You have a clever mind," he said. "Why don't you apply it wholly to God's books?"

Before Lemmy could answer, Benjamin took a step toward the door. "Shall we go?"

On the way to the synagogue, the rabbi rested his arm on Benjamin's shoulder. "I hope you concentrate on the teachings of God, not on stories of the Goyim."

"We study together." Benjamin walked stiffly under the weight of the rabbi's arm. "The two of us, every day, all day."

"Apparently, my son finds time for idleness." He spoke as if Lemmy was not behind them. "But not you. God blessed you with a pure soul. Our people need leadership and guidance. Continue to study hard, and one day you'll be a great rabbi."

The synagogue appeared before them with its tall windows and massive wood doors. The forecourt was filled with men, and they rushed to greet the rabbi.

Redhead Dan pushed through the crowd. "Rabbi! Have you heard the news? On Sunday morning the Knesset will approve the final abortion law! God wants us to fight! The death of babies takes precedence over the observance of the Sabbath!"

Everyone started talking at the same time, but Rabbi Gerster only smiled, lifted his arms into the air, and began singing: "*Heighten your heads, gates, exalt yourselves!*"

Confused, the men of Neturay Karta stopped arguing.

"*Doorways of the universe,*" he sang, "*the King of Honor, God is coming!*"

The men joined, and the rabbi started from the beginning. Quickly the singing intensified, and circles formed around him. Their faces grew more cheerful as they danced around him faster and faster, proceeding into the synagogue. Inside, the men's singing filled the hall, their hands on each other's shoulders, dancing with their beloved rabbi around the elevated bimah, under the glistening lights of the crystal chandelier. "*The King of Honor, God is coming!*"

Lemmy danced, his arms locked with the men, whose faces glowed with sweat and spiritual joy. The dancing grew faster, the singing louder. Someone broke between Lemmy and the man to his right. It was Redhead Dan, his round, freckled face full of excitement. He sang at the top of his voice, and slapped hard on Lemmy's shoulder. "*Heighten your heads, gates! Exalt yourselves!*"

As he danced, Lemmy thought of the mysterious box and Redhead Dan's talk of fighting. What was he up to? Yoram must have told the rabbi, but did anyone realize how crazy Redhead Dan really was? And who would Tanya tell about this, and what would they do?

Rabbi Abraham Gerster danced with his men, his hands bound with theirs, his eyes closed, his face lifted to the glowing chandelier. It went on and on, until the rabbi suddenly pulled free and leaped on top of the nearest wooden bench.

The men stopped dancing and stood still, watching him.

When the synagogue was completely silent, the rabbi filled his lungs and, very slowly, began singing again: "*Raise!*"

He paused, his hands reaching up. "*Your heads!*"

His face creased in great devotion. "*Gates, exalt yourselves!*"

Everyone looked up at him, holding their breath.

Like a conductor leading his orchestra, he suddenly waved his hands, and his forceful baritone bounced from the walls, "*Doorways of the universe!*"

They joined him with a wonderful, earthshaking roar, "*The King of Honor, God is coming!*"

The men of Neturay Karta danced in circles, their pace faster, their unbuttoned coats flying around them, their faces red with ecstasy, brilliant with sweat, their legs going up and down with boundless energy, their black shoes drumming the floor in honor of their beloved rabbi, who had returned to lead them.

But Lemmy broke off from the circle and went outside to the forecourt. The breeze was cool on his moist face. The sun had descended below the horizon. Sabbath had arrived.

"Turning your head saved your eyes." The doctor on call at the Sharay Tzedek Hospital smeared ointment on Elie's left cheek, neck, and upper chest, where the tea had scalded him. "Eyes are like eggs. Hot water would boil them." He was young and not too happy about having to work on Friday night.

Elie wasn't listening. His mind was filled with vengeful images of Tanya suffering all kinds of torture. But those images would have to remain in his mind. Hurting Tanya in any way was outside the realm of possibility. It had been his fault anyway. His infatuation with her had loosened his tongue, and he had bragged like a schoolboy on a pubescent date, receiving his just reward in the form of second-degree burns. Now she was under guard at a safe house on the outskirts of Jerusalem, where she would remain until after tomorrow morning's operation.

The doctor put down the ointment jar and pulled off the gloves. "We'll keep you overnight with a fluid drip. I can prescribe something to make you comfortable."

"No." Elie gave him a look that discouraged any argument. "Pain isn't a problem. I'll take this." He pointed at the jar of ointment.

Ten minutes later, he walked out of the hospital, all the records of his treatment already in the trash. He wore a cotton undershirt, separating the rough khaki shirt from the ointment and his angry-red skin. One of the agents was waiting for him in the car.

"Drive me to the police compound at the Russian Yard," Elie said. "They're waiting for me."

The Special Force combined experienced police officers and veterans of elite IDF units, men who engaged in extreme violence without raising their pulse. The group filled a conference room on the second floor of the building. Pinned to the wall was a street map of the Rehavia neighborhood, marked with green, blue, and black pushpins that represented the troops, the commanders, and the attackers respectively. The prime minister's residence was circled in red.

Elie listened as Major Buskilah assigned men to positions, discussed the chain of command, the range from each position to the targets, the lines of fire assigned to each team, and the need to avoid civilian casualties.

When Major Buskilah was done, Elie addressed them. "This operation is based on a tip we received from an informant that two members of Neturay Karta plan to attack the prime minister in the morning. We don't know their identity or appearance," he lied, "and unfortunately, senior members of the media have already been invited to a press conference tomorrow on the roof of the prime minister's residence." He cleared his throat, and the movement shot burning pain across his scalded skin. "We suspect that the conspirators have obtained some kind of explosives. We're still investigating how and what they have, but time is running out."

He looked around the room, waiting for his lies to sink in. The faces he browsed showed no doubts. They were eager and attentive, open faces of men accustomed to trusting their commanding officers and adhering to a plan of action.

One of them raised his hand. "Why don't we raid Meah Shearim tonight and search door to door?"

Elie was ready with an answer. "The political situation, especially with the abortion vote coming up, would make such a search appear to be politically motivated to harass the religious community."

Another man said, "We can shoot them on approach, before they attack."

"Israeli forces don't shoot at unarmed Jews," Elie said, "especially while a bunch of journalists are watching from the roof. A mishap like that could turn the whole Jewish world against this government. As you know, our desperate armament needs depend on the generosity of the Diaspora, especially American Jews."

Some of the men nodded.

"You may only—and I emphasize the word *only*—shoot after you have clearly witnessed one or both of them using deadly weapons. Now, that's me." He pointed to a black pushpin at the intersection of King George and Ramban streets. "I'll be scouting their probable approach path, dressed as an ultra-Orthodox Jew for the occasion, so make sure not to shoot me."

Several of the soldiers laughed.

"Remember that on Sabbath morning many religious Jews go to their synagogues. Watch carefully, but do not engage anyone until you witness an actual attack. That's your license to kill. Any more questions?"

Someone asked, "Why don't we stop and search black hats who approach the area? If they carry nothing, let them walk. Why take the risk?"

It was a good question that Elie had expected. "We can't stop and search religious Jews randomly. It would be viewed as police harassment of the innocent Orthodox community. And if we're lucky enough to actually stop these two, they might detonate and kill themselves and the arresting officers. Either way, it's bad. Better let them go through with whatever they've planned and act according to the orders you have received."

There were no more questions. Major Buskilah dismissed the troops until sunrise.

The tall windows of the synagogue grew darker. Lemmy watched from his bench in the rear as his father mounted the dais and kissed the blue velvet curtain of the Ark. The silence was deep, almost unreal for a hall filled with hundreds of men. The moment of truth had arrived. Their rabbi was about to reveal his decision: How would Neturay Karta combat the Zionists' most infuriating sin to date.

Rabbi Gerster's face was white under the black hat. He opened his arms as if he wanted to embrace his followers. "I love you, my sons, as I love my Creator, His name be blessed." He sighed. "I have sought His guidance. I have prayed and studied the words of the sages."

A murmur passed through the hall.

"Yes, we all want the Zionists to put aside their heretical law that sanctions the murder of innocent Jewish babies. And, yes, we want them to embrace God's law, so that one who commits an abortion shall be punished as a murderer."

Before Rabbi Gerster could continue, Redhead Dan sprang up from his seat and yelled, "Kill Levi Eshkol!" His payos wriggled wildly as he turned left and right and yelled again, "It is written: *He who comes to kill a Jew, kill him first!*" He earned loud applause, which encouraged him. "Smash the head of the snake! Bring down the defiler of God!"

Lemmy noticed Yoram, who sat next to Redhead Dan, raise his beady eyes to his admired study companion. It was neither a glance of support nor of admiration, but of fear.

"Our learned friend," Rabbi Gerster said, "wants to kill the Zionist prime minister."

"It's God's will," Redhead Dan yelled.

The rabbi nodded. "It reminds me of the story about a man who stood in line at the post office with a package."

The men hushed each other. They loved the rabbi's stories. Redhead Dan sat down.

"After waiting for three hours to send his package, the line was still long. His feet hurt terribly, his shirt stuck to his back with sweat, and he got so angry that he dropped the package and screamed that he was going to kill Prime Minister Eshkol. A woman standing in line behind him promised to keep his spot, and he ran off to kill Eshkol."

A few men laughed.

Rabbi Gerster took out his white handkerchief and wiped the sweat from his face. "An hour later he returned. The line had moved forward a bit, and the woman who had kept his spot asked, So, did you kill him? The man answered, No, I couldn't, because the line there is even longer!"

The hall exploded with laughter.

Redhead Dan stood up, ready to speak.

"Some of us," Rabbi Gerster said, "believe the abortion law is a reason to go to war against the Zionist regime even today, when millions of Arab enemies are gathering to attack this sliver of the Promised Land from all directions. Some of us believe God demands that we raise our hands against our misguided brothers. But I disagree."

A collective sigh came in response—a sigh of relief or of disappointment, Lemmy couldn't tell.

"God is our beacon," the rabbi declared, "the divine luminary that guides us. How could we spill blood because of laws made by foolish, faithless men in the Knesset?"

Redhead Dan's round face was crimson. "Kill the *Rodef* to save the babies!"

"The law of *Rodef* is an extreme exception, narrowly defined." The rabbi looked up in contemplation. "As Talmud tells the story of Yoav and Asa'el, God permits striking a pursuer in the fifth rib to disable him, but killing is allowed only if nothing else would stop the *Rodef* from murdering another Jew. Now, even if we assume that the Zionist prime minister is a pursuer who is intent on killing—"

"He is!" Redhead Dan looked around, seeking support. "God expects us to cut him down before—"

"And even if his demise would cause their Knesset to drop the abortion legislation and instead pass a law that *banned* abortions altogether, it would still be a meaningless law, wouldn't it?"

The cryptic question ignited a flurry of hushed exchanges as the men consulted their study companions.

The Zionists enacting the opposite law?

The Knesset banning abortions?

Meaningless?

Why?

"No!" Redhead Dan must have felt compelled to respond, as if the question had been directed at him. "It wouldn't be meaningless! It would be God's law!"

The rabbi's voice remained calm. "Do you really think that a law passed by the secular Zionists would stop faithless women from promiscuity? Prevent unwanted pregnancies? Save innocent babies from the abortionist's blade?" He caressed his beard.

"Such a law would only send confused women to back alleys in search of help."

The crowd muttered in agreement.

"All we can achieve by fighting the Zionist laws is to endanger the lives of mothers on top of the babies. You remember Solomon's judgment, yes?"

Many of the men nodded.

"Laws inscribed by human hands are meaningless," Rabbi Gerster said. "Without faith in God, women wouldn't know any better. It's a waste of time to fight against Zionist laws, an exercise in futility that won't help them see the light."

Redhead Dan yelled, "But they're blind!"

"By studying Talmud, by setting an example of a righteous life, by praying to God for an end to sins, we can bring out the light of Judaism. I therefore decree that in this community we shall never again mention the laws of the Zionists." Rabbi Gerster shut his eyes, his face turned up, his hands stretched out in a gesture of begging, and his sad baritone filling the hall: "*This world is just a very narrow bridge.*"

The men of Neturay Karta joined their rabbi's singing, "*Leading to Heaven; so don't be afraid, no fear at all.*"

Their voices grew stronger, their bodies swayed back and forth, and they joined in a forceful, repeated affirmation of faith, "*This world is just a very narrow bridge.*"

From the rear of the hall, Lemmy's lips moved with the words, yet his voice was mute. His body swayed, yet his heart remained indifferent. He looked at Benjamin, whose eyelids were shut tightly, his hands pressed against his chest, his voice trembling, "*So don't be afraid, no fear at all.*" Watching his devoutness, Lemmy knew the gap between them had widened. Tears filled his eyes, and for the second time that night, he left the synagogue unnoticed.

Chapter 23

At sunrise, the marksmen took their positions on the roofs near the prime minister's residence and in discreet locations along the street. Major Buskilah had direct command. Elie went up to the third-story roof, which was set up for the press briefing with folding chairs, hot coffee, and maps of Jerusalem pinned onto plywood.

General Yitzhak Rabin leaned on the railing. "Got a cigarette, Weiss?"

Elie held out a pack of Lucky Strike for the chief of staff.

Rabin pulled a few cigarettes, put one between his lips, and pocketed the rest. "My wife wants me to quit," he said with a lopsided grin. He drew deeply, holding the smoke for a long while before releasing it into the air in a long, straight thread. "Rumor has it that your *Nekamah* campaign has killed more Nazi officers than the Allied forces managed to kill."

"An exaggeration. Many of them continue to live with impunity." Elie lit a cigarette. The burns on his neck itched as hell, and he struggled to keep from scratching.

"They say that you caught an SS officer raping a Jewish girl, cut off his genitalia, and shoved it down his throat."

"Not his throat."

General Rabin chuckled. "An inspiring story nevertheless."

"I like working with blades," Elie said. "I find it nostalgic."

Rabin's cigarette stopped midway to his lips. "Nostalgic?"

"My father, rest in peace, was a kosher butcher."

The young general laughed. But when he realized Elie had not been joking, he tried to control himself, his face turning red. "Sorry, Weiss, it just sounded funny."

"I understand." Elie hid his anger, thinking how this ignorant sabra knew nothing of Jewish life in old Europe. A *shoykhet* was the only person trained in the ritual slaughter of livestock. Without him, the community would have no kosher meat and starve through the harsh winters, losing children to simple infections. A *shoykhet* should have been more important than a rabbi, yet the Jews of his childhood had revered Abraham's father, Rabbi Yakov Gerster, while Elie's father, Nahman Weiss, was treated like the carpenter, the shoemaker, or the blacksmith. *How the tables had turned!*

"*Jerusalem!*" It was his father's voice. "Wake up!" Lemmy got out of bed and opened the door. Rabbi Gerster was dressed and ready. "We must go now."

On Saturdays, morning prayers were held later, giving the men of Neturay Karta an opportunity to observe the command: *And on the Sabbath you and your livestock shall rest from all the work that you have done.* But for some reason his father was up early.

When they left the house, Rabbi Gerster turned in the opposite direction from the synagogue. Lemmy followed, still not completely awake. They entered an apartment building at the edge of Meah Shearim and went down a damp staircase. The rabbi knocked on a door.

Redhead Dan was still in his pajamas. He held the door open, and they entered a small room packed with a table, a sofa, and a bookcase. A baby started crying in the next room.

"Good Sabbath, Dan," Rabbi Gerster said. "I believe you have in your possession something that a God-fearing Jew should not possess."

Redhead Dan's mouth opened for an instinctive denial, but he thought better of it.

They waited as he disappeared into the other room. The baby cried harder, and a woman's voice comforted him. A moment later Redhead Dan returned with the box, which he placed on the table. "God had ordained this," he said. "A righteous man was jailed with me and we just knew that God—"

"You were tricked by the Zionists." Rabbi Gerster opened the box. "These things could have killed you and your family." He took out each of the grenades and checked the fuses. "And the neighbors too."

Redhead Dan sat down, his face buried in his hands.

The rabbi closed the box. "Tonight, when the Sabbath is over, you'll pack a suitcase and take the bus to Safed, where Rabbi Shimon Elchai will take you into his yeshiva on probation. Your wife and son will remain here, and the community will take care of them. One year from now, not a day earlier, you may return. If I find your repentance sincere, you'll be allowed to return to this holy community and reunite with your family."

Lemmy carried the box up the stairs. He shuddered at the sound of Redhead Dan crying and realized that his father had taken him along to witness the banishment of a Neturay Karta member and to hear his sobs.

It was a lesson.

A warning.

The alleys of Meah Shearim were still deserted. At the gate, Rabbi Gerster turned east toward the border. They heard soldiers chattering in Hebrew and an occasional laughter from the concrete bunker facing the rolls of barbed wire and the Jordanians across. The entrance to the bunker was surrounded by sandbags. Two soldiers sat outside, their backs against the sandbags, smoking.

Rabbi Gerster said, "Shalom!"

The soldiers were startled.

"We found this box." He motioned for Lemmy to put it on the ground. "Please be careful."

One of the soldiers opened the box. "Hey! Look at these puppies!"

"Have a good Sabbath." The rabbi walked away.

"Wait! What's your name?"

He kept walking, his pace fast but not rushed. Lemmy kept up. They turned a street corner, the soldiers' excited voices fading behind.

An aid came up to the roof to summon General Rabin and Elie Weiss downstairs. Prime Minister Eshkol was sitting alone at the kitchen table, sifting through a pile of newspapers. A black-and-white television set was tuned to the BBC without sound.

"Look at this!" The prime minister threw a copy of the daily *Ha'aretz* across the conference table.

Elie read the front-page headline: *New Delhi Summit: Tito, Nasser, and Mrs. Gandhi Express Support for the Legitimate Rights of the Palestinian Arabs.*

"Look at the rest," Eshkol said impatiently, "look!"

Elie scanned the front page.

Anti-American riots in Manila.

Washington to cease bombing N. Vietnam if political solution is found.

Syrian deputy prime minister accuses Israel of preparing to attack Egypt and Syria.

British spy George Blake escaped London prison via ladder of knitting needles.

"Look here!" The prime minister flipped the pages. "Only here, in the corner of page three, they finally mention it: *Eshkol Appoints Galilee as Information Minister.* A charade, that's what it is!"

Rabin and Elie read the piece, which quoted Prime Minister Levi Eshkol's speech before the Knesset assembly: *The new Information Ministry will direct the provision of information to the public. While information is not a substitute for policy, the government must communicate clearly its sound policy to the Israeli citizenry.*

"Can you believe this?" Eshkol shook the newspaper. "A knitting English spy belongs on the first page, but the prime minister of Israel is dumped in the corner of the third page, next to wedding announcements."

"After this morning's operation," Elie said, "every word you utter will make the front page, and you'll have public support to make difficult decisions."

"That would help." The chief of staff shifted uncomfortably. "The army needs permission to call up the reserves. At least forty thousand troops."

"Not so simple," the prime minister said. "It could signal aggressiveness, make us look bad. Our best defense is an American guarantee. And a UN declaration."

"Those won't protect us from a joint Arab attack, which would be deadly without our reserves stationed along the borders. In fact," Rabin said, "it would be deadly even if our troops are fully engaged, but we'll have a better chance of survival."

"That's my point! We can't win!"

"I didn't say that."

"I won't authorize anything that would give the Americans an excuse not to help us." Prime Minister Eshkol gestured at the window. "Weiss, I feel like a sitting duck here."

"We have men on the roofs," Elie said, "and along Ben Maimon Avenue. As soon as the attackers throw the grenades, we'll finish them off."

"The operation," Rabin said in his slow, contemplative tone, "required a few adjustments. When they approach, an officer will shout a warning. If they don't lie down and surrender, they'll be shot in the leg."

"That's not the plan," Elie protested. "Where's the deterrence if you don't kill them?"

"We don't kill Jews."

"They're criminals. Assassins. And where's this sudden righteousness coming from? You shot Menachem Begin's ship in 'forty-eight. Jews died on the Altalena."

General Rabin's face turned red. "That was a tragedy I won't repeat. There will be no killing unless it's unavoidable."

Prime Minister Levi Eshkol stood up, signaling the meeting was over. "Good luck. I'll see you when it's all over."

Elie was seething. The two Neturay Karta men had seen him, and even with the fake beard, they might be able to recognize him later. They had to die! He touched the bulge on his hip, where the long blade was sheathed.

In the large foyer of the residence, Elie stood aside as the newsmen arrived. He knew them from the extensive files SOD maintained. All the major news outlets were represented, including the evening papers, *Yediot* and *Ma'ariv*, the laborite daily *Al-Ha'mishmar*, the English-language *Jerusalem Post*, and the national radio *Kol Israel*, as well as a cameraman from the nascent Israeli Television. Yaakov Even-Khen, a poet and the Jerusalem reporter for the National Religious Party's daily *Hatzofeh*, entered the foyer breathlessly, having walked from his home in observance of the Sabbath. The bureau chiefs for *Time, Newsweek,* and the *Associated Press* arrived together from Tel Aviv, followed by a woman who wrote for *Le Monde.* Eshkol's press secretary accompanied them up to the rooftop for refreshments, followed by Rabin's presentation and Eshkol's Q&A session.

Elie went to his car, put on the black coat, and stuck on the fake beard. The wide-brimmed black hat completed the picture. It was time to rendezvous with the two Neturay Karta men.

The synagogue was full. Cantor Toiterlich led the Sabbath prayers. Lemmy thought of Redhead Dan and his impending exile. Would the sect's firebrand have cried so badly if his wife and child were allowed to join him? And would he, Lemmy, also cry if exiled from his parents and Benjamin? He glanced at his study-companion, whose melodic voice pronounced the verses.

Suddenly a hand came between them and tapped Benjamin's shoulder.

Lemmy looked up. It was Nachum Learner, a frail scholar whose thin beard had started to turn gray. He rarely left his seat in the first row, praying and studying from dawn to midnight every day. His wife and seven children lived on the weekly allowance from Rabbi Gerster. "Benjamin Mashash," he said, "the rabbi wishes to see you."

Lemmy watched Benjamin follow Nachum Learner down the center aisle. Rabbi Gerster huddled with them for a moment.

When Benjamin returned to their bench, Lemmy asked, "What does he want from you?"

Benjamin collected his books from the table.

"What are you doing?"

He piled his books one on top of the other. "I'll be sitting next to Nachum."

"*What?*"

The men around them raised their eyes from the prayer books.

Lemmy grabbed Benjamin's forearm. "You can't sit with Nachum! You study with me!"

"Not anymore." Benjamin finished collecting all his books and hugged them to his chest. "Your father decided that I'll be studying with Nachum from now on."

"But—"

"Someone saw you with a Zionist woman in uniform." The tears welled up in Benjamin's dark eyes. He tried to say more, but couldn't. He turned and walked away from the bench they had shared since they were young boys, where they had studied daily for twelve, fourteen, even fifteen hours, arguing complex Talmudic theories, pounding each other with words and sometimes fists.

His father was standing at the front, near the ark, and their eyes met. They stared at each other over the rows of men, who swayed and chanted the prayers, oblivious to what had just happened. Rabbi Gerster put a finger to his lips.

The prayer book was still in Lemmy's hand. He dumped it on the bench, grabbed his black hat, and made his way to the exit in the rear of the hall. Tears blurred his vision as he ran through the foyer to the forecourt. A cold breeze slapped his burning face.

Elie Weiss waited at the intersection of King George and Ramban streets. He watched the bend in the road where the two Neturay Karta men would appear. They were late, and he began to worry that the media briefing would end before the attack.

"Weiss!" Major Buskilah beckoned him from the street corner. Elie walked over.

"We received a call," the major said. "Two black hats dropped off a box with hand grenades at a bunker near Meah Shearim."

"When?"

"An hour or two ago. The description fits Rabbi Gerster and his son."

"And how did this particular bit of information find its way to you so quickly?"

"Impressive, isn't it?" Major Buskilah grinned. "General Rabin issued an all-units order last night to report immediately any unusual incident involving black hats."

"I see." Elie realized he had underestimated the young chief of staff.

Rabin was waiting outside the prime minister's residence. He conferred with Major Buskilah about relieving most of the Special Forces. "Keep two on the roof across the street, two in a car, and two on patrol." He looked at the house and shrugged. "I'll tell the prime minister it's a no-show."

Elie headed for his car. Had Abraham's son told him about the grenades? That boy had spirit, which could be harnessed for useful purposes. A plan began to form in Elie's mind.

"Weiss!" Rabin caught up with him.

"I didn't take you for a backstabber."

The chief of staff smiled. "These things happen."

"Not to me." Elie realized he should have lined up a backup team of attackers to ensure redundancy.

Rabin tilted his head toward the residence. "Eshkol is a good prime minister. He's a capable mediator between the coalition parties. But he must give up the defense ministry. We need a decisive man to order a draft and authorize a preemptive strike against the Arabs before they hit us."

"You support Dayan?"

"He's popular. He knows the IDF. And he's got balls."

"What do you want from me?"

"I'm a soldier. But you could pull a few levers behind the curtain."

"We're not in Kansas anymore," Elie said.

"Excuse me?"

"What do you read to your kids at bedtime? Carl von Clausewitz?"

Lemmy ran home. He wanted to get into his room, shut the door, and bury his face in his pillow. How could he live without Benjamin? For the first time, he understood the phrase he had read in one of Tanya's books: *A broken heart.*

"Jerusalem?" His mother appeared from the kitchen, "What's wrong?"

The way to his room blocked, Lemmy turned to the wall. He was still panting from the run home. He hid his face in the crook of his arm and burst out crying.

When he calmed down, his mother took him into the kitchen and made him sit down. She sat next to him and held his hand. Her hand was cold and moist, and an odor of dish-washing soap came from it. He looked away and saw the adjoining dining room, the Sabbath table ready for lunch, a white cloth, shining silverware, braided challah bread, and a bottle of sweet red wine. He thought about Redhead Dan's young wife and the baby, waiting at the Sabbath table in the basement apartment, their year-long separation imminent.

"What happened?"

"Father took Benjamin away from me."

"I'm sorry."

"He hates me!"

Temimah sighed. "He doesn't hate you. He is your father. It's his duty to raise you to as a faithful, God-fearing Jew."

"Then he's doing a lousy job!"

"*Oy vey.*" Temimah took a deep breath. "Your father is a strict man. I know my husband. But he is also strict with himself. And he means well."

"No, he doesn't!" Lemmy pushed her hand away.

"With time, you will understand the reasons—"

"He hates me, and the sooner I accept it the better!" Determined not to cry again in front of his mother, Lemmy rushed to his father's study.

"Jerusalem!" She hurried after him. "Don't!"

He shut the door in her face.

"Master of the Universe!" She sighed behind the closed door. "What am I to do?"

Sitting in his father's chair, he grasped the carved lion heads. He looked for *The Zohar*, but couldn't find it on the desk. He opened the first and second drawers, which contained pens, blank papers, and other office supplies. The bottom drawer refused to open. He searched for a key in the other drawers, taking out each bundle of papers and shaking it. Kneeling, he searched underneath the desktop. At the far corner, in the back, on the rail that supported the drawers, he felt the shape of a key. His pinkie edged it out.

It fit into the lock.

There were no papers in the bottom drawer, only a small case made of dark wood, about the size of a book. He took it out, placed it on the desk, and removed the top.

A handgun.

He took it out of the case and examined it closely, moving a finger along the barrel, which was cold and oily. The magazine bay seemed large enough to hold a pack of cigarettes. Between the trigger and the barrel, the model name was etched in the steel: *Mauser Bolo 96*

He aimed the gun. The tiny bump at the end of the muzzle moved along the shelved books across the room. The handle was warmer than steel, plated with a smooth, off-white material.

Along the steel barrel, tiny letters were engraved: *K.v.K. 1943 Deutschland Über Alles*

He turned it. Along the other side of the barrel, a rougher carving had been forced into the steel. He rubbed it on his sleeve a few times until the Hebrew letters surfaced: *Nekamah. Revenge.*

"Jerusalem!" His mother knocked on the door. "Your father is coming!"

Lemmy replaced the box in the drawer and slammed the drawer shut. He knelt and stuck the key under the desktop. Standing up, he realized he had forgotten to put the handgun back in the box. He shoved it under his belt in the back, the cold steel against his left buttock. He pulled his coat over it and slipped out of the study.

Rabbi Gerster entered the apartment. "Good Sabbath, Jerusalem."

"Good Sabbath, Father." Lemmy tried to keep his voice even. He felt the Mauser as big as a tree under his coat. The open window let in the neighbors' singing of the Sabbath's *Zemiros*.

The rabbi tugged at his long beard. "Your mother and I feel that we have done you wrong." He glanced at Temimah. "When we married, two Holocaust survivors, alone in this world from large families, we didn't expect much from life. Definitely not a child. You were a miracle—"

"An accident," Lemmy said, shocked at his own chutzpah.

His father shrugged. "A gift perhaps, for which we were unprepared, but nevertheless grateful to the Master of the Universe."

His mother's face broke into a brief smile.

"It appears," his father continued, "that we failed as Jewish parents by overindulging you."

After the circuitous introduction, this was more in line with Lemmy's expectations.

"We gave you everything on a silver platter. Your own room. Your own bed, bookshelves, and desk. Your own little universe of privacy, which you have recently begun to abuse."

Lemmy opened his mouth to protest.

His father silenced him with an open hand. "All that is in the past. You're grown now, a learned young man who can serve God. You're ready to assume responsibility for others."

"We're very proud of you," Temimah said.

"Proud of your capabilities," his father clarified. "We have never asked anything of you, except what every Jewish parent hopes for: To see his child grow up to study Talmud, marry well, and do good deeds. Is it too much to ask, considering what we've given you? Your meals are prepared by your mother. Your clothes are washed. Your sheets and blankets are pressed. Your room is cleaned every day. Have we deprived you of anything?"

Lemmy shook his head.

"Our only expectation is that you continue on the path of our tradition, be studious and righteous as God expects of you, and over time assume the honor of leadership. Is that too much to ask?"

His urge to argue was stifled by his mother's sad eyes.

"Do you think," Rabbi Gerster asked, "that we want what's bad for you?"

Lemmy shook his head.

"Do you think we want you to be unhappy?"

He shook his head again.

"Do you think we want you to have a bad life?"

"No."

"Very well." The rabbi put his hand on Lemmy's shoulder. "It's settled. Blessed be He, Master of the Universe."

"Amen," Temimah said. "Amen!"

"Now," the rabbi clapped his hands, "I want you to know that I've given a great deal of thought to your future. I've decided that you need a mature study companion, a man whose wisdom and knowledge can help you navigate those perfectly natural doubts and occasional confusion."

Lemmy held his breath. Was his father going to become his study companion? It would be hard work to keep up with Rabbi Gerster's intellectual intensity, but the prospect of such daily closeness—

"Cantor Toiterlich has agreed to take you on as his protégé, so to speak." Rabbi Gerster glanced at Temimah, who was glowing with joy. "Which makes perfect sense considering that we'll be family soon!"

"God willing," Temimah said.

"You see," the rabbi held his big hands together, fingers interwoven, "Cantor Toiterlich and his wife have given us their final consent to engage Sorkeh to you in marriage immediately. Therefore, tomorrow night, after the evening prayers, we will meet to celebrate your engagement—a wonderful, blessed union!"

His parents took turns hugging and kissing him, congratulating each other, "*Mazal Tov! Mazal Tov!*"

Lemmy knew he should insist that he didn't want to become engaged yet, that he wanted time to think, to explore his feelings, to read more about the world and its marvels. But he remained silent, unable to speak up. In his mind, like a broken record, the words replayed: *Mazal Tov! Mazal Tov! Mazal Tov!*

Chapter 24

Tanya pointed at the figure standing by her house, and Elie slammed on the brakes, which made the tires screech as the car rocked back and forth on its soft suspension.

"That's Abraham's son," she said. "You don't want to meet him."

"No," he said. "Not yet."

"What do you mean?" She looked at him, alarmed.

"Only kidding. He's all yours."

Tanya collected her coat from the rear seat.

"I assume our deal is still on?" Elie did not turn to her, keeping the burnt skin out of her view.

"Next time you screw with me, it won't end with hot tea."

"Do not threaten me." Elie pulled the wool cap down to his eyebrows. His head hung forward, his aquiline nose almost touching the steering wheel. Would Abraham's son recognize the car as the one that had delivered the grenades to Redhead Dan? Even if he did, the cheap Deux Chevaux was a common car in Israel.

She waved at the boy through the windshield. He waved back.

"Ah," Elie said, "the allure of youth."

"Jealous?"

"Through and through."

One foot already outside the car, she pointed at the beggar's cloak he was wearing. "That thing stinks like somebody pissed on it."

Lemmy watched Tanya get out of the little Citroën and walk up the street toward him. The driver sat low, his wool cap showing over the steering wheel. Did they work together? Another translator of secret documents? Or a lover? For a moment, Lemmy felt foolish for rushing to see her, for waiting by her door like a desperate suitor. But there was no one else he could talk to.

The car U-turned and drove away, leaving a trail of bluish fumes.

"Who's the mystery man?"

Tanya reached and pinched Lemmy's nose between a finger and a thumb.

"Nice car."

Tanya unlocked the door. "Sarcastic today, aren't we?"

"No, really." He followed her inside. "It's a Citroën Deux Chevaux—very innovative!"

"A piece of French junk." Tanya went into the bathroom and washed her hands and face.

"He was Jewish, Andrea Citroën, the largest car maker in Europe before the second world war. He asked farmers what's important to them, and they wanted a car to transport eggs to the market on dirt roads *and* drive to church wearing a top hat. That's why it looks like a frog. And there's no axle—the first car in history to have an individual suspension for each wheel."

"Where did you learn all this?" She started brushing her teeth.

"I read it in one of your magazines. Citroën built one hundred prototypes for a media demonstration, but the Nazis invaded France. All cars were destroyed, except two that were hidden in barns in the south of France. When the war ended, he was long dead, but one of the prototypes survived and was used to build millions of Deux Chevaux cars."

Tanya clapped her hands. "Bravo!"

Lemmy bowed, taking off his black hat, holding it to his chest, and then throwing it behind his back. She turned to him while undoing the bun in her hair. He took her face in his hands, her carved cheekbones aligned with his thumbs. He kissed her hungrily, his hands moving down her back, to her buttocks, pressing her slim body against him. She balked at his sudden assertiveness and drew back. But then, she gave in, reached up, and pulled down his head, her fingers in his hair, their tongues exploring each other. His yarmulke fell to the floor. They moved together toward the sofa, Tanya's shoe leaving a dusty footprint on his black yarmulke.

"We should stop doing this," Tanya said. It was late in the afternoon. Her hand was on Lemmy's bare chest, and he was examining the lines on her open palm. "I'm twice your age."

"More than twice," he said.

She laughed.

"It doesn't matter. Love has nothing to do with age."

"You're not in love with me." Tanya's finger circled his bellybutton. "You're infatuated. It will pass."

She was wrong, but he said nothing.

"I'm too old for you, and not only in years. By the time I reached your age, I'd been through enough to fill a hundred years of life. I could never fall in love again."

"Again?"

She bit her lower lip.

"Then maybe I should start seeing Bira. We had a good time walking to the city together."

"No!" Tanya pulled away from him. She collected her shirt from the floor and put it on.

"I'm joking." He placed his arms around her waist. "Bira is way too young for me."

"She's three years older than you, silly!" Tanya turned within his embrace.

"I only have eyes for you."

"That has to change."

"Why? Are you still in love with my father?"

She sighed. "Whatever happened between me and your father was a long time ago. In another life. I doubt we'll ever speak again."

"Tell me more."

"No."

"I found a Mauser in his study last night." He reached down to the floor, where his clothes lay in a pile. "It must have belonged to a Nazi once. Look!" He showed her the engraved inscription: *K.v.K. 1943 Deutschland Über Alles.* "And someone scratched *Nekamah* in Hebrew on the other side." He turned the gun to show her.

Tanya looked away. "Your father is a foolish man for keeping this gun. And you must return it."

"But—"

"Promise me you'll forget you've ever seen this gun, and never ask me about your father again."

"But why—"

"No more questions! Otherwise, I won't see you anymore."

"That's not fair!"

"Promise!"

"Okay, I promise." He held the Mauser in his hand, feeling its weight. "On one condition: That you teach me how to use it."

"Hell, no!"

"What if I'm attacked on my way home?"

"Oh, please!" Shaking her head, Tanya plucked the gun from his hand. "I'm going to regret this." She held the gun up. "Magazine release." She pressed the release, letting the magazine drop to her open hand. "Magazine in." She pushed it in. "Loading." She held the gun with one hand and pulled back the barrel with the other hand, letting it spring forward. "Cocked. Bullet in the barrel." She aimed at the opposite wall. "Safety switch, secure position." She flipped the switch with her thumb. "Safety off. Ready to shoot."

"Let me try."

Tanya secured the Mauser and handed it to Lemmy, handle first. He repeated the process, only that when he cocked the gun, the bullet already in the barrel popped out.

She picked up the bullet. "If you ever have to shoot, press the trigger slowly until it goes. Otherwise, you'll spoil your aim by shifting the direction of the gun."

"I'll remember that." He released the magazine and added the bullet back in.

"And no more questions!"

"It's not fair."

Her face softened. She touched his lips with a finger. "You're young, smart, and handsome. You have a great life ahead of you." With both hands she manipulated his dangling payos behind his ears, out of the way. "Your father is a prisoner of a horrible past, serving a life sentence. As I am. But you are free to read, explore, choose your own way in the world."

Suddenly, as if a chandelier had turned on inside his head, the dim twilight of doubts cleared up and he knew what he must do. He looked deep into the green pools of her eyes and kissed her.

"Elie Weiss! Just the man I wanted to see!" Prime Minister Levi Eshkol leaned over the wide desk, extending a hand, which Elie shook. "So? The black hats stood you up?"

"Seems so."

"At least they didn't riot this morning after the Knesset approved the abortion law. Great job, Weiss!"

"Thank you."

"I have another thorn in my side, and I decided you're the man to pull it out."

"I'm better at sticking thorns in than at pulling them out."

The prime minister laughed. "Pull this one out of my side and stick it in someone else's side, if you know what I mean."

"Moshe Dayan?"

"Exactly."

Elie felt in his pocket for a cigarette. He had already guessed what Eshkol wanted. Now it was time for bargaining. "You want me to meddle in politics?"

The prime minister pulled off his spectacles. "Politics *schmolitics!* It's about our survival! That pirate will launch a war we can't win!" He wiped sweat from his head with a handkerchief. "The public is fooled by his cheap charisma. But Israel needs mature leaders, not a young sabra who shoots from the hip."

Elie nodded. Did Eshkol know that Rabin wanted Dayan? The situation was becoming more and more interesting. "From what I hear, the generals are anxious for a preemptive strike on Egypt, and they feel Dayan is more likely to authorize it."

"Because he's reckless. We have two hundred jets, and Weitzman wants to launch all of them at first light, fly across the desert, and bomb Nasser's airfields—a suicidal mission if there ever was one."

"Why?"

"They'll know we're coming as soon as the first plane takes off. The UN radar in Jerusalem will pick it up in a second. General Bull will tip the Jordanians, and they'll bombard West Jerusalem to death while alerting the Egyptians to scramble their planes into the air before we've even crossed the Suez Canal!"

Elie was impressed. The prime minister had outlined a viable doomsday scenario. "Do we know the UN radar's capabilities yet? Perhaps it's not powerful enough to see planes take off in the Negev or Galilee?"

"We must assume the worst. With our luck, it can track every *gefilteh* fish in the Mediterranean Sea and all the way to the Cyprus!"

"What exactly do you want me to do about Dayan?"

"You're creative. Bring him down, and I'll appoint you."

"Chief of Mossad?"

"I promise!"

The deal done, Elie got up to leave. "You can rely on me."

Chapter 25

Sunday morning arrived with a bright sun shining through the window over Lemmy's bed. He sat up and realized he had slept in. His parents must have decided to let him enjoy a bit of leisure ahead of tonight's engagement to Sorkeh. He thought of Benjamin, already studying with someone else. Sweet, wise Benjamin. One day he would make a great leader for Neturay Karta.

Denunciation and Faith was the title of the book that rested on the floor by Lemmy's bed. It was a thin volume. He had read it twice since returning from Tanya's house last night. He smiled at the memory of her delicate hands on his face, on his lips, his own hands giving her pleasure the way she had taught him, making her twist and moan and cling to him breathlessly.

When he had left near midnight, Tanya put *Denunciation and Faith* in his coat pocket. Now he knew why. This book spoke simultaneously of fantasy and reality—*his* reality. It had been written a generation earlier by the poet Uri Zvi Greenberg. In verse and metaphors, it blasted the Socialist-Zionist camp of David Ben Gurion, who had betrayed to the British authorities Jews from the right-wing guerillas of Menachem Begin's EZL and Yitzhak Shamir's LHI. The beauty in Uri Zvi's verses did not diminish the violence of his prophecy, which reminded Lemmy of the way Neturay Karta's charitable communal life did not diminish the fervor of its religious ideology. The battles were different—internal Zionist divisions compared with the ultra-Orthodox against the whole Zionist camp. But the similarity was striking—a readiness to stone, to set on fire, to spill Jewish blood, to hate fellow Jews who held conflicting beliefs.

Lemmy had made his choice. His doubts were gone. He would follow his conscience.

He dressed quickly. The thought of washing his hands and reciting the morning blessings passed through his mind, but he dismissed it. He pulled the Mauser from under the mattress and shoved it in his belt.

In the kitchen, refreshments and wine bottles awaited tonight's engagement celebration. Cakes were baking in the oven. His mother stood at the sink, scraping glassy scales off a large carp. Another fish stared at him from the counter by her elbow. She worked with a serrated knife, which she applied to the fish in quick, sharp movements.

He was already in the foyer when his mother caught up with him. "Good morning, my son." She handed him a mug and watched him bring it to his lips.

Turning away from the fish odor that came from her, he took a sip. The hot chocolate soothed his mouth with warm sweetness. He embraced the mug, his hands warmed by it. He tilted the mug higher and higher with each gulp, the aroma of hot chocolate comforting, until the rim of the mug reached his nose. Another, more potent scent came from his fingers, forcing its way through the smell of hot chocolate, filling his nostrils with sweetness that was not sugary but flowery. It was the scent of Tanya's passion.

A wave of heat went through him, and he choked on the last gulp. Coughing hard, he handed back the mug.

"What's wrong?" Temimah patted his back. "Are you okay?"

He pushed his hands deep in the coat pockets. "I'm fine."

She fixed the hat on his head, tilting it slightly to the right. "Study well. It's a big day."

"It's a great day!"

Passing by the synagogue, he headed for the gate and turned left toward Jaffa Street. From there he followed King George Street to Rehavia, a tree-lined neighborhood of stone houses inhabited by intellectual Zionists and government officials. Young women pushed strollers, taking advantage of the unseasonably warm sun. His black coat and hat drew curious glances.

He entered a barber shop, and a bell tolled above the door. Two teenage boys about his age sat in the waiting chairs. The barber held a blade over the lathered face of an elderly man. Everyone stared at Lemmy while a ceiling fan creaked above. He sat down, picked up a magazine and pretended to read. The Mauser pushed against his spine.

The barber resumed his conversation with the customer. A few moments later he let the man out of the chair, collected a few bills, and turned to the two teenagers. "Who's first?"

The one with dark curls pushed his friend to go first, laughing in a way that resembled Benjamin.

The teenager said, "I'm joining the army tomorrow."

"A soldier already?" The barber put a white cape around his neck. "Only yesterday your mother pushed your stroller. How come you grew up, and I never got older?"

"My father says that a true Zionist remains young forever."

"Your father should be in politics." The barber's hand messed up the boy's honey-colored hair. "Let's clean you up for the army!"

A few minutes later, the two shorn teenagers paid the barber and left, teasing each other. The barber showed Lemmy into the chair and swept the piles of hair to the corner of the shop. Lemmy removed his hat and looked at his reflection in the mirror. His blond hair covered his forehead, the spiraling payos came down to his shoulders. His heart raced.

The barber propped the straw broom against the wall and tied a cape around Lemmy's neck. "What will it be, son?"

He tilted his head in the direction of the door. "Like them.

The barber touched Lemmy's payos. "These too?"

Swallowing hard, Lemmy nodded.

A pair of scissors appeared in the barber's hand. A single snip, and the spiral chunk of hair, which had never been touched by scissors, dropped to his right shoulder, rolled down his chest, and rested in his lap.

The left one followed.

Lemmy shook the white cape, sending his payos from his lap to the floor. The deed was done. There was no way back.

As the barber picked up the electric clippers, Lemmy noticed the blue number tattooed on his forearm. The clippers buzzed over his head, clumps of hair falling off.

The barber removed the white cape. Lemmy glanced at the stranger in the mirror, got out of the chair, and pulled out his wallet.

"Keep your money," the barber said. "For good luck."

"I don't understand."

"I also was a true believer, a God-fearing Jew, in Poland. I had payos—beautiful, long payos, just like yours." His hand motioned at the floor. "Until the Nazis took us to the camps. My parents, my brothers, all of us." His voice broke, and he took a deep breath. "We were the Chosen People—chosen all right, chosen to die like animals while our God, *Adonai*," he spat the word in disgust, "did nothing to save us. But I'm still here—and no thanks to Him! He doesn't have my faith anymore, and I'm glad to see He doesn't have yours either!" The barber grabbed Lemmy's hand and shook it vigorously. "Good luck, son!"

Shmattas took one look at Lemmy and uttered a frightened whimper, followed by a long, unintelligible monologue in Romanian, accompanied by face twisting and hand wringing. He sifted through her stock and found khaki pants, a blue shirt, and a windbreaker with a fake fur collar. He changed behind a screen and offered Shmattas some money. She waved her hands at him and began another monologue in Romanian, interspersed with, "*Oy vey, Rabbitzen!*"

He wanted to explain to Shmattas that the black coat and hat were not a Jewish tradition at all, merely an imitation of the Polish aristocracy of a few centuries ago, which Jews had adopted for no religious reason. But he knew she wouldn't understand.

Lemmy emerged a clean-cut, blue-eyed young man, with a bundle of black clothes under his right arm and a Mauser stuck in his belt under the windbreaker. His head felt cold, neither hair nor a hat to protect it. He strolled down King George Street, enjoying the sun. The secular women glanced at him differently now, some smiling openly. He smiled back.

When the sun touched the rooftops in the west, he headed home. He knew his parents would be shocked, but they would have to let him live according to his principles. They had to understand and accept him in this new phase of his life as a modern Jew. After all, he was their only child. The threat of banishment was empty, Lemmy was certain. His father had preached: *Our child is our creation. Once we give birth to a child, it's ours, flesh and blood, for better or for worse.* As to the rest of the sect, Lemmy did not care what they thought. He was done studying Talmud from morning to night, and his future did not include marrying Sorkeh, he was certain of that. Maybe she could marry Benjamin?

His mother opened the door. She gasped and stumbled backward until her back met the wall. Slowly her knees gave way, the whites of her eyes appeared, and she descended to the floor.

"Mother!" Lemmy knelt beside her.

The hinges creaked as the study door opened. Lemmy looked up at his father, who seemed calm, as if he had expected his son to come home with his payos chopped off.

"Fetch water for your mother."

Lemmy ran to the kitchen and brought a glass of water. He held it to her lips while his father supported her head. Her eyes slowly came into focus.

They held her up and walked her to her room, where she collapsed on the bed. Lemmy took her hand, but she pulled it away.

"You are the same," she whispered, "the two of you, the same." She closed her eyes and rolled onto her side, facing the wall.

Rabbi Gerster left the room and waited for Lemmy in the hallway. "Did Tanya tell you to do this?"

"No. She told me to make my own choices."

"I see." There was no anger in his voice. "Is this your final decision?"

"Yes."

"You feel you have no other choice?"

"Correct."

"Then I have no choice either." Rabbi Gerster gestured at Lemmy's bare head. "Put on your yarmulke. We're going to the synagogue."

"The synagogue? I don't think it's a good idea."

"Obey me, Jerusalem, this one last time."

As they were leaving the house, Lemmy saw *The Zohar* in his father's right hand. Why was he taking the book of Kabbalah to the synagogue? Lemmy's heart beat faster as thoughts raced through his mind. Was his father planning to cast a spell on him? No. That was a ludicrous idea! More likely, his father would use the book to somehow make the men accept Lemmy in his new form. And if they refused? He touched the bulge of the Mauser against the small of his back. The men in the synagogue would be shocked by his snipped payos, his Zionist outfit, his proverbial slap in the face of his father, their beloved rabbi. Would they scream? Wave fists? Throw rocks?

His legs weakened, and his throat went dry. He had expected his choice to cause discomfort, maybe even a bit of acrimony with his parents, but he had not planned to follow his father, like the first Abraham, to an altar. *And Abraham held up the slaughterer's knife to slay his son.*

Entering the synagogue behind his father, Lemmy was blinded by the glow of the crystal chandelier, which burned with a thousand drops of light. He realized it had been turned on in honor of his scheduled engagement, in celebration of continuity, of the first step in the rabbinical succession at Neturay Karta.

The two of them entered the hall and stood behind the rows of men, who swayed as they studied, unaware of Rabbi Gerster and his only son, who was no longer a faithful member of their community.

"Good bye, Jerusalem." His father started to turn away, but suddenly changed his mind, took Lemmy in his arms, and pressed him tightly.

Lemmy's hands hung listlessly at his side. He wanted to speak, but no voice came out. His father had not hugged him since he was a toddler.

Rabbi Abraham Gerster let go, turned, and walked down the aisle. A thousand crystal tears rustled above him. Row after row, the men's voices quieted. They noticed their rabbi's slow pace and bowed head. They watched him climb onto the dais and kiss the blue curtain.

The rabbi turned and faced his men. "Rabbi Shimon Bar Yochai wrote this book eighteen hundred years ago." He held it up.

The men murmured, "*The Zohar! The Zohar!*"

"This book lists the secret names of God." Rabbi Gerster's hand pointed up, toward the ceiling. "God's names are divided into three groups: Names related to Adam, the source, the first father. Names related Eve, the first mother, who was created out of Adam's rib. And names related to the son, who is like *Malkhoot*, the kingdom of continuity."

From the rear, Lemmy saw rows of heads in black yarmulkes or hats. The men focused on Rabbi Gerster. None of them looked back yet to see Lemmy's missing payos, his pale face, and his right hand, which emerged from under the jacket, clenching a handgun.

"A son represents continuity of faith. For every Jewish father and mother, a son is the focus of all sacred things, a cherished vessel to carry God's Torah onward to the next generation." Rabbi Gerster closed his eyes and turned his face up in meditation.

Lemmy's heart beat hard. He wanted to flee, but his legs wouldn't move. His fingers clung to the ivory handle of the Mauser.

"God entered into a covenant with our patriarch Abraham." Rabbi Gerster's voice roamed through the synagogue. "*You shall be the Father of multitudes, and the land of Canaan shall be for you and your seed to possess forever. I shall be your God.*"

Now Lemmy knew what was coming: Abraham sacrificing his son! A voice screamed inside his head: *Run!*

Rabbi Gerster sighed. "Our sons are the essence of the eternal covenant." He opened his hands in pleading. "But here I am, Abraham Gerster, your rabbi, standing before you today in shame!"

Many asked loudly, "What? What? What?"

Lemmy's thumb pushed the safety latch of the Mauser.

"Shame, dear God, so much shame!" The rabbi's voice was broken. "I have failed to raise my own son to honor the covenant." He pointed above the men's heads to the back of the hall.

The air froze in Lemmy's throat. His forefinger slid into the trigger slot.

Hundreds of faces turned to him, bearded faces with bewildered eyes that looked at his blue shirt and khaki pants, at his shaven sideburns. He felt naked without his black coat and black hat. He was *The Painted Bird*, surrounded by its own kin, who were ready to lynch him. Fear screamed inside his head.

He saw their disbelief giving way to rage. They tore up from their seats, hands clenching into fists, lips spitting words of revilement, a collective howl of damnation, which grew louder as they advanced at him. Behind them, his father stood high on the dais, eyes shut, face upturned, hands stretched to the sides, palms open upward.

Lemmy's hand rose, the Mauser appearing between him and the mosaic of red faces. The muzzle aimed at the black of their coats, their heaving chests.

His finger applied pressure to the trigger while his hand rose higher, across their faces, above their heads, until the bump at the end of the barrel found his father's chest at the opposite end of the synagogue. It lingered there, while the men were almost upon him.

He raised his hand farther up and pressed the trigger.

The recoil threw him back, the explosion tenfold louder than he had expected. He fell down and saw the ejected casing hit the floor nearby. But when he looked up, he froze in terror.

The crystal chandelier, still burning bright, detached from the ceiling. The giant cluster of lights descended, gaining speed until it hit the center of the synagogue and exploded. The noise was terrifying, and the glistening crystal tears bounced up in the air and landed on the floor with ringing chimes, spreading throughout the center aisle and between the benches and under the hundreds of shoes of stunned men, who slipped and dropped to the floor with flailing arms.

The brightness of the chandelier disappeared. Twilight engulfed the synagogue, and an eerie silence.

"There's no punishment," Rabbi Gerster roared, "no punishment for the dead! Only the judgment of the Lord!" He brought his hands to his chest, gripped the lapel of his coat, and pulled his hands forcefully in opposite directions, ripping the black cloth apart. It made a loud tearing sound, like a hoarse cry of pain. His eyes closed, the rabbi pressed his fists to his chest, against the torn cloth. With a voice full of agony he recited the mourners' prayer for the dead: "*Blessed be He, Master of the Universe, the true judge.*"

"Amen," the men chorused, rising from the floor. "Amen." None of them looked at Lemmy anymore. For them, and for their rabbi, Jerusalem Gerster was dead.

Chapter 26

Lemmy spent a week with Tanya—reading, talking, and making passionate, tender love. When she sat for hours with the oversized headphones in the other room, he slept as if recovering from months of insomnia. For his eighteen birthday, she baked a chocolate cake and opened a bottle of wine, which they finished together. Now that he was officially an adult, she took him to a government office, where he obtained an Israeli ID card and received his military draft papers.

They barely slept that night. In the morning, they showered together and took the bus to an open field in West Jerusalem, where the IDF had set up a processing center for mandatory draftees, most of them recent high-school graduates. Several rows of military trucks waited in the sun, and female soldiers in olive-green uniform and hoarse voices tried to keep order.

Standing among hundreds of young recruits and their families, Tanya hugged him tightly. She smiled through her tears. "Keep safe, will you? And no more rebellions. Once in uniform, you must obey orders."

Lemmy made a mock salute. "Yes, Madam!"

She waved as he climbed onto the back of the truck. "Don't forget to write!"

He blew her a kiss and mouthed, "I love you!"

The trucks departed in a cloud of dust and engine fumes. The families, many with younger children, waved at the convoy until it made the turn onto the main road to Tel Aviv. Fathers put on brave faces while mothers wiped tears.

Tanya walked to the main road, where she planned to catch a local bus back home. She noticed Elie's car, parked farther up the road under a tree.

Tanya got in. "You're becoming too predictable for a spy."

"It's all part of the plan." His face seemed even gaunter than before, his dark eyes sunken beside the protruding bridge of his nose. He was wearing a brown wool cap, pulled down over his ears. He emitted a medicinal smell, which she assumed came from the ointment on his burns. She watched the families leave the field, some getting into their small cars, others walking, or waiting for the bus. "The army is the best thing for him."

"I made a few calls. He'll be assigned to Paratroopers Command. Their boot camp lasts six months, so even if war breaks out, he'll still be in training, safely away from battle."

She thought of Lemmy in uniform, so different from the Talmudic scholar he had been only a week earlier. He was free now to make new friends, gain confidence in himself, and become a normal Israeli. "Have you spoken to Abraham?"

Elie uttered a strange chuckle, something between clearing his throat and blowing his nose. "He's too furious to speak with anyone. Blames you for brainwashing his boy."

The thought of Abraham being angry with her gave Tanya mixed feelings—a satisfaction in prevailing over him to set Lemmy free and a lingering doubt as to whether she had done the right thing, tearing a boy from his family and community.

"Better keep away from Abraham," he added. "He's got a temper, you know."

His tone made Tanya wonder whether Elie was telling the truth, or was he up to his usual manipulations. "Lemmy told me that his father was sad, that he hugged him before addressing the men, and tore his coat in mourning, as if his son had died. But you say he's furious?"

"Abraham isn't furious with his son. He's furious with you. But he's a soldier in our fight for survival. A secret agent of his caliber doesn't get distracted from his job by personal problems."

"He's not a machine. Losing a son is a tragedy for any parent."

"Abraham's job is to keep the ultra-Orthodox under control, not to babysit a troublesome teenager whose very existence was an error and whose behavior undermines Abraham's authority. It's better that *what's his name* is gone from Meah Shearim."

"His name is Jerusalem."

"Right. Jerusalem." Elie tapped the steering wheel. "Of course, to begin with, it would have been better if you had left the boy alone. Abraham's standing in the sect would have been stronger with a devout son to follow him. But once you exposed the boy to secular culture and to carnal pleasures, it's better he's out of the sect. They'll forget about him soon enough, except maybe his mother. Abraham is very concerned about her."

Tanya thought of the woman she had seen briefly that Sabbath morning months ago, when she had visited Abraham's home.

"He's her only child," Elie added as if Tanya didn't know. "I would have her committed to a mental institution, but Abraham thinks she'll recover better within the sect."

"She'll recover only when she's reunited with her son. A mother is a mother, no matter what religious differences separate them."

"You don't know Neturay Karta."

"I know motherhood. She can write to Lemmy and meet him when he's on leave."

"I'll suggest it to Abraham." Elie turned on the engine. "Shall we conclude our business?"

Tanya took a deep breath. She was about to hand over the ledger, breaking her promise to the first man she had loved, SS General Klaus von Koenig. But she wasn't doing it for her own personal gain, or for wealth and influence. She was buying Lemmy's freedom. And the money—even if Elie somehow managed to get it from the Swiss—would be used to defend Israel and protect those who had survived the Nazis' camps. It was justice, yet the ledger belonged to Klaus, who had saved her life and turned her into a woman, who had taught her art and music, who had treated her with kindness and affection while the rest of the world was engulfed in cruelty and death. She had not been blind—Klaus was a cultured, polished technocrat, who had applied his education and energy to serve mass murderers. But with her he had shared only his warmth, humor, and strength, forming a peaceful cocoon in a stormy world, earning her heart in that all-consuming passion of a teenage girl's first love. And that Klaus, the one she had known and loved, would have understood why she was trading his ledger for Lemmy's freedom.

"Here." She held up the pocket-size booklet, bound in black leather, stamped with a red swastika. "But promise me that you won't interfere with the boy. Ever."

"Abraham's son?" Elie made a dismissive gesture. "What would I want with him?"

"Swear!"

He raised his hand. "I solemnly swear that I won't interfere with Jerusalem Gerster."

She watched Elie's thin fingers turn the pages. Each page listed precious stones and jewelry, categorized by size and quality, with meticulous notations of quantities and totals for each category. On the last page, hand-written in faded blue ink, it said: *Deposit of above-listed goods is acknowledged this day, 1.1.1945 by the Hoffgeitz Bank of Zurich. Signed: Armande Hoffgeitz, President.*

Chapter 27

"As of this moment, you will forget your mommy and daddy and your *coochie-moochie* girlfriend!" The officer, stout with a freckled face, paced down the three-deep line of fresh recruits, holding up his machine gun in the air. "Your Uzi is your new mother, father, and girlfriend!"

"Yes, sir!" Lemmy yelled in chorus with the others.

"Hug your Uzi every morning, kiss it every evening, and sleep with it every night!"

"Yes, sir!"

"Now, get around the building! Thirty seconds!"

"Yes, sir!" The company of about sixty soldiers broke into a sprint, raising dust and spinning pebbles. Lemmy held the Uzi to his chest and ran as fast as he could. Beside him, a dark-skinned recruit tripped over a rock. Lemmy stopped and helped him up, and they chased after the others around the building, rejoining the line in attention.

"You!" The officer pointed at Lemmy. "Did you have a nice stroll? Did you enjoy the view? Shall I call a taxi for you next time?"

Lemmy yelled, "Yes, sir!"

Everyone burst out laughing. Even the officer laughed, suddenly appearing almost as young as the recruits. "Thirty seconds! Go!"

This time, Lemmy was the first to return. When the rest arrived and lined up, the officer clapped slowly. "A bunch of old ladies. Do you want to play bingo now?"

"Yes, sir!"

He grinned. "My name is Captain Zigelnick. But you can call me God."

"Yes, sir!"

"Drop and give me twenty pushups. Now!"

Lemmy kneeled carefully and strapped on the Uzi so that it rested against his back while he dropped forward on his hands. He heard the officer berating the soldiers who had put their machine guns on the ground.

By the tenth pushup, he was surrounded by grunts and groans. Lemmy gritted his teeth, ignored the burning in his muscles, and counted in his mind. At twenty, he stood up.

Zigelnick pointed at him. "Give me another twenty!"

After more running and pushups, they marched into a rectangular building with bathrooms and showers at one end, an office at the other, and rows of metal-framed beds with foam mattresses in between. Lemmy picked a bed next to the soldier he had helped—Sanani, who spoke Hebrew with the crisp accent of a Yemenite Jew, which also explained his dark complexion.

It rained outside as they lined up. Captain Zigelnick led them down a rocky crevice. Soon, their new boots were caked in mud, and the rain soaked their uniforms. Some of the trainees cursed under their breath, but to Lemmy the wet uniform felt better than any dry black coat. They started up a new hill. Sanani raced him to the top. When the rest of the company gathered, they lined up three-deep and someone started singing, *"Jerusalem of Gold, and of bronze, and of light…"*

It was a popular song by poet Naomi Shemer, infused with Jewish longing for the Old City, as if the threatened war with the Arabs was not about Israel's very survival, but about recovering the ancient Israelite capital.

Others joined. *"The enchanted city, which sits alone, a wall across her heart."*

Captain Zigelnick joined the singing. "*And no one travels to the Dead Sea, by way of Jericho.*"

Their voices rose louder, echoing from the surrounding, barren hills. "*Jerusalem, which is made of gold.*"

Lemmy stood shoulder to shoulder with his fellow paratroopers-in-the-making, a chorus of devotion to the Old City he had watched from across the border every Friday of his young life, listening to his father's prayers. He thought of the narrow alleys and the smell of fish from his mother's hands. And the sound of Benjamin's laughter.

"**R**ead our history, and you'll know the future!" Elie watched the two agents push aside their cups of coffee and gaze at the open book. This page of *Samuel II* told of a hot day in Jerusalem, when King David had enjoyed the cool evening breeze on the roof of his royal palace. He noticed a beautiful woman bathing in a pool of rainwater on a nearby roof and sent a courtier to summon her to his royal bed. When she became pregnant, the king assigned her husband to the front line, where he died in battle. The widow married the king and gave birth to an heir. '*And God disapproved of the evil which King David had committed.*'

The younger agent, Dor, looked up with a grin. "Naughty boy, the king of Israel."

"Like he had a choice? Bathsheba was irresistible." Yosh was an older man, whom Elie had recruited over a decade earlier.

Elie closed the book. "Great men are all alike—three thousand years ago, and yesterday. You know the rumors about Moshe Dayan. I want facts about his affairs: Who he's seduced, where, when, and what happened to their husbands—names, ranks, and service records, especially if they died."

"It's not going to be easy," Dor said. "Dayan is a popular man and a member of the Knesset. We'll have to sniff around his former military staff, his driver, his neighbors, his friends—"

"I don't like it." Yosh pushed *Samuel II* aside. "I didn't sign up with your department to assist inept politicians in a lascivious blackmail operation to keep Dayan out of the defense ministry."

"Who said anything about the defense ministry?"

"Oh, come on!"

"And you signed up with me because you were kicked out of Shin Bet for equally *lascivious* activities." Elie paused to let his rebuke sink in. "Now go and do your job!"

Chapter 28

Three weeks after she had accompanied Lemmy on his first day in the army, Tanya found a letter from him in her mailbox. He described how the harshness of boot camp had forged the company into a tight-knit group. He was learning new skills and growing stronger after a bout of the stomach flu. There was a long paragraph about a five-day hike they had taken in the desert as part of a drill involving a mock attack on a tank-battalion base which, he wrote, *was a lot of fun!* As if anticipating her question, Lemmy added at the end of the letter that he had been thinking of his parents and wondered whether Tanya could find out how they were, *especially my mother.* From this Tanya deduced that he had received no letters.

Late that night, after the chatter on the UN radio dwindled down to silence, Tanya turned on the automatic recording device and called a taxi.

When they reached Meah Shearim, she asked the driver to wait for her at the gate. Dressed in an overcoat and a knitted wool cap, she walked quickly through the alleys and climbed the stairs to the third-floor apartment.

Rabbi Abraham Gerster opened the door wearing black pants, a white, button-down shirt, and a black yarmulke.

"Shalom, Abraham."

He glared at her. She feared he would slam the door in her face. But he beckoned her into his study.

"You got some nerve coming here." He leaned on his desk. "How is my son?"

"He's in basic training. Paratroopers corps." A reading lamp by the cot shed light on an open book by his pillow, but otherwise the small room was dim. She could not decipher the expression on Abraham's bearded face. "He's doing well," she added.

"I can't say the same for us."

She pulled off the wool cap and unbuttoned her coat. "I had to rescue him from this fundamentalist concentration camp."

Abraham grimaced and stepped forward, coming at her with quickness she had not expected. She retreated, her back hitting the book shelves. He closed his arms around her, tightly, as if trying to smother her. But then he uttered a deep, painful sigh, and she gave in to his embrace, placing her arms around his waist, resting her head on his chest, which rose and sank with quick, halting breaths.

After a long time, they let go of each other. Abraham blew his nose into a handkerchief and sat on his cot. She sat next to him.

He took her hand and kissed it. "You did him a favor. He deserved better. I should have sent him away years ago, but I couldn't bring myself to do it."

"How could you? Parents can never let go, even under the best of circumstances."

"Not only that. I was afraid for him. Still am."

"Basic training will take six months," she said. "He'll be safe when the war comes—if it comes. Eshkol will do anything to avoid war."

"It's not war that I fear. This place is close to the border." Abraham gestured at the walls. "He would be more likely to get hit by a Jordanian cannonball here than while serving in the IDF."

"So?"

"It's Elie. I've always worried that he would somehow ensnare Lemmy, turn him into another cog in his machine. That's why I kept my son here."

"You don't need to worry about Elie." Tanya squeezed his hand. "I made him swear that he won't interfere with the boy. And I paid dearly for it."

Abraham turned sharply. "You gave him the ledger?"

She nodded.

"God almighty!" He stood up, suddenly regaining the stature of Rabbi Abraham Gerster, leader of Neturay Karta. "Think of how he gave those grenades to Redhead Dan! Now, with this kind of money, there's no limit to what he'll do!"

"Elie won't get the money." Tanya stood, facing him. "Klaus chose his banker carefully—a schoolmate whose personal loyalty is to Klaus. The Swiss will find an excuse to deny Elie access to the account."

"But he has the ledger!"

"It won't be enough." Tanya gestured at the open door. "How is your wife?"

"She barely eats, doesn't go out, keeps crying. During the day, the women of the sect care for her, and the men pray."

"Why hasn't she written to Lemmy? I asked Elie to tell you."

"I haven't seen Elie since before the grenades debacle."

"That's odd." Tanya reflected on Elie's description of Abraham's anger. Should she mention it? He didn't seem hostile now, but raising it could reignite his anger. Her visit had one purpose, and Elie's games were no longer important. "Maybe I misunderstood him," she said. "Anyway, please tell your wife to write to Lemmy. It will be good for him and good for her. Address it to the IDF and write his name and military ID number on the envelope." Tanya jotted down the number.

"I'll do it first thing in the morning." He caressed her hair. "You are kind and generous. In my heart, we are forever together, you and me—"

"*Abraham!*" Temimah Gerster stood at the door, wrapped in a sheet, her shaved scalp exposed.

He moved fast, catching her as she collapsed.

"You touched her," Temimah cried.

"She brought us news from Jerusalem." He lifted her in his arms, cradling her as a child.

"Tell her to go!"

"He is in the army. A soldier."

"My Lemmy?"

"He's doing very well." He carried her down the hallway. "We'll write to him tomorrow. It will make you happy, yes?"

Tanya buttoned up her coat, slipped on the wool cap, and left the apartment.

Chapter 29

"I'm not doing this!" Sanani pointed up at a wooden platform affixed to the summit of a giant eucalyptus tree. A thick rope came down from the platform, across a wide gulch, ending in a knot around the trunk of another eucalyptus.

"I need a volunteer," Captain Zigelnick said, "to show Sanani how to be a man."

The soldiers looked up. No one stepped forward.

"I'll show him." Lemmy raised his hand, and the captain tossed him a bent steel bar.

Short sections of wood were nailed to the trunk, forming a makeshift ladder. He stuck the metal bar in his belt, shifted the Uzi so it rested on his lower back, and started climbing. The trunk was smooth. It had a sharp smell. He climbed one rung after another. His muscles began to ache.

His friends clapped rhythmically. "Gerster! Gerster! Gerster!"

Lemmy paused and looked down. Their upturned faces surrounded the base of the tree, approximately four stories below him. He held on with one hand, his feet planted securely, and pretended to unzip his fly. They scattered, hooting.

A light breeze was blowing from the north, and the tree swung from side to side. The platform was built like a raft of rough-cut logs tied together with wires, the cracks between the logs wide enough to put his hand through. He made the mistake of looking down. Far below, his friends seemed small.

He reached up to the rope, which was tied to the trunk over his head, and slowly rose to stand on the platform. It swayed under his weight, creaking in protest. The rope was as thick as his arm. It dropped steeply about two-thirds of the way then curved in a gradual slope before leveling off near the opposite tree.

Gripping the rope with both hands above his head, Lemmy inched forward until the tips of his boots lined up with the edge of the platform. The chanting below stopped. He heard Zigelnick yell something.

Acting against every survival instinct, Lemmy let go of the rope with one hand and pulled the hooked bar from his belt. Slowly, without disturbing his careful balance, he slipped the hooked bar over the rope, slid his other hand to the opposite end of the bar, and eased forward into the air.

The acceleration was blinding. The friction of the metal bar on the rope produced a high-pitched whizzing. He heard himself howling.

The pressure on his arms and shoulders grew as his slide changed direction and leveled off. The deceleration was as drastic as the initial acceleration, and his vision cleared just in time to see that he was hurtling head-on toward the trunk of the opposite eucalyptus. He let go before colliding with the tree, curled up, and rolled on the ground several times, coming to rest in a cloud of dust.

A moment later, his friends were all over him, and someone emptied a bucket of water on his head.

Cursing and laughing at the same time, Lemmy got up. His knees were weak and his hands trembled, but he knew he could climb all the way up to the flimsy platform and rappel down again right now. But it was Sanani's turn, and everyone goaded him up the eucalyptus tree.

Elie was summoned to a strategy conference at the King David Hotel. From the top-floor suite, the border with Jordan passed practically under the windows, which offered sweeping views of East Jerusalem and the Old City. A light breeze diluted the smoke of cigarettes.

Minister of Foreign Affairs, Abba Eban, who had arrived straight from the airport, spoke first. "My consultations in Paris left me with an unequivocal conviction that King Hussein has in fact received our non-aggression communiqué through the French consular intermediary."

"You mean," Eshkol said, "they told Jordan we don't want war?"

"Precisely. The French ambassador to Amman personally conveyed our fervent preference for a non-confrontational détente in lieu of Jordanian participation in the belligerent military campaigns currently contemplated by Egypt and Syria."

"And?"

"The Elysée Palace remains utterly concerned." Eban's British accent, usually a cause for chuckles among the sabra generals, somehow seemed appropriate in this opulent hotel suite. "Our diplomatic overtures, notwithstanding their sincerity, have been spurned decisively by the royal Jordanian court. The king's counselors misinterpreted the message as insidious machinations, contrived merely to lure His Majesty toward injurious inaction while we surreptitiously prepare to launch the IDF at his prized territorial and theological possessions."

"You mean," Eshkol concluded, "the Jordanians think we're bluffing."

"A poignant understatement," Abba Eban said. "The Jordanian consorts infused their analysis with undertones that historically have been accorded to our Jewish race, such as underhandedness in commerce and money lending. They advised King Hussein to array his armed forces in a forthcoming posture, cohesive with the other Arab armies, and to issue a proclamation soliciting the incursion of Iraqi and Saudi battalions into the West Bank as fortification of Jordan's combat units."

"Hussein is inviting the Iraqis into Jordan?" General Rabin threw his cigarette out the window. "If they reinforce the existing Jordanian units in the West Bank, we're doomed. There's no way we can defend the coastal strip. They'll cut us in half between Natanya and Herzlia, then march south and north to take Tel Aviv and Haifa."

"During our meeting," Abba Eban continued, "President De Gaulle was lucidly unambiguous about the pertinence of Israeli non-aggression. He assured me that he's a loyal friend of *l'Etat Hébreu,* but insisted that we unequivocally forgo war. When I left, De Gaulle pressed my hand and admonished me: *Ne faites pas la guerre!*"

"The French want to teach us national defense?" Prime Minister Levi Eshkol looked around the table. "It took Hitler three days to conquer France and gobble up all their baguettes!"

In the midst of laughter, Chief of Staff Yitzhak Rabin remained serious. "De Gaulle might be right. If Jordan fights us, the war will be a blood bath."

"But look at this!" General Ezer Weitzman, CO of operations, went to the window and pointed. "How can we pass up the opportunity to recover the Old City? Return to our historic capital? It's crazy!"

Now Elie understood why the prime minister had chosen to hold this strategy meeting on the top floor of the King David Hotel rather than at the Pit. The unobstructed views created an irresistible temptation for the sabra generals, whose lives had been dedicated to recreating the ancient Jewish kingdom in the Land of Israel. The glorious sights provoked them to say what they really had in mind.

"We must," Weitzman said, "recapture our ancestral land, all the way to the Jordan River."

"That's enough," Rabin said.

But Weitzman couldn't hold back, "What kind of a Jewish state is it without Jerusalem? What kind of Jewish warriors are we without the courage to restore King David's glory?"

"That's a political question." The prime minister shook his finger like a scolding teacher. "You boys harbor impossible dreams!"

Chief of Staff Rabin lit another cigarette.

"Strategic decisions," Abba Eban said, "must be contemplated in conjunction with the appropriate analysis of all diplomatic, strategic, and fiscal ramifications. Acquisition of our ancient biblical sites, tempting as it might be, could jeopardize our very chance of national survival. The pending wholesale attack by the Arab nations could pit us against Soviet-supplied firepower of great magnitude. We must utilize diplomatic maneuvers to preempt a war through UN and American guarantees. The Egyptians won't fight the United States!"

"In other words," Eshkol said, "the Arabs are idiots, but not *meshuggahs*."

"We have to assume," Eban said, "rational behavior by our adversary."

"Exactly!" The prime minister looked at Chief of Staff Rabin. "We shouldn't let the holy places tempt us into a ruinous war." He waved at the window. "The Arabs will throw us in the Mediterranean—a second Holocaust!"

Elie saw Yitzhak Rabin cringe, as if the word Holocaust was a slur. "Israel isn't a *shtetl* in Poland," the chief of staff said. "The IDF is stronger than the sum of our units. It's a matter of sequence and allocation. And sacrifices. But we can win."

"Ah!" Eshkol groaned. "Gambling with our lives!"

There was silence in the room, which Elie guessed was not because of General Rabin's interjection, but due to the attendees' shock at the prime minister's explicit panic.

"It could be a pyrrhic victory," Abba Eban said. "The territories biblically known as Judea and Samaria, where our forefathers once dwelled, will come into our proverbial hands with multitudes of hostile indigenous inhabitants whom we must feed, clothe, and treat medically. The costs would drastically surpass our financial means, deplete our scarce material resources, and overburden our bureaucratic infrastructure. Furthermore, ruling over an Arab population dominated by paternalism, tribalism, and primeval customs would conflict with our democratic, pluralistic, and modern social fabric. In time, this conflict could undermine Israel's international standing."

"That makes no sense," Weitzman said. "Wouldn't the world support our modernity?"

Abba Eban shook his head. "We must remember that democratic nations are, and will remain, a minority among the global community, while dictatorships and banana republics will continue to dominate the most powerful international organizations."

Elie heard one of the generals whisper to his neighbor, "What the hell is he talking about?"

"Pardon me," Abba Eban stood. "I am obliged to use the lavatory."

As soon as the foreign minister was out of the room, Prime Minister Eshkol shook his head. "*Der gelernte Narr!*"

Everyone laughed. By calling Eban *The learned fool,* Eshkol punctured the foreign minister's inflated aura. Unlike the erudite, highly educated Eban, who had taught at Oxford before devoting himself to the Zionist movement, the sabra generals were at best high-school graduates. They distrusted his wordiness, tailored suits, and oversized spectacles, yet recognized the value of his ability to meet world leaders as an equal and deliver awe-inspiring speeches in world capitals. Eban's startling ability to communicate Zionist concerns with Churchillian oratory had won many of Israel's existential diplomatic battles, as well as the breathless pride of Diaspora Jews everywhere. But the sabra warriors never accepted him as a true Israeli, and Prime Minister Eshkol's contemporaries, the older generation of pioneers and party apparatchiks, mocked Abba Eban behind his back.

"Our strategy must be logical," General Rabin said. "If diplomacy succeeds and the Arabs stand down, then all is well. But if diplomacy fails, we'll have to disable the Egyptian fighter jets and bombers before they mobilize. If we achieve air superiority, then we can destroy their armored forces in Sinai and turn to Syria."

"If. If. If." The prime minister took off his eyeglasses and made like he was throwing them away. "If we had enough locusts! Or frogs! Or if we could turn their rivers to blood, or kill their firstborn, ah?"

"Those would work too." Rabin drew from his cigarette. "But whether or not we can fend off Egypt and Syria, Jordan is the wildcard. If the king orders an attack, fifty thousand Jews will die in West Jerusalem, and Jordanian forces in the West Bank will roll across the coastal strip and slash Israel in half."

Elie was impressed with Rabin's ability to offer a clear analysis that solidified a consensus in the room. The soft-spoken Chief of Staff was cleverer than his boyish appearance implied—no less a politician than a soldier. He raised his hand. "The Armistice

Agreements forbid military activity in West Jerusalem, but we can mobilize civilians to dig trenches as shelters."

General Rabin nodded. "Trenches are defensive in nature. Very clever. But who's going to dig?"

"The ultra-Orthodox."

Everyone burst out laughing.

Elie lit a Lucky Strike and took a deep draw, waiting for the laughter to die down.

"Do you really think," Rabin asked, "that the black hats would come out of their synagogues and yeshivas to dig trenches?"

"They avoid military service because they object to Zionism, but they'll pick up a shovel to keep the Arabs out of West Jerusalem."

"Why?"

"Because they remember 'forty-eight. Many of them saw with their own eyes what happened when the Jordanians captured the Jewish Quarter of the Old City—the burning of Torah scrolls, the raping of girls, the indiscriminate killing of defenseless Jews." Elie drew from the cigarette again, letting them digest what he'd said.

"Okay," Rabin finally said. "There's no harm in trying."

Abba Eban returned, carrying a cup of tea. The discussion turned to diplomatic efforts to obtain a U.S. promise to honor its 1956 guarantee to punish Egypt if it attacked Israel. Eban explained that President Johnson was already overwhelmed by losses in Vietnam. Prime Minister Eshkol was unmoved, insisting that only an American declaration would prevent war—and Israel's demise.

As everyone was leaving, an aide asked Elie to join the prime minister in his car for a moment.

Elie sat on the jump seat, facing him.

"Excellent meeting, right?"

"Yes," he said, though he didn't think so.

"My job is to prevent war. But these sabra hotheads want to use their toys, conquer and pillage like King David. They're children who dream childish dreams!"

"They beat the Arabs before."

"But not the Soviet Union. What chance do we have?" Eshkol formed a circle with his finger and thumb.

"Soviet weapons and a few thousand advisors, but the commanders and soldiers are Arabs, and Rabin seems confident—"

"Yitzhak Rabin is a nice boy." Eshkol made a dismissive gesture. "A *schmendrik*, that's what he is. I'm not worried about him. He'll follow my orders. My problem is Moshe Dayan. He's a warmonger, strutting around with the fancy eye patch. Who's ever heard of a Jewish pirate?"

Elie touched the scabs over his burns. "My agents are combing his past. I'll let you know as soon as we find something useful."

Chapter 30

For several weeks, Tanya seldom left her house. She spent day and night listening to UN communications. The European and Indian officers spoke primarily English in varying accents. She was especially attuned to any mention of the UN radar at Government House. Formerly the seat of the British High Commissionaire, in 1948 Government House had become the UN Middle East headquarters. It occupied a high ridge that controlled the southern approaches to Jerusalem as well as the road to Bethlehem and Hebron. It was the highest vantage point in the region, and her equipment tapped into its wireless radio channels and its physical phone lines. Finally, on a morning that brought blooming scents of early spring through her window, Tanya heard a revealing conversation. She wrote down the exchange, switched the equipment to automatic recording, and left the house.

At the IDF command in West Jerusalem, she was taken straight into the office of Brigadier General Tappuzi, military commander of the city.

He looked up. "Good or bad?"

"They'll open the gates to Jordanian troops as soon as war begins, no matter who started it."

"And the radar?"

"Goes with the territory."

"*Damn!*"

"There's more," she said. "Bull allowed them to bring anti-aircraft batteries up to the ridge, just outside the UN compound."

Tappuzi called a group of officers into the room. They congregated around a map. It quickly became clear that only a massive Israeli air strike at the outset of war could prevent the Jordanian artillery from turning Jewish West Jerusalem into a deathtrap. But with the UN radar and Jordanian anti-aircraft guns working in sync, IDF aerial activities anywhere near Jerusalem would be suicidal.

Tappuzi accompanied Tanya outside. "We have to destroy that radar."

"You want to attack the UN Mideast Headquarter?"

"What choice do we have?"

"The diplomatic consequences would be catastrophic."

"Not as catastrophic as Jordanian carpet bombing of West Jerusalem!"

"A lot worse," Tanya said. "Attacking the UN will make us an international pariah. We'll lose any support, any chance for armaments or parts for our jets and tanks. The world will install a complete embargo on Israel—no flights, no shipping, no imports of food and oil—"

"Okay. Okay." He raised his hands. "I got it. No attack on Government House. Fine. But you must find another solution for that radar. I won't sit still and wait for Jordan to massacre our people!"

The unusually hot spring day made Elie sweat under the beggar's cloak. The burns on his cheek and neck had almost healed, the scabs dry and peeling off. But the new skin was still red and tender against the rough cloth.

A book landed in his lap. He glanced up and saw Abraham enter the public urinal. The door let out a whiff of stench.

Elie opened *The Zohar* and leaned over it so that his cloak sheltered it from the eyes of men entering and leaving the foul place. There was no note inside the book. He stuck an envelope between the pages. It contained cash and a note describing the planned recruitment of ultra-Orthodox residents of Jerusalem, including Neturay Karta, to dig trenches in the streets. Abraham was to enlist his own men, as well as convince other rabbis to have their followers join the life-saving effort. The new Office of Civil Defense, which Elie had set up at the IDF command in West Jerusalem, would hand out shovels and city maps showing them where to dig.

Abraham exited the restroom, but rather than pick up the book from Elie's lap, he walked away. Elie got up and followed him at a distance. Exiting through the long passage onto King George Street, they merged with the midday pedestrian traffic. Farther down the street, Abraham entered an old building. Elie did the same.

The unlit landing was barely enough for them to stand, facing one another beside a rusted stairway railing, which served as an anchor for a dusty bicycle, chained together.

"I decided to quit," Abraham said. "Immediately. I'm done!"

Elie pulled out a pack of Lucky Strike and tore off the cellophane wrapping. This development was not completely unexpected. Abraham's rebelliousness had occasionally reared its head over the years, requiring careful manipulation by pressing the correct buttons of grief and guilt, grandiosity and gullibility, which still dominated this powerful-yet-vulnerable man. "What about your fiery disciples?"

"Neturay Karta won't cause any trouble. I've ruled that they must study and pray to make the world better, never attack another Jew. My work is done."

"Until the next instigation causes them to riot? To throw rocks at innocent people?"

"That's your problem. I'm quitting."

"You can't quit. You're a spy. A mole. A non-believer among the believers. It'll take years to find someone like you."

"I don't have years. My wife will wither and die before summer."

"Now isn't the time for faintheartedness." He pointed with his cigarette at the book. "Look inside."

Abraham took out the note and read it by the light from the entrance, where pedestrian traffic kept flowing by. "You think a few trenches will protect us from the Jordanian cannons?"

"A few? We'll dig up every street and save thousands of lives."
Elie waited a moment to let the image sink in. "Don't shirk your
duty. Israel needs you. Your people need you."

Stuffing the envelope inside his coat pocket, Abraham looked
down at Elie. "My wife cannot live without our son, and our son
cannot live among Neturay Karta. And I cannot let her suffer
like this. She's a good woman."

"Didn't you tell me that you wanted to leave her for Tanya?"

He didn't answer.

"You're a secret agent in a crucial post. You made a
commitment!"

"Twenty years ago, after you made me believe that Tanya was
dead."

"I told you what I found in the forest. It was true. You drew
the conclusion."

"Enough with the lies! I had nothing to live for in 1945, so
I agreed to dedicate my life to this job. But I cannot sacrifice
my wife's life. It's not mine to sacrifice. And my son should not
be an orphan while his parents are alive. He hasn't replied to
Temimah's letters. It's up to me to fix the situation. I'm a father
and a husband—that's my duty now!"

"How noble." Elie tried to control his anger. "And what about
your duty to our nation?"

"Cantor Toiterlich can lead the sect for a few years until
Benjamin Mashash, my son's study companion, is ready. Neturay
Karta will remain peaceful after I leave, I assure you."

"You have to wait until after the crisis. Two, maybe three
months."

Abraham nodded.

Satisfied, Elie leaned on a bicycle handlebar. A brief delay
was all he needed. Soon, Abraham would have no reason to leave
Neturay Karta. "We'll have to plan carefully. The departure of
Rabbi Abraham Gerster could raise suspicion."

"I'll tell them that God spoke to me, told me to go and live
among the sinners in order to bring them back to His grace.
Then I'll find a tolerant community, where Lemmy can live with
us while pursuing his own aspirations—religious or not." He
paused. "Do you know where he's serving?"

"Not a clue." Elie raised a hand as if taking an oath. "Tanya made me swear to stay away from your son."

"He must be very angry with me. It was a terrible spectacle."

"I heard he shot down the chandelier."

"He didn't mean to. The bullet hit the hook, broke it off the ceiling. A fluke." Abraham chuckled sadly. "Our very own *Kristallnacht.*"

Chapter 31

After several months of intense training, the time came for the first of three dives, which were required to earn the paratrooper pin. Lemmy's company hiked all night, arriving with first light at an air force base somewhere in the Negev Desert. They spent the day cleaning their weapons, arranging their gear, and memorizing topographical maps.

As the sun was setting, they strapped on the parachutes and boarded the plane, whose tail was marked with a blue Star of David. It accelerated down the runway, and the two engines snarled as the plane detached from the ground and gained altitude, heading west into the sunset.

The soldiers sat on metal benches along the fuselage, their Uzis loaded and secure, their pouches stuffed with ammunition, and their parachutes strapped on snugly. Lemmy sat sideways and peered out through the small window. Sunsets reminded him of Fridays in Meah Shearim. A white tablecloth. Burning candles. *What do you know tonight that you didn't know this morning?*

But now Benjamin alone was there to answer the questions at the Sabbath table, to debate the subtleties of Talmud between dishes, and to recite the blessing after the meal. Life in Neturay Karta had continued to exist, a parallel universe of worship and study, of Sabbath meals and strict observance of myriad rules. But Lemmy was no longer part of it. For them, he was dead.

His eyes caught a herd of mountain goats, like white shadows in the twilight, fleeing into a ravine, frightened by the roar of the plane. He tried not to think of the initial drop and freefall, the immense height, and the speed at which he would hit the ground should his parachute fail to open. Instead he thought of the navigation challenges that awaited him once he was safely on the ground.

Their training had been put on a tight schedule in order to prepare them for a fighting role. The consecutive drills left little time for sleep and even less time for reflection. Like his fellow soldiers, Lemmy lived out of a military duffel bag that contained everything he owned—his uniform, folded and pressed, his only set of civilian clothes, and Uri Zvi Greenberg's *Book of Denunciation and Faith*. His proudest possession was a wooden box containing his father's Mauser. He also had a black yarmulke, which he hadn't put on since leaving Meah Shearim.

His friends knew he came from an ultra-Orthodox family that had banished him, but they never pried into his past. With endless grueling exercises across the Negev Desert, soldiers judged each other on integrity and teamwork. The outside world of family, money, or education was irrelevant, and Lemmy had won their trust.

"Get ready!" Captain Zigelnick's stocky figure appeared in the glow from the cockpit.

The red light above the door came on. Two minutes to destination.

Lemmy was first in line. He clipped the automatic-release strap to the metal wire that ran along the ceiling. If the canopy failed to open, he would use the emergency strap for manual opening in midair.

Captain Zigelnick walked down the aisle between the two opposite rows of soldiers, his hand moving along the metal wire, verifying that everyone's release strap was properly attached. The inside of the plane was dark. The soldiers were quiet, their faces tense. It would be their first time leaping from a speeding plane, followed by a night of solitary navigation through the desert.

When he reached Lemmy, the captain patted his shoulder. "Nervous, Gerster?"

"No," he lied, reaching up to unclip the strap from the wire. "I don't need this."

The light above the door made the captain's face red, adding mischief to his grin. "Count to three, then pull the strap."

"Yes, sir!"

A minute later, the red light turned yellow. When the light turned green, they would jump in twenty-second intervals, which meant a half a mile between each soldier. After landing, he would be on his own. They had memorized individual routes through dry streams and over rocky hills. Like a nighttime treasure hunt, each soldier had to find and jot down codes painted on rocks at various destination points and reach the gathering spot by dawn.

Lemmy shut his eyes and imagined the topographic map he had memorized. He recalled the desert paths that served deer in search of water, the *wadis*—dry streams—that were always at risk of flash floods, the sharp-edged palisades that spiked along the rolling dunes. For a good navigator, the maps gave rich information in shades of brown and green that told of the forms taken by the earth. Lemmy's Talmudic mind, trained to digest complex facts and weigh conflicting scenarios, found it easy to interpret the map, visualize the three-dimensional landscape, and memorize the details of his route. The rest depended on his stamina.

The green light went on. Zigelnick pushed open the door, and wind whirled into the plane. Lemmy shut his eyes, leapt into the darkness, and immediately regretted it. The wind grabbed his body and tossed him like a piece of paper. A moment later his fall stabilized somewhat as the colossal magnet of the earth pulled him downward with relentless force. The acceleration screamed in his ears. The pressure grew in his chest as his guts rose to his throat. He searched blindly for the release strap, his mind intoxicated by the thrill of free fall. A voice inside his head counted, *Twenty-one. Twenty-two. Twenty-three. Twenty-four.*

He reached farther down for the strap.

His hand grabbed empty air.

Grabbed again.

Nothing!

Elie Weiss examined the photograph closely. The woman was smiling. A lock of light hair dropped nonchalantly across her forehead. Moshe Dayan, in uniform, stood behind her, his hands on her hips. They were looking up, possibly at a bird or a plane. Behind them was Dayan's staff car and in the background, a sandy beach and a cluster of buildings. The date on the back of the photo placed it about a year before Dayan retired from the IDF.

"Bella Leibowitz," Agent Yosh said. "Her husband was Lieutenant Colonel Gabriel Leibowitz. He was found dead in their apartment, his service Uzi set on automatic. The place was quite a mess. She discovered the body and called Dayan, who was then chief of staff. He sent army medics to clean up. It was ruled an accident, but there were rumors."

Elie touched the photo. "Did he leave a note?"

"None was found."

"She probably destroyed it." Having run out of cigarettes, Elie took one from his agent's pack—Royal, a filter brand. He lit it and, taking a draw, twisted his face in disgust. "Any evidence? Letters? Witnesses?"

The agent examined his notes. "Her neighbor said Dayan had visited her whenever the husband was away. Dayan stayed for an hour or two while his driver waited in the car. It went on for a few months but ended when the husband died. His mother made a scene at the funeral, but it was all hushed up."

"We need more evidence," Elie said.

The other agent, Dor, pointed to a photo of Dayan holding a ceramic object.

"What's this?" Elie looked closely. "A cow?"

"A wine jar shaped like a bull." Dor pointed to the eyes and ears. "Wine pours out of the mouth. It's at least three thousand years old. Biblical." He took out another photo, showing an outdoor collection of antique jars, tapestries, small fountains, and tools. "Dayan's backyard garden. It's full of these. Worth millions."

"So?"

"Ancient artifacts must be handed over to the Antiques Authority." Dor pulled another photo, showing General Dayan standing near a gaping hole in a hillside with a group of young soldiers holding shovels. "And Dayan regularly used military personnel and vehicles on his private digging expeditions."

"It's a good start." Elie collected the photos. "Keep digging."

The speed of descent was beyond anything Lemmy had expected. The voice in his head kept counting. *Twenty-five. Twenty-six.*

He had to find the strap and pull, or in a few more seconds he would hit the ground and die.

Twenty-seven.

He felt the strap on the tip of his fingers. Then it was gone again.

Twenty-eight.

It touched his palm, and he clasped it, pulling hard.

Nothing happened.

Twenty-nine.

Crack! The canopy popped open, and the straps yanked his shoulders. The howling wind suddenly quieted, and he was swaying in midair, surrounded by silent darkness. The plane's buzzing sound faded into the night. He looked down, trying to estimate the distance to the ground. It was too dark.

The rocks appeared suddenly, leaving him little time to bend his legs, double over, and roll.

Everything hurt, but he managed to move all his limbs. He unstrapped the parachute, folded the canopy, and stuffed it into a backpack.

The skyline separated the starry sky from the hills. He recalled the map, visualizing the topography. From his landing point he was supposed to see a wadi ascending north, with steep rocks forming the right bank and more shallow, round hills on the left. He looked at his compass. The tiny arm glowed with yellow phosphorus, pointing north. He followed the skyline and exhaled in relief, recognizing the formation he had memorized back at the base.

He made sure the Uzi was loaded and the safety latch secured. The Egyptian border was only a few miles south, a porous line often crossed by Palestinian terrorists heading for the Israeli farming communities in the Negev Desert. Their attacks had intensified recently. Only a few days earlier Lemmy had read in *Ha'aretz* that Egyptian president Gamal Abdul Nasser had ordered his generals to transfer all remaining Egyptian forces from Yemen, where they had taken part in a bloody civil war, to the Sinai Peninsula, declaring: *The Arab nation is ready to remove the last foothold of imperialism from our land.* PLO leader Ahmad Shuqairi had told reporters at his headquarters in Gaza: *Very soon the Jews will be repatriated to the countries they came from, but I estimate that none of them will survive the war.*

The thought crossed Lemmy's mind that PLO infiltrators might be lurking in the darkness, ready to welcome him with a burst of automatic fire. He pushed the thought away and focused on the task ahead. With a strip of cloth tied around his head to keep the sweat from his eyes, Lemmy ran up the narrow wadi, his boots stomping the rocks. He counted his steps to measure the distance. After two thousand steps, he held up his compass and searched the skyline, finding the boulder at the top of the hill on the right—a massive rock, wide and flat, reminiscent of the boulder his father had mounted every Friday to pray in view of Temple Mount.

Once on top of the boulder, he cupped his flashlight with his hand and turned it on. The series of letters and numbers had been painted on the boulder in black, and he copied them down on a piece of paper. He shoved everything back into his pouch, leaped off the boulder, and ran.

By the third target, Lemmy's feet ached, his leg muscles burned, and his shoulders grew sore from the heavy backpack. The landscape had flattened, the skyline harder to decipher. He looked at his watch. He was making good time, but one erroneous turn and his advantage would disappear. He closed his eyes and concentrated, imagining the path ahead: Down a moderate slope at exactly thirty-seven degrees from the north, turn right and head east into a wide valley. He adjusted the strap of the Uzi and shifted the backpack slightly higher.

At the bottom of the hill he turned right. His throat was dry and his shirt was wet with sweat. But he kept going, determined to reach the final destination before anyone else. The army had become his new home, his new family. He hoped to be chosen for officers' training and pursue a military career like Captain Zigelnick.

A wide valley should open before him any minute now. He had not been able to tell from the map whether the valley would be bare or cultivated. Such valleys had rich alluvial soil, and farmers from the kibbutzim traveled hours on their tractors to farm every piece of fertile land.

Lemmy sprinted across the field, happy to gain some distance at high speed, but his boot hit a hard object, and he fell. The packed parachute landed on his head, pushing his face into the dirt. He cursed, rolled over, and spat out the sand.

When he realized what had tripped him, his anger turned to joy. He lifted the watermelon with both hands and let go. It dropped and split open. A second later, his teeth sunk deep into the juicy, sweet flesh. It filled his mouth, dripping on his chin and onto his shirt.

Earlier that year, Israel had opened the largest manmade waterway in the Middle East, connecting Lake Kinneret in the Galilee to the Negev Desert through open canals and underground pipes. The immense project had been the brainchild of Prime Minister Levi Eshkol, whose dedication speech predicted: *This waterway will transform our barren land into fertile soil, like blood flowing in countless arteries to every part of the human body.*

The Syrians responded with efforts to divert the Yarmuch River, intending to dry up Lake Kinneret. When diplomatic mediation proved futile, Israeli fighter jets destroyed the Syrian dams. Lemmy thanked the anonymous IDF pilots whose attack had kept the water flowing south to nourish this watermelon field.

He was chewing on the last piece when rocks tumbled from a nearby hillside. He placed the watermelon on the ground, rubbed his sticky hands against his pants, and reached for the Uzi.

A man's silhouette appeared against the starry sky.

Lemmy pressed the Uzi to the inside of his forearm, aimed at the figure, and threaded his forefinger into the trigger slot.

A watermelon burst open.

Lemmy's forefinger eased out of the trigger slot. He picked up a piece of watermelon skin and tossed it.

A cry came in response, and an Uzi was cocked.

"Don't shoot," Lemmy yelled, laughing.

"Gerster! I'll kill you!" It was Ronen, who had jumped from the plane right after Lemmy.

"Chill out. And let me help you with this watermelon."

"Steal your own watermelon!"

"I already did. They're so good." Lemmy strapped on his backpack and shouldered the Uzi. "How many targets have you found?"

"Only two. The first was real close, but I got lost, had to go back and start over."

"Don't shoot anyone unless they speak Arabic." Lemmy started running, and a piece of watermelon chased him.

Chapter 32

The IDF lent Elie Weiss four reservist officers to assist him in setting up the Civic Defense operation. They put up a tent near the entrance to the IDF command center and posted signs in Hebrew and Yiddish. It was Passover Eve, and large numbers of Orthodox men showed up to volunteer. He watched with satisfaction as they arrived by foot or by bus, chattering in Yiddish as they queued up to register. The stories of Arab atrocities in the Old City in 1948 had been told and retold over the intervening two decades, and now the Jews of Jerusalem seemed determined to prevent a repeat.

Per Elie's instructions, each volunteer had to present a form of identification and provide the names of their community, yeshiva, and rabbi. For Elie's Special Operations Department, this was a treasure trove of new information, to be added to the existing files. He estimated that the next few days would double his already vast database of potential religious agitators who were hostile to secular Zionism.

Many of the black hats mentioned Rabbi Abraham Gerster's proclamation, which had been printed and plastered on walls all over West Jerusalem: *The duty to guard Jerusalem supersedes the duty to study Talmud until the evil forces of the Muhammadians have been repelled from our sacred city.* Such words from the leader of Neturay Karta—the most virulent anti-Zionist sect in Jerusalem—left all the other rabbis no choice but to permit their followers to volunteer for the trench-digging effort.

The reservists at the makeshift desk took down the information, handed out the shovels, and sent the volunteers to dig trenches near their homes, not only for their convenience, but to create a closer association between the physical work, which they were unaccustomed to, and their own families' safety.

Shortly before noon, Elie noticed Tanya Galinski arrive at the building. She wore a light-blue dress, and her hair was gathered under a khaki cap. Elie followed her inside.

The office of Brigadier General Tappuzi was filled with officers, who congregated around a map of the city. Elie poured himself lukewarm coffee in a paper cup and stood in the back, listening.

"I have some bad news," Tanya said. "General Bull has allowed the Jordanians to run cables from their anti-aircraft batteries to the UN radar station. There was some talk about safe passage for UN personnel to the airport in Amman, where General Bull's private plane is kept."

"There you have it," Tappuzi said. "If we don't disable that radar, Jerusalem is lost!"

"Not if the front remains quiet," Tanya said. "We're still hoping to avoid war or at least keep Jordan out of it."

While they argued, Elie elbowed his way between the uniformed men and looked closely at the map. He found Government House on a ridge south of the city, controlling both parts of Jerusalem while guarding the roads to the southern half of the West Bank and east to Jericho and the Jordan River.

Tappuzi fingered the point on the map. "I'd like to get over there and blow up the radar, but there's the Armistice Line, the Jordanian bunkers and patrols, the UN observers, the fences and landmines around Government House—"

"Getting caught by the UN," Tanya said, "will make Israel look like the aggressor and destroy any chance of obtaining American and French support.."

"And in the hands of the Jordanians?" Tappuzi passed a finger under his throat. "Immediate execution!"

One of the officers said, "How about destroying the radar with artillery shells in the first moments of the war? We could later claim it was a mistake, a misfire, or something."

A major in olive drabs and a large mustache said, "I don't have precision artillery for something like this. The radar operates on Antenna Hill in the rear of the compound, protected by sandbags and concrete. It would take a lengthy barrage to do real damage, and I'll probably hit the main building multiple times, kill a couple of hundred UN observers, and so on."

"Forget it," Brigadier General Tappuzi said. "The only option would be an attack from the air, which can't be done until the radar is disabled, It's the chicken and egg thing."

"Same with the Jordanian anti-aircraft batteries," the artillery major said. "Their bunkers are vulnerable only to surprise attack from the air, but our planes would be detected by the radar and shot down."

Elie had heard enough to outline an operation in his mind that would save Jerusalem from Jordanian bombing *and* allow him to pluck Abraham's son from the paratroopers' corps. But a room full of loudmouthed sabra officers wasn't the right forum. He would approach Tappuzi in private.

Lemmy reached the final destination in the early morning, finding Captain Zigelnick and a driver roasting potatoes by a campfire. He showed Zigelnick the codes he had jotted down at each of his destination points, which the captain compared to a list. They were correct.

Sanani showed up almost an hour later and cursed at the sight of Lemmy chewing on a piece of potato skin. His dark face shone with sweat as he dropped to the ground, panting. "I'm going to beat you next time, Gerster!"

"Good luck," Lemmy said.

The rest of the soldiers trickled in, handed in their lists of scribbled codes, and unloaded their gear while sharing experiences with the others. Meanwhile, the surrounding yellow dunes began to heat up under the morning sun.

Captain Zigelnick beckoned Lemmy. He was only a couple of years older than his trainees, but his rank and seniority made him seem like an adult. "Training is almost over. You feel ready for battle?"

Lemmy realized his commander wasn't joking. He was talking of a real battle, with Arabs shooting to kill, with blood and death all around, like the war stories Lemmy had read in Tanya's books. "I'm ready," he said. "We'll beat them back and then some."

Zigelnick smiled. "That's the spirit. Just remember, you don't have to prove anything to anybody."

"Prove?"

"Your father is a famous man."

Lemmy felt his face blush. How did Zigelnick find out? Pretending to watch the other soldiers load the gear into the canvas-covered back of the truck, he regained his composure. "He's not my father anymore."

Captain Zigelnick's forehead creased.

"I'm dead to him."

"Then you don't have a reason to die again." Zigelnick patted his shoulder. "I don't care about your father. He can go on preaching nonsense. But I don't want to see you showing off when bullets start flying. Understood?"

"Yes, sir."

Once the truck was loaded, Zigelnick jumped in the cabin next to the driver, and they began the long drive back to the camp in the hills south of Beersheba. Lemmy sat with the rest of the soldiers in the back of the truck, surrounded by piles of gear and backpacks.

As always, Sanani was the center of attention, drawing on his endless fountain of jokes. "Do you know why the black hats grow long payos?" Sanani paused for a moment then answered his own query. "So that when they walk down the street and see a sexy woman, they can cover their eyes with the payos but still see her tits through the hairs."

The roaring laughter was louder than the constant humming of the truck.

"And why do they wear black hats and black coats?" Sanani looked around. "Because it makes them invisible when they prowl the parks at night to find a whore."

Lemmy said, "Sanani could just go naked," which caused even more laughter.

"And do you know why the Orthodox don't turn on the lights on Friday nights?"

"Because they're cheap," suggested someone, to the cheers of the others.

"Also," Sanani declared, "because they rather not see their ugly wives coming to bed!"

The soldiers booed. They despised the Orthodox for refusing to serve in the IDF and defend Israel like everybody else.

"And why don't they take off the black coats even during the hot summer?"

Someone shouted from the other end, "Because they like to stink!"

"Because they can't take it off. It's stuck!"

The soldiers mimicked vomiting.

Sanani's teeth showed against his dark skin. "And why do they pile shit in the corners of a black hat wedding-hall?"

No one had an answer to that.

"To keep the flies away from the bride!"

When the laughter calmed down, Lemmy said, "You're wrong. That smelly brown stuff in the corner isn't shit. It's a bunch of Yemenite relatives!"

Sanani laughed with everybody else, taking no offense.

The soldiers were chronically sleep-deprived, and soon everyone was out. But Lemmy couldn't sleep. This Passover would be the first holiday away from his parents. He thought of the intense preparations in Neturay Karta, the cleaning of apartments and scrubbing of pots and pans. Under his father's supervision, every dish and tableware was dipped in the water of the mikvah to cleanse them of all remnants of bread or other leavened food. Bottles of wine and boxes of matzo were distributed to needy Neturay Karta families, and the women spent three days cooking for the Seder dinner. Lemmy thought of last year's Passover, the room full of guests, singing praiseful melodies from the *Hagadah* of the Israelites' exodus from Egyptian slavery. Would they miss him this year? Or next year? Would his parents ever forgive him, or agree to see him again? He imagined walking into Meah Shearim one day, many years ahead, dressed in his IDF general's uniform, an Uzi slung from his shoulder. He would enter the synagogue, wearing a military cap rather than a black hat, and face Father, whose beard would be white, his back bent with years. And then what? A handshake? A hug? Or a cold shoulder?

The truck traveled along a dirt road, raising a storm of dust. When it slowed down to cross a dry stream, a dust cloud caught up, filling the back of the truck and covering his friends' faces with a ghost-like white layer.

Chapter 33

The day after Passover, Elie Weiss boarded a Swissair flight to Zurich. The plane was packed with well-to-do Israeli families fleeing the country—a recent phenomenon that demonstrated new cracks in the idealistic spirit that had typified most Israelis until the Eshkol government began to fumble indecisively while the Arabs prepared to attack. The children were oblivious to the tension, marveling at the airplane and its accoutrements, but the adults furtively glanced at each other in a camaraderie of shame.

Elie kept on his wool cap and sunglasses. He was travelling under the name of Rupert Danzig, a junior SS officer, who in January 1945 was raping a woman at her kitchen in a village near Munich while his comrades ransacked the house. Abraham pulled Danzig off the woman and held him while Elie clipped his vocal cords with a quick stab. They prodded him out the back door and deep into the forest, where they tied him to a tree, his pants still down at his knees.

Danzig eagerly answered Elie's questions by nodding or shaking his head while air gurgled through his perforated vocal cords. With the war about to end, Danzig had planned to don civilian clothes and avoid capture by the approaching American forces. That explained the passport and cash in his pocket. After removing his identification tags, papers, and uniform, Elie used his *shoykhet* blade to peel off the rest of the Nazi's identity. When he finished, Danzig had no face, only a mask of raw flesh, bare jaws exposing a perfect set of teeth, and lidless eyes glaring downward at the puddle of blood on the soft carpet of pine needles.

Since the war, Elie had maintained bank accounts and a tiny apartment in Paris under Rupert Danzig's identity. He travelled to Europe often to continue his private hunt for SS veterans. The years had thinned out their ranks, but had also lowered their guard. He used them as cash cows, making them pay for their past sins and current freedom, making them work hard for money he then used to finance his SOD operations in Israel and Europe. And those who refused to pay, or ran out of money, were found dead. In most cases, no one ever detected the surgical entry point under the right ear, where Elie's blade had severed the brainstem without external bleeding.

But this trip was different. By gaining control of the fortune Tanya's Nazi lover had stashed in Zurich, Elie would no longer have to chase the aging small fish. Rather, he would put his energy into a revolutionary reversal of the global balance of power between the Jews and their enemies.

When the plane leveled off over the Mediterranean, Elie unzipped his leather briefcase and took out a bunch of envelopes held together with a rubber band. He had arranged with the IDF postmaster to stop all mail addressed to, or from, Private Jerusalem Gerster. Checking the stamps on the envelopes, Elie opened Temimah Gerster's first letter, dated approximately six weeks earlier:

> *My dearest Jerusalem,*
> *Your father gave me the address in the Zionist army and allowed me to write to you. With God's help, after many weeks, I am recovering from the terrible shock. What you did is still incomprehensible to me. I know that young men sometimes desire to assert their independence, to rebel against authority. But why did you have to go to such extremes? And why didn't you speak with us first, before stripping yourself of all that distinguishes a God-fearing member of our community? You defied your father, rejected our whole way of life, and broke God's laws. I cannot understand it. I pray that you realize your error soon. I beg of you, my son, to think of what you have done. I plead and implore you*

to repent. It's not too late—as the Talmud says, 'He who repents and corrects his ways shall be treated with compassion.' God will show you the way when you are ready to see it. Meanwhile, make sure to eat and sleep well, and say your prayers. I ask God every day for your safe return to us. May the Master of the Universe watch over you, my son. Please write back.

Your loving mother,
Temimah Gerster.

The stamp on the second envelope was from about a week later. The letter inside was written on the same type of paper, and with the same blue pen, as the first letter:

My dearest Jerusalem,
You haven't responded to my previous letter. Perhaps you are away on military drills. Today is Thursday, and I went out of the apartment for the first time since that terrible day, when your father, in his understandable anger, excommunicated you. Everyone was very happy to see me at the synagogue, and most of the donated clothes are gone. I asked Benjamin to take the rest to Shmattas to be exchanged, and he did it well. He also misses you very much and prays for your return. Please write a few words to let us know how you are. Your father agreed that you may come home to celebrate Passover with us, provided that you respect God's laws while under out roof. Please, I beg you to come, even if you have to go back to the army after the holiday. Maybe you don't understand what it means for me to think of sitting at the Passover table without you. When you have a child one day, God willing, you will understand my agony. So please come home for Passover. I pray for your safe return.

Your loving mother,
Temimah Gerster.

Elie folded the letter and slipped it back into its envelope. He read the next one, and the next, until he had read all six of them. With each successive letter, her tone grew more anxious, her pleas more urgent, especially with the approaching holiday. In the last letter, under his wife's signature, Abraham had added:

Jerusalem,
   Please respond to your mother, whose heart is broken. Cruelty
is the gravest sin, while forgiveness is the finest virtue.
   Your father,
   Rabbi Abraham Gerster.

Elie wondered what would have happened if the boy had received these letters. Would Lemmy have gone home for Passover? It was a question that would never be answered. Both Abraham and his son had their separate roles to play in the historic struggle for Jewish survival, and Elie was determined to prevent any reconciliation between them. As to the mother's grief, it was unfortunate. Collateral damage. But she would get over it soon. In the grand scheme of Jewish destiny, Elie could not afford to worry about Temimah Gerster's spoiled Passover plans.

The pilot announced that the plane would land in Zurich in three hours. Elie lowered his seatback and closed his eyes. The constant engine noise soon put him to sleep.

Tanya's phone rang near midnight on Saturday night. It was Lemmy, calling from a payphone at the central bus station. He had won a one-day leave at a sharp-shooting contest.

She drove Elie's small Citroën, which he had left with her yesterday before departing for Europe. Lemmy waited at the curb, carrying an Uzi and a duffel bag. She took him home, and they fell into bed without turning on the lights. He smelled of dust and sweat and grease. His embrace was forceful, and his hands on her skin felt coarse in a way she found incredibly arousing. He was tireless, his breathing not labored even as their lovemaking intensified, sending her again and again beyond the limits of her self-control.

Tanya woke up with first light. She used the fast-forward feature on the recording device to scan for any UN communications that had occurred overnight, finding only a few casual exchanges. She called Brigadier General Tappuzi to tell him there was no news.

Around noon, Lemmy appeared at her side in his khaki boxer shorts. "What a setup you have here! What is it for?" He touched a knob on one of the receivers.

She slapped his hand, not too hard, but enough to make him recoil and laugh.

Daylight afforded Tanya a good look at him. She was amazed by the transformation. He seemed taller, with a narrow waist and sculpted shoulders. His muscles bulged like those of a man who worked with his hands. "I'm wondering," she said, "where's my skinny Talmudic scholar?"

"He's gone. I'm all you've got."

"You'll have to do, then." She stood and kissed him, reaching up to caress his cropped hair. "I've arranged a room for you in Tel Aviv. At Bira's apartment. You can stay there during leaves from the army. It's a fun group, around your age. You'll be comfortable there."

"I'm comfortable here."

She traced the line of his jaw with her finger. "It's not safe here, not until things settle down. And you're better off with young people."

His blue eyes were hurt. "Who says?"

"I do." Tanya detached from him and went to the kitchen to make coffee. She had to ease him away, no matter how painful it was for her. It would be the height of hypocrisy to keep him hooked in a dead-end relationship after tearing him apart from Neturay Karta. She had to complete what she had started, set him free to experience a normal life, to date girls his age, to have fun like any other young secular Israeli, to pursue a career and eventually start a family with a woman who could give him a partnership of equals and a bunch of cute kids. "It won't be long," she said, "before you lose interest in me."

"How do you know?"

"There's no future for us together."

"Forget the future." He hugged her from behind. "Right now, it's really good."

Tanya poured coffee into two mugs. He was right, of course. It was more than "really good." Their night together was a hundred times better than the hesitant, tender love they had made during their brief time together, before he had joined the army. The experience was like a sudden, wild storm that tossed her back in time, not only in the sense of a physical joy, of reaching heights she had assumed herself too old to experience again, but also emotionally, an overwhelming sense of wholeness and completeness that must have been false considering the enormous gaps in age, life experience, and *realism*—a word better than *cynicism*—that she had acquired through witnessing true evil time and again. How could their bond be anything but an illusion, when Lemmy didn't know the evil she knew, when he didn't understand that the evil of Jew-demonizing and Jew-hating and Jew-killing was everywhere, that the evil which had robbed her youth and killed her family and put her life on a path of clandestine armed struggle, the evil that won again and again, the evil that was clever and resilient and unbeatable, the evil that hid behind inspiring ideologies, behind nationalism and fascism and communism and even humanism, that evil which spoke grammatically-correct French, German, English, or Arabic, was everywhere, yet unfamiliar to this boy-turned-man, who was embracing her and breathing in the scent of her hair as if it were life-supporting oxygen. How could Lemmy's love be true, when he didn't know what she knew, that Gentiles sipped the loathing of Jews with their mother's milk, goat milk, or coconut milk, that it flowed smoothly into their veins and hearts and minds with each shot of Rémy Martin under the Eiffel Tower, or a squirt of fig juice under a palm tree. The worlds she and Lemmy occupied weren't overlapping at all. And why should they? He lived in a world of optimistic youth and patriotic hopes, a world without an end, while she lived in a dark world, a world lurking with death, a world of kill or be killed—or better said, a world of kill, kill, kill, and eventually be killed for being a Jew.

By now, Tanya was crying silently, her face away from him, her hands holding the two coffee mugs, her shoulders shaking.

He kissed her earlobe, then her neck, not in passion but in the tenderness of those early explorations of last year, when he had still worn a black coat and a black hat and those golden, ringlet side locks. And as she leaned back into his arms and surrendered to his gentleness, the onslaught of her sorrow began to recede, and she stopped crying.

"You think too much," he said. "Don't over-analyze what we have. It feels good, so it must be good. Leave the hair-splitting to the Talmudic scholars."

The mugs safely on the table, she blew her nose and wiped her eyes. "I'm sorry. The last few months have been tough." She stopped there, not explaining further, not sharing with him the terror of a victim's *déjà vu*, of recognizing the rising ghosts from another war, gathering again, circling gleefully with the single goal of exterminating the Jewish people. It was Hitler all over again, only that his incarnation had taken the three-headed identity of Nasser, Assad, and King Hussein. They spoke Arabic instead of German. They propagated Pan Arabism instead of Nazism. But just like Hitler, their language and ideology was but a masquerade for their true aim. And among their chosen prey, among those they sought to murder, were the two people she truly and unconditionally loved. But unlike the Nazi Holocaust, which caught her as a budding and hapless young teen, this coming war would include her as a fighter. All her training and skills were now going to count in the struggle to prevent this war from following the Nazi Holocaust with an Arab Holocaust. And the fight would require her total commitment, all her physical and mental resources, as she would be fighting not on the front lines, but in the back alleys of Marseilles, or the power hallways of Paris, where armament, money, and military secrets could give Israel the upper hand in what seemed like an unavoidable calamity. And for her to win the secret battles under her command, Tanya had to regain the single-minded ferocity of a hunter who was simultaneously being hunted. She had to focus, to forget everything else, including the two souls that occupied her heart—Bira and Lemmy—a daughter she loved by force of motherhood and two decades of a perilous-yet-joyous life together, and a boy she loved by force of fate, or coincidence, or sheer stupidity and feminine weakness for which she had only herself to blame.

"Enough," he said as if reading her mind. "There's only here and now, okay?"

They held each other for a long moment.

Tanya breathed deeply. She rebuked herself silently for letting gloom and fear take over. Israel wasn't a Shtetl, or a ghetto, but a Jewish state with an army of dedicated men and women, ready to defend it. And she had a vital role in that effort. "My assignment here will end soon. I'll probably be sent back to Europe. This house might be empty or occupied by someone else when your next leave comes around."

"I've never been abroad. Can I visit you?"

There was no way she could see him in Europe. Mossad life didn't allow for casual visitors. To change the subject, she asked, "Have you received any letters from home?"

"Are you kidding?"

Tanya was surprised. Abraham had clearly said that his wife would write to Lemmy. "Your mother didn't write to you?"

"She probably forgot about me already."

"Don't be stupid!" Tanya immediately regretted her sharp tone. "There's nothing my daughter could do to make me forget her. Your mother will never—"

"What do you know about Neturay Karta?"

"I know how a mother feels."

"Not my mother. She feels what my father allows her to feel, which obviously can't include feelings for a banished son."

"That's not what—"

"I don't want to talk about it!" Lemmy put down his coffee and left the kitchen. She heard him enter the bathroom, and a moment later the water was running in the shower.

Elie Weiss had spent the night at the Pension Naurische, a small hotel run by an elderly couple near Zurich's train station. When he came downstairs, Frau Naurische handed him a thick envelope addressed to *Herr Danzig*. Taking his breakfast in the cozy lounge, Elie used a butter knife to open the seal.

One of his agents had collected background information on Armande Hoffgeitz. Technically it was a violation of Israeli law, which limited all overseas clandestine activities to Mossad. But

Elie had never considered his operations to be subjected to this or any other law. Only the best interest of the Jewish people counted.

He pulled out a manila folder, which contained approximately twenty black-and-white photographs. In the first photo, a family was seated on the deck of a sailboat, chewing on sausage sandwiches. The parents were pudgy, but the two children seemed athletic. The note on the back of the photo read: *Armande, wife Greta, daughter Paula, and son Klaus V.K. Hoffgeitz.*

Another photo showed a thin, tall man in a dark suit and a tie standing by a Rolls Royce. The note on the back read: *Günter Schnell, long-time assistant to Herr Hoffgeitz.* In the next photo, the family entered a church whose front was adorned with three stained glass windows that seemed familiar. The agent noted that the Hoffgeitz family regularly attended Sunday afternoon mass at the Fraumünster on the Limmat River, which apparently was opened to tourists in the morning hours.

As he walked to church through the streets of Zurich, Elie remembered walking with his father to the synagogue through the muddy roads of the shtetl, both of them in black coats and wide-brimmed hats. At the door of the synagogue, Rabbi Yakov Gerster greeted them with his son, Abraham. The rabbi asked how Elie had been progressing as an apprentice *shoykhet*, and while Elie's father bragged about his son's proficiency with the slaughter of livestock, Abraham scrunched his face in revulsion.

With this memory on his mind, Elie mounted the stone steps of the Fraumünster church and entered the cavernous space, which was braced by multiple cross-arches high above. The three aisles of the gothic basilica were lit by the rays of the sun, filtered through the stained glass windows. Less than a third of the pews were taken. The Hoffgeitz family sat up front. The organ played a thunderous tune, and the parishioners sang a hymn. He sat in the rear, far to the right. It was chilly, the damp air scented with candles. He hesitated before removing his wool cap, but he had no choice.

The pastor, in a black robe, signaled to the organ player, who picked up the pace, bringing it to a roaring climax. The organ was enormous in size, with hundreds, perhaps over a thousand pipes rising to different heights.

"This is a special day," the pastor began, his German spoken with a French accent. He pointed to the front of the choir room and the stained-glass windows. "Thanks to the generosity of our faithful and the divine gift of the inspired artist, we are blessed with the presence of prophets Elijah, Elisha, and Jeremiah."

This jolted Elie's memory. Months earlier he had read in a newspaper article criticizing the elderly Jewish artist Marc Chagall for accepting a lucrative commission to create biblical scenes for a Swiss church, including one of Jesus Christ, in whose name countless Jews had been murdered over the past centuries. Elie shifted in the pew to get a better look.

While Elijah was rising to heaven in a chariot of fire, Jeremiah hovered in a hazy blue cloud. The next stained window showed Moses looking down on the Israelites in the midst of battle. Jacob occupied the next, his ladder reaching for the sky while a seraph wrestled him to the ground. Elie almost laughed at the next scene, which had the walled city of Jerusalem descending from a yellowish sky while King David and Bathsheba looked on amorously.

The pastor, meanwhile, crossed over to the most striking depiction, a greenish-orange creation that starred Mary, Baby Jesus, a floating tree, a lamb, and the crucifixion, with an adult Jesus ascending to divine heights that required Elie to crane his neck to look at the top, near the ceiling, where their Messiah was finally free from his earthly suffering.

The pastor's sermon went on for a half-hour, extracting lessons of modesty and charity from the lives of Elijah, Elisha, and Jeremiah, concluding with Jesus. Elie watched the Hoffgeitz family, the mother nodding approvingly, the daughter glancing at her watch, and Herr Hoffgeitz's chin resting on his chest while he napped. The son, who was about twelve, seemed captivated by the colorful biblical scenes.

The service ended with another hymn. Elie put on his wool cap and moved to the shadow of a thick stone column. The Hoffgeitz family lingered to look up at the windows, while the pastor spoke animatedly, gesturing at each of the scenes. He paused when Herr Hoffgeitz spoke and leaned forward in deference.

Elie slipped outside and chose a discreet vantage point. A dark Rolls Royce glided into the plaza. The driver came around to open the door. *Günter.*

A rattling engine noise drew everyone's attention as a yellow VW minibus arrived, stopping behind the Rolls Royce. It was filled with teenagers with longish hair. The daughter jumped in, and only young Klaus waved at the departing VW, which left behind a smell of burnt oil. Across the rear of the minibus, a crudely painted serpent slithered between purple letters *LASN*, which Elie suspected stood for Lyceum Alpin St. Nicholas, the Swiss boarding school once attended by SS General Klaus von Koenig and Armande Hoffgeitz. It appeared that the prestigious boys' school had become coed.

Lemmy tied a towel around his waist and went to the living room. He felt at home among Tanya's books, the music from the wooden box of the radio, and Bira smiling from her photo on the wall. He found Ayn Rand's *The Fountainhead* and flipped through the pages, finding familiar passages.

When he put down the book, Lemmy noticed a cigarette lighter leaning against an empty ashtray. He picked it up, surprised by its heavy weight. With his thumb he opened the tiny cover and pressed. It worked. He thumbed the cover, extinguishing the flame. He could see the glint of silver under the greenish coat of aging.

Tanya entered the room, carrying two cups. "You didn't finish your coffee." She sat on the sofa. "I made you a fresh cup."

"I'm sorry for ending our conversation so abruptly."

"Apology accepted."

"No one can possibly understand Neturay Karta unless you've been part of it." He sat next to her and picked up the cigarette lighter. "Have you started smoking?"

She put down the cup, splashing hot coffee on the table. "Give it to me!"

He held it up, away from her, and pulled out the Mauser with his free hand. The long shining barrel lined up with the oxidized rectangle of the lighter. Both had the same engraved initials. "Who is *K.v.K.*?"

Elie crossed the Limmat River and headed back to the Pension Naurische. Sunday traffic was sparse. The tram rumbled by, throwing electric sparks from the overhead wires. On Bahnhofstrasse, near the entrance to the central train station, he bought the Sunday edition of the German-language daily *Neue Züricher Zeitung*. Farther down, he found a small café off the main road and sat at a round table outside, raising his collar against the early evening chill, and lit a cigarette.

The waitress noticed the Lucky Strike pack on the table and asked, "*Amerikaner?*"

"*Nein*," Elie said. "*Ich bin ein Berliner.*" It amused him to name another divided city when lying about where he lived. Before she could ask more questions, he ordered black coffee and *Erdbeertoertli*, a traditional Swiss dessert of strawberries and whipped cream in a pastry cup.

The front page carried a long article about a proposed ban on foreign-controlled banks in Switzerland. A headline on the second page reported that Mahmoud Riad, the Egyptian foreign minister, had gone to Jordan to negotiate a military pact with King Hussein. Until now, the young king was not receptive to the idea. But the events of April 7, almost three weeks earlier, had created a different mood. According to UN observers, Syrian cannons atop the Golan Heights had released a barrage of 247 shells on the Israeli farmers at Kibbutz Gadot on the shore of Lake Kinneret. The IDF air force sent a squadron to destroy the cannons, and the Syrians scrambled their planes into the air. In the ensuing dogfight across the clear sky over Damascus, Israeli Mirage jets shot down five Syrian MiGs. This intimidated the Jordanian leadership enough to support joining an Egyptian-led alliance against Israel.

Elie put down the paper and nibbled on the Erdbeertoertli, its crust practically melting on his tongue. The confetti strawberries were too sweet for his palate, and he washed it down with a bit of coffee. The steam rising from the coffee made him rub his neck, still tender after several months of healing. The news of an Arab joint command, dominated by the belligerent Nasser, was a realization of Israel's worst fears. Elie knew he had little time to waste. As soon as the Hoffgeitz Bank began transferring Klaus von Koenig's fortune to the accounts in Paris, he would return to Jerusalem.

"K.v.K. stands for Klaus von Koenig." Tanya looked away from the Mauser and the cigarette lighter, two personal objects Klaus had carried on him every day until his death. "He was in charge of budget and finance at the SS Central Command, reporting directly to Himmler."

"You knew him?"

"I lived with him."

Lemmy's face paled. "As a sex slave?"

"As a lover."

"You loved a Nazi?"

"I loved a man, a wonderful man, despite who he was, or *what* he was."

"I don't understand."

"It didn't start that way. I was only thirteen." Tanya closed her eyes, taking herself back to that horrifying day. "We arrived in the morning. My mother. My little sister, Edna. A train filled with Jews from Lindau, Germany, our hometown. My father had died a year earlier. He had always thought of himself as a German first and a Jew second. But when they burned down his bookstore, it just broke his heart. At least he didn't live to see us arrive at Dachau. Three days in a cattle car, no room to sit, no water, no toilet. No dignity. We were made to strip naked and line up by the doors to the showers, shivering from cold and fear. The doors opened. My mother and Edna were pushed in, but someone grabbed my arm and pulled me aside. I wanted to go with them, but my mother shook her head. She knew."

Tanya wiped her eyes. It had been a long time since she had allowed these memories to surface. She felt Lemmy's hand on her arm. "To this day I cannot remember my mother clothed. She's forever naked in my mind, holding Edna's hand as the steel doors were shut behind them. I know she was a beautiful woman, always dressed tastefully. I know it, but I cannot visualize her the way she had been before Dachau. I can't, and there are no photos left to remind me. It's as if our past, our nice little family life in Lindau, never existed." Tanya took a deep breath. "Anyway, there I was, standing with my hands over my breasts. It was so cold. I saw a tall man in a long coat and an officer's cap. The others looked like midgets around him. He took off his coat and draped it around me." Tanya rubbed her neck with her hand. "I can still feel the stiff collar chafing against my skin."

"And then?"

"I was lucky." She shrugged. "Not only to stay alive, but to be with Klaus."

"Lucky?"

"I was numb with grief, alone in the world, with no one to protect me. He could have used me and put me back in line, but he didn't. He took me to his home and nurtured me back to life like a precious bird with broken wings."

Lemmy's mouth was slightly open, his expression incredulous.

"You think I should have hated Klaus?"

He nodded.

"Because he was a monster, responsible for killing millions of innocent people, our people, right?"

"Yes."

"And you're correct. He was part of that evil machine. But with me he was someone else. He was a confident, impeccable man, who showed me only kindness and devotion. He was the first man I'd ever been with—as a woman. He was there for me, strong and caring, very patient and considerate. I know it sounds crazy, but I knew that he really loved me. I was his angel, and he was mine."

"But he was a Nazi!"

Tanya rolled a lock of her hair around her finger, as a girl would do. "If you were a young woman, perhaps you would understand. I was just becoming a woman then. My body and my emotional universe revolved around those feelings. Klaus von Koenig loved me, *really* loved me, like no one else before or after. He was a formidable man. Senior SS officers trembled before him. But with me he was different. He saved my life, but he treated me as if I saved his. There was nothing he wouldn't do for me, and I was happy with him, would have stayed with him even after the war, would have gone to Argentina and borne his children. I would have."

"Then why didn't you?"

"Because we were ambushed by two starved, half-frozen Jewish partisans, one of whom was your father."

Lemmy held up the gun. "That's how he got this Mauser?"

She nodded. "Abraham shot Klaus in the head just before dawn, on the first day of 1945. My seventeenth birthday."

"I didn't know my father was a partisan."

"War turns everyone into something else, often irreversibly. They had come from a shtetl, two Jewish boys, raised to take over their fathers' peaceful professions. The war transformed them into soldiers of *Nekamah*. Revenge. An eye for an eye."

Lemmy put down the Mauser. "So you went from the Nazi to my father?"

"Don't judge me." Her voice softened. "You should have seen Abraham when he was your age. Lean and strong, with blond hair and piercing blue eyes." She gestured at Lemmy. "You look like him. We could have built a life together, but the Germans were losing the war, and he was obsessed. *Nekamah. Nekamah. Nekamah.* I thought he would quit, but he didn't. He is that rare kind of a man—totally committed, but not to a person, not to a lover, not to an offspring, but to a higher cause." She choked with emotions that had long been suppressed. "And then we lost each other and have remained separated all these years. But I'm glad I found out Abraham was alive, because it led to our first encounter, remember?"

"How could I forget?" Lemmy touched her forehead where the bruise had long healed. He pulled her closer, and Tanya rested her cheek against his bare chest, smooth and taut over his hard muscles, scented with soap. He cradled her face in his hands and leaned down to kiss her lips.

Chapter 34

The Hoffgeitz Bank resided in a three-story stone mansion at the corner of Bahnhofstrasse and Augustinergasse. Elie rang the bell. The lock clicked, and an elderly man opened the door. "*Guten morgen*," he said with a curt bow.

Elie handed him a business card that carried only the name Rupert Danzig and a P.O. Box in Paris. "I'm here to see Herr Hoffgeitz."

The cozy lobby could have been a living room in an old-money residence. The leather sofas were worn yet elegant, and the oil portraits on the walls told of a long ancestry. When the man held out his hand for Elie's coat, Elie noticed a ring on his finger, the familiar serpent intertwined with *LASN*. The cuff of his dark-navy suit shone with age, but the creased face was carefully groomed, the gray eyes alert, and the back not yet stooped.

The man hung Elie's coat in a closet and picked up a telephone on a side table. A moment later Günter Schnell appeared through another door. "How can we assist you, Herr Danzig?"

"Greetings from my commander, Obergruppenführer Klaus von Koenig."

A facial twitch was all that revealed Günter's surprise. He gave a shallow bow and beckoned Elie. They went down a hallway with closed doors, accompanied by the muffled sounds of typewriters, men's voices, and ringing phones, and entered a windowless room with a round mahogany table and straight-back chairs.

Elie waited alone. No sound penetrated the walls or the door, but he detected a trace of cigar smoke. He lit a cigarette.

More than a half hour passed. Elie noticed a rotary phone on a small shelf, picked up the receiver and listened. There was no dial tone, but he could tell someone was listening at the other end. He put down the receiver.

Not a minute later the bank's owner appeared. He was a bit taller than Elie and weighed three times more. His ruddy cheeks told of good food and plenty of drink. He shook Elie's hand. "I am Armande Hoffgeitz."

Elie clicked his heels. "Untersturmführer Rupert Danzig, at your service."

The banker sat across the table from Elie. Günter remained standing, his hands on the back of a chair, showing the same ring as the man downstairs. It appeared Herr Hoffgeitz only hired fellow graduates of Lyceum Alpin St. Nicholas.

Elie had planned this conversation carefully. "Obergruppenführer von Koenig often speaks of the delightful school years you shared."

Herr Hoffgeitz nodded and blinked a few times.

"He sends sincere regrets for the long years of silence."

"I see."

"We had to exercise extreme caution, considering what happened to Adolf." Elie intentionally used only the first name, leaving it to the Swiss banker to guess whether the reference was to Adolf Hitler, who had committed suicide after killing his dogs and lover at his command bunker in Berlin, or to Adolf Eichmann, picked up by the Israelis in Argentina, tried in front of the world's media, hanged, and cremated, his ashes tossed into the Mediterranean.

"Well." Herr Hoffgeitz pursed his lips. "You can understand our need for verification before any discussion can take place, yes?"

"Herr Obergruppenführer ordered me to convey his gratitude for naming your son after him and his best wishes to your lovely daughter for success in her Alpine schooling."

"Ah." The implication that Koenig had been watching his private life from afar seemed to unsettle the banker. "Is that so?"

Elie pulled out the black ledger and placed it on the table between them, the red swastika facing up.

Herr Hoffgeitz put on silver-rimmed reading glasses and picked up the ledger. He turned the pages that listed the huge quantities of plundered diamonds, gems, and jewelry. His fingers trembled as he put it down on the table.

Elie didn't touch it. "Herr Obergruppenführer trusts you have liquidated the valuables and converted all into growth investments."

The banker didn't respond.

"Transfers will need to be executed. Funds are required for certain needs."

Herr Hoffgeitz looked at Elie over his reading glasses. "There was much gold, sent by sea to Argentina."

"It's an expensive business," Elie said, "to hide from the Jews for twenty-one years."

Even Günter allowed himself a smirk.

"These are three accounts in Paris, kept under my name for confidentiality purposes. Herr Obergruppenführer instructed me to transfer half the funds—"

"*Half?*" Herr Hoffgeitz's shock confirmed the immense size of Klaus von Koenig's account. Elie's assessment, based on the quantities in the ledger, pinned it at several hundred million U.S. dollars—perhaps more if the banker had taken his time to dispose of the diamonds in small portions during high-market periods over the years while investing the proceeds wisely.

"My credentials," Elie said, and placed Rupert Danzig's passport and SS identification card on the table. "I have served Herr Obergruppenführer since the beginning of the war. I have executed all his orders diligently. He is still my master."

Armande Hoffgeitz examined the SS card without touching it. "I wonder why he didn't contact me directly."

"He is," Elie said, "contacting you directly—through me. He awaits the day that speaking with you face-to-face would no longer endanger him, or you."

The hint of personal peril was sufficient to get the banker off the subject of direct communications. "But why does he wish to withdraw the funds? Does he doubt our reliability?"

Elie had an answer ready. "Herr Obergruppenführer has determined that it is time to begin preparing for the Fourth Reich."

The Swiss banker put both hands forward as if trying to ward off the words.

"And the first step," Elie continued, "is to help the Arabs complete the Führer's final solution. Our men have kept in top shape, ready to serve under the new leader of the German people: Obergruppenführer Klaus von Koenig. Crack teams of veteran experts—battle strategists, armament specialists, engineers, pilots—will take undercover lead in the Middle East as part of the Egyptian joint-Arab command. Herr Obergruppenführer has decided that the narrow territory inhabited by the Jews in the Holy Land is perfect for a blitzkrieg—cut them in half through Jerusalem and the West Bank to the Mediterranean Sea, then thrust north and south simultaneously in a rapid annihilation of their primary population centers along the coast. It's a very expensive project, but necessary. As long as the Israelis are still around, Herr Obergruppenführer's personal safety is in danger. The destruction of the Jews will open the door for the return to power of our *Nationalsozialistische Deutsche Arbeiterpartei* in Germany and the rest of Europe. It's time!" Elie stood up, clicked his heels, and raised his arm in a Nazi salute. "*Heil Hitler!*"

Armand Hoffgeitz's cheeks lost much of their ruddiness. He rose slowly and buttoned his suit jacket over his protruding belly. "My assistant will handle the formalities."

"Thank you."

"And please tell my dear friend Klaus that I look forward to seeing him in person." Pausing at the door, Herr Hoffgeitz said, "By the way, how is his beautiful friend?"

It took a moment for Elie to understand he was referring to Tanya. "The Jewess?"

"Yes."

"She's dead."

When his boss left the room, Günter Schnell opened a file. The top document was a blank form. He started filling it out, copying the information from Danzig's passport and SS card.

Elie pulled out a new pack of Lucky Strike and tore off the wrapping.

"Account number please?"

Elie wasn't ready for this question. "You don't know the number?"

"Standard procedure. Like every other client, General von Koenig chose a number and a password. This bank will not take instructions or reveal account information before a client provides these two pieces of information. Surely he told you, yes?"

"Of course." Elie coughed to mask his ignorant surprise. "Now let me think. It's been several weeks since I left Argentina."

Günter waited.

Trying to keep a straight face, Elie had to make a convincing show of forgetfulness. "He didn't want me to write it down. I'm afraid the memory escaped me momentarily."

"Well, then." The banker put down his pen. "We cannot do anything until you provide the account number and password."

Sudden rage hit Elie as he realized that Tanya had tricked him. "May I use the telephone?"

When they left Tanya's house, Lemmy thought he heard the phone ring inside. She was already by the car, reaching to open the trunk for his duffel bag.

"Isn't that your—"

"I have an idea." She held the trunk open. "Let's stop by Meah Shearim, and you'll run in to say hello to your mother."

"*What?*"

She patted his Uzi. "No one is going to mess with you. Just go in and tell her you're doing fine, not to worry. What's the worst that could happen? They'll ignore you?"

"Great idea!" Lemmy threw his bag in the trunk and slammed it shut. "Should I stop by the synagogue to say hello to my old friends? Check out the new chandelier?"

Tanya drove along the border, where hundreds of Orthodox men of all ages were digging up the sidewalks and filling up pillowcases in lieu of sandbags.

"You don't understand," he said. "I defied their God, spat on their sacred rules, made a farce out of their divine truth."

"You didn't spit on anything. You took a different path, that's all."

"My father once hit me for asking an inappropriate question. For a question!" He gestured at his uniform. "This is a million times worse than a question, more than blasphemy. For them, it's *Khilool Ha'Shem*—Desecration of God in the worst way! Don't you understand what Neturay Karta is all about?"

"But still, your mother loves you no matter what."

"You love me too, right?"

"Of course."

"Then imagine that I went to Tel Aviv and raped Bira, completely and violently ravished her, left your darling daughter violated, bleeding, broken, sprawled on the sidewalk. Would you still love me? Would you want me to stop by and say hello?"

"It's not the same thing."

"Yes, it is! I raped their Talmud, ravished their faith, crapped on their holy way of life, and shot down their chandelier."

"That was an accident."

"You don't get it, do you? I'm dead to them, especially to my parents." He hit the door of the car with a clenched fist. "Worse than dead!"

After a few moments of driving in silence, Tanya said, "You might be right."

"What do you mean?"

"Don't be angry at me, but I went to see your father."

Lemmy was too shocked to say anything.

"Many weeks ago. I gave him your address in the army so your mother could write to you." Tanya sighed. "I don't understand why she didn't."

"Because I've been excommunicated! I don't exist anymore!"

At the central bus station, Tanya parked and accompanied him inside. Hundreds of soldiers milled about, some young like Lemmy, others much older, reservists in haphazard combinations of uniform and civilian clothes.

A group of kids sat on the ground in a circle, singing a popular tune: "*Nasser sits and waits for Rabin, ai, yai yai, and he should wait 'cause Rabin is coming, ai, yai yai, to bang him on his head, ai yai yai.*"

They stopped to watch the kids sing. She took his hand. "Sorry I yelled at you."

She pulled him toward the row of buses. "You'll miss your ride."

"Will you attend my graduation ceremony next month?"

They reached his bus. "I can't leave my post. We're sitting on a cinder box."

"That's okay," he muttered. "My friends would be surprised to see anyone showing up for me."

"My poor little Jerusalem." She held him tightly. "I shouldn't tell you this, but just to make you feel better, I really can't travel. The fate of the city is hanging in the balance. We need as much information as possible."

The bus began to back up from the dock. He bent down to kiss her lips, but Tanya offered her cheek instead.

The overseas telephone number had many digits, and Elie tried again, fingering each digit, impatient for the dial to rotate back, the pulses to travel the lines to Jerusalem. But the telephone in Tanya's house rang and rang without an answer.

He dialed her number again every few minutes for almost an hour, but there was no response. He wondered whether she even knew the account number and password. It would have been careless for her Nazi lover to give her the ledger *and* the codes. Was it possible to guess them? Back in 1945, SS General Klaus von Koenig must have realized it would be many years before he could return to Zurich. He had to use a memorable pattern. Perhaps the name of a place or a person? Something related to Tanya? Elie jotted down *TANYA 1945*. Below he wrote in reverse order: *AYNAT 5491*.

A while later, Herr Hoffgeitz's assistant reappeared. Elie showed him the page. Günter checked the file and shook his head. "Please return when you have the correct information, Herr Danzig. Or, better yet, suggest to General von Koenig that he comes here in person."

Elie collected the passport, the SS identification card, the ledger, and the list of the Paris accounts. He put everything in his inside breast pocket.

The elderly attendant helped Elie into his coat, and Günter Schnell held the front door open. "By the way, Herr Danzig, how did you like the Chagall windows at the Fraumünster?"

"I didn't," Elie responded without missing a beat. "Typical *Juden* kitsch masquerading as art. Don't you agree?"

Chapter 35

Late at night, after turning on the recording devices, Tanya went to bed with an Agnon book. The story was titled *Agunot – The Forsaken Wives*. It dramatized the traditional marriage that kept a woman bound by the strictures of Talmud long after all the other aspects of matrimony had dissolved. Sad, but beautifully written. She was so caught up in the world that Agnon had created that the knocks on the door seemed to belong in the story rather than in reality. But they sounded again, insistent, loud.

She wrapped herself in the blanket and went to the door. "Who is it?"

"Abraham Gerster."

When she opened the door, only his face, beard, and payos stood out in the darkness, the rest of him as black as the night. He was panting hard.

"You walked here?"

He nodded.

"Why in the middle of the night?"

"I waited until my wife fell asleep." He coughed. "She's going out of her mind. I have to do something. You must help me!"

"How did you know where I live?"

"My son." He gasped for air. "I followed him one Saturday when he—"

"When he came for my books?"

"Was it only books he came for?"

Tanya thought of their Saturday afternoons together, Lemmy's clothes on the floor, easily visible through the window.

He leaned against the doorpost. "Oh, Tanya, what have I done?"

She reached up and caressed the side of his face. "It's not your fault."

"Who else?" He grabbed her hands and pressed them to his chest. "My heart belonged to you! Always! But I agreed to live a lie! I made a terrible mistake marrying her!"

Her heart racing, Tanya spoke with difficulty. "Did you tell your wife to write—"

Noise outside made them turn.

Out of the darkness, in the dim light from the door, a woman appeared. She wore a gray headdress, her face bright with sweat, her body covered in a black coat—a man's coat, which Tanya realized must be Lemmy's old coat. Below it, her shins were exposed, very white, and her bare feet.

"Temimah!" He let go of Tanya's hands.

She stepped closer. Her feet left wet prints of blood. "You stole my son!" She pointed a trembling finger at Tanya. "Now you want to take my husband?"

"No," Tanya said, "please, you don't understand—"

"*Vixen!*" Her voice had a primal pitch, like an animal screeching at the moment of death. "*I curse you!*"

"Temimah," Abraham's pleaded, "enough."

"*God will bring you sorrow! Grief!*" Her eyes rolled up and she collapsed.

Chapter 36

The weeks since his visit to Tanya's home in Jerusalem had flown by with exhausting drills and endless hikes in the desert. Bits of news reports told the trainees of the rising tensions in the country as tens of thousands of reservists, called up to guard the borders, sat idly in makeshift camps and waited for the government to tell them whether to fight or to return home to their families and jobs. But Prime Minister Eshkol continued to plead with the Americans to confirm the ten-year-old guarantee issued by President Eisenhower to use U.S. forces against Egypt in the event it attacked Israel, and the Arabs continued to build up their massive forces in the Sinai Desert, the Golan Heights, and the West Bank.

On the eve of Independence Day, Zigelnick informed Lemmy and Sanani that they would carry the flags at the main parade in Jerusalem. They tossed a coin, and Sanani won the national flag, Lemmy the IDF banner.

The soldiers had spent the night oiling guns, ironing shirts, and shining shoes. A military barber set up a chair near the outdoor showers, and the kitchen supplied hot coffee and cold sandwiches to keep everyone awake.

At sunrise, they lined up three-deep, and Captain Zigelnick inspected each soldier's appearance. "Listen up," he said. "You'll represent the Paratroopers Brigade, but it's not because you're so good looking."

Everyone laughed.

"But because everyone else is on alert along the borders." The captain looked at them for a moment, letting the implication set in. "So wipe the milk from your lips and march like real soldiers. And don't expect lots of adoring crowds. The Voice of Israel told listeners to stay home and enjoy the live broadcast of the parade, followed by the National Bible Bee." He grinned. "Let's load up!"

It took another hour to get all the gear on the truck. They left the camp as the heat of the desert began to rise. Sanani led the company in singing Israeli folk songs, which he modified to his own lyrics, mostly involving female body parts that rhymed with the names of Arab leaders.

The heartbreaking confrontation with Temimah Gerster had left Tanya shaken up. She wanted to call an ambulance, but Abraham disappeared into the night, carrying his wife in his arms. He must have feared a public scandal.

As the days passed, the intensity of UN communications rose steadily. Her work consumed every waking moment.

One morning, soon after Tanya finished her first cup of coffee, she picked up a radio conversation between UN General Odd Bull and one of his officers—an Indian by his accented English. Bull instructed the officer to alert the UN observers stationed at the Mandelbaum Gate that he would be crossing over to the Israeli side later to protest the Israelis' Independence Day parade, which he called "That damned Jewish provocation!"

Tanya was still writing down the last sentence of their conversation, translated into Hebrew, when Elie arrived. He came in with a burning cigarette dangling from his thin lips. She held up an ashtray for him to stub it. He had been showing up occasionally since his return from Zurich weeks earlier, trying to pry open her memories of the years with Klaus. She had been honest in her denials. Klaus had never told her the account number and password. But fearing that Elie would somehow interfere with Lemmy's new life, she forced herself to treat him cordially.

"I have to call in a report," Tanya said. "General Bull is upset, even though Eshkol cut the parade down to a joke."

"What choice did he have?" Elie removed his wool cap and rubbed his gaunt skull. "All the foreign ambassadors are boycotting our Independence Day. In all fairness, the Armistice Agreement bans heavy weapons in Jerusalem."

"That agreement is long dead. The Arabs are violating it." Tanya poured him a cup of coffee. "The Sinai and the West Bank are filled with their tanks and cannons."

Elie took the cup from her hand cautiously. "It's the diplomacy of oil."

"It's the diplomacy of turning the other cheek. Eshkol has no right to downgrade Israel's national birthday. A parade is an opportunity to showcase the IDF's power to our nervous population."

"What's to showcase? President Johnson suspended delivery of the new Patton tanks and Skyhawk jets on condition that we allow American inspections of the nuclear reactor in Dimona. And the French are holding up the weapons we've already paid for. You think a parade would reassure the nation?" Elie took a sip of coffee. "Listen, I was thinking. Do you remember von Koenig's birthday?"

"Sometime in 1910. April, I think."

"You didn't celebrate it?"

"Not really." Tanya recalled Klaus returning from a field inspection, aching from endless hours in the car. When he saw the cake she had baked for him, he kissed her and asked her to give it to his driver, Felix. Instead of blowing out candles, they soaked in a hot bath. At first they listened to Wagner, but as Klaus's mood improved, they piled more embers under the bath and started reciting lines from a play he had taken her to see in Berlin a month earlier. They ended up laughing so hard that the bathwater splashed all over the room.

"Tanya?"

"Yes." She shook her head to drive away the sadness. "Klaus didn't like to celebrate his birthday. But he was important enough that the date should be on record somewhere." Before Elie could ask another question, she headed to the other room. "I must return to my work. Please let yourself out."

Elie put down his cup of coffee. "Have you heard from Abraham?"

Something in his voice made Tanya pause. "Why should I hear from him?"

"Well, that's interesting."

"Why?"

He pulled the wool cap down over his ears and opened the front door. "It's just that I assumed he would run straight to you with the bad news."

"Bad news?" Her chest constricted with dread. "What bad news?"

The drive from the Negev Desert to Jerusalem took over three hours, providing time for much-needed sleep. They woke up in the city, which was crowded despite the government's call to stay home. Lemmy sat in the back of the truck and took in the incredible sight of thousands of Israelis in white shirts and blue pants, the children waving little flags, the windows and balconies along the road packed with cheerful spectators.

The soldiers jumped off the truck and assumed formation for the parade. Lemmy adjusted the flagpole against his hip and glanced at Sanani, who struggled to do the same. Just ahead, two half-tracks rolled into position. On a stage farther down, a band played a fast-paced tune while dignitaries took their seats.

His eyes searched the crowds. He knew his parents would never attend an event celebrating the Zionist state, and neither would Benjamin. But could Tanya be among the revelers, unaware that he was marching with his unit? He sought her pale, delicate face, framed by black hair, even though he knew how unlikely it was for her to leave her post. No. She was sitting dutifully inside that half-ruined house, wearing the bulky headphones, eavesdropping on secret communications across the nearby border.

The music stopped, and the thousands of spectators gradually quieted down. On the stage, the loudspeakers crackled, and a woman's voice announced, "Prime Minister Levi Eshkol!"

Lemmy saw a stout man stand up and wave, earning isolated applause.

The announcer said, "The Chief of Staff, General Yitzhak Rabin."

A man of average height and build, dressed in khaki uniform and an officer's cap, stood up and saluted. Cheering swelled up and down the boulevard, and many launched into spontaneous singing, "*Nasser sits and waits for Rabin, ai, yai, yai...*"

Barely heard over the singing, the announcer kept listing the names of civilian and military leaders on the stage. But the singing persisted, "*And he should wait 'cause Rabin's coming, ai, yai, yai...*"

There were no speeches, which was a good thing as the sun was beating down on them with full force. But before the marching commenced, the announcer invited the chief rabbi of the IDF to recite a blessing. Lemmy stood on his toes to get a better look at the contradiction—a rabbi in uniform. At Neturay Karta, Zionism was equated with blasphemy, and those who called themselves rabbis while supporting the state were mocked. But Rabbi Shlomo Goren, now a full general, had transformed the IDF into a Jewish army, with kosher kitchens and observance of Sabbath, enabling religious soldiers to serve without compromising their faith.

The rabbi recited a prayer for the soldiers of Israel in battle and victory. Then he chanted, "*If I forget thee, Jerusalem, my right hand shall wither.*" Many voices joined him. "*My tongue shall stick to my palate, if I don't remember thee, if I do not put Jerusalem ahead of my own happiness.*"

Lemmy recalled his father atop the squat boulder in view of the Old City, chanting the same mournful song, defying the Jordanian sniper, whose bullet perforated the black hat. He remembered his father's arm, resting on his shoulders as they descended the hill. Had that gesture reflected love? No, Lemmy thought, a loving father wouldn't rip the lapel of his coat and declare his son dead while that son was standing, very much alive, in the back of the synagogue.

A whistle sounded. An officer took the microphone and called the units to attention. The civilian crowds swelled as more people arrived. The police barricades threatened to topple over under the pressure. Lemmy kept his face forward, the flagpole at the correct angle. But his eyes moved left and right, stubbornly searching for Tanya among the sea of faces.

The band played the tune for *Jerusalem of Gold, and of bronze, and of* light, and the crowd sang, arms interlocked, thousands of Israelis swaying from side to side, until the last line.

Breaking into a fast military march, the band caused a dramatic change of mood. The spectators started clapping and waving flags. Zigelnick barked an order, Lemmy and Sanani raised the flags, and the company marched forward. Passing by the stage, they half-turned and saluted.

Elie Weiss heard the cheering from a distance. He didn't like crowds. Instead of attending the parade, he borrowed a vehicle from the IDF car pool and drove along the border section of West Jerusalem to inspect the progress of trench-digging. Tanya had borrowed his Citroën for the drive to the base in the Negev where Abraham's son was apparently stationed. She insisted on telling him face to face, rather than allow the army to deliver the news.

The ultra-Orthodox volunteers surpassed Elie's expectations. Men who spent their lives as sedentary Talmudic scholars instead worked around the clock to create a system of deep trenches and walls of sandbags along the border. Beside the military benefit, Elie was pleased to see them out of their synagogues and yeshiva halls, where anti-Zionist fever would have peaked during such perilous times, when even secular Zionists doubted the Jewish state's chances of survival. And for good reason. Jordan's cannons could easily decimate the civilian Jewish population of West Jerusalem. Transportation of Israeli ground forces from the south or the north, even if some units could be spared, would take too long to reach the city in time.

The trenches would save some lives, but the only way to effectively defend the Jews of West Jerusalem would be a massive attack by Israeli jets on Jordanian artillery positions in East Jerusalem—a suicidal mission because of the UN radar at Government House, connected to the Jordanian anti-aircraft guns. Brigadier General Tappuzi and his team desperately needed a solution, and Elie believed he might have it.

He parked by an abandoned building and climbed to the roof, which offered unobstructed views eastward. The Old City's ancient walls surrounded the densely populated quarters, and the two mosques on Temple Mount resembled domes of nuclear reactors. He focused his binoculars on Government House, high on the southern ridge. Two UN sentries in khaki uniform and blue caps lounged on a bench. The guard towers at opposite ends of the compound were not manned. The massive building was made of local stone. On the roof was a storage room, which served as a base for the steel mast carrying the giant UN flag. In the rear of the compound, Antenna Hill swelled up, topped by a wall of sandbags around a concrete structure, half-sunk in the ground. A huge reflector antenna rotated on top. Behind the radar station he could see gasoline tanks—a useful feature for faking an accidental explosion.

Lowering his binoculars to just outside the fence, Elie traced the Jordanian anti-aircraft batteries along the ridge, only the tips of the barrels showing above the surrounding defenses.

A commotion in the courtyard drew his attention. A white vehicle with the UN insignia drove around to the front of the main building. The driver stepped out to open the door. General Odd Bull emerged from the front doors and got in. The gate opened, the two sentries saluted, and the vehicle drove through. Elie followed it with his binoculars. The commander of UN forces in the Middle East was driven around the Old City, disappearing from view for a few moments behind the ancient walls. He reappeared near the Mandelbaum Gate and was waved through by the Jordanian border guards. The UN observers saluted, and the Israeli soldiers did the same. Once in West Jerusalem, he drove south to the IDF command center. Elie knew that, after the parade, Chief of Staff Yitzhak Rabin was going to take Bull on a helicopter tour along the borders in order to refute the Arabs' allegations that Israel was preparing to attack them.

He got down from the roof and drove off. The streets filled with civilians. Locals walked home, and a string of buses with out-of-town revelers crawled toward the city exit. He turned on the radio for the 1:00 p.m. news. The Voice of Israel reported that over two hundred thousand Israelis had attended the parade, which instigated an immediate UN resolution declaring Israel in violation of the Armistice Agreement. Egyptian President Nasser again threatened to remove UN observers and blockade the Straits of Tiran, cutting off Israel's shipping routes to Asia and its oil supplies from Iran. A blockade, Elie knew, would mean war.

He found General Bull's vehicle parked in front of the IDF command in West Jerusalem. He walked around it, taking a closer look. It was a Jeep Wagoneer, which resembled a tall station wagon with large tires and an elevated stance for off-road driving. The white paint seemed fresh, and the UN insignia on the doors shone as if the letters had been polished that morning.

"Is there a problem, sir?" Bull's driver was a young, dark-skinned UN sergeant, who spoke English with his native singsong Indian accent.

"To the contrary." Elie returned his salute. "Happy Independence Day."

It took an hour for the army truck to get through traffic, but Lemmy and his friends didn't mind. They sang patriotic songs and ate candy that civilian pedestrians tossed in through the open back. The hearty adoration infused the soldiers with a sense of purpose that months of drills could never have achieved.

Once out of Jerusalem, on the open road to the Negev Desert, the excitement gave way to exhaustion. Lemmy's mind was still racing with flashes of the day's events. He was a real Israeli soldier, ready to defend the nation with his life, to fight shoulder-to-shoulder with his friends. His old life in Neturay Karta seemed like a distant memory. He hugged the Uzi to his chest and remembered what Zigelnick had said to them on the first day of boot camp: *Your Uzi is your new mother, father, and girlfriend!*

He dozed off.

After what seemed like a few minutes, the truck's hydraulic brakes screeched and groaned, waking everyone up. A thick cloud of desert dust penetrated through the back and filled the truck.

"You have ten minutes," Zigelnick yelled, "to change and get ready for tonight's drill. Come on, ladies! Ten minutes!"

Sanani cursed in Mehri, an Arabic dialect from Yemen that his parents still spoke, making Lemmy laugh. The soldiers unloaded all the gear from the truck and changed into olive field drabs.

"Hey, Gerster," someone yelled, "you have a visitor."

In the parking area outside the camp, Lemmy saw a gray Citroën. The driver stepped out—a woman in a sleeveless, white-cotton dress and black hair. He ran over and took Tanya in his arms.

Elie watched the military helicopter approach from the south. The landing area near the IDF command was barely enough to clear the rotors, and the evening wind had picked up enough to challenge the pilot, who struggled to keep the craft pointing into the wind, its stubby nose downward. As soon as it landed, an aide ran to open the sliding door.

Chief of Staff Yitzhak Rabin stepped down, followed by UN General Odd Bull, who held his blue cap as they jogged from the helicopter, which departed immediately.

The Indian driver held the door for the UN general, and a moment later the Jeep drove off. Elie glanced at his watch, noting the time.

"Weiss!" Rabin noticed him and came over. "Impressive work with the black hats."

"Fear is a great motivator."

They strolled to the end of the parking area and stood by a stone wall, which offered southern views across a ravine, the border fence running north to south, and Government House on the opposite ridge.

Elie turned his back to the wind and lit a Lucky Strike.

Rabin pulled one from Elie's pack and used his burning cigarette to light it. His fingers shook, and his eyes were bloodshot.

"Is Bull going to help?"

"A pompous old stiff." Rabin drew deeply and held the smoke inside. It drifted from his mouth when he spoke. "I took him everywhere—the Galilee, the coastal strip, the Negev. Wherever he pointed, the pilots went. He kept looking for the attack forces we're accused of building up along the borders, but all he saw were our thin lines of defense, manned by our regulars and some very frustrated reservists. It confirmed what we've been telling him. He couldn't argue with his own eyes, but he said that the

Arabs have legitimate concerns about our belligerent intentions. *Legitimate concerns!*"

"They're lying to justify attacking us first."

"Bull said they're afraid of us because of Dimona. Can you imagine? *They* are afraid of *us!*"

"Nuclear bombs are a scary thing."

"But we don't have anything useable!"

"Not yet."

General Rabin took another cigarette from Elie's pack and lit it with the stub. "I need a vacation," he said. "Maybe we'll all end up together in a POW camp—a long vacation."

"You don't really believe that, right?"

"No. There won't be any POW after an Egyptian first strike." Rabin made a cutting gesture. "They'll demolish our air force on the ground and own the sky. Their tanks and infantry will swarm us like *arbeh!*" He used the biblical word for the locusts God had sent to scare the Egyptians into freeing the Israelite slaves. "The Jordanians and Syrians will jump in, and we'll be dead in twenty-four hours."

The wind, which had calmed down for a while, suddenly lashed at them. The chief of staff shielded his cigarette. "Our only chance," he said, "is a preemptive strike."

"What about the UN radar?" Elie motioned at Government House across the gulch. "Won't they notice our jets taking off?"

Rabin sucked on his cigarette as if it were oxygen. "I'm still waiting for a Mossad assessment of the radar system's range. We know it can detect planes approaching Jerusalem. But if this radar is strong enough to track our jets over the Negev and the Mediterranean, then Bull could alert the Egyptian high command. That kills our first-strike option. Which is our only option."

"I'm not an expert in radars," Elie said, "but the rotating reflector on that thing is huge."

They stood together, gazing at the radar on the hill behind Government House, smoking their cigarettes.

"Whatever the range of this thing," Rabin finally said, "without an order from our government, there won't be a first strike. I need Dayan to take over the defense ministry."

Elie pulled a few photos from his pocket. They showed Moshe Dayan holding various antiques for the camera, directing uniformed IDF soldiers at an archeological dig, and sitting in his garden among valuable treasures.

"Everyone is entitled to one vice." Rabin lit a third cigarette with the stub of his second. "Or two."

"A thief as defense minister?"

"You're looking for an honest politician?" Rabin sneered. "Good luck!"

"There's a difference between dishonesty and criminality."

The chief of staff watched the smoke drift away from his mouth. "Most of my career I've served under Dayan. He's arrogant. Dishonest. A braggart. But he has steel balls. As defense minister, he'll give the green light and save Israel. That's all I care about right now."

Across the gulch, on the Jordanian side, they could see the white ant that was General Bull's Jeep. It approached Government House from the east. Elie glanced at his watch. Eleven minutes since leaving the IDF command in West Jerusalem. "Eshkol promised me the top Mossad post."

Rabin smiled. "Why would you want such a headache?"

"To save our people from another Holocaust."

"Get over it, Weiss. The Nazis lost the war. They failed to exterminate us. Look around. We're still here."

"You're a naïve sabra," Elie said. "No offense."

"None taken."

"You haven't seen your family butchered like sheep on market day, haven't smelled the crematoria, still glowing red with our people's ashes."

"I've lost comrades in battle," Rabin said. "I've fought for Israel since my Bar Mitzvah."

"Playing defense. That's why you boys call your army the *Israeli Defense Force.* It's delusional to think that the Holocaust ended with the Third Reich. The Final Solution didn't start with Hitler, it didn't end when the Americans reached Auschwitz, and it will continue until we finish it off!"

"You're paranoid."

"The way I see it, our people have been the subject of a Final Solution campaign for thousands of years, since the day idol worshippers chased the patriarch Abraham from his home, through the Egyptian slavery, Amalekite attacks, Canaanite raids, the Babylonian exile, the Greek massacres, the Romans burning down the temple, crushing Masada—"

"I don't need a history lesson." Pointing with his cigarette at the border, Rabin said, "I'm worried about the here and now."

Elie looked over his shoulder at the staff car awaiting Rabin, his driver and aide standing by, watching. "The here and now include the Final Solution. Think of the crusaders, who killed more Jews in Europe than the Muslims they had set out to vanquish. And the Inquisition, another phase in the Final Solution. The expulsions from Spain, Portugal, and England. The pogroms in Poland, Latvia, the Ukraine, and Russia. Stalin's mass murder of Jews." He paused to take a draw, blowing the smoke into the wind. "Hitler's camps were just another phase in the effort to exterminate the Jews. And now? Are you listening to Nasser's speeches? He's the leader of the Arab world, and what did he declare in Cairo's giant square last week? *Annihilate Israel! Throw the Jews into the sea!* Isn't it the familiar language of the Final Solution?"

"What do you want?" Rabin's voice rose in anger. "We're ready to move! We're ready to fight! We're ready to win!"

"This time, maybe. But what about next time? And the next?" Elie's cigarette burned his fingers. He dropped it. "When I escaped our village in 'forty-one, powerless to stop the butchery of my parents and siblings, I vowed to dedicate my life to *our* final solution. I call it: *Counter Final Solution.*"

The chief of staff looked at him, waiting for an explanation.

"Exterminate our enemies before they exterminate us."

"You want to kill all the Gentiles in the world?"

"Only those who want to kill us. A dose of preventative medicine."

"Easier said than done."

"Kill Nasser, for example, and you've eliminated a charismatic leader capable of marshalling a Pan-Arabic military attack on Israel."

"There would be another Nasser."

"We kill him too." Elie pointed at his own chest. "When I'm in charge of Mossad, the game will change. I'll set up a worldwide network of fearless Jewish assassins and go after our enemies preemptively."

"Sounds expensive," Rabin said.

"Money is available. Our agents will operate on every continent. They'll identify our enemies and eliminate them. We'll muzzle up preachers who plant seeds of hate, silence demagogues who fan anti-Semitic flames, and bring down the businessmen who sponsor the factories of hate and terror. Under me, Mossad will act as a powerful antidote—dispensing the ultimate vaccination against infectious anti-Semitism."

General Rabin tossed his cigarette over the low wall. "Human beings are not a disease."

"Some humans are a deadly virus that must be eradicated."

"Viral strains can be controlled, not eradicated."

"A few might slip through the cracks," Elie conceded. "But even they will know that those with Jewish blood on their hands—or on their minds!—will never sleep in peace again. We'll hunt them to the ends of the earth. *Counter Final Solution!*"

General Rabin peered at him through creased eyes. "You're a dangerous man, Weiss."

One of the guys whistled, which reminded Lemmy they were not alone. He let go of Tanya. "I was looking for you at the parade. But there were so many people—"

"I didn't know you'd be there," she said. "Could have saved me the long drive."

"You missed me?"

Her eyes smiled and hurt at the same time. She reached up and caressed his hair. "I have bad news."

"You're leaving for Europe?"

"No, not yet. It's about your mother." Tanya held his hands. "She passed away."

He heard her words, but they didn't sound real. How could his mother be dead? "That's impossible."

"I'm so sorry."

"But she wasn't sick."

"I wish it wasn't true, but she died yesterday and, you know, buried last night." That wasn't unusual, because Talmud required same-day burial in Jerusalem, lest the rotting dead sullied the holy city.

"It's my father!" Lemmy kicked the dirt, filled with sudden rage. "He broke her heart! I hate him!"

Tanya waited while he informed his commanding officer and packed a small bag.

The car struggled up the Judean Mountains, its small engine screaming in a high pitch. The narrow road detoured around Arab villages. She steered through tight curves, avoided gaping potholes, and passed under precipitous boulders that seemed ready to drop. She stopped at the side of the road while long military convoys made their way to the Negev Desert. Army trucks towed tanks, heavy artillery, and armored personnel carriers. Civilian trucks with hastily brushed-on camouflage ferried troops, most of them reservists still in their street clothes.

Lemmy watched in silence. He pushed away any thoughts of his mother, of his life before the army. That boy in Neturay Karta had been someone else, not him.

It was dark when they entered Jerusalem. Tanya drove quickly through the narrow streets. Closer to the border, Lemmy saw Orthodox men dig trenches under the glare of electric lights. Women carried heavy shopping bags with food in anticipation of shortages. It was a far cry from the jubilant mood at this morning's Independence Day Parade.

Chapter 37

As the sun was rising, Elie Weiss made his way through the narrow alleys of Meah Shearim to the small apartment where Rabbi Abraham Gerster had resided for almost two decades. He climbed the stairs and found the front door ajar, as was customary during the mourning period, letting out the voices of chanting men and the aroma of baking bread.

A mirror in the foyer was covered with black cloth, and men in black coats swayed while reciting prayers. Someone handed Elie a prayer book, and he stood by the wall, pretending to read from it. He took quick glances, registering the open doors to a dining room on the left, a hallway straight ahead, and a study on the right, all filled with men.

Rabbi Gerster was leading the service. Elie could not see him, but the tone of his voice said it all, and for a moment Elie was beset by regrets. He had not expected this to happen, had not wished it to happen, and should not be responsible. It had been Abraham's mistake. He had insisted on marrying Temimah, arguing that a wife would be necessary for a leader in Neturay Karta. And he had compounded that mistake by satisfying his wife's initial childbearing urges. Eighteen years ago, Abraham had dismissed Jerusalem's birth as a token of happiness for his wife. Now she had paid back that token, plus interest, and Abraham would contend with grief and guilt and anger for the rest of his life. But from an operational point of view, Elie noted to himself, the woman's departure eliminated a major risk of exposure, which her intimate presence in Abraham's life had always threatened.

Everyone quieted down when the rabbi recited the Kaddish. He reached the last sentence of the mourners' prayer: "*He who brings Shalom to heaven ...*" The men joined him for the last words, "*He shall bring Shalom upon us and upon all the people of Israel, and we say Amen.*"

While the men removed the black straps of their *tefillin* and folded their prayer shawls, a few women in long sleeves and tight headdresses brought out bread and coffee. The men lined up to wash their hands, recited a blessing, and ate quickly.

Elie watched them file into the study, each man sitting for a few seconds next to Rabbi Gerster and reciting the traditional shiva farewell: "*God shall comfort you among the mourners of Zion and Jerusalem, and you shall not know sorrow again.*" As they departed, the men glanced at Elie, who stood in the foyer in his plain khakis and wool cap, clearly out of place in Neturay Karta. He made sure to keep his face down, pretending to recite Psalms. No one asked him anything—a house of mourning was open to all who wished to pay a shiva call.

When the apartment finally emptied, he entered the study.

Rabbi Gerster was sitting on a low cot without a mattress, as was the custom during the seven days of mourning. His blue eyes were half-closed, his face gray. He looked up. "*You?*"

It was a loaded question. This visit violated the strict rules of separation they had followed for two decades. But Elie had a reason to take this risk. "I had to bring you my condolences in person. It's a tragedy. Absolutely terrible."

"I told you. It was killing her."

"If we could only turn back the clock."

"I shouldn't have waited."

"But you reached out to the boy, didn't you?"

"Temimah wrote to him, but he didn't respond. I can't understand it. Why couldn't he at least send a short reply, a postcard, something?"

Elie didn't respond. What could he say? That Jerusalem Gerster had not received any letters? That he had no knowledge of his mother's repeated pleas? That his letters had to be diverted, or he surely would have responded? No, Abraham should never know why his son had not responded, because in his web of conflicting loyalties and heightened emotions, even an accomplished agent of his caliber couldn't accept that it was necessary to isolate the boy, who had a destiny to fulfill.

"It would have been different if we moved out of Neturay Karta. It would have given my son a message, louder and clearer than a hundred letters, that we really forgive him, accept him, want him back. And then she would still be alive."

It was true. Abraham had wanted to relocate so that his son and wife could reunite, but he had agreed to wait. Duty came first. That's why Elie had never contemplated starting a family of his own, which by its nature necessitated painful choices at the expense of loved ones. And the leader of Neturay Karta could not just get up and leave, especially not on the eve of war, when it would not be beyond the messianic elements in the sect to advocate a treasonous patronage pact with the Jordanians, as some in Neturay Karta had proposed back in 1948.

The cot creaked under Rabbi Gerster. "I sent a telegram to him yesterday. Look at it."

On the desk rested a carbon copy of a postal telegram. Elie picked it up, though there was no need. He had the original in his pocket, having received it last night from his contact at the IDF postmaster office, who had intercepted the telegram on its way to the Negev. But for the sake of appearance, Elie held the copy and read it:

> *Jerusalem; your mother went to be with the Master of the Universe; she is at peace now; please come home to sit Shiva for her; she loved you more than life itself; signed: your father, Rabbi Abraham Gerster;*

"I'm sure your son is on his way here," Elie lied. "Perhaps he's delayed by all the military convoys."

"I don't think so." He reached inside his black coat and pulled out another telegram.

Elie took it and again pretended to read, though he had drafted and sent it to this apartment last night—a short and clear response on behalf of Abraham's son:

Rabbi Gerster; you're not my father anymore; I am free of your cruelty; and so is Mother, who will no longer suffer under you; signed: Jerusalem Gerster;

Elie put down the telegram. "The boy must be upset. He'll come around eventually, I'm sure of it."

"But this response has maliciousness in it, which I've never seen in my son. I don't understand it."

"He was responding to the news—"

"I must find him, speak with him. After the shiva, I will travel to his base and talk to him."

"You might cause the opposite result to what you're hoping to achieve."

"Why?"

"Give the boy some time. Don't contact him for a while." This was Elie's purpose in visiting Abraham in person—to keep the father and son apart. "Let him work it out emotionally. For a few months, at least."

"But I'm worried about him. Such anger could cause Jerusalem to take unnecessary risk. You know how it is when one is consumed by anger."

Elie nodded. "Do you want me to make some calls, check on him?"

"Yes! Get the IDF to assign him to an office, a clerical job. For now. He's very smart, almost fluent in German. Some English too."

"Absolutely. I'll make some calls, get him transferred. He'll be safe."

"Do it! If I lose him," Abraham's voice broke, "I'll have nothing. Nothing at all."

A young man entered the study with a plate of food and a cup of tea. Elie recognized him—the study companion, Benjamin Mashash. It was time to start a file on him.

Elie stood and headed to the door, murmuring the traditional condolences: "*May God comfort you among the mourners of Zion and Jerusalem.*"

Lemmy sat with his legs over the side of the bed, his feet resting on the cold tiles. There was light in the window. Tanya was asleep, curled under a heavy comforter. He went outside. The air smelled of Jerusalem sage, a blooming carpet of yellow flowers along the rusting barbwires and warning signs: *Border Ahead! Danger!*

He heard a distant ambulance siren, but he couldn't tell whether it came from the Jewish or the Jordanian half of the city. He thought of his mother, in constant motion, cooking, mopping, hanging wet linen on wires outside, or helping young mothers with babies. How could she be dead? The finality of it seemed impossible.

He heard the radio inside come to life, warming up with static. A series of beeps preceded the hourly news broadcast on the Voice of Israel.

Tanya got up and poured a glass of milk for him. They stood together by the wooden box of the radio, listening. The lead news was the U.S. declaration of a weapons embargo on Israel until it allowed an American inspection of the nuclear reactor in Dimona, to which Moshe Dayan responded, "With friends like this, who needs enemies?" The White House also denied Eshkol's claim that the Americans promised that the Sixth Fleet would intervene should Egypt attack Israel. President Johnson issued an explicit statement: "*There will be an absolute neutrality by all American forces in the Middle East under all circumstances!*" To top it all off, the Voice of Israel reported that Abba Eban had failed to convince the UN Security Council to issue a resolution calling for cessation of hostilities and commencement of peace negotiations.

When the announcer moved on to news about the results of the National Bible Bee, Tanya asked, "Do you want something to eat?"

Lemmy knuckled the radio box. "Why are we begging the world for help? If the Arabs want a fight, let's give them a fight!"

"It's not so simple. Eshkol and his ministers are old men who grew up in Eastern Europe, where Jewish survival depended on the Gentile authorities' protection."

"But now we have an army!"

"A small army, poorly equipped, and outnumbered by massive Arab militaries equipped with the best Soviet death machines."

The voice of opposition leader Menachem Begin sounded from the radio: "At this time of historic peril for our nascent

Zionist dream, we must put aside personal and political rivalries and call upon David Ben Gurion to return as prime minister and lead Israel to victory!"

"There's a sign of panic." Tanya shut off the radio. "The wolf calls the lion to fight off the hyena."

The Deux Chevaux took a few attempts to start. He placed the Uzi in his lap and folded up the half-window, bolting it in the open position. The car had the sour odor of burnt nicotine, but Lemmy did not ask Tanya whose car it was or who had smoked in it. She was twice his age, beautiful, smart, and independent. A woman like Tanya Galinski couldn't be satisfied with an eighteen-year-old yeshiva dropout, let alone a soldier who was away most of the time. This must be the reason she had arranged a room for him with Bira.

They reached the hills west of the city. The road followed a long fence, ending in a dirt parking lot near an iron gate. A sign read: *Sanhedriah Cemetery.*

The sight hit Lemmy with the reality of the situation. His mother was buried here. He hesitated before getting out of the car. How could she be dead? He shut his eyes and felt her presence, smelled the raw fish and dish-washing soap, and saw her hand tighten her headdress. He thought of the hot chocolate she had made for him every morning, and his throat constricted. He pushed the memories away, determined not to cry in front of Tanya, and stepped into the sun.

Through the gate he saw a vast hillside dotted with tombstones. Farther to the right, beyond the stones, a group of rabbis formed a cluster of swaying black coats. They chanted prayers while one of them piled stones to form a marker. The group marched a good distance away and repeated the process of praying in the open field while another stone marker was erected.

Tanya asked, "What are they doing?"

Lemmy had never actually seen this done, but he knew the relevant Talmudic rules. "They're expanding the burial grounds," he explained. "Before a Jew could be buried, certain blessings must be recited over the soil to sanctify the site as a Jewish cemetery. Only then it is ready to provide a resting place until the Messiah comes and announces the Day of Resurrection." He watched the group march again, almost out of sight, where they repeated the ritual. "That's a lot of sacred grounds," he said. "Are they expecting a plague or something?"

"A war," Tanya said. "A terrible, bloody war."

An old man at a flower stand accepted a few coins and handed Tanya a small bouquet. Lemmy was not sure whether his mother had liked flowers. She had never had any in the house.

"Let's go." He headed to the gate.

"Not there."

He stopped and turned to Tanya.

"We need to go around." She gestured. "Your mother is buried over there."

"But this is the only entrance." He pointed at the gate.

Tanya's face, usually as smooth as porcelain, was creased in pain. She reached to touch his arm. "She's buried outside the fence."

Lemmy tried to digest the information. Again he felt as if in a dream, or a nightmare, where things seemed real but were not. *Outside the fence?*

Tanya wiped her tears with the back of her hand. "She hanged herself."

A fleeting image of his mother at the end of a rope made Lemmy groan. He could see the noose tighten around her white neck, tilting her head sideways, her mouth agape, her tongue stuck out, thick and purple, her eyes wide and focused on him.

He grabbed the fence and shook it, fighting to control himself, to drive away the image.

But then the comprehension shocked him again. His father had buried her outside the sanctified grounds of the cemetery! Lemmy no longer believed in those rules, but *she* had believed! According to Talmud, she would be excluded from the ultimate resurrection of the righteous. And until then, her stone would stand out, attracting derision and mockery. "He is evil," Lemmy yelled. "Evil! How could he do this to her? She lived for him!"

"He had no choice."

"He could've done her this last favor!"

Tanya put her hands around him. "It was a suicide. Your father had to bury her outside the fence—"

"That's a lie!"

Brigadier General Tappuzi shut the door to his office. "Okay, Weiss. What's on your mind?"

"The UN radar." Elie approached the map. His finger traced the road from Government House, circled east of the Old City to the Mandelbaum Gate, across the border, and over to the IDF command, which was marked with a blue Star of David. "About twelve minutes of driving."

"So?" Tappuzi tapped the table with a pencil.

"I could get a man in there, blow it up."

"That's it? That's your plan?" Tappuzi grabbed a bunch of papers stapled together. "This, for example, is a plan for a military operation. It has three parts: *When? Where? What? How?*"

"That's four parts."

"Who's counting?"

"Do you want to hear my plan?"

"But Galinski said Mossad won't risk sending in a team!"

"Mossad is a bureaucracy. My SOD is different. That's why it's called *Special*. We can do it."

Tappuzi sat down. "Give me a step-by-step."

"Forty-eight hours before the IDF launches first strike, you summon General Odd Bull to a meeting here. We disable his car, and an identical vehicle, driven by an Indian-looking soldier in UN drab, crosses the border to Government House. A second man hides in the Jeep with a bag of explosives. He slips into the UN building, the driver turns around and drives back across the border to a safe house. General Bull's car is fixed, your meeting with him ends, and he goes back. Our guy at Government House hides and waits. Moments before war starts, we give him a signal and he blows up the radar. Mission accomplished."

"Daring, but full of holes. And even assuming everything works out, how will you get him out?"

"Same drill. You call Bull for an emergency meeting, which will make sense considering the breakout of hostilities, and we send our fake UN Jeep to pluck out our boy."

"Odd Bull is not dumb," Tappuzi said. "He'll suspect a ploy when I call him minutes after his radar blew up."

"It'll look like an accident. There are gasoline tanks behind the radar station."

"And how will our man know where to go inside Government House?"

"I've set up an intense training program for the two—the driver and the mole. The candidates are young soldiers, just finishing boot camp. I'll have them reassigned to SOD and prepared for the mission."

"What about the car?"

"I've located an identical Jeep Wagoneer in Haifa. A wealthy contractor had it special-ordered from Detroit. It's perfect."

"You'll need authority from Northern Command, Armament Division, to confiscate a civilian vehicle. Tell them to call me."

Elie was at the door. "It's already in the safe house. The owner wasn't too happy."

"I'm sure he wasn't." Brigadier General Tappuzi laughed. "Way to go, Weiss!"

"A lie!" Lemmy tore out of Tanya's embrace. "He could have buried her inside the cemetery!"

"Listen, please," Tanya begged, "your father had to follow the rules—"

"You know the rules?"

"Suicide is a desecration of God's image, in which we're created. Talmud requires burial outside the fence, right?"

"But there's an exception!" Lemmy hit his fists against each other. "The sages said there's always regret in the last second of life, between the act of suicide and the actual departure of the soul. This last-minute repentance cleanses the deceased from the sin of suicide. Any rabbi would permit burial within the sacred grounds—a proper burial! Any rabbi except my father, the *tzadik!*"

"Lemmy, please, don't hate him. Your father couldn't extend leniency to his own wife. He's the leader of Neturay Karta. His people watch what he does—"

"Why do you defend him?"

She hesitated. "One day you'll understand."

"I understand it already. He's cruel and fanatic, a self-righteous, merciless tyrant. He's a monster!"

"*Jerusalem!*"

The way she shouted his name, the anger it carried, was like a slap in the face. He looked at Tanya, finally comprehending a reality that had simmered between them since the beginning. "You're still in love with my father, aren't you?"

She shook her head once, but her eyes confirmed his suspicion.

"You've never stopped loving him. That's why you defend him."

Her lips tightened as if she was holding back a cry.

"Is that why you seduced me?"

She groaned as if he hit her.

"That Sabbath, when you came to our home, you argued in his study. Why?"

Tanya opened her mouth to explain, but no words emerged.

"Did you ask him to leave Neturay Karta for you? And he refused, right? So you took me instead." It was almost like one of the novels he had read. Tanya was the spurned lover who took revenge on the man who rejected her by stealing his only son. "You knew I would fall for it. A horny teenager who had never seen the skin of a woman's elbow, suddenly reading romantic novels while a beautiful woman offers him paradise on earth." Lemmy laughed bitterly. "You must think me such an idiot!"

"I don't."

"And after you took away his son, you pushed his wife over the edge. How biblical!"

At this Tanya physically shook, the knot in her hair collapsing, the black locks descending around her. "Don't say that!"

He gestured at the fence. "Is that why my mother killed herself? Did she catch the two of you in the act?"

Tanya grabbed his arm, her fingers digging into his flesh. "I didn't mean for this to happen! Your father and I did nothing wrong!"

"Killing my mother isn't wrong?"

"Would you listen to me?"

"*Enough!*" He turned away from her and faced the rows of tombstones covering the hillside, each with a Star of David. He straightened his olive-green uniform, tilted his red beret until it sheltered his right ear, and adjusted the Uzi strap across his chest. "I'm going to say good-bye to my mother now." He took the flowers from Tanya. "I'll hitch a ride back to the base."

"But—"

"I don't want to see you ever again."

"Oh, please!" She was crying now. "Let me explain—"

Choking on his sobs, Lemmy ran along the outer fence of the cemetery.

Chapter 38

The Antique Authority resided in a drab office building near the west campus of the Hebrew University. The director, Professor Amos Gileadi, had the leathery skin of a farmer and the thick glasses of a habitual reader. His white hair was unruly, and the breast pockets of his shirt were stuffed with papers and pencils. Like Elie Weiss, he was a German Jew who had lost his entire family in the Holocaust. They met had years earlier, when Elie brought in a box filled with ancient Torah scrolls that a veteran SS officer had kept as souvenirs. Professor Gileadi had traced the scrolls to a synagogue in Berlin, and before that, to a congregation in Cordova whose members disappeared in the 1492 Spanish Expulsion. The restored scrolls were now displayed at the Museum of the Book in Jerusalem. Since that first encounter, Elie had continued to help Professor Gileadi with cash to purchase invaluable archeological pieces, mostly from the Bedouins who travelled freely across the borders to Sinai and the east bank of the Jordan River.

The professor examined the photos of Moshe Dayan's backyard, filled with antiques. "These photos don't do justice to his magnificent collection."

"He showed it to you?"

"Of course. We've authenticated and dated all these pieces."

"What's Dayan's collection worth?"

"It's hard to set monetary value to any archeological items when so many of them are bought and sold by collectors in the black-market. But such a massive assemblage of precious pieces?" Professor Gileadi shrugged. "Millions of dollars."

"Isn't the law clear that the state owns everything?"

The professor sighed. "Shouldn't you worry about more *contemporary* crimes?"

Elie pulled off his wool cap and rubbed his head. "I worry about the ascendance of a criminal to the defense ministry. Don't you?"

He laughed. "General Moshe Dayan isn't a criminal. He's an idealist, a first-rate Zionist, who has risked his life many times for Israel."

"Yes, yes, I know. But this," Elie held up a photo, "is proof that he is enriching himself by stealing state property, correct?"

"For God's sake, Weiss! Dayan grew up in a kibbutz. He cares nothing for money." The professor pointed to the photo of the ceramic wine jar shaped like a cow. "A Bedouin trader bought it in Jordan and offered it to Dayan. I authenticated it. Second Temple era, two thousand years ago. The Hebrew letters indicate ritualistic usage by the Levites at the Temple. We couldn't afford it, so Dayan took a personal loan and bought it himself. He garnished six months of paychecks as a Knesset member."

"Why would he do that?"

"The sabra boys aren't like us. They're not Yids from the shtetl. They're *Israelis.*"

"What's the difference?"

"I see it with my students. Judaism isn't a religion for them. It's an ideology, the foundation of their nationalism. They didn't experience the Diaspora like us. In fact, they mock Diaspora Jews as servile, honorless wimps, who'd rather beg the Goyim for mercy than fight like men. Israelis don't believe in God and the divine concept of the Promised Land. They believe we are an ancient nation that has returned to reclaim the homeland stolen from it by the Romans. That's the reason they're obsessed with archeology. Every piece adds additional proof that our nation is entitled to ownership of this land. This ancestral claim is the core of the Zionist ideology for which they fight and die."

"They die for clay pieces?"

"For the land once inhabited by the ancient Israelites, whose descendants are back in *Eretz Israel*. That's why I have two former IDF chiefs of staff—Yadin and Dayan—in addition to countless other Israeli-born war heroes, spending their free time and the money they don't have on archeological evidence of Jewish life on this land."

The mention of Yigael Yadin, who had spent years digging on Mount Masada, triggered Elie's memory. Major General Yadin, by now an archeology professor in his own right, had been able to substantiate the myth of the last Jewish rebellion against the Romans with unearthed lodgings, a synagogue, a ritual bath, and even pieces of clay used in the last lottery among the zealots to select those who would help the rest die rather than fall into Roman hands—a story recorded by the original chronicler of the rebellion, Josephus Flavius. "But Yadin is different," Elie argued. "He is a scholar, and he doesn't keep the antiques."

"They're all the same. I call it: *Ideology by Archeology*. It's got nothing to do with money." Professor Gileadi pulled open a filing cabinet and took out a heavy binder. "Every piece Dayan finds, he brings here to authenticate and log."

Elie examined the hand-written lists of ancient items and descriptions. "But who owns all these antiques?"

"Technically, the State of Israel." The professor closed the binder and put it away. "But as director, I may permit a collector to keep items for private display."

Rather than provide Elie with the substantiation he had hoped for, the meeting deflated his case against Moshe Dayan. "But what about the use of soldiers for private digs? And military equipment? And what about selling some items? I have proof that Dayan sold antiques to foreign collectors for large sums of money. Do you know that?"

Professor Gileadi nodded. "He occasionally sells a piece that's not unique, such as coins or Byzantine household wares, things of which there are many examples."

"To profit personally!"

"To have money to acquire other pieces from the Bedouins."

"How do you know? Does he provide an accounting?"

"I trust him." The professor stood. "Weiss, I do appreciate your help over the years, but General Moshe Dayan has been devoted to our archeological studies of ancient Israel, not to mention his service to our national defense. I can only guess who put you up to this destructive endeavor, but this department shall have no part in it." He shook Elie's hand. *"Auf Wiedersehen!"*

Tanya had spent most of the night on an urgent translation of documents stolen by a Mossad agent from the Moscow office of a German firm. The text included chemical formulas of poison gas, manufactured in liquid form, which the firm had supplied to Egypt at the behest of the Soviets in the past few years. The difficult translation to Hebrew was tiring, but the implications kept her awake. The quantities of poison gas Egypt had acquired would suffice to kill all the inhabitants of Israel several times over. She thought of the cemetery, Lemmy explaining the religious significance of the ritualistic expansion of the sacred burial grounds. Would anyone remain alive to bury the dead?

She cringed at the memory of his explosive anger, so uncharacteristic of him, yet so understandable for a son whose mother had hung herself and was buried outside the fence as a pariah. But was he right? Had their relationship been rooted in her unresolved feelings for Abraham? Or had she loved the boy for his own qualities? Would she ever know the answer? Probably not, but whatever subconscious motives had driven her, there was no question that by luring Lemmy away from Neturay Karta, she had set those tragic wheels in motion.

Forcing her mind to concentrate on her work, Tanya finished translating at sunrise. The eavesdropping equipment came to life, and she put on the headphones to listen. The exchange was initiated by General Rikhye, an Indian officer who commanded the forty-one observation posts along the Egyptian border with Israel. Four thousand five hundred UN observers served as a buffer that stretched from Gaza, across the Sinai Desert to Eilat and Aqaba, and down to Sharem Al-Sheikh and the Straits of Tiran. Rikhye insisted that General Bull be woken up and read to him verbatim a letter from General Fawzi of the Egyptian High

Command. The Egyptians demanded the UN move out of Sharem Al Sheikh, warned that Egyptian forces were already on the way there, and that any attempt to stop them would cause "clashes." General Bull asked how much time they had, and Tanya was shocked by General Rikhye's response: "The Egyptians want us out immediately." The Indian officer then launched into an angry monologue about UN Secretary General U Thant, who apparently had failed to respond to Rikhye's repeated warnings about the risk of war and the need for an emergency mediation mission. Bull, whose voice betrayed something close to astonishment, asked if Rikhye had told the Egyptians that a UN departure could trigger war. Rikhye replied that he had said exactly that, and that the Egyptian general had declared: *We shall meet next in Tel Aviv!*

Tanya reported by phone to headquarters. She knew others would be listening in on the UN international phone lines and would soon be able to hear General Bull's discussions with the UN headquarters in New York. If the UN agreed to evacuate its posts, Nasser would be emboldened to act on his threat to blockade the Straits of Tiran. The worst-case scenario was unfolding into reality!

Elie arrived shortly afterward to collect his car. Tanya told him about Lemmy's accusations.

"It sounds like the normal process of grief," Elie said. "Shock, pain, anger, guilt, and finally, acceptance. You shouldn't blame yourself. If anyone is responsible, it's Abraham. She was his wife. How could he miss the signs of her desperation?"

Surprised by Elie's criticism of Abraham, Tanya said, "I'm only telling you all this because I'm worried about Lemmy. He hates his father, and now he hates me too. With no one in the world, if war breaks out, he might feel that he has nothing to lose."

"I wouldn't worry about that," Elie said. "He's still in training, right?" Tanya nodded.

"The IDF will use trainees for support services, not front-line fighting. They're only kids, after all."

"You think?"

"I'm sure of it," Elie said. "And in a few weeks, he'll probably come back to you with an apology."

"I don't need his apology. I just want him to be safe and happy."

"I see no reason to worry."

"Maybe it's for the best," she said. "Like Cortez, who burned down his ships upon reaching the New World, Lemmy can now start a new life on a clean slate. He's finally free from our sins—mine, Abraham's, and yours."

Chapter 39

The graduation ceremony began late in the afternoon on May 18, 1967. The field was divided into squares for each company of graduating trainees from various divisions of the IDF. Lemmy's company was assigned to the front. They lined up, their olive-green uniforms neatly pressed and their red berets tilted to the right. Zigelnick assumed position a few feet ahead of his soldiers, facing them, his hands behind his back. A three-man military band tuned its instruments, and a senior officer approached the lectern, looking through his notes.

"Gerster," Sanani whispered without moving his lips, "do you know why Zigelnick wears a mustache?"

"No."

"Because he wants to look like his mother."

The word *mother* jolted Lemmy, but he chuckled, struggling to keep a straight face.

Zigelnick must have heard them. "Sanani, I heard your mother ran into the rabbi who circumcised you at birth, and he yelled at her for raising the wrong piece!"

Some of the soldiers began repeating the joke to the others, and soon dozens were laughing openly.

The officer cleared his throat at the microphone. "Soldiers! The chief of staff!"

Everyone stood to attention as General Yitzhak Rabin's helicopter descended behind the stage. It was a great surprise.

No one had expected him to attend the ceremony. Only a few hours earlier the Voice of Israel had reported that UN Secretary General U Thant had not only caved in to the Egyptian demand without bringing the issue to the General Assembly in New York, but had gone even further by ordering *all* UN observers to leave the Sinai Peninsula. Egyptian forces had already taken control of Sharem al Sheik, poised to blockade the Straits of Tiran.

Rabin climbed the stage and jogged to the podium. "Soldiers! Several months of training might not be enough. But time is a luxury we don't have. Therefore, on behalf of the Israeli Defense Force, I welcome you. Our enemies have an ambition. To destroy our Zionist dream. And to throw us into the sea. They think they can succeed."

Standing so close to the stage, Lemmy was surprised at how young Rabin looked—and how tired.

"If we must, we *will* fight," he continued. "For our families. For the land of our ancestors. And for Israel's future."

There was an audible exhalation of pride among the troops.

"Last but not least," he continued, "for the graduates who earned the highest grades in each unit." He held up a pocket-size copy of the Bible. "We are the People of the Book. This is our history and the story of our homeland."

The officer next to Rabin looked at a list and announced, "Private Jerusalem Gerster!"

Everybody applauded while Lemmy ran forward. He accepted the military-issued, plastic-bound copy of the Bible from the chief of staff, who returned his salute and said, "Good luck!"

"Thank you, sir!" Lemmy ran back to his place, holding the small Bible. He returned Zigelnick's wink.

A few other soldiers were recognized for graduating first in their units. When the last one was back in line, the graduates sang the national anthem, *Hatikvah*. "*As long as at heart, deep inside, a Jewish soul longs; and to the ends of east, far ahead, an eye for Zion longs.*" For all of them, this moment was the culmination of months of hard training, of leaping from tree summits and speeding planes, of rushing up hills in mock attacks, and of delicate training in explosives. But for Lemmy, this moment was also the culmination of a personal journey from Neturay Karta's abhorrence of Zionism to the IDF's patriotic spirit, from singing melancholy prayers in the synagogue to singing the Israeli anthem. *"Our hope still lives, two millennia old, to be a free people on our land, the land of Zion and Jerusalem."*

Lemmy's heart pounded with excitement. He felt warm inside. The words of *Hatikvah* emerged from his heart, where prayers had once originated. He felt as if he had regained his faith, only that it was a different faith. He was finally an Israeli.

Following the national anthem, the band broke into a lively tune, and each instructor decorated his own soldiers. Zigelnick attached the coveted parachute pins to their shirts and beckoned Lemmy to take his place up front. Having graduated first in his unit, Lemmy had earned the honor to lead them off the field. He marched forth, turned right, and passed before the stage, where Major General Yitzhak Rabin stood in attention and returned his salute.

Elie Weiss stopped at the central post office in Jerusalem and collected a package that was waiting for Rupert Danzig. It came from his agent in Munich and contained a few newspaper clippings about a house fire in a nearby suburb, which killed a man and injured his son, age sixteen. The victim, Manfred Horch, was a widower who owned an auto repair shop. He had served in the SS during the war. The son, Wilhelm, was a high-school dropout who worked as an apprentice with his father. He was hospitalized with severe burns. Elie's agent scribbled in the margin: *Son died during the night. Death not reported in the news. No living relatives or close friends. Body cremated and hospital records altered to show that Wilhelm was transferred to private clinic near Zurich for further treatment.*

Beside the news clippings, the agent sent a copy of an admission application for Lyceum Alpin St. Nicholas, the prestigious Swiss boarding school.

Elie filled out a blank telegram form, addressed to his Munich agent. In the block reserved for the text, he wrote only one word: *Proceed.*

Mossad headquarters ordered Tanya to prepare for a quick departure. With war appearing imminent, she had been assigned to run a weapon-acquisitioning operation in Europe.

Twenty minutes later, a retired agent, summoned back to service, showed up at her door. She adjusted the headphones to fit him and spent an hour explaining how to use the eavesdropping equipment.

Having experienced Mossad life for so many years, Tanya was accustomed to sudden, life-altering orders, accepting them with equanimity that was rooted in the trust she had in her superiors. But there was no way to stop her mind from engaging in the endless game of speculation: *Where? Why? What?*

She knew Israel had ordered and paid for large quantities of French armaments, from bullets to cannons and Mirage jets. But earlier this morning President De Gaulle had followed the American example by announcing a complete embargo on all weapon supplies to the Middle East—a disingenuous announcement, considering that only Israel was affected by it while its Arab enemies continued to receive huge quantities of modern weapons and jets from the Soviet Union.

Paris required a different dress style than Jerusalem. She pulled a silk scarf from her closet and faced the mirror. The cheerful red, green, and yellow fabric contrasted with the heaviness in her heart. She thought of Abraham's wife in her tight headdress and sad eyes while looping the scarf around her neck and forcing on a smile. "*C'est la vie, Mademoiselle Galinski.*"

"*Oui?*" the agent in the other room yelled, "*Es-tu parle le moi?*"

"No," Tanya said. "I was talking to myself."

The soldiers spent the afternoon preparing for redeployment. No one had yet told them where the company of fresh-minted paratroopers would be sent. Most hoped for the north, where the cool Galilee Mountains would be a pleasant relief from the desert heat. A few argued that, having trained for months in the south, they would fight better in the familiar topography of the Negev.

Before dinner, Captain Zigelnick summoned Lemmy and Sanani to the command tent. It was dimly lit, only one bare lamp hanging from the pole in the center, shedding a circle of light on a field desk. He returned their salutes. "Congratulations on your achievement, Gerster."

"Thank you, sir."

"And congratulations to you too, Sanani."

"What for?"

"For not getting kicked out before graduation."

"Why would you kick me out?"

"For all your bad jokes."

They laughed.

Lemmy registered the glow of a cigarette in the dark corner of the tent. A small figure stepped forward. When the light reached the face, Sanani made a funny little noise. The face was gaunt and sickly, and burn scars covered the left cheek and neck, down into his collar. And the strangest eyes—tiny and black—were separated by an aquiline nose. He wore a wool cap, pulled down to his ears, which stuck out.

Zigelnick said, "This is Agent Weiss from the Special Operations Department in Jerusalem."

They saluted him, but he extended his hand instead. It was small and clammy. He immediately retreated back into the shadows.

"SOD needs two volunteers," Zigelnick said, "for a secret mission. It's your choice whether or not to volunteer. You can take your time and let me know tomorrow."

"I'm in," Lemmy said.

"Same here," Sanani said.

"Very well." Zigelnick shook their hands for the first time, and probably the last. "Get your gear and follow Agent Weiss. Good luck!"

Tanya met the rest of the Mossad team at Lod Airport. The head of the Europe Desk briefed them on the whereabouts of the weapons Israel had purchased from France, the identities of sympathetic government officials, industrialists, and army officers. While De Gaulle and his advisors at the Quai d'Orsay were intent on neutrality, the French military brass was still smarting from a series of defeats in Algiers and therefore eager to see Israel deny the Arabs a certain victory.

Most pressing was the IDF's severe shortage in artillery pieces, half-tracks, light guns, and ammunition supplies, in addition to replacement parts for jets and other French-made weapons Israel had purchased over the past decade. Tanya's team would use every possible mean to gain access to various military and factory warehouses where the goods were kept, take possession, and transport everything to the Mediterranean coast. A fleet of fast cargo ships was already on its way from Haifa to Marseilles.

Especially daring was the plan to take possession of the twenty-three new Mirage jets, which the French refused to deliver even though Israel had already paid for them. Mossad had learned that the jets were stored in a military air field south of Paris. A group of IDF pilots was on high alert, ready to board a cargo plane for a flight across the Mediterranean as soon as Mossad had secured access to the jets.

Tanya's contact was the chief procurement official at the French Defense Ministry, a charming man of distant Jewish descent, whose repeated marriage proposals Tanya had rebuffed over the years while obtaining priceless concessions for Israel. She would coordinate the whole operation from a Paris apartment, making sure that the different teams played their roles in a synchronized manner.

She knew some of the Mossad agents in the room from past operations. Others were new faces. All thirty-six men and women were fluent in French and versed in the social subtleties required to blend in without being noticed.

The briefing was conducted strictly in French to acclimate everyone to the field, and the questions went down to the smallest details.

Before going out to the tarmac, where a plane was waiting to fly them to Paris, a table was rolled in, loaded with food. Everyone descended on the trays of chopped salad, humus, fries, and roast lamb. Tanya grabbed a piece of pita bread and went to the departures terminal. It was crowded, people trying to catch flights out of the country, angry exchanges in many languages, and frustrated airline attendants with no seats to offer.

She crossed over to the arrivals terminal and went to the IDF counter, which had been set up to process returning Israelis. The lines there were even longer, Israeli men rushing home from abroad to join their reservist units.

Flashing her credentials, Tanya found the supervising officer and gave him an envelope addressed to Bira, which contained pocket money and a loving note. A second envelope had Lemmy's name on it. It held a longer letter she had written intermittently over the past few days, confessing that, even though she had initially seen him purely as Abraham's son and a means to remain connected to a lost lover, she had come to love him for who he was, for his quick mind and sense of humor, for his kindness and easy laugh. He had every right to be angry, she added, but anger should give way to understanding and forgiveness. She would be away for a while, so during his vacations he should stay with Bira in Tel Aviv. "*And when I return, we'll talk about what happened and discuss the future. Keep safe. All my love, Tanya.*"

The officer promised to forward the note to Paratrooper Command, where they would make sure it reached Jerusalem Gerster.

Back with her team, Tanya stood at the door of the plane and exchanged a few words with each one as they boarded. These men and women were professionals, having participated in multiple overseas operations. But this wasn't just another operation. They were leaving behind families and friends whose survival, and the survival of Israel, depended on what would happen in France over the next couple of days.

The plane rose into the dark night. Tanya watched through a porthole. From above, Tel Aviv appeared like a carpet of glistening lights, which ended in a straight line at the Mediterranean coast. She had not prayed in a long time, not since Dachau. But craning her neck to catch a last glimpse of Israel, Tanya mumbled a short prayer for Lemmy and Bira, and for herself as well—that she would see both of them alive again. Then she rested her head back, shut her eyes, and thought of Abraham Gerster—not the bearded rabbi from Neturay Karta, but the blond youth who had sung to her during the snowy nights of 1945.

Chapter 40

Lemmy and Sanani stayed in a vacant stone house that had been deserted by its Arab owners back in 1948. Plaster was peeling off the walls and laying a crunchy carpet on the floor. The empty rooms stunk of urine, and the smell of cooking fires drifted from across the nearby border. An IDF-issued outhouse and a rusty water tank occupied most of the enclosed rear patio.

Two agents in civilian clothes, Yosh and Dor, brought in food and newspapers every morning. The food was homemade and delicious, but the newspapers were depressing. On May 19, the papers reported that Foreign Minister Abba Eban had protested the Egyptian ousting of UN observers from the southern border and declared that Israel would view a blockade of the straits as an act of war. The next day, Prime Minister Eshkol sent him back to Washington to beg again for reaffirmation of President Eisenhower's 1956 guarantee that Red Sea shipping lanes would remain open. But the entanglement in Vietnam and pressure from American oil companies caused the Johnson White House to insist that the Eisenhower commitment was invalid because it lacked ratification as a treaty by Congress. Johnson issued a vague statement: *In the interest of peace, we hope Egypt does not interfere with free maritime travel in the Gulf of Aqaba.*

As the days passed, Sanani had perfected his imitation of the wails of the muezzins, who summoned the believers to prayers five times a day. Lemmy practiced dismantling and assembling his Mauser until he could do it with his eyes closed. They also played countless rounds of backgammon.

Agent Weiss had told them nothing about the mission, but people without names came by to teach the two young soldiers skills that seemed totally irrelevant to the coming war: A middle-aged Jewish couple, originally from India, taught Sanani to speak English with their funny accent, which he used to throw Lemmy into fits of laughter. An elderly nun with a wooden cross on a ropelike necklace, insisted on addressing Lemmy as *Herr Horch* and tutored him in English, which she spoke with a German accent not much different than Yiddish. A police pensioner, who had once commanded a bomb-defusing unit in the Galilee, brought in a suitcase full of wires, timers, and fake dynamite sticks. He taught them how to construct explosive devices from different components and told stories from his long service about Arab terrorists and their affinity for booby-trapping playgrounds and bus stations.

On May 23, the shoe dropped. Lemmy read in the newspaper about President Nasser's declaration: *The Gulf of Aqaba constitutes Egyptian territorial water. Under no circumstances will we allow the Israeli flag to pass through.* His declaration fired up the Arab streets everywhere, and the armies of Lebanon, Kuwait, Saudi Arabia, and Iraq mobilized to help Egypt, Syria, and Jordan fight Israel. In response, Prime Minister Eshkol sent Eban yet again to Washington to press for an American guarantee of Israel's security. At the same time, political maneuvering in the Israeli Knesset became intense. Opposition leaders Menachem Begin and Shimon Peres demanded the appointment of Moshe Dayan as defense minister. Eshkol hinted that Dayan was morally unfit for a ministerial position, to which the opposition responded with demands for evidence.

After lunch, as they were doing pushups in the unfurnished living room, Sanani suddenly rolled on his back. "These politicians," he yelled, his voice echoing in the empty space, "play musical chairs while we're dying here!"

The word *dying* hit Lemmy with the image of his mother in a noose. He turned away from his friend to hide his grimacing face.

"Screw this!" Sanani tossed a piece of broken plaster at the wall. "I'm sick of it!"

Lemmy swallowed, pushing away the image. "You'd rather stay in the Negev? Eat sand?"

"I'd rather be fighting in Cairo than beg the Americans to save my ass!"

"I have a feeling," Lemmy said, dropping for another set of pushups, "that you and I aren't going to Cairo any time soon."

"So where *are* we going?"

"I figure, either Germany or India."

Elie Weiss parked on Ramban Street and walked the rest of the way to the prime minister's residence. The street had changed since the staged assassination attempt had failed. The trees had recovered from the winter frost, and the bushes along the sidewalk bloomed with purple flowers as big as fists. A brick wall had been erected around the house.

An aide showed Elie into the kitchen. The prime minister sat alone, his untouched dinner before him, his feet in brown socks, resting on another chair. "Weiss," he said, "they're drinking my blood. *Dayan. Dayan. Dayan.* Why? Because that pirate will pull the trigger! And cause disaster!"

Elie sat down.

"They call me a coward because I'm trying to avoid war. Arik Sharon said I'm disarming our most powerful weapon—the Arabs' fear of us." Eshkol sneezed.

"*Gesundheit*, but Arik is not alone in worrying about our declining deterrence."

"Deterrence is when the other side fears your threats." Eshkol's voice rose. "But deterrence disappears when you actually attack! What do you think will happen if war breaks out? *Blut vet sich giessen vie vasser!*"

Elie imagined blood running like water in the streets of Jerusalem. "Rabin told me that the IDF can win."

"You believe in miracles?" The prime minister held up a bunch of papers stapled together. "I believe in intelligence, facts, analysis. The Arabs have the best weapons in Moscow's arsenal—planes, tanks, cannons, short-range rockets, long-range rockets, air-to-air missiles, air-to-land missiles, land-to-land—"

"I get the picture."

"Nasser has amassed hundreds of thousands of troops in Sinai. King Hussein has turned the West Bank into a launching pad for his armored divisions. And the Syrians engage in daily target practice from the Golan Heights. The Arabs are like a giant *shoykhet* standing over a skinny lamb!"

Elie thought about his father, back in the shtetl, holding a sharp blade to a lamb's neck while explaining how the smoothness of a single pass of the perfect blade would cause the animal an instant, painless death.

"Why do they hate us so, Weiss?" The prime minister's eyes moistened behind his glasses. "Why?"

"Jealousy," Elie said. "Plain old jealousy."

"*They* are jealous of *us*?"

"Started with the patriarch Abraham. While he claimed to be on a first-name basis with the mightiest God, all-powerful and invisible, the Goyim had to make do with wooden idols on a shelf."

"True."

"Moses parted the sea. King David built an empire. Solomon had a thousand wives. And for centuries the exiled Jews could read and write in many languages while their Christian neighbors couldn't even sign their own names. Are you surprised they hate us?"

"But the Germans were an advanced nation. Why would they be jealous?"

"Because emancipation opened the shtetl's gates by giving Jews equality and opportunity. And the Jews became more equal than others. By 1936, every other German doctor or lawyer was a Jew, prestigious university positions and industrial leadership posts—"

"But look at us now!" Eshkol pointed at himself. "We've lost six million in the camps, we're eighty percent new immigrants, a Babel of languages in the tiniest country, with a majority living in poverty, and no allies to stand with us against a unity of Arab nations. What's to be jealous of now?"

"We have this land."

"For this tiny patch the Arabs envy us? Our single grain of sand to their vast territories? Our puny Lake Kinneret to their oceans of oil? Our dripping Jordan River to their Nile and Euphrates?"

"They linger in the Stone Age while we've arrived at the Nuclear Age. The Dimona reactor is driving them meshuggah. And the Soviets aren't happy either."

"You're right." Levi Eshkol wiped his forehead with a handkerchief. "Not only I have a lingering fever, I also exemplify Isaiah's words: *Your destroyers shall come from within.* How can I save our people when my own party leadership betrays me?"

Elie placed the Dayan file on the table. "Perhaps this will help."

"Ah!" Eshkol's face lit up. "You got the goods on the pirate?"

"As promised." He pulled photos and notes from the file and commenced his presentation. There was the excavation at Megido, where Dayan had used soldiers, army trucks, and even a helicopter to remove hundreds of archeological objects of unimaginable value. A mosaic floor of an ancient synagogue near Nazareth, which Dayan had lifted—literally—courtesy of the IDF corps of engineers. Statements from officers and civilians attested to General Dayan's actions, including testimony from a middleman who had delivered Dayan's antiques to a buyer in Brussels.

When Elie finished, the prime minister clapped his hands. "Weiss, you're a man of your word!"

"General Dayan is a compulsive risk-taker. I think his courage under fire matches his contempt for the law, especially the law governing archeological findings."

"This stuff will sink him." The prime minister blew his nose into a handkerchief. "You know, Abba Eban once told me that Moshe Dayan is the first Jew ever to succeed in violating all Ten Commandments!"

"Funny." Elie put everything back into the file. He didn't tell Eshkol about his meeting with Professor Gileadi at the Antique Authority. Let Dayan defend himself.

An assistant walked in and handed Eshkol two pages held with a clip. "Your speech, sir. We've made additional changes to clarify some points."

Elie saw the penciled scribbling between the printed lines and along the margins. He knew Eshkol was due to speak directly to the nation in a live radio broadcast that night. "You should have it retyped. It would be easier to read."

"Nonsense. If there's one thing I do well, it's talking!" Eshkol stood, sliding his feet into his slippers. "Leave the evidence here. I'll give Dayan a chance to withdraw his candidacy quietly. He'll take a reserve command in the south, keep himself busy."

"Of course." Elie got up, holding the file to his chest. "As soon as you announce my appointment as Mossad chief."

"Right now? Let's deal with the Egyptians first!"

"A deal is a deal."

"The country is on the ropes, and you worry about a deal? Mossad isn't running away. Once the crisis is over, we'll see what can be done, okay?"

"I'd rather not wait." Elie pointed to a newspaper on the table. "Meir Amit screwed up. He estimated there was no risk of war until 1970 at the earliest. I heard him say that. His mistake gives you a perfect excuse to dismiss him and appoint me."

Prime Minister Eshkol sat back, shaking his head. "I can't do that. Not now."

"But you promised."

"Yes, but I didn't promise to keep my promise!"

"Not funny."

"Come on, Weiss, how can you expect me to dismiss the chief of Mossad at a time like this? And appoint someone like you, with limited experience—"

"My experience, Prime Minster, has been more diversified than you can imagine."

Eshkol gave him a wary look. "Let's first get rid of Dayan," he said, almost pleading. "Those sabra boys are daredevils. The good of the country demands it."

"The good of the country," Elie said, turning to leave, "demands that Dayan take over the defense portfolio. That seems to be the consensus."

Even though it wasn't cold, the summer evening was cool enough to give Lemmy the idea of starting a fire in the brick stove that had once been the center of the house. They found a broken chair in one of the rooms and smashed it into small pieces that fit into the stove. Sanani used yesterday's newspapers as kindling.

The fire spread quickly to the dry wood, but the smoke drifted out the front of the stove and began to fill up the room. Sanani tried to close the steel door of the stove, but the smoke kept coming around the ill-fitting door.

"The chimney's blocked!" Lemmy ran to the rear patio to bring water in the two empty tin cans they used as drinking cups. He heard a hissing sound from the living room and found Sanani urinating into the stove. He joined him, and the fire died down. They laughed until their eyes ran with tears.

The house stunk of smoke. They went to the rear patio and sat against the wall, reading the newspapers under two candles.

Going through *Ma'ariv*, Lemmy saw a photo of black-garbed men leaning on their shovels and picks, smiling at the camera. The caption read: *Neturay Karta Members Complete Trench from Meah Shearim to Musrara Neighborhood.* He examined the tiny, familiar faces in the photo. Benjamin wasn't there. Lemmy folded the newspaper and put it away. He had nothing in common with the men in the photo, as if the years at Neturay Karta and his friendship with Benjamin had been experienced by someone else.

Sanani showed him the report in *Ha'aretz* that Egyptian submarines had reached the Straits of Tiran, while heavy guns were deployed at Sharem Al-Sheikh. UN General Rikhye predicted a major Middle East war, declaring: "*I think we will be sorting it out 50 years from now.*" Meanwhile, in Jerusalem, Citizens for Eshkol, an organization that had helped Eshkol win the 1965 elections, turned against him: *Give Dayan the defense portfolio before it's too late!*

That night, Lemmy and Sanani decided that, in the morning, they would demand a brief furlough from their confinement. They crawled into their sleeping bags determined to see the outside world tomorrow, or to hear a good explanation as to why they were wasting time on learning to speak English with funny accents while their friends were preparing to fight the real enemies of Israel.

After the initial rage had subsided and murderous images receded from his mind, Elie decided that Prime Minister Eshkol's broken promise was a good omen. Assuming the top

Mossad position would be better *after* acquiring Klaus von Koenig's vast fortune. And without the account number and password, he would have to plant a mole inside the Hoffgeitz Bank, which hired only graduates of Lyceum Alpin St. Nicholas—a long-term operation that would require careful planning and execution.

He arrived at the IDF Jerusalem command to find everyone huddled around the radio in anticipation of Eshkol's speech. By that night, May 28, every Israeli citizen was on edge, desperate for reassurance that the Arab posturing did not pose existential danger to the Jewish state. The prime minister had to convince the people that his diplomatic overtures would avert war.

At first, Levi Eshkol sounded confident. He greeted the nation and read verbatim the text of the government's decision to send Abba Eban to America yet again. But when he turned to speak about the IDF's readiness to defend the country, Eshkol stuttered and became incoherent. The broadcast continued while the prime minister whispered to an assistant, mumbled in confusion, and attempted to read on, his voice breaking into incessant coughing.

The crowded room uttered a collective groan. Brigadier General Tappuzi turned off the radio.

Elie saw some of the men wiping their eyes. A young officer said, "Eshkol is leading us to another Holocaust." Some nodded in agreement.

As the men ambled out of the office, Elie stayed behind.

"Can you believe it?" Tappuzi's voice shook. "If our leader is afraid, what are we supposed to do?"

"He's not afraid. He's got a bad cold, bad eyes, and a bad copy of a poorly typed speech that even Ben Gurion would have a hard time reading."

"Ben Gurion spoke without notes, from the heart."

"Nostalgia is a waste of time," Elie said. "Have you seen the Mossad report on the UN radar?"

"Worse than we expected." The gray-haired officer dropped into his chair. "It's an American-made system, built under contract for the UN." He pulled the papers from a pile on his desk. "Semi Automatic Ground Environment radar, model AN/SPS-35, shipped directly from Alabama to Amman on a UN cargo plane. It operates at 420 to 450 megahertz, capable of tracking planes up to two hundred miles away, which means they see all of Israel and well into the Sinai and the Mediterranean."

"That far?" Elie lit a cigarette.

"The antenna reflector is over eighty feet wide!"

"If that's true, defending Jerusalem is the least of it." He drew deeply, and the smoke petered out as he spoke. "The UN boys won't miss more than two hundred planes taking off from every airfield in Israel and heading for Egypt. They'll report to the Arabs within minutes, every Egyptian plane will take off, and our first strike will turn into a one-way trip."

"You don't say." Tappuzi tossed the Mossad report back on his desk. "If your plan fails, this radar will cost us the war, possibly our very survival!"

"It's a good plan." Elie stubbed his cigarette in an ashtray that resembled a step-triggered landmine. "But it's going to rest on very young shoulders."

Chapter 41

Lemmy woke up at sunrise and sat on the patio to read a travel book about Munich. He had been ordered to memorize a second cover story as a backup in case his first cover, as a UN observer, was blown. His name was Wilhelm Horch, born and raised near Munich. He had been recruited into the youth training program at the BND, the West German secret service, which had sent him on a practice drill to infiltrate the UN Mideast Command and obtain details of the American-made radar system, which was far more advanced than anything Germany was making.

When the two civilians showed up later that morning, Lemmy and Sanani were ready with a speech demanding a day off. Yosh carried a cardboard box with pastries, still warm from the oven. Dor brought a thermos of coffee and the morning newspapers. "Let's eat," he said, "then go for a drive."

Lemmy looked at Sanani, who shrugged and reached into the box of pastries.

Outside they found a dark-green Jeep Wagoneer, an expensive vehicle that few Israelis could afford. Dor tossed the keys to Sanani, who cheered and broke into a little dance.

New-car smell welcomed them like perfume. The dashboard, doors, and seats were smooth and shining. Sanani had a wide grin on his face as he turned the key. He floored the gas pedal, causing the engine to roar. "Mama, I'm in love!"

"Drive," Yosh said from the back seat, "if you know how."

"This beauty?" Sanani engaged first gear. "It'll drive itself!" He threw the clutch, and the tires screeched. They sped down a narrow street of deserted Arab homes, the Jeep rattling over potholes, and stopped at the corner.

Nablus Road stretched in both directions. A short distance to the left was the border crossing at the Mandelbaum Gate, which sported Israeli, Jordanian, and UN flags.

"Turn right," Yosh said. "And take it easy."

The road passed through the Musrara neighborhood, occupied mostly by Sephardic Jews and recent immigrants from Arab countries. Farther to the right was Meah Shearim. When the Jeep crossed Shivtay Israel Street, Lemmy caught a glimpse of his former neighborhood.

A few minutes later, Sanani veered to the shoulder and stopped.

"Look over there." Dor pointed at the Old City. "From the Mandelbaum Gate, down Salah Al-Din Road, you end up at Herod's Gate. Do you see it?"

Sanani pounded the steering wheel. "If only we could go there!"

"You will," Dor said. "Very soon."

Lemmy thought the civilian was joking, but his tone was serious.

"At Herod's Gate, you'll turn left, down Jericho Road," Dor said. "We can't see it from here, but Jericho Road goes around the eastern wall of the Old City, just under the Mount of Olives, past the Lions Gate, and ends in an intersection—left to Jericho and the Dead Sea, right to Government House. That will be your destination."

"Dressed as UN observers," Lemmy said.

"Correct."

"But how do we cross the border?"

"All in good time." Dor tapped Sanani's shoulder. "Drive."

They continued south, the border on their left, and beyond it the views of the Jaffa Gate, the Zion Gate, and the Abu Tor neighborhood. On the high ridge ahead, the massive stone building of Government House flew the UN flag. The radar reflector rotated atop a concrete structure on a low hill in the rear of the compound.

"There," Dor said, "you'll be coming from the other side, up from the intersection with Jericho road, to the gate of Government House."

"Easy," Sanani said. "We'll roll down the window and yell *Open sesame!*"

"Seriously," Lemmy said, "what do we say to the UN sentries? *Boker tov?*"

"Good morning," Sanani announced in the singsong Indian accent he'd been practicing, "we brought you samossas, beef biryani, chicken masala, and basmati rice. Do you want some chutney with that?"

Elie drove to Tel Aviv that afternoon. He went down into the Pit. The IDF underground complex was a beehive. In the operations center, a meeting of the general staff was just getting underway, the concrete ceiling almost invisible through the cloud of cigarette smoke.

Chief of Staff Yitzhak Rabin said, "When U Thant pulled all UN observers from Sinai, I thought of a fire brigade that runs away at the first sign of fire." He waited for the laughter to die. "As some of you already know, on the same day, May seventeen, two MiGs flew over our reactor in Dimona, probably taking photos."

There was something different about the chief of staff, and Elie suddenly realized that the characteristic slow delivery was gone, replaced with a confident, eloquent presentation that kept the officers' attention. Perhaps it was the experience of witnessing the disastrous impact of Eshkol's stuttering broadcast, or the prepared notes Rabin was holding, which appeared to be cleanly typed.

"Nasser has about one hundred thousand soldiers in Sinai," Rabin continued, "eight hundred tanks, and over a thousand artillery guns, with more pouring in. He placed a de facto blockade on the Straits of Tiran while pursuing a joint command with Jordan and Syria, reinforced by Iraq and Saudi Arabia, as well as smaller units from other countries. Meanwhile our government continues to seek international support." He glanced at his notes. "The Americans won't interfere. De Gaulle again told Abba Eban, *Ne faites pas la guerre!* As if we started this crisis. British Prime Minister Harold Wilson declined to make a statement in our favor. And Soviet Ambassador Chuvakhin, who has accused us of amassing aggressive forces along the borders, declined a helicopter tour to see for himself, saying that his job is to repeat Soviet truths, not to check their veracity."

Everyone laughed, and General Ariel Sharon said, "Maybe Chuvakhin should become our defense minister."

"Arik!" Rabin shook a finger at him. "What you say here appears on the front page of *Ma'ariv* tomorrow."

When the room quieted down, Rabin continued. "Our enemies are optimistic. PLO Chief Shuqayri said yesterday that he expects Israel's complete destruction, and Hafez al-Assad predicted the eradication of Zionist presence in the Arab homeland. We have reports of Iraqi units moving into Syria, Saudis into Jordan. All over the Middle East, the Arab street is in fever. Meanwhile, our reservists are sitting idle in their tents, and their families are anxious. The politicians are still trying diplomacy, but we must prepare to attack as soon as we get government approval."

"Or without it," General Sharon said, earning another finger-shaking from Rabin.

Moshe Dayan stood up. He wore a dusty uniform, and even his trademark eye patch was more gray than black. "I toured the southern front and watched the Egyptians take over the UN monitoring posts. They're mobilizing for an invasion. War is inevitable. If the Arabs attack first, Israel will be destroyed."

No one argued with Dayan.

"I think Abba Eban is coming around," Yitzhak Rabin said. "He told the ministers yesterday: *A nation that could not protect its basic maritime interests would presumably find reason for not repelling other assaults on its rights.* As the song goes," Rabin smiled, "Nasser sits and waits for Rabin, and Rabin waits for Eshkol, and Eshkol waits for his cabinet, and the cabinet waits for Eban, and Eban waits for President Johnson!"

The room exploded in laughter, and Rabin beckoned Chief of Operations Ezer Weitzman to take over.

The famed fighter pilot swiveled the pointer with a swagger. "Code name, *Mokked*," he announced. "The plan is aimed at capturing air superiority by destroying all Egyptian runways and strafing all their grounded planes." Weitzman held up a diagram. "Our scientists have designed bombs with delay fuses, set to explode only after penetrating deep into the runways. The damage will take weeks to repair. We have detailed plans of every military airfield in Egypt, Jordan, and Syria, including exact locations, lengths of runways, construction materials, and types of planes kept at each airfield." He pointed at Chief of Mossad Meir Amit. "I don't know how your guys got it all, but thank you."

Elie saw the Mossad chief nod in acknowledgment.

Weitzman went into some details about schedules, risks, and the necessity of acting before the enemy realized what was happening. "This is a first-strike plan," he concluded. "If the Egyptians attack us first, they'll destroy Dimona and all our airfields. What I need is a green light for a preemptive strike."

"Call Eshkol," someone said.

"What about detection?" General Arik Sharon shoved a piece of cake into his mouth, but continued speaking with a mouthful. "Our planes will be in the air for at least a half-hour, right? Won't the Egyptians notice us? And scramble their jets to meet us?"

"They're practically blind," Weitzman said. "The Soviets gave them the best weaponry, but the most primitive radars."

"Ever since Prague," the Mossad chief, General Amit explained, "the Soviets are careful not to provide their client-states with defensive measures that could hamper a Soviet attack, should the friendship turn sour."

"But still," Arik Sharon said, "the Egyptian forces along the Sinai border could notice our planes and alert the airfields inland. How will you avoid that?"

"By flying fast and low," Weitzman said, but Elie could tell he was not telling the whole truth.

The chief of Mossad stood, which brought immediate quiet to the room. "Timing is key. By the time an Egyptian soldier notices a couple of planes pass overhead and makes the decision to bother his direct commander, our pilots will be close to their targets. The hierarchical nature of the Egyptian army means that a warning from a junior officer in the front would have to climb up rung by rung all the way up to headquarters. And it won't make an impression unless many other such sightings are reported simultaneously. By then, even if the Egyptian generals realize what's happening and send orders down to each airfield, they'll be too late. Our pilots will have already hit their respective targets."

"But there's a weakness," Weitzman said.

"Correct." The chief of Mossad glanced at Rabin. "The new radar system at the UN Middle East headquarters at the Government House is the most powerful ground-based radar America makes. It sits on the highest piece of land in the region and is powerful enough to track our jets from the moment of takeoff and all the way over Sinai and the Mediterranean. They'll see our pilots take off, and General Bull could call President Nasser directly and tell him the radar is tracking two hundred and thirty Israeli jets heading south. Nasser would shoot orders down to the bases, and all their planes will take off just in time to give our boys a deadly welcome."

Arik Sharon said, "What about cutting off the electrical power to Government House?"

"The UN has its own generators and gasoline depot behind the radar station." The Mossad chief must have anticipated Sharon's next question, adding, "And no, Arik, you may not attack the UN Mideast headquarters."

Sharon grinned. "You have a better option?"

"Our technical experts are looking into jamming as an option, but it doesn't look promising."

On the drive back, they stopped at a payphone and Dor gave Sanani a fistful of tokens to call home. Lemmy watched his animated face as he happily spoke to each of his many family members and blew loud kisses. When Sanani was done, Dor beckoned Lemmy, who shook his head. He would have liked to call Tanya, but what could he say to her? *I still love you even though you used me.*

A gray-haired woman with a husky voice and a beautiful British accent came in the afternoon, carrying a cardboard model of Government House, where she had worked before 1948 for the British High Commissioner. She pointed out to Lemmy and Sanani the gate, the front courtyard, Antenna Hill in the rear, and the building itself, where a side entrance led into a stairwell made of matches and pieces of fabric. She explained the internal setup of the building, especially the three alternative stairways up to the roof, where a storage shed served as a base for the massive flag mast. When she left, the model stayed behind.

Yosh and Dor showed up a while later with cans of paint and brushes and a photo of a UN Jeep Wagoneer. "Have fun," Yosh said. "Try to make it look professional."

Sanani walked around the green Jeep, cradling his cheeks in mock grief. "It's a crime against humanity!"

After taping over the glass and chrome, as well as the headlights and turn signals, they stripped down to their boxer shorts and began painting.

Lemmy was working on the bottom of a door when he felt a wet brush travel down his spine. "No!" He turned and smacked Sanani on his head with his brush, turning the black curls into white hair that was pasted down Sanani's forehead.

The brushes became swords, marking their naked chests and backs. Sanani was quick, feigning, thrusting, and hooting at the top of his voice. His back against the Jeep, Lemmy suddenly tossed his brush at Sanani, and while his friend was busy trying to catch it with slippery hands, Lemmy ran for the rear-patio shower.

"There's another issue," the Mossad chief said. "We have evidence that the Egyptians have transported into Sinai their whole poison gas stockpile. We've obtained the original shipping documents from the German manufacturer. Chemical analysis shows they have enough to eliminate approximately ten million humans, theoretically speaking. In reality, efficacy depends on accurate delivery, topography, population density, wind conditions, and humidity. Our sources report that the

Egyptians have rigged up some of their artillery pieces to launch the canisters at our army units. They'll use planes to drop the rest on our cities."

He passed around photos of poison gas victims in Yemen, where the Egyptian army had eliminated whole villages. The photos travelled around the large table in complete silence. Elie passed them on without looking. He had seen the real thing in Nazi Germany and had no need to refresh his memory.

Amit said, "I showed these to Eshkol this morning. He is sending me to Washington to show them to President Johnson." The Mossad chief chuckled. "The way Eshkol put it: Tell that big Texan goy that we're dealing with *chayes! Vildeh chayes!*"

Wild animals, Elie thought, was exactly what the Arabs were. And the Germans too. And the Austrians, Polacks, Ukrainians, Romanians, Hungarians, and Russians. In fact, all Christians and Muslims were *vildeh chayes* when it came to killing Jews. Even Johnson wasn't much better, refusing to stand by Israel as its enemies were gathering to destroy it with full Soviet support.

Rabin announced a break and beckoned Elie to accompany him outside the room. They stood in a concrete hallway near the restrooms, where a large vent was sucking air into the underground purification system.

"You heard it, Weiss," the chief of staff said. "It's not just Jerusalem. The whole success of *Mokked* depends on your radar operation. If Bull warns them before we reach Egyptian air fields, we'll lose our entire air force. And once they control the air, our ground forces have no chance against their massive numbers and equipment. We'll all be dead within a week."

"I'll disable that UN radar for you," Elie said. "Even if I have to do it myself."

"Tappuzi has doubts about your plan. What are the chances of success?"

"One hundred percent."

"That's never the case," Rabin said. "And what can you do about Eshkol and his geriatric ministers?"

Elie knew what he was asking. "Going to war is a political decision."

"They're fearful old men. They'll wring their hands and pontificate in clever Yiddish while I carry the burden alone. But I'm a soldier! I need orders! Dayan is the only—"

"I have a file full of dirt on Dayan."

Rabin grabbed Elie's arm. "Burn it! Just burn it!"

"Eshkol promised to appoint me to run Mossad."

The chief of staff turned away, and Elie was afraid he would bang his head on the concrete wall. This was a crucial moment. The bargaining would be short and decisive. "But I'd rather deal with a sabra."

Rabin turned back, and a boyish smile cracked his face. "Weiss, you're a *mamzer!* Wicked!"

"My price is the same. Give me your word, and I'll burn Dayan's file."

"But I don't appoint Mossad chiefs."

"Not yet. But you will when you become prime minister."

"Me?" Rabin laughed. "You are meshuggah. I'm a hundred years too young for that job."

"I'm a patient man."

"Sure. I give you my word. When I'm prime minister, I'll appoint you to run Mossad." Yitzhak Rabin patted his shirt pockets. "Damn, I'm out. Give me a cigarette, will you?"

Chapter 42

On Saturday morning, June 3, Lemmy went outside to check if the paint on the Jeep had dried. He passed his hand on the hood, feeling no stickiness, only tiny specs of dust embedded in the paint.

He woke Sanani up, and they cut molds for the letters U and N out of cardboard pieces. The car doors were open, and the Voice of Israel played Hebrew ballads on the radio.

At ten a.m. the radio uttered the familiar series of beeps preceding the news, and they stopped to listen. The lead item was that King Hussein had piloted his own plane from Amman to Cairo to sign a treaty with Nasser, submitting the Jordanian army to Egyptian command. The second item was an announcement from Prime Minister Eshkol, welcoming Moshe Dayan as defense minister in a unity government that also included opposition leader Menachem Begin.

"Yes!" Sanani lifted the paint brush, which he had just dipped in black.

"Don't start!" Lemmy grabbed his hand.

"Why?" Sanani was laughing as he tried to free his hand and splatter Lemmy with paint.

"Because I think today is our day."

Elie Weiss was not surprised to see the prime minister deflated, barely bothering to look up as government ministers and IDF generals filed into the conference room. The new defense minister, Moshe Dayan, appeared in khaki uniform that carried no rank or insignia, placing him in a gray area between the civilian and military leaders. He took a seat next to Yitzhak Rabin, who raised his glass of water in a symbolic toast. Dayan grinned and patted the chief of staff on the shoulder.

Abba Eban spoke first. "I must report with indelible regrets that our repeated excursions across the oceans have come to diplomatic naught. This is the last word from President Lyndon Johnson." The foreign minister read from a piece of paper. "*I'd love to see that little blue and white flag sailing down the Straits of Tiran, but I can't do anything at this time.*"

Eshkol sighed.

"The American president's final decision," Eban continued, "must be analyzed prudently. For example, embodied in the latter part of his message is an expression of absolute negation—*anything*—regarding American intervention. However, he left a door poignantly open by utilizing words of friendly intonation, such as the emotional *love* and the endearing *little* in reference to our national flag."

OC operations, Ezer Weitzman, sneered and tossed a pencil on the large table.

"In diplomatic terms," Abba Eban said, "the phraseology is carefully chosen to deliver a secondary message. I believe Johnson intended to give us a non-explicit permission to engage in active self-defense. I submit to you therefore that the United States has assented implicitly to our pending engagement in a unilateral military endeavor."

No one responded to Abba Eban's short dissertation which, Elie suspected, was due to the attendees' difficulty in comprehending it.

"I agree." Chief of Mossad, Meir Amit, was disheveled after a long flight from Washington via Paris. "The Americans blew us off. We're on our own. But they won't punish us for taking action. Our CIA liaison, Jim Angleton, is a good friend, and he told me as much. He took me to meet McNamara, and we showed him the evidence of Egyptian poison gas stockpiles. They agree we must act, but they'll stay out for fear of instigating World War Three."

"Exactly," Moshe Dayan said. "And the Soviets are afraid of the same thing, so they won't step in to fight for the Arabs."

"Unfortunately," Amit said, "the Soviets are better at saying one thing and doing another."

Eshkol perked up. "What do you mean?"

"Our analysis shows that these reconnaissance flights over Dimona went to fifty-thousand feet. Only MiG twenty-fives can go that high, and only Russian pilots fly them. I believe Moscow is determined to stop our nuclear enterprise, even at the risk of a limited American intervention."

"God help us," Eshkol said. "We're starting a nuclear war between the superpowers!"

"Not likely," Abba Eban said. "Despite a level of unpredictability, Moscow and Washington are disinterested in a major conflagration. It would counteract their strategic game plans, which are founded on gradual expansionism of their respective ideologically favorable hemispheres."

"I don't need the Americans to fight for us," Rabin said. "But will they send us supplies and replacement parts for the weapons we've bought from them?"

Amit shook his head. "The only thing Johnson approved was a plane full of gas masks and nerve-gas antidote. I caught a ride on that plane—a strange flight, let me tell you."

There were a few chuckles in the room, fading quickly.

"Our team in France had better success," the Mossad chief continued. "The new Mirages are already in the air, somewhere over Greece." He glanced at his watch. "They'll start landing at Ramat David in two hours. Also, three cargo ships left Marseilles last night with artillery pieces, half-tracks, light guns, ammunition, and replacement parts."

The dozen or so elderly ministers seemed lost for words. They looked expectantly at the new defense minister.

Moshe Dayan asked, "What's the bottom-line recommendation of Mossad?"

Amit didn't hesitate. "The Egyptian forces are poised to attack. We are facing an existential threat. I recommend a preemptive strike against Egypt, while keeping Jordan and Syria out of the fighting, if possible."

Dayan turned to Rabin. "Yitzhak?"

"I concur."

His single eye focused on Prime Minister Eshkol. "I request," Dayan said, "a cabinet vote authorizing me to determine the exact timing and scope of the war."

Elie sat and listened as the elderly ministers tried to probe for renewal of diplomatic efforts. Dayan seemed almost petulant, dismissing their concerns with laconic responses. Eventually, Eshkol called for a vote, which Dayan won. He now had full and autonomous authority over Israel's armed forces. No one in the room doubted his inclination to launch an attack as soon as possible.

Before the meeting formally adjourned, Elie left and drove to see Brigadier General Tappuzi. As they had planned in advance, Tappuzi called UN General Odd Bull, asking him for an urgent meeting to discuss Israel's protest over the entry of Jordanian armored units into East Jerusalem in violation of the Armistice Agreements.

Tappuzi put down the receiver. "He'll be here in about an hour."

"Good," Elie said. He felt the handle of his father's *shoykhet* knife against his hip. "Make sure someone distracts his driver while I deflate his tires."

"How long do you want me to keep Bull here?"

"An hour or so. Tell your mechanics to take their time."

Lemmy and Sanani showered and shaved in the rear patio, shivering under the freezing water. The plan had been made clear to them, and the time for jokes was over. They folded their olive-green uniforms and put on UN khakis and blue caps. Sanani wore large sunglasses, which apparently were an exact copy of the shades worn by Bull's driver.

Lemmy stuck the Mauser in his belt in the back. "Better keep this place tidy while I'm away. And no peeing in the oven!"

"Maybe I'll stay at Government House with you," Sanani said.

"Next time," Lemmy said, and they laughed.

The Jeep was clean and fueled up. It smelled of fresh paint but otherwise looked like a real UN vehicle. Lemmy loaded a khaki duffel bag marked with a UN insignia on both sides, which contained explosives and detonators. A backpack held a jar of water and two loaves of bread.

The two civilians showed up. "It's time, boys." Dor held out his hand, and they gave him their military ID tags and personal identification papers.

Meanwhile, Yosh fixed a new license plate to the rear of the Jeep: *UN-1*

Lemmy got in the rear, and Sanani covered him with blue tarp. General Bulls' Jeep was supposedly protected from Jordanian inspections, but this one was a fake. In the event of exposure, their orders were to speed up and reach Government House. A capture by the UN would be preferable to falling into the hands of the Jordanians, whose likely response upon catching an Israeli spy behind the lines would be a bullet to the head.

The Jeep shook over bumps in the road. The hard floor of the trunk provided Lemmy with no cushion.

"Approaching Mandelbaum Gate," Sanani announced. Lemmy had asked him to describe what he was seeing, especially once they entered the eastern part of Jerusalem, which he had longed to visit since childhood.

Sanani downshifted, and the Jeep slowed down. Lemmy held his breath.

"Good morning," Sanani yelled through the window, hiding the quiver in his voice behind a good imitation of an Indian accent. "Nice weather!"

The Jeep kept moving. Again Sanani slowed and greeted someone, probably the Jordanian guards. He rolled up the window and drove off slowly. "We're through," he said. "*Mazal Tov!*"

"Speak English," Lemmy said from under the tarp, worried that Sanani would slip into Hebrew at the wrong time.

"I'm approaching the Old City. What a view!"

Lemmy lifted the corner of the tarp and peeked through the side window.

Sanani swerved, almost hitting a donkey cart. "Keep your head down."

They reached the intersection with Jericho Road, and Lemmy caught sight of Herod's Gate—wide and tall and more impressive than he had imagined. He lowered his head as Sanani turned left, passing a crowded outdoor market along the ancient walls.

A few moments passed. The Jeep hit more bumps and potholes.

Lemmy peeked again. On the left was a hillside dotted with olive trees and gravestones.

"The Mount of Olives," Sanani said with wonder in his voice. "And down there, Absalom's tomb!"

With the Old City walls so close, Lemmy wished they could stop and go over to touch the ancient stones. Instead, he got back under the tarp.

A few minutes later, Sanani hit the brakes. "Jordanian roadblock."

"Don't stop."

"Have to. It's an intersection. Left to Jericho, right back up the hill to Bethlehem Road."

"Slow down, wave, smile, and turn right."

The Jeep was barely moving. Lemmy heard Sanani roll down his window. Someone yelled in Arabic, and the Jeep stopped. More Arabic, and a series of bangs along the vehicle, as if someone was tapping it with a truncheon. He heard the trunk lid open up.

Elie stood at the edge of the parking lot near the IDF Jerusalem command, the binoculars pressed to his eyes, aimed at Bethlehem Road as it rose from the east toward Government House. He had expected the boys to appear ten minutes ago, and with every passing moment his worries grew. Had they been stopped by the Jordanians? An experienced agent would know to be chatty, joke around, and charm his way out of a tight spot. But a young soldier might convey nervousness, inciting suspicion.

Behind him, two IDF mechanics were busy with General Bull's car. They had already removed the two tires Elie had punctured with quick jabs from his *shoykhet* blade. Now one mechanic was lying under the Jeep, pretending to spot an oil leak while the

Indian driver stood beside his disabled vehicle, chatting with Tappuzi's pretty secretary.

Elie returned his eyes to the binoculars. The distant road across the gulch was still empty. Had he erred in using Abraham's son for this operation? Had he tried to catch too many birds with one stone, committing the cardinal sin of impatience? Had he caused a failure, or worse, the boy's immediate execution? That would be an unfortunate setback, Elie thought, considering the next clandestine job he had in mind for Jerusalem Gerster.

The trunk lid was open, and a voice said something in Arabic. Lemmy didn't move. He heard Sanani get out of the car and yell in Indian-accented English, "No search! United Nations!"

Lemmy felt the tarp being pulled. He grabbed it from underneath, holding for dear life.

The Jordanian switched to English. "*Vod yo hab ear?*"

"What I have here?" Sanani laughed. "I have Umm Kooltoom, Allah bless her soul!" He started imitating the famous singer, her Arabic lyrics somehow accented to sound the way an English-speaking Indian would be singing. It was an impressive performance, and the Jordanian soldiers started clapping. The trunk lid closed, and he came around to the driver's door, still singing. As they moved off, he yelled, "*Ahlan Wa'Sahalan, ya habibi!*"

Lemmy said, "You're a madman."

"I think I wet my pants," Sanani said.

Elie let the air out of his lungs in a long whistle. His binoculars followed the white Jeep Wagoneer over the crest of the hill toward Government House. The gate opened, and the Jeep drove through without stopping, circled the courtyard, and turned around, coming to a stop at the far corner of the main building. The rear of the Jeep faced away from the courtyard and the gate, but Elie could see Sanani coming around. The trunk lid rose, and Lemmy slipped out with the duffel bag and the backpack and disappeared in the doorway that led to the rear stairway.

Shifting his focus to the roof, Elie waited. Moments later Lemmy appeared, carrying the load quickly across the roof to the shed. He pushed the door—it was not locked, which was a fact they had not been able to ascertain before—and entered the shed.

Sanani waited five minutes and drove the Jeep back to the gate. The sentries opened it, and the vehicle passed through and turned east. No one seemed concerned about the quick turnaround.

Elie walked by Bull's real Jeep. He caught the eye of one of the IDF mechanics and nodded once. In fifteen minutes, the repairs would be completed, the UN general would be driven back to Government House, and the nail-biting wait would begin.

Chapter 43

On June 5, at 7:00 a.m., Elie was in Brigadier General Tappuzi's command center in West Jerusalem, drinking black coffee and smoking another cigarette. Almost two days had passed since Sanani had returned from Government House, through the three sets of border checkpoints, to the safe house well before General Bull's Jeep was ready to leave. He was a smart kid from a poor family of Yemenite immigrants, and Elie had been impressed by his tale of distracting the Jordanians at a roadblock. But the launch of *Mokked* had been delayed due to clouds over Egypt, and by now Lemmy must be hungry and thirsty. How long could he survive cooped up in that dark rooftop shed?

"It's a go!" Tappuzi ran into the office, waving a telegram. "It's a go!"

Elie took the sheet of thin paper. It was a printout of a secret order, issued moments earlier by Air Force Chief, General Motti Hod, to the 230 pilots about to take off:

Mokked is the word. The Spirit of Israel's ancient braves soars with you today, from Joshua Bin-Nun, to King David, and the Maccabee warriors. Fly, ascend over the enemy, destroy him, and spread his remains over the desert dunes, so that our nation can live safely on our ancestral land for eternity.

Elie headed to the door. "I'll give the signal."

"Hurry!"

Across the parking lot, at the edge, Elie inspected Government House through his binoculars. It was a clear morning, and he saw nothing out of the ordinary at the UN headquarters. He focused on the rooftop storage shed under the fluttering UN flag. The door was slightly ajar, just enough for Lemmy to peek through. Elie put down the binoculars and removed the cap from the flare. Gripping it with two hands, he slammed the bottom of the cylinder on a rock.

The yellow flare shot up into the sky, trailing a white wake. It drew a wide arc and began a slow descent.

Elie focused his binoculars on the shed. A moment passed. He assumed Lemmy was gathering the bag of explosives and straightening his blue cap.

Another minute passed. *7:04 a.m.*

The jets would be taking off from every Israeli air field in eleven minutes. What was Lemmy doing?

The flare was like a lever, releasing all of Lemmy's pent-up stress. *Action!* But as he bent down to lift the duffel bag, he realized that a different type of pressure had built up inside him during the three hours he'd stood at the door to watch for the signal. He had visited the restroom on the top floor during the night to relieve himself and shave. But now, the UN staff were arriving at their offices, and he could not risk a chance encounter with an inquisitive UN officer.

Have to go!

Lemmy faced the wall and unzipped his pants. His mind began counting, just like during a nighttime navigation drill. *Twenty-one. Twenty-two. Twenty-three.*

At twenty-eight, he was done. He grabbed the duffel bag and ran out. The sun blinded him after the darkness of the shed. He stopped, covering his eyes.

No time!

He sprinted to the stairwell at the east end of the roof and paused at the top landing to listen. All quiet. The smell of fried eggs rose from the ground-floor kitchen, which Lemmy wished he had time to visit, having sustained himself on dry bread and water for two days.

One floor down, he heard a commotion in the hallway. "Look at that flare," someone said. "What's that supposed to be?"

Lemmy froze. If the UN observers realized the flare was a signal for military action, the whole front could go up in flames, sabotaging Israel's preemptive strike.

"It's nothing," another voice answered in heavily accented English. "Some Jews playing around."

Breathing in relief, he resumed his descent.

At the bottom, he used a door on the east side of the building, out of view for anyone in the courtyard. He peeked around the corner of the building. Across the courtyard, two gate sentries sat on white plastic chairs and smoked. He adjusted his blue cap, shouldered the duffel bag, and started across the open area.

A moderate incline toward Antenna Hill formed the east grounds of the UN compound. He looked up and saw the enormous radar reflector rotate atop the concrete station like a giant sail, curved in with a good wind. He kept a calm pace, resisting the urge to run. Anyone walking in the courtyard, sitting at an office window, or guarding the gate, could see him carry the duffel bag toward the radar station. He imagined eyes following him, and his back felt as if ants were crawling all over it.

Across the open area, he approached Antenna Hill without anyone disturbing the sounds of normal activity at the UN headquarters, with which he had grown familiar.

The radar station was half-sunken in the ground. A tall wall of sandbags surrounded it, and the entrance formed a narrow zigzag, barely wide enough for one person. As Lemmy reached it, already panting from the hike, a gray-haired man in UN uniform appeared in the passage. "Good morning," he said, his *g* and *r* throaty.

Lemmy swallowed hard and saluted. "Good morning," he said, struggling to say it with the same accent. But he had not spoken to anyone in two days, and his words came out hoarsely. He forced himself to smile and repeated, "A *very* good morning, sir!"

The UN officer paused, blocking the narrow entrance, and measured Lemmy up and down.

Still smiling, Lemmy prepared to drop the duffel bag and reach behind his back to draw the Mauser.

The officer said, "X. Y. Z."

Lemmy hesitated. What did it mean? He began to lower the duffel bag. There was no time—the whole IDF air force depended on him!

"X. Y. Z," the officer repeated.

"Weiss!" Tappuzi called from across the parking lot. He stood at the entrance to the IDF command center, tapping on his wristwatch. "Noo?"

Elie shrugged. It was 7:13 a.m. More than two hundred heavily armed fighter jets waited in multiple airstrips across Israel. Any delay meant missing the window of time when all the Egyptian pilots were eating breakfast while ground crews fueled their planes after the early morning sorties. He had seen Abraham's son emerge from the rooftop shed on Government House two minutes behind schedule and disappear in the south stairwell. The rest of his route to Antenna Hill was not visible from where Elie stood, more than three miles away, but the partial view of the courtyard showed no unusual activity, the UN observers going about their business in customary leisure. Had he been stopped inside the building? Had he been exposed?

General Rabin had said he would go forward with the strike even if Elie's operation failed to disable the UN radar. But that meant a UN alarm, communicated to the Egyptians, who would have enough time to scramble their planes into the air and hone their anti-aircraft batteries. In other words, it meant the lives of countless Israeli pilots, the failure of *Mokked*, and possibly the loss of the war before it had even started.

"Weiss! Talk to me!" Tappuzi sounded desperate. The UN radar, once connected to the Jordanian anti-aircraft guns, meant a free range for their cannons and tanks. Such an artillery barrage would result in wholesale slaughter in West Jerusalem, whose defense was Tappuzi's responsibility.

Elie kept his eyes glued to the binoculars. He could see the radar reflector rotate in defiant laziness. He spat the cigarette and said out loud, "Come on, Jerusalem Gerster! *Blow it!*"

The UN officer repeated: "X. Y. Z." He was wearing an array of brass symbols on his shoulders and an assortment of war decorations on his chest. A chrome nametag said: *O. Bull*

Lemmy was desperate. Were the letters some kind of a UN code? What was the appropriate response? He reached behind his back, digging under the khaki shirt for the Mauser. To stall for a few more seconds, he said, "A. B. C."

"*Ya! Ya!*" The officer laughed, pointing at Lemmy's crotch. "X. Y. Z. Examine. Your. Zipper."

"Oh!" His face burning, Lemmy zipped his fly, saluted, and grabbed the duffel bag. He entered the narrow passage through the wall of sandbags and heard the officer chuckle while walking away.

A path took Lemmy around the radar station to the rear. Five gasoline tanks were lined up next to a silent generator. In the rear wall of the station, large wooden doors allowed delivery and removal of heavy equipment. The doors were locked, and he was out of sight between the station and the perimeter fence. Above his head, a buzzing sound came from the electric motor that kept the radar reflector turning.

He found the drainage faucet at the bottom of the first gasoline tank and opened it. Fuel began to pour out, flowing toward a depression in the asphalt, where it formed a puddle. From the duffel bag he removed a small device, about the size of a book, and placed it near the growing puddle. The ensuing conflagration was supposed to create the false impression that the destruction of the radar was caused by an accidental ignition of the fuel. It would take time to find traces of explosives, and by then operation *Mokked* would be over, and the UN observers would be too busy monitoring a raging war to investigate the explosion.

He placed a much larger pack of explosives by the electric board next to the loading doors and pulled the fuse on each of the devices.

One minute.

Running around the corner to the front, Lemmy was about to exit the zigzag passage through the sandbag wall when he heard voices through the open door of the radar station. Someone was talking while a second voice hooted.

In a flash, Lemmy realized the UN observers inside were young soldiers not much different than him, having fun just like he, Sanani, and the other guys back in boot camp.

He turned and ran inside.

The large control room was well lit. Bulky sets of electronic equipment occupied most of the walls. Two UN soldiers sat at the tracking monitors. Three others were busy throwing darts at a full-body poster of a naked Marilyn Monroe, fixed to the loading doors behind which the explosives were about to detonate. Several darts were already stuck in Monroe, primarily around her chest.

One of them turned to Lemmy. "*Ya?*"

"Get out," Lemmy yelled. "Fire!"

The soldiers laughed. One of them, who seemed Indian, plucked a dart from Monroe's chest and offered it to Lemmy. "Fire! She's very hot!"

"Get out!" Lemmy tore the headphones off the two soldiers at the monitors. "Now!" But their expressions told him that they still thought it was some kind of a joke. He wasn't getting through to these men, who were about to be incinerated by his bombs. He grabbed one by the shirt and shoved him toward the door. "*Out!*"

Finally grasping the urgency, the UN soldier sprinted out. The others bolted as well. Lemmy chased them out through the sandbag passage, just as an explosion pounded him square in the back. It threw him face-down to the ground, and a wave of heat washed over him.

Elie's hands jerked up instinctively as the fireball leaped into the sky, followed a second later by the sound of the explosion. He stumbled backward, shocked by the size of the eruption. As the initial cloud of smoke and debris began to settle, he looked through his binoculars.

The radar reflector was gone from the skyline. He aimed the binoculars lower and saw the giant steel-mesh reflector in the courtyard of Government House. By now Lemmy must have melted into the hundreds of UN soldiers running around in confusion while flames engulfed the radar station. Lemmy had been instructed to watch for Bull's Jeep leaving the compound, which would be his signal to wait near the gate for Sanani to pick him up twenty-four minutes later in the fake jeep.

Back at the command center's front steps, Brigadier General Tappuzi held an upturned thumb.

A group of reservists and staff hurried outside at the sound of the distant explosion and watched the flames across the valley. Someone speculated about a Jordanian attack on the UN compound. Another mentioned old landmines left from the British rule two decades earlier.

At the communications center, Elie phoned Rabin at the Pit. "The sky has just cleared up in Jerusalem," he said.

"About time." Rabin hung up.

Replacing the receiver, Elie said, "You're welcome."

Tappuzi slapped his back. "You got it done, Weiss! Your crazy plan worked!"

But Elie knew that toppling the UN radar was just the beginning. Everything was still at stake—the aerial attack on Egypt, the subsequent raids on Syria and, if it joined the fighting, on Jordan too, and the ground war on three fronts. Israel's survival was still at stake, as were his own plans to change the paradigm of Jewish-Gentile relations in a way that would altogether eliminate the risk of future wars against Israel.

Mokked required radio silence while IDF planes took off from every Israeli air base at specific, predetermined times, so that all squadrons reached their various targets deep inside Egypt simultaneously. Because Egyptian airfields were located at different distances from Israel, Mokked had to reach a level of precision never tried before by any air force in history. The plan resembled a three-dimensional jigsaw puzzle, calculating the exact duration of each plane's expected travel distance from its base to its designated target, factoring in speed, wind conditions, fuel capacity, and type of armament. It was crucial that all the Egyptian targets were hit at the same time, preventing the enemy from raising the alarm before all targets had been destroyed. With the farthest Egyptian target being its airfield in Luxor, the various Israeli squadrons had to fly low over the Mediterranean, the Red Sea, the Negev Desert, or the Sinai Peninsula, enter Egyptian territory at multiple points undetected, and converge simultaneously over eleven disparate targets after flight times varying between twenty and forty-five minutes.

For Elie, chain-smoking in Tappuzi's office in West Jerusalem, the wait was torturous. If Mokked failed, Israel would lose control of the air, and Egypt could launch its massive arsenal of poison gas and destroy Dimona. After fifty years of losing land and pride to the Zionist enterprise, the Arabs would surpass even the Germans in the enthusiastic killing of Jews.

"Let's go downstairs," Tappuzi finally said, having bitten his nails down to the flesh.

An hour passed without news. Another thirty minutes.

That was as much as Tappuzi could wait. "Make the call," he said, "please!"

Elie dialed the number for the operations center at the Pit. After several more connections, Rabin's voice came on the line. "Yes?"

"We're wondering," Elie said, "how's the weather in Tel Aviv?"

"Sunny," the chief of staff said. "Our pigeons are back in the nest for a quick drink before flying south again."

"Shall we call the big house to extend an invitation?"

"Go ahead. And tell Tappuzi to let us know if his neighbors to the east get rowdy. I'll send him a few pigeons if that happens."

Elie put down the receiver. He smiled. "It worked. Our boys are back safely, getting ready for the second raid."

Tappuzi looked up and yelled, "Thank you, God!"

"Time to sound the alarm. Let's get the population into bomb shelters and trenches. The Jordanians might start shelling our neighborhoods if they think Egypt is winning. Let Rabin know and he'll send a few planes."

Brigadier General Tappuzi ran out. A moment later, the air-raid sirens started whining all over West Jerusalem. As planned, he would call General Bull to complain that Egyptian jets attacked

Israeli defenses in the Negev, a lie that was intended to prolong the confusion as much as possible and provide an excuse to demand a meeting with Bull.

Elie went outside to wait for General Bull's Jeep. He felt the handle of the *shoykhet* blade hidden against his hip. The UN chief would be suspicious when his tires went flat again, especially after his prized radar had been blown up, but what could he do? Call the police?

Across the gulch, other than the fire behind Government House, the Jordanian side of Jerusalem seemed quiet. But for how long? They must be wondering about the sirens on the Jewish side.

"Weiss!" Tappuzi emerged from the building, beckoning him. "Bull is raging crazy. The fire is out of control there, and he heard from his people in Egypt that Israeli planes have attacked. He's accusing us of destroying the radar. He claims that—"

"Doesn't matter what he says. He's got no evidence. And he should not have colluded with the Arabs."

"He warned me to stay out of the Old City."

"Fool's dreams," Elie said. "Dayan won't pass up the opportunity to recapture Temple Mount—the mother of all archeological treasure troves."

"It gets worse. Bull saw our saboteur earlier near the radar. They're looking for him."

"That's bad." Elie watched the column of smoke rise behind the white mansion with the light-blue flag. If Lemmy broke down and talked, the whole operation would be exposed, causing a diplomatic nightmare for Israel, let alone derailing all of Elie's well-laid plans.

"What do you want me to do?"

"Call Bull back," Elie said. "Tell him that if he's not here in fifteen minutes, you'll order our artillery to bomb Jordanian positions in East Jerusalem."

"We don't have any artillery!"

"Bull doesn't know that. When he gets here, have someone disable his Jeep. I can't wait any longer."

"But what if Bull doesn't show up? What are you going to do about that kid over there?"

"For all we know, he might already be dead."

The voices were garbled, some shouting, even fearful, others calm and reassuring. Lemmy felt hands lifting him. He opened his eyes and tried to brush off the dirt that stuck to his eyelids. How long had he been lying here? He craned his head and saw the flames rising from the ruined radar station.

Success!

They put him on a stretcher, face down, and carried him across the courtyard toward the building. Someone said, "It's okay. Stay down."

Many UN personnel milled about, some pulling water hoses, others removing sandbags to facilitate access to the burning radar station.

The stretcher reached the main building entrance just as the gray-haired officer emerged from it. His face was red. He slammed the blue cap on his head and got into his white Jeep. For a second, Lemmy mistook the Indian driver for Sanani. But it was the real driver. He hit the gas and raced across the courtyard toward the open gate. Lemmy tried to look at his watch, but it was gone. How would he know when to expect Sanani? As they carried him on the stretcher into the building, it dawned on him that he might be too badly injured to make his way to the gate.

The room smelled of antiseptics. They transferred Lemmy onto an examination table, still on his belly, and left him. He tried to rise but was overwhelmed by dizziness.

A woman in a white coat rushed in, a stethoscope around her neck. She spoke to him in a foreign language, which he guessed to be Norwegian. He didn't answer, but tried to rise. She made him stay down and used scissors to cut his pants, starting from the bottom near his boots. He stopped her by kicking at her hand. She yelled something, pulled off a piece of the shirt from his back and held it in front of his face. It was singed black. Lemmy reached behind and touched his lower back. The skin was raw.

She left the room.

After a while, Lemmy felt strong enough to stand. He rolled off the examination table, legs first, and stood, shaking. The front of his body was unharmed, the UN khakis dirty but otherwise in good shape. Looking over his shoulder at his back side, he saw blackened skin. His head hurt badly, and his right ear was developing a blister along the edge.

He tried the door. It was locked. He went to the sink and put his head under cold water. It hurt, but he was coming back to his senses. He had to get to the front gate to rendezvous with Sanani. How long had it been since General Bull had left? In the small mirror above the sink, his face was bruised, a gash over his left cheekbone trickling blood. He pressed a towel to the wound. His head was pounding, and the room started spinning. He stumbled, held on to the sink, and collapsed.

The risk that Lemmy might be caught and interrogated forced Elie to make a swift decision. He drove to the safe house and changed into UN khakis—an extra set he had ordered with the sets made for Lemmy and Sanani. Elie's shirt was adorned with the insignia of a UN general, copied from a photograph of General Bull.

Sanani was waiting outside by the Jeep.

"Let's bring your friend home," Elie said.

They left the safe house and drove to the corner of Nablus Road, where they waited in the shadows until Bull's car passed by on its way to Tappuzi's office.

Mandelbaum Gate was a minute away. Sanani drove through the three checkpoints while Elie returned the hesitant salutes of the Israeli, Jordanian, and UN guards, all of whom must have wondered about the unfamiliar UN general being driven in Bull's Jeep moments after it had gone the other way.

As they approached the Old City walls, Elie saw the Arab merchants pushing their carts away from the market. The wailing sirens on the Jewish side of the city must have freaked them out. Sanani kept pressing the horn, but the road was crowded with slow-moving traffic. Elie put his hand on the soldier's arm. "Calm down. Your friend can wait another few minutes. He's in no danger."

Lemmy regained consciousness just as the door flew open. A dark-skinned UN officer entered, followed by two soldiers. "What's the meaning of this?"

With difficulty, Lemmy stood up, his legs wobbly.

The officer walked around him, examining his backside. "Who are you?" His English was spoken with an Indian accent, just like Sanani.

Lemmy didn't answer.

"We will find out!" The officer beckoned the two soldiers. "Search him!"

Lemmy clenched his fists, ready for a fight, but a sudden cramp in his lower leg caused him to bend over and grunt in pain. He reached behind his back, feeling for the Mauser.

"Looking for this?" The UN officer held up the Mauser. He put on silver-framed reading glasses and peered at the gun. *Deutschland Über Alles.* He looked at Lemmy. "What is this? Are you German?"

Nodding, Lemmy tried to estimate whether he could snatch it from him and aim properly before the three of them acted. The Mauser was always cocked and ready to fire with a quick release of the safety, but they were three and he was alone. Chances were poor, even if the gun was still loaded, which was in doubt. Whoever had found it in the courtyard might have disarmed it.

"You're not a member of the United Nations staff, correct?"

Lemmy nodded.

"Then take off our uniform!" He pointed the Mauser at what was left of the khaki UN shirt. "Now!"

With effort, he unbuttoned the shirt and took it off.

"You are a saboteur! A spy!" The Indian UN officer pointed at the door. "We'll hand you over to the Jordanians!" He gestured to his subordinates, who stepped toward Lemmy.

"Don't touch me!"

"Get out!" The officer held the door open.

"My name is Wilhelm Horch," Lemmy lied. "I work for the *Bundesnachrichtendienst*—the West German secret service."

"The BND?" The Indian officer seemed taken aback.

"Yes! The BND!"

"Who is your commanding officer?"

"I report directly to General Reinhard Gehlen."

"Really? Gehlen? Wasn't he a Nazi commandant during the war?"

Lemmy shrugged.

"Then surely he wouldn't employ a Jew, right?"

"*Ich nicht ein Juden!*"

"Let's check." The Indian officer motioned to the two soldiers, and they pulled down Lemmy's pants, exposing his circumcision.

Elie sat next to Sanani, controlling his impatience as the Jeep slowly advanced at the pedestrian pace of the merchants and their carts. Finally, at the next roundabout, Sanani was able to speed ahead.

They approached the roadblock at the intersection with Jericho Road. Elie pulled the UN blue cap down to his eyebrows. "Don't stop."

The Jordanian soldiers stepped into the road, blocking it.

"Drive," Elie said. "They won't shoot at a UN vehicle."

Sanani slowed, rolled down his window, and waved. One Jordanian lifted his hand while his partner aimed a machine gun.

Sanani kept going at a slow pace and stuck his head out the window. "*Ahlan Wa'Sahalan!*"

The Jordanians didn't move aside, and Sanani had to hit the brakes. They approached the Jeep, one on each side.

"Let him come to your window," Elie said. "When he's close enough, open your door fast and hit him as hard as you can."

"Are you crazy?"

"Do as I say!"

The Jordanians came closer. Elie's window was down, and he held up a blank piece of paper he had found on the floor of the car. Meanwhile, his right hand unsheathed the *shoykhet* blade. "Here," Elie said, "my credentials."

The Jordanian came to the window and extended his hand to take the paper.

Pulling up his pants, Lemmy took a step back. "You can't do this! The Jordanians will kill me!"

"That," the UN officer yelled, "is between you and His Majesty's troops. *Out!*"

The two soldiers positioned themselves behind Lemmy, and the Indian officer led the way. They left the room and marched down a long hallway, passing a dining room that still smelled of fried eggs. The lobby let them out to the courtyard, where UN personnel ran back and forth with buckets of water.

The fire had spread to a field of thorns and tumbleweed beyond the reach of the hoses. The smoke was overwhelming, and flecks of ash drifted in the air. Lemmy was shocked to see the enormous radar reflector resting in the courtyard, its massive center hinge pointing up, mangled as if it had been torn out of its housing.

The officer headed to the main gate. When they were two-thirds of the way across the courtyard, Lemmy saw a Jordanian army truck arrive at the gate, the open box filled with soldiers in camouflage uniform. A Jordanian officer stepped down from the cabin.

The UN officer ordered the gate opened and exchanged salutes with the Jordanian. "This man," he said, pointing at Lemmy, "is an Israeli spy." He held up the burnt remnant of the UN shirt Lemmy had worn.

The Jordanian officer yelled something in Arabic, and the soldiers started jumping off the back of the truck. Two of them grabbed Lemmy by the arms and marched him toward the side of the road, where a telephone pole waited as an ideal place of execution. Meanwhile the soldiers lined up with their rifles.

The Jordanian sentry's hand entered through Elie's window, reaching for the paper. Making like he was handing it to him, Elie instead grabbed his hand and ordered Sanani, "Hit your guy now!"

Sanani's door flew open, followed by a loud bang.

Elie pulled the Jordanian's hand downward, bringing him closer to the window, and jabbed the blade upward at the Arab's exposed neck, right under the chin, into the brainstem. He opened the car door and used it to shove away the sentry, who collapsed, no longer in control of his limbs.

With the dripping blade pointed at the ground, Elie got out of the Jeep and walked around the hood. He found Sanani locked in a wrestling match, the Jordanian on top, his hands clasping Sanani's throat. Elie rested his hand lightly on the back of the soldier's head, searched with his thumb for the soft spot just under the cranium, and slipped the blade in with little effort, all the way to the handle, its tip emerging through the gaping mouth.

Sanani's eyes popped wide as he watched his opponent fall sideways onto the road. "What the hell!"

"Let's go." Elie wiped the blade on the dead soldier's pants and sheathed it. Up the road, where they had come from a moment earlier, a few merchants lifted their long robes and gave chase, yelling in Arabic.

Sanani drove forward, between the two corpses. "We're being pursued by a mob," he said in a tremulous voice as he glanced at the rearview mirror.

"Make the turn and go fast. It's too far for them to catch up."

He pressed the pedal all the way, and the Jeep raced up the hill.

Four minutes later, they cleared the crest and saw Government House engulfed in smoke. On the right, Antenna Hill was burning. A Jordanian army truck stood by the gate.

"Not good!" Sanani slowed down.

"Drive up to the gate and stop."

They turned into the access road and reached the gate, which was open. The UN guards saluted.

"Oh, no!" Sanani pointed. "They're executing him!"

Elie saw Lemmy stand with his back to a telephone pole, blindfolded, his upper body exposed to the sun. A line of Jordanian soldiers stood in the ready. An Indian UN officer watched from the gate.

Elie punched Sanani's leg under the dashboard. "Stop the car."

The soldiers cocked their weapon while their officer raised his arm, ready to give the order.

Lemmy knew he was doomed. The Jordanian officer tightened the blindfold and said something in Arabic that included the word Allah. Weapons were being cocked, and he heard an engine roar nearby. He was struggling to stay on his feet, erect and proud, not to show them how terrified he was. Would it hurt when the bullets pierced his chest? Or would he die before the nerves managed to transmit the pain to his brain?

His chest constricted. His breathing stopped. His muscles tensed up, expecting the sound of shots and the bullets to tear into him. He heard the Jordanian officer yell something in Arabic—an order to shoot!—and his mouth opened to scream.

But no shots sounded.

The air raid sirens on the Israeli side of the border continued to whine. He heard voices arguing and shook his head to loosen up the blindfold, which dropped to the bridge of his nose.

The Jordanian officer stood by Bull's white Jeep. The UN general was sitting in the front passenger seat, and Lemmy realized with a sinking heart that Sanani was not coming. Would General Bull step in to save an Israeli saboteur from execution? Considering the enormous mayhem he had caused, Lemmy doubted the angry general would show any mercy.

General Bull's door opened, and he came out.

Lemmy gasped in shock. It wasn't Bull, but the skinny little man from Zigelnick's tent! *Agent Weiss!* He was dressed in a UN uniform with lots of insignia that made him very important as long as no one realized he was a fake.

The Indian officer stared at the unfamiliar UN general. The guards at the gate stood still, unsure what to do.

Elie Weiss shook hands with the Jordanian officer. "Good morning," he said in heavily accented English. "I'd like to question the spy for a couple of minutes. You can shoot him when I'm done." He turned and marched through the gate into the UN compound.

After a brief hesitation, the Jordanian officer untied Lemmy and led him by the arm after Elie. The Indian officer sent the two UN soldiers off to assist in the fire fighting and joined the procession. Sanani drove the Jeep across the courtyard.

Elie entered Government House and strode across the lobby. UN soldiers, running back and forth with buckets of water, noticed his rank and stopped to salute him. He turned down a side corridor and entered an office on the left, which Lemmy realized he'd chosen because it had no windows facing the front of the building. The group followed him, and a moment later Sanani joined them, shutting the door.

The office had a single desk, file cabinets, and family photos on the walls. It probably belonged to a low-ranking UN administrator. Elie sat in the chair behind the desk, adjusted his blue cap, and grabbed a pen and a few blank papers.

Lemmy positioned himself to the side, against the wall. It gave him a clear vantage point and forced the Jordanian officer, who carried a pistol in a hip holster, to stand beside him, rather than behind him.

Elie's black eyes focused on the Indian officer. "Identify yourself."

"Major Raja Patel, operations commander for this United Nations facility. And who—"

"Thank you," Elie cut him off. "What's the situation with this young man?" He gestured at Lemmy.

The Indian officer started describing the events that led to Lemmy's exposure. When he reached the part about his clever idea, that the former Nazi now running the West German BND would not employ a Jew, he turned to Sanani, who stood the closest to him. "We pulled like this," he demonstrated, reaching down to pantomime on Sanani's pants, but paused and took a second look at Sanani's face. "Who are you? I don't recall you!"

Sanani was caught unprepared. He smiled and looked at Elie.

The UN officer switched to Hindu, uttering a long sentence.

"Well spoken," Sanani said, regaining his edge. "As Mahatma Gandhi said, *An eye for an eye makes the whole world blind.*"

The Indian officer stepped back and drew Lemmy's Mauser. "Who are you people?"

Elie stood up. "Calm down, Major."

The Jordanian officer hesitated, shocked at the sudden conflict between the UN officers.

Major Patel stepped backward toward the door, aiming the Mauser at Sanani. "What is going on here? Tell me!"

Lemmy heard Elie whisper to Sanani in Hebrew, "He hasn't cocked it. Knock him down!"

"No!" Lemmy reached forward to stop him, but Sanani had already leaped forward and tackled the Indian officer. A shot sounded, muffled by their intermingled bodies.

Lemmy rammed the Jordanian officer, and they both fell to the floor. Lemmy started rising, but what he saw stopped him. A long blade appeared in Elie Weiss's hand, the shining steel at least as long as his forearm. He swung it across, almost too fast for Lemmy to see, the point passing under the chin of the Jordanian officer, leaving a thin red line on his throat. The blade continued over Sanani's bowed head and swished below Major Patel's jaw. It returned in a figure-eight for another cut across the Indian officer's neck and passed by Lemmy's face, its glistening point swiping just above the shirt collar of the Jordanian officer, who attempted to draw his gun.

The two men held their twice-cut throats. They dropped to the floor, writhing.

"Sanani!" Lemmy kneeled by his friend, whose shirt was soaked red. "*Sanani!*"

Elie felt his neck. "Your friend is dead."

"*No!*"

"Put on this guy's uniform." Elie gestured at the Indian officer.

"But—"

"Quick, before his blood soaks it!" He fished the car keys from Sanani's pocket.

In a daze, Lemmy undressed the dead Indian officer. Meanwhile, Elie was removing the uniform from the dead Jordanian, whose eyes stared vacantly at the ceiling. He tossed away the shirt, pants, and boots, and removed the identification tags from the Jordanian's neck, replacing them with tags that Lemmy recognized as his own IDF tags.

With difficulty Lemmy buttoned up the UN shirt, whose collar was warm with Major Patel's blood, pushed it into the oversized pants, and buckled up the Indian's belt. He glanced up to see what Elie was doing and would have vomited had there been anything in his stomach.

The long blade was dancing in his small hand, making rapid cuts in the Jordanian officer's dead face. Pieces of skin and flesh flew up from the blade as the face grew naked, the pink bones emerging in unnatural clarity. He poked the eyes, carved off the brows, and removed the ears. Then he held up each hand and peeled the skin off all the fingertips with quick slicing motions.

Lemmy managed to say, "What are you doing?"

"Amazing how similar we all look under the skin."

He gagged, covering his mouth.

Elie took a hand grenade from his pocket and placed it on the corpse's groin. "And this should count as a kosher circumcision, right?"

Voices filtered through the closed door, men talking excitedly, someone issuing orders.

Lemmy cleared his throat. "What now?"

"Now?" Elie reached down for the fuse on the hand grenade at the corpse's groin. "Now we're going to kill you."

Chapter 44

A clear sky spread over Jerusalem. A gentle breeze stirred thousands of blue-and-white flags, which flew from every pole and balcony. The reunited city was celebrating its return to Jewish sovereignty.

Elie Weiss leaned against a pine tree on the hillside overlooking the military cemetery on Mount Herzl. He watched the army truck crawl up the path between the graves. A group of paratroopers marched behind it, olive-green uniforms clean and pressed, red berets tilted to the right. A military rabbi followed the group, reciting from Psalms in well-rehearsed mourning. Farther back, dozens of black hats clustered around Rabbi Abraham Gerster.

Operation Mokked had succeeded beyond expectations. Within two hours, the Egyptian air force had been decimated, hundreds of jets left smoldering on the runways. When the Jordanians joined the war with a murderous artillery barrage on West Jerusalem, Israeli jets attacked. During the fighting at Government House, which the UN had handed over to the Jordanians at the outset of hostilities, Israeli shells destroyed General Bull's Jeep Wagoneer. And while strafing a Jordanian airstrip in Amman, an IDF bomber hit the UN general's private plane, which burnt down to its steel frame. A formal apology was issued by the Israeli Foreign Ministry, but it did little to calm Bull's ire. It took four more days to push the Jordanians back from East Jerusalem and the West Bank.

Fooled by President Nasser's false claims of advancing on Tel Aviv, the Syrians also joined the war, forcing Israel to fight on a third front. The IDF reservists—farmers, teachers, laborers, lawyers, and shopkeepers—took the battle to the enemy's territory, away from their families and homes. They suffered heavy casualties, but managed to drive the Syrian army to the gates of Damascus, the Jordanian Legion over to the east bank of the Jordan River, and the Egyptian army across the Suez Canal. Egyptian soldiers, most of them poor farmers pressed into service, took flight with bare feet, leaving the Sinai Desert dotted with Soviet-made boots. Many died of thirst, and hundreds drowned trying to swim across the Suez Canal.

After six days of battle, when the guns finally quieted down, Israel had tripled its size. The stunning victory over those who had sought the Jews' total annihilation was mixed with grief for the many civilian and military casualties. Funeral processions followed each other from sunrise to midnight in every cemetery in Israel, and the hospitals were filled with the wounded and their tearful families. But the short war had changed the Middle East forever, and Elie was eager for the future.

Only a few powerful men knew how Elie's UN radar operation had saved the day. The risk to Israel's position at the UN General Assembly in New York required that the operation would forever remain secret. No record was made of the bodies recovered from a ground-floor office at Government House. Instead, two paratroopers' names were added to those who fought courageously on the northern front. Sanani's large family had attended his military burial in the morning, and now it was Lemmy's turn.

Elie lit a cigarette and gazed through his binoculars.

The bearded black hats followed the military procession slowly, heads bowed, cylindrical payos swaying back and forth by their faces.

The truck stopped by an open grave. Six paratroopers carried the coffin out of the truck. It was a wooden coffin, draped in a blue-and-white flag, the Star of David on top. They lowered it into the grave while the military rabbi chanted a prayer. The paratroopers lined up, cocked their rifles, and aimed at the blue sky. The captain, stout and muscular, stepped to the head of the grave. Elie remembered him from the tent in the desert.

Rifle shots cut through the air. Frightened birds flocked from a nearby tree. At the sound of a second salvo, Elie stirred and moved his hand over his bald head. Another round, and they lowered their Uzis and stood in attention while the military rabbi recited a final prayer.

A shovel rested by the grave. The paratroopers took turns to cover the coffin with soil. The captain was last. When the grave was filled, he saluted and marched off, followed by the others.

Only then did the bearded men approach the grave. Their black coats fluttered with the wind. Benjamin Mashash helped Rabbi Abraham Gerster kneel down by the fresh mound of soil.

A small cardboard sign on a wooden stick had been placed at the head of the grave. Through his binoculars, Elie could read it:

Private Jerusalem ("Lemmy") Gerster
Killed in Battle, June 7, 1967
In the Defense of Israel
God Will Avenge His Blood

A taxicab appeared on the gravel path leading to the site. It stopped, and two women came out of the backseat. Elie watched Tanya and her daughter hurry toward the grave. A few black hats turned to face them, forming a human barrier. Tanya stumbled, and Bira supported her.

At the foot of the grave, Rabbi Abraham Gerster suddenly fell forward. The palms of his hands sank into the fresh soil. A terrible cry tore through the air: *"Jerusalem!"*

Among the pine trees, Elie's gaunt face twitched. He dropped the burning cigarette and pressed it into the earth with the sole of his shoe. From his pocket he drew a telegram, which had arrived from his agent in Munich that morning, and read it again:

Wilhelm arrived on flight as scheduled. He's recovering well. The burns will leave only minor scars on his back. He's already making excellent progress with German pronunciation and grammar, but less so with French. Mood is dark at times, but he enjoys the driving lessons, albeit with youthful recklessness. Admission to Lyceum Alpin St. Nicholas confirmed for coming school year.

Elie put the telegram back in his pocket, satisfied. Soon Lemmy would grasp the importance of his mission and embrace his new life as a secret agent in the service of Israel. It was the life he had been destined for since birth. He was his father's son. A natural.

Turning to leave, Elie paused at the sound of Tanya's sobbing. He returned the binoculars to his eyes and watched her push through the black hats and drop to her knees next to Abraham, where they cried together by the heap of fresh soil.

THE END

Note to the Reader

While the characters and their deeds are fictional, the political and military leaders, as well as the historic events of 1966-67, are described as accurately as possible. The dire conditions in the divided city of Jerusalem, Israel's international isolation in the face of an all-out Arab assault, and the Egyptian preparations to engulf the Jewish state in a cloud of poison gas, are all part of a well-documented historic record.

It is interesting to note that on June 19, 1967, the Israeli government passed a resolution offering a return of the captured territories to the Arabs in exchange for peace. The response came three months later, when the Khartoum Arab Summit issued its famous three No's: "No peace, no recognition, and no negotiation with Israel." The closure of that small window of opportunity seems tragic in retrospect.

My research has benefited from the works of many scholars and biographers, particularly those who participated in the political and military actions. I'm especially indebted to recent researchers, such as Michael Oren, who enjoyed unfettered access to previously secret sources, including Israeli, Jordanian, and Egyptian veterans of the Six Day War.

For readers interested in further exploration, a list of my primary bibliographical sources appears next.

In writing this book, I had the privilege of loving friends and family, whose enthusiastic support has sustained me along the way. Special thanks to editors Aviva Layton, Natalie Bates, Richard Marek, and Renee Johnson, as well as the professional staff at CreateSpace.

Bibliography

Oren, Michael. *Six Days of War: June 1967 and the Making of the Modern Middle East*. New York: Oxford, 2002.

Segev, Tom. *1967 – Israel, The War, and the Year that Transformed the Middle East*. New York: Metropolitan, 2007.

Moskin, J. Robert. *Among Lions: The Definitive Account of the 1967 Battle for Jerusalem*. New York: Arbor House, 1982.

Schleifer, Abdullah. *The Fall of Jerusalem*. New York & London: Monthly Review Press, 1972.

Narkis, Uzi. *The Liberation of Jerusalem*. London: Vallentine, Mitchell, 1983.

Mulligan, Hugh A., et al. *Lightning Out of Israel – The Arab-Israeli Conflict*. Englewood Cliffs: Prentice Hall, 1968.

Nakdimon, Shlomo. *Ahead of the Zero Hour – The Drama that Preceded the Six Day War*. Tel Aviv: Yediot, 1968 (Hebrew).

Efrati, Yigael, Dir.: *Follow Me – The Story of the Six Day War*. Jerusalem: IDF/Israel Film Service, 1969 (VHS).

Teveth, Shabtai. *The Tanks of Tamuz*. New York: Viking, 1969.

Rabin, Yitzhak. *The Rabin Memoirs*. New York: Random House, 1979.

Harris, Bill (Director). *Yitzhak Rabin – Biography*. New York: A&E Television, 1995 (VHS).

Arel, Yehuda. *Warrior and Statesman – Moshe Dayan*. Tel Aviv: 1968 (Hebrew).

Dayan, Moshe. *Story of My Life*. New York: Morrow, 1976.

Dayan, Moshe: *Living with the Bible.* New York: Morrow, 1978.

Meir, Golda: *My Life.* New York: G.P. Putnam's Sons, 1975.

Eban, Abba. *Personal Witness – Israel Through My Eyes.* New York: G.P. Putnam's Sons, 1992.

Sadat, Anwar el. *In Search of Identity – An Autobiography.* New York: Harper & Row, 1978.

Dallas, Ronald. *King Hussein – A Life on the Edge.* New York: Fromm Int'l, 1999.

Mansfield, Peter. *Nasser's Egypt.* New York: Penguin, 1969.

Lacouture, Jean. *Nasser: A Biography.* New York: Alfred A. Knopf, 1973.

Raviv, Dan, and Melman, Yossi. *Every Spy A Prince – The Complete History of Israel's Intelligence Community.* Boston: Houghton Mifflin, 1990.

Raviv, Dan, and Melman, Yossi. *The Spies: Israel's Counter-Espionage Wars.* Tel Aviv: Miskal – Yedioth Ahronoth Books and Chemed Books, 2002 (Hebrew ed.).

Katz, Samuel M. *Soldier Spies – Israeli Military Intelligence.* Novato, CA: Presidio Press, 1992.

Carroll, James. *Constantine's Sword – The Church and the Jews – A History.* New York, Boston: Houghton Mifflin Company, 2001.

Made in the USA
Columbia, SC
07 October 2017